AUTHOR	CLASS
BOOTH, M	F
TITLE Hiroshima Jo	No
	~~18545081~~

D0410548

HIROSHIMA JOE

HIROSHIMA JOE

Martin Booth

HUTCHINSON
London Melbourne Sydney Auckland Johannesburg

Copyright © Martin Booth 1985

First published in Great Britain in 1985
by Hutchinson & Co. (Publishers) Ltd

An imprint of Century Hutchinson Ltd
17–21 Conway Street, London W1P 6JD

Hutchinson Publishing Group (Australia) Pty Ltd
16–22 Church Street, Hawthorn, Melbourne, Victoria 3122

Hutchinson Group (NZ) Ltd
32–34 View Road, PO Box 40-086, Glenfield, Auckland 10

Hutchinson Group (SA) Pty Ltd
PO Box 337, Bergvlei 2012, South Africa

ISBN 0 7126 1014 6

Typeset by Inforum Ltd, Portsmouth
Printed in Great Britain in 1985 by
Butler & Tanner Ltd, Frome, Somerset

CONTENTS

ACKNOWLEDGEMENTS

IN WRITING THIS novel, I am indebted to a number of people from whom I obtained much help, advice and encouragement. I am most grateful to Dr A.H.R. Coombes, MBE, and M.M. Swan, ISO, for their recollections of the fall of Hong Kong and Japan; to N.H. ('Yagi') Colley for his memories of the sinking of the *Lisbon Maru* and his liberation; to G.P. Adams for his knowledge of prison camps in Japan and for his informative book *Destination Japan*; to the librarian of the Embassy of Japan in London; to J. Teicher, who researched details of the despatches of General MacArthur in the Library of Congress, Washington D.C.; to Harry Guest, for helping me through the complexities of Japanese maps; and to my parents, who provided jarring memories of the Hong Kong of my childhood throughout the writing of this book.

Finally, I owe considerable thanks to Miss Yasuko Fujiwara in Hiroshima who invaluably researched the year of the bomb for me, corrected my Japanese, sought out the most obscure details on Japanese wartime life and generally guided me through the web of detail. Without her, the story would have been infinitely poorer.

Martin Booth
Somerset, 1985

PART ONE

Hong Kong: Spring, 1952

SANDINGHAM WOKE WITH a jerk, puppet-like, life surging through him as if he were in the hands of some impatient grand controller, someone who had snapped a switch that coursed a charge of electricity through him. His dream was already forgotten in the panic of coming round. His left hand was folded under his chest. It was numb, and this had been a part of the dream, although now he was unable to say how. His right hand was lying on the pillow next to his face and in the semi-darkness of the room it looked whitely ill. His entire body was damp with sweat and the cotton sheet that covered him stuck to his back and clung to his vertebrae where they showed through the skin.

Slowly, he reached for the battered alarm clock that rested on the glass top of the bedside table. Under its cracked leather case was arranged a set of hotel rules and a tariff card; between these he had lodged a tattered photograph of a young man in loose army drill shorts and a battle-dress blouse. The person in the photograph was wryly smiling, as if aware of what fate and the years held in readiness for him. Beneath his feet, across the dry grass of a lost Malayan summer, was scrawled in blue ink, 'Bob: Penang, 1939'.

The night before, as on the nights before that, he had forgotten to wind the clock and it had run down at 2.09. Even after seven years he could not get used to turning the key before sleeping. He had forced himself to grow so much out of the habit of counting time. It was enough just to let the days slip past, unheeded and uncared for. Every so often, though, he found a deep need to time-keep, and this worried him. He knew he should

not count the days and yet sometimes he did. To mark off a
mental time-sheet was a sign of optimism, anticipation, a readying for a time to come; yet he knew he had nothing for which to
prepare.

He shook the clock viciously and it started ticking again. As
soon as he put it down, the mechanism stopped. The tips of the
hands phosphoresced dully but the spot of luminous paint over
the twelve had peeled off, to leave a grey spot, like a blind eye.

He turned on to his back, then sat up and rubbed his forearm to
regain circulation. As he worked at the skin he noticed, as he so
often did, its faint pallor and coarseness. His massage also caused
tiny shards of tissue to flake off, as if his arm had dandruff. The
minute jabbing pains that he felt as his hand passed over the flesh
made him wince.

With his arm restored, he leaned over and tugged open the
drawer of the bedside table. His fingers fumbled through the
contents – an old army paybook, some dog-eared letters in
airmail envelopes, nearly a dollar's worth of change in ten-cent
coins, a fountain pen with a cracked case, a comb with a thick
conglomeration of grease accumulated at the base of the teeth, a
used khaki handkerchief, a British passport and a cardboard
pocket calendar for 1952 – until they found a half-empty packet
of Lucky Strike and a box of matches with a yellow and red label
decorated with two world globes illuminated by a single match
and a pair of Chinese characters. He lit one of the cigarettes and
lay back upon the pillow, concentrating only on blowing the
smoke into the air. His fingers' first joints were stained by
nicotine and they quivered, almost imperceptibly.

Outside, the last of the night was close and warm. Although it
was less than an hour to dawn the buildings still retained some of
the heat of the previous day. The window of his second-floor
room was open, but it faced only a bleak concrete wall which was
punctuated, some yards off, by the vertical line of frosted glass
panes to the stairwell of the next building. Somewhere above him
he could hear the clatter of mah-jong tiles across a hardwood
table top and the laughter of the players rising and falling. The
game had lasted through the night and it too had played an
indecipherable part in his dream.

With the cigarette smoked down as near to his fingers as he

could stand, he pinched it out and, certain that the flame was extinguished, crushed the remaining quarter of an inch into a dented tobacco tin. This he placed at the rear of the bedside-table shelf, covering it with the Bible that came with the room. It was not that he was afraid that one of the hotel roomboys would steal it: he knew they wouldn't. And it wasn't because he was ashamed to hoard the fag-ends in order to roll remnants up later. It was just that he was used to doing this, had done it for many years. Like not winding the clock, it was something to which he was accustomed by training; perhaps even by instinct. He did not know and he could not tell.

Balancing on one elbow, he reached for the cord of the faintly blue venetian blind. He pulled firmly and the slats of the blind shuttled together loudly as he raised it. Dawn had come while he was smoking and daylight had already overpowered the glim of the neon street lamps.

The metal window-frames were warm to his touch. Gripping them he peered out of the window, craning his head sideways to catch a glimpse of the papaya tree at the end of the alleyway between the two buildings. He could just see it, the fruit hanging down pendulously from under the canopy of broad leaves. The tree reminded him of another papaya, one that had been so close to him for so long and had yet been wholly unobtainable. He had watched the fruit on that other tree grow and fill, turn from dark to light green and then to a peachy cream that developed into the soft, subtle yellow of maturity. From the present tree he had never seen any fruit drop. It was always picked by someone unseen. It was as if they came in the night and spirited the goodness away: often staring at the fruit in the mornings, he could actually taste the firm sweetness of the pinkish flesh in his mouth. Once he had even seen the debris of black pips just outside the wire, and had tried to reach them with his hand. They were too far off so he had gone to get a bamboo broom, but by the time he returned with it two speckle-breasted birds had pecked clean the spot in the dust. They had flown off guiltily as he approached.

It was while leaning out of the window that he made his decision. Today he would have a papaya fruit. The lowest was very nearly ripe. If he took it now and kept it on his windowsill it might just r:pen. Of course, the roomboys might find it. But then he could hide it in the cupboard, under his dirty clothing, until they had finished cleaning the rooms on his corridor, and place it on the sill afterwards. They usually reached his room by half-past nine each morning.

The sunlight, reflected off the wall outside, should be sufficiently strong to ripen the fruit. After all, in nature they ripened under the shade of the leaves. If it did not ripen then he'd eat it however it was.

He dressed stealthily in a creased, off-white shirt without a collar and a pair of loose underpants. Over these he pulled a pair of dark trousers, with frayed turn-ups. They were old and slightly long for him – hardly surprising, as they had not been tailored to fit him. He put on unwashed grey socks and slipped his feet into scuffed brown brogues with rubber soles. He owned two pairs of shoes – the other pair was black with leather soles – but, at this moment, brogues seemed the more appropriate. He wouldn't be heard walking in them and they would give him added grip.

He opened the door. The verandah corridor outside his room was deserted. It ran along to the left then, at a T-junction, joined the main corridor. Across the central courtyard he could see the pebble-glass window of the ground floor office where the night-duty porter would now be sitting, dozing. The strip light was still on over the desk.

Turning right, he came to a navy-blue painted door and slipped the catch. It clicked loudly and he glanced through it, shutting it gently but firmly behind him.

He was on a staircase that was never seen by ordinary guests of the hotel. It was made of bare concrete and its walls were white-washed. Upon each step was piled cleaning equipment – mops, galvanised buckets, brooms, boxes of lavatory cleaner and Mansion floor polish.

By the head of the stairs, at a thin landing from which a door opened out to the flat roof of the hotel, lived the gardener. He slept there in a folding camp-bed, his belongings stored in two small apple crates and a cheap suitcase which he secured by parcelling it up with a length of chain and a brass padlock.

It was imperative not to awaken him for he was easily angered and his gaunt, tight-skinned face was quick to mirror his mercurial soul.

With the skill of long practice, Sandingham crept up the stairs to the last angle before the gardener's bed. It was not an easy manoeuvre, for the equipment and stores that were kept there were, in places, precariously balanced. He had to be very careful not to touch anything. One object knocked over would be sure to domino into others below it. That would be disastrous. From overhead came a grunt and a volley of exhaled breaths: the gardener was soundly asleep.

As he went deeper into the well, Sandingham saw the articles change from cleaning materials to tins of soup, vegetables, fruit and meat products. These were new: they had not been there the last time he had edged his way down. The lower flights had held only bundles of newly-delivered laundry then. He was certain the food would remain there for a short time only, until the shelf space was found for it in some storeroom.

At the foot of the staircase was a metal door with a Yale lock. He opened this, being careful to put it on the latch, for he wanted to return this way.

A narrow passageway led off to the right from the door and he took it, careful not to disturb the lids of dustbins that stood alongside it, against the street wall of the hotel grounds. From over the wall he could hear footsteps moving along the pavement. They fell with slow deliberation and he visualised a Hong Kong police constable on his beat, black leather belt, revolver holster and peak cap glinting in the early light. Standing on an empty tea chest, Sandingham looked warily through strands of barbed wire strung on metal posts along the top of the wall. His fears were instantly soothed. Instead of a policeman walking the pavement an elderly man in a loose-fitting suit of black cloth was counting through a thin wad of dollar bills. He had come out of the back yard of the building next door.

Sandingham stepped off the tea chest and continued around the corner of the hotel. The ground-floor windows were guarded by wavy, wrought-iron grills. He frowned. He hated bars and these bars in particular for, at the rear of the hotel, they protected the storerooms.

The alley beneath his room window was narrower than the other passageway and he had to squeeze along, stepping gingerly over broken glass. He was not afraid of cutting himself but he knew from personal experience that glass makes a distinct, loud crunch when stepped on, especially in a confined space.

At the end of the alley he came to the top of a grass bank, twenty feet wide, ten feet high and overlooking the arc of the hotel front drive. Cautiously he put his head around the corner of the building.

The main entrance was deserted, like the rest of the hotel. He could see the marble steps leading up to the foyer clearly, the small door that revealed steps leading down to the hotel garage beneath the front lawns. He ducked under a bush and inched forward, using a hunched, squatting technique, to the foot of the papaya tree. Here he paused.

Near him he could hear muted voices coming from the open window of one of the downstairs front suites; the sound of lovers in the early morning. He heard a man's cough, then the quiet whisper of a woman.

The tree was younger yet also higher than he had expected. Stretching his arms up he found he was still some four feet short of the bottom-most fruit. He looked around.

Another wall, five feet high, separated the hotel frontage from the garden of the next building, a block of flats. This wall was made of concrete covered with plaster that had cracked in the summer heat; like the rear wall, it had three strands of barbed wire running along it.

He held one of its metal stancheons and lifted himself on to the wall, placing a foot on each side of the wire, which he used to keep his balance as he edged precariously along to the tree. Here the fruit was hanging level with his face, but several feet away from the wall. Judging the distance carefully, he let himself fall outwards to the tree. He hugged the trunk tightly as it swayed away from the wall, then returned to its original upright position. With one hand he grabbed the ripest papaya and twisted it. Its stem bent, then snapped. He carefully dropped the fruit to the ground, where it bounced under a bush.

He lifted one leg clear of the wire and was about to lift the other, to swing himself on to the tree trunk, when the young tree juddered and again took him away from the wall. This time it did not straighten but started to bend dangerously and he thought it might break. The leg of his trousers caught on the wire and ripped down the seam from the knee to the turn-up. He swore inwardly, and pulled hard. The wire released him, but one barb dug into his ankle as he broke free.

The tree shuddered and two more papaya came loose, one hitting him on the shoulder before falling into the bushes below. He slithered down the trunk, searched for the ripe fruit on all fours. It was nowhere to be seen.

Puzzled, he looked over the bush. The papaya had slipped through the bushy undergrowth, rolled down the bank and hit the concrete drain at the side of the drive. Bouncing over this, it had struck the concrete driveway and split open. Its sections had then rolled down the slope of the drive and out into the gutter of the main road.

He heard a swishing sound. The main foyer doors had been opened. The night clerk had obviously heard the fruit falling on the drive and come out to investigate. He glanced right then left. An unripe papaya had toppled after the ripe one and was now rolling crazily, like a rugby ball, down the drive. The clerk, a fresh-faced Chinese man in his early twenties, walked briskly after the fruit and stopped the papaya with his foot. He looked up the bank.

No one there.

Once in safety around the corner of the building, Sandingham stopped to regain his breath. Another sound, above his head – no more than a bird might cause – made him look up.

From a window on the second floor peeped the face of a boy. He was a European, blonde haired and with blue eyes, and it was obvious that he had seen everything. Their eyes met. For twenty seconds the boy looked at the man and the man at the boy. The boy's eyes were wide with wonder at what a grown man was doing, at the crack of dawn, before most adults were awake. The man's eyes were squinting with fear as he tried hard to think how he could avoid the beating that would inevitably follow.

In the end he did nothing, said nothing; just went back down the alleyway, around the rear and in through the metal door, slipping the deadlock into its closed position. On his way back upstairs he found that two of the food boxes had already been opened. From them he took three tins of pineapple cubes and two of tomato juice. His scrounging trip, after all, had not been entirely in vain.

Back in his room, he lowered the venetian blind – although there was no way anyone could see in without a long ladder – rummaged in the chest of drawers, found a rusting tin opener and prised open the top of a can of pineapple. He ate the contents with his fingers and drank the sweet syrup straight from the tin, cautious not to cut his lips.

He hid the other cans in the hollow pedestal of the wash basin and flattened the empty one with his foot. Once it was out of shape, he wrapped it in newspaper and put it in the wastepaper-basket. He stood for an instant, indecisive. It was not worth the risk of the roomboys finding it, so he took it out again and placed it in a drawer, planning to dispose of it later in the day.

It was after doing this he sensed his ankle was wet, tacky with blood. Tugging off his trousers, shoes and socks, he lifted his foot into the wash basin and ran cold water over the cut. It was not as deep as he had feared it might be. The water stopped the bleeding long enough for him to take from under the mattress a strip of clean cloth hidden there, wrapped in newspaper for just such an emergency. This makeshift bandage tight, he lay back on his bed, crudely stitched the rent in his trousers and dozed.

'Mistah Sandin'am. You wake up please.'

He grunted and turned on to his side, facing away from the roomboy who stood on the parquet floor by the bed, looking down at him.

'Mistah Sandin'am. I do you room now. You please ge' up.'

Sandingham sat up and felt, as he did so, a twinge in his ankle. He looked blearily at the man standing over him. He wanted only to sleep longer, a desire in him that was deeply rooted and one which he always found inexplicable, even to himself. Lying-in was a luxury of which he had been for so long deprived that now, with it accessible, he treasured it.

As if anticipating his first words, the roomboy said, 'It ha'f-pass ten. It time for you to ge' up.'

Sandingham swung his legs over the edge of the bed and reached to the alarm clock for confirmation. It still showed 2.09. Daylight filled the room, so it was obvious that dawn had come and gone: it was not afternoon, for he would have sensed that, and, besides, the roomboys always did their rounds in the morning. He reasoned all this quite clearly in the half-concious state into which he had sat up.

'Five minutes,' he said. 'I'll be out in five minutes. Do the next room first.'

The roomboy, who had turned aside upon seeing that the man was semi-naked, said nothing in reply. He was used to it. He simply left. Sandingham could hear him clattering a metal dustpan and broom outside, followed by the jangle of a bunch of brass keys.

His ankle hurt him. He rubbed it and the pain increased. The makeshift cloth bandage had slipped during his sleep and now he was rubbing the material of his trouserleg against raw flesh.

With difficulty, for he was stiff in every joint, he lifted his foot into the sink once more and bathed the wound with warm water, rubbing the hard, hotel-courtesy soap into it. This increased his pain but he knew it would stop any infection. He tried to remember how he had come by the cut and then it came back to him: barbed wire. Had he really tried to climb over the wire? No; he had merely swung on it. But why? Then he recalled the papaya and the birds eating seeds.

Stiffly, he lifted his foot out of the basin and let the grimy water run away. Then, under a clean flow from the tap, he rinsed and wrung out the bandage before tying it back around his cut.

The knots of the damp material held better and he tightened them firmly. Even twisting the cloth to wring it out and then to tie the knot caused his fingers to ache. He ached so much these days, especially in the mornings. Sometimes his head ached as well, a sly throb that was not centred on his brow or at the back of his head, like a migraine, but which came from the very core of his skull, the deep tissues of the brain. This morning, however, he noted with a certain detachment that the headache was absent.

He relieved himself in the small toilet that adjoined his room. His urine was richly yellow, almost amber, and it smelled bad again. Some mornings it was almost clear, a pallid stream that burned as it flowed; on others it was like today.

As the flush operated, he checked behind the cistern. It was loosely mounted a quarter of an inch out from the wall and into this crevice he had stuffed a tiny parcel, wrapped in several layers of silver foil taken from expensive cigarette packets that he had found off and on in the ashtrays of the hotel. It was safe. So far, no one had found it. He took it out and sniffed it. There was a faint scent working its way out through the foil, a scent that could have been a delicate mixture of sandalwood oil, rosewater and exotic herbs, had it not been a third of an ounce of opium.

The odour made him want it. He started to unwrap the foil but then stopped. Discipline: one could only stay alive by discipline. Hadn't Willy always said that? And lived by the motto? And died by it, tied to a wooden cross on a beach? Besides, the roomboy was nearly through with the next room and this was his emergency cache, not one for a morning's indulgence. He returned it to its hiding place, noting that the overhanging cistern lid still effectively hid it from view both from above and each side. Roomboys were hardly likely to lie on the ground behind the cistern and look up to catch the dull glint of the foil. To be safe, though, he took the opium out again and wrapped the foil in a sheet of lavatory paper to mask the possible gleam.

'You can do my room now,' he said as he left it; the roomboy was closing the door of the adjacent room. He spoke with what he hoped was dignity.

The roomboy replied politely, 'T'ang you, Mistah Sandin'am,' but he knew the truth about this shabby customer. He was one who seldom paid his room charge, never tipped, seldom ate in the hotel restaurant but was more likely to be found at food stalls in the streets of Mong Kok. The roomboy had seen him one evening, seated at a food stall in Tung Choy Street, eating plain rice with some green vegetables and a sliver of fish. It was probably all the man could afford.

Trying not to limp, Sandingham walked down the corridor through the floor lobby to the main hotel staircase. The floor captain ignored him: he was busy defrosting the refrigerator in which the guests kept soft drinks and perishable luxury foods which they ate in their rooms.

Sandingham glanced at the interior of the fridge with the expert eye of one trained in scrounging, his mind at once registering what there was that might be edible should he later have the luck of discovering the floor desk nearby unattended.

The stairs took him down to the hotel lobby. When he had reached the mock marble floor of the hotel entrance, he paused and surveyed what he could see. To his right was the door to the establishment's restaurant with a lime-green plastic surround to it that was back-lit by neon strips at night. Across from that, beside the door to the ground floor corridor, was the bar. Behind it, the inverted bottles of spirits, glasses, chrome shakers and ice buckets and other paraphernalia of cocktails glittered in the coarse glare from a row of concealed electric bulbs. The barman was wiping the green marble top with a duster. Opposite, and to his left, was the round curve of the hotel reception desk with the staff seated behind it – the girl clerk who handled registration, the two Chinese clerks who prepared the bills, operated the telephone switchboard, sorted the mail and took reservations in halting English, and the manager. Immediately to his left, under the stairs, was a cubby hole in which the porter by night, and the bell-hop by day, lived while awaiting work. Ahead of him was the hotel's main entrance, two glass doors with large metal handles in their centres bearing the initials of the hotel and its crest. Outside, sunlight blazoned off the front lawn and off the rows of porcelain plant pots containing chrysanthemums and asters: these lined the low front wall which, in turn, overlooked the street below. A taxi, a Morris saloon painted red with canary yellow Chinese characters on the doors, was just driving off. The bellboy, a Chinese lad about twelve years of age, wearing a white uniform with a matching pork-pie hat, was standing on the steps leading up to the glass doors. He was counting a tip.

The manager swivelled in his chair to talk to the register clerk. Then he stood and crossed the office space behind the desk to consult the register itself.

He was a tall man, much taller than the rest of the Chinese staff, and spoke the local Cantonese with a misplaced accent. Sandingham understood this local dialect and he knew a strange accent when he heard one. The manager's height and intonation indicated clearly that he was from northern China. Since the Communist take-over vast numbers of well-to-do northern Chinese had flocked south and those unable to afford passage to Malaya, the Philippines or the USA had settled as refugees in Hong Kong. Those who had been well educated, especially in mission schools or overseas, had been able to obtain reasonable employment. The rest had come to form the basic labour force of the colony.

Mr Heng, the manager, was an impressive figure of a man and not just because of his height. He was in his late forties, strongly built, with close-cropped grey hair. His head was squared off on top, the shape exaggerated by his haircut, and he wore gold-framed bi-focals. He was always dressed in a smart charcoal grey or light blue suit. Sandingham coveted those suits. The man's hands were large and although his voice was quiet he had an awesome temper. The staff of the hotel respected or feared him. He was not one of them. He was like a mandarin lording over his albeit small domain.

Sandingham backed up three steps. No one could see him except the bellboy, who was still preoccupied counting his small change.

The manager came out from behind the desk and walked towards the main entance, his back to Sandingham. His highly polished shoes clicked on the floor, and then softened on the carpet that ran from the large, sunken main doormat to the stairs.

As soon as Heng's back was to him, Sandingham went smartly down the remaining steps, turned left and walked as quickly as he could along the ground floor corridor.

It was cool there, for the corridor was bordered on one side not by a wall but by flower beds in which grew an assortment of small frond-like palms and broad-leafed bushes. He reached the rear door of the hotel unseen. It was open and he noticed that the dustbins had been taken out into the street and were now piled alongside the tea chests upon which he had earlier stood.

The street at the rear of the hotel was deserted. From over a high stone wall opposite drifted the chanting of school children learning mathematics by rote, in Cantonese. The flag above the gate of the playground and basketball court indicated that this was a Communist school.

Within fifty seconds, he had reached the end of the street and disappeared around the corner.

He was now in Soares Avenue. The buildings on either side were mostly pre-war and he could vaguely remember some of them. They were made of grey concrete in the blunt style of the thirties with small shops giving directly on to the pavement. Between the buildings lay dank alleyways, down the centres of which were gutters running with slow trickles of stinking water. When the typhoons came in the late summer months, these alleyways were awash with garbage.

As he passed the shops, he looked in them. One was a sweet-shop, its window displaying a varied assortment of Chinese confectionery in shiny paper with blue, red and green printing on the wrappers. Another was a fruit and vegetable shop. Outside this, he paused and rummaged in his pocket for a coin. A hand-painted cardboard notice, stuck vertically into a box of tangerines, stated in Cantonese that the fruit was five cents each. Sandingham understood the characters. From his pocket he drew a ten-cent coin and the woman in the shop came out from the doorway to serve him. He gave her the coin and helped himself.

This was not a shop where a European would normally go – it was in a back street, halfway up the Kowloon peninsula. Euro-peans shopped at the southern end of Nathan Road and even then seldom bought food. They purchased clothes, consumer goods, jewellery, curios of soapstone, jade or ivory. The buying of food was invariably left to their servants.

However, the shop owner was not surprised. She had seen Sandingham before, wandering the streets, standing by the bus stop, reading the previous day's issue of the *South China Morning Post*. She assumed that he was a poor White Russian.

The tangerine was small even for such a fruit, and the peel stung when he wedged some under his fingernails. He had dis-covered recently that the quick on his thumbs was raw under the nails and, on occasion, it wept a straw-coloured liquid. Once, the previous week, he had woken to find the nail badly bruised, but he could not recall having caught or banged it.

He reached Argyle Street and crossed over through the mid-morning traffic to the bus stop going east. Behind him, up a low hill, Kadoorie Avenue and Braga Circuit wound through trees and past the houses of the very wealthy. He looked along the street to see if there were a bus in sight, and saw instead a large American convertible come to a halt at the junction leading up the hill. At the wheel sat a beautiful Eurasion girl in her mid-twenties. Her cheekbones were soft, her skin the cool cream so

common in such a mixture of races and her deep brown eyes
shone. Her auburn hair was short and she was wearing a blouse
of sky-blue cotton. As she spun the steering wheel, Sandingham
could see her gold ladies' Rolex wristwatch catch the bright
sunlight. He pondered how much such a watch, not to mention
the girl herself, might fetch where he was going.

The bus, with its red sides and off-white roof, was not long in
coming. He put his hand out to hail it and the conductor yanked
on the silver grid gate at the front entrance of the vehicle. Sandingham boarded the bus and sat down on a wooden slat seat. The
conductor pulled twice on the thin cord rope that ran the length
of the vehicle and the bell dinged by the driver. He paid the
ten-cent fare and received a flimsy ticket made of something very
like thin greaseproof paper. He folded this once and put it in the
breast pocket of his shirt. He would need it later.

After it had circled a roundabout, the vehicle slowed down and
stopped at Kowloon Hospital where at least half the passengers
alighted. This took several minutes, for the bus was full.

It was a section of the route that Sandingham did not like. As
the bus pulled away from the kerb he looked at the floor between
his shoes to avoid seeing anything out of the window. But there,
in the rubbish under the seat, was something that rudely jarred his
memory. Such was the connection with this road in his mind that
even garbage on the floor reminded him of it. He smiled ruefully.
It was perhaps fitting that it was such trash that did cause his
brain to think back. That was what it had all been about, really.
On the floor was the screwed-up silver lining of a chocolate bar.

The bus halted for an amber traffic light. He looked up from
his feet and automatically from right to left. A few houses with
deep-set balconies now stood where gardens had once been laid
out. But the soil was poor and vegetables had found it hard to
gain sustenance. So had men.

An elderly Chinese in black baggy trousers that seemed to be
made of tarred cloth, and a loose-fitting jacket of the same
material, was crossing at the lights. Ahead of him he was pushing
a home-made wooden trolley mounted on four pram wheels, and
piled high with Chinese cabbages.

Bemused, Sandingham watched the man advance slowly across
the road. Once, that could have been him: except that they had

had their trolley made out of the chassis of a wrecked Baby Austin from which anything worth salvaging had been systematically removed and spirited away.

His eyes followed the pedestrian to the entrance of the Argyle Street camp, outside which stood a young British soldier. His rifle was at the slope and his knees were pinkly sunburnt. He was sweating profusely and had dark semi-circular stains under his armpits. He could not have been more than eighteen or nineteen. For a split second Sandingham thought he was wearing a soft, khaki peaked hat but then he blinked as a quick flash of sun came off a black Humber staff car, turning in through the gates, and he realised that the hat was actually the squaddy's hair.

No longer able to watch, he looked at the floor again. The silver paper was stirring in the breeze. Squeezing his hand down between his legs, Sandingham picked up the foil and smoothed it out carefully on his thigh, taking great care not to tear or cause additional creases in it. Once flattened out, he held it up to the bus window. There was a pin-prick of light shining through it. Someone must have trodden it on to a sharp rivet on the floor. It was no use. Even a miniscule hole invalidated the whole sheet. If there were the slightest hole it would never have done for the condenser for the radio.

The huge open space by the fence to the airport at Kai Tak was surrounded on three sides by the intersection of three main thoroughfares – Prince Edward Road, Argyle Street and Ma Tau Wai Road. Sandingham looked at the area of dust and scrubby grass. Through the centre of it ran a depression, once a deep ditch, the sides of which had now been eroded smooth: he had been one of those who'd dug it.

Dotted around the area were small groups of people sitting or standing by low hovels made of cardboard boxes, plywood scraps, hessian sacking and splintering planks. They were the occupants of the lowest spoke on the refugee wheel of fortune – squatters who had nothing and who lived by petty crime, begging and the hardest of labouring jobs. By many of the makeshift shelters, cooking fires were smoking under oil cans and broken plates upon which the most basic of foodstuffs was being prepared. He remembered how he, too, had once cooked with empty tin cans and not all that far away, either.

Kowloon City was walled not merely by an actual structure but also by history and atmosphere. Out of the jurisdiction of the Hong Kong Police, unmapped and with no published street plan, it was like a tiny sovereign state of its own in which the monarchs were the leaders of the Chinese criminal fraternity. Secret society bosses – the Triads and the Tongs, the Chinese 'mafia' – ruled with hands of iced jade and the assistance of well-trained thugs and a cast-iron oath-taking system which no one, once sworn in, dared ever violate. No European would think to enter Kowloon City, yet Sandingham did. In a manner of speaking, one of the local bosses knew him. They had met for the first time a decade before and there was, he felt, a mutual bond of shared experience between them.

He stepped down from the bus and began to walk up Lung Kong Road, weaving through the throng of shoppers who were purchasing vegetables from a large group of street hawkers. Then, looking about cursorily to make sure he was not in sight of a policeman, he crossed into the walled city. Word of his arrival, he knew, had travelled ahead of him down the narrow streets and passages, carried by small urchins operating under the orders of lookouts posted in the surrounding streets.

He was heading towards Mr Leung's house, a building at the end of a narrow alleyway that was a cul-de-sac and therefore easily guarded.

'What you name?'

The demand came with a firm thrust into his chest from a bunched fist. It wasn't a punch, only a hard push, yet it moment-arily took his breath away. His chest was not strong.

'Joseph Sandingham,' he said, adding in Cantonese, 'Mr Leung is waiting for me.'

'Mr Leung wait for no one,' replied the Chinese firmly and in English, stepping from the shadows into a thin shaft of sunlight that had succeeded in reaching down into the alleyway. He wore a modern American-cut suit with an expensive cotton shirt under the lightweight jacket. The hand that had not pushed against Sandingham's chest held a small calibre pistol. He knew enough about small arms to recognise it as an Imperial Japanese Army issue weapon and he wondered what rank of soldier had been garrotted with piano wire for it to be 'liberated', as they had put

it. Guns were a rare sight in Hong Kong unless they were attached
to policemen's lanyards; but then this was Kowloon City. Hong
Kong was a hundred and fifty yards away.

A peephole in a door at the end of the alleyway opened and
a voice, muffled by the wood, spoke through it. The minion
lowered his hand but not the barrel of his pistol.

'Okay. You go to door. No turn roun'.'

The door opened and Sandingham entered. He had not been in
the building for over six weeks and he had forgotten how its
interior fragrance differed from the odours of the open *nullahs*,
rotting vegetables and overcrowded streets and tenements outside. It was cool, too. As soon as the door closed he felt chilled,
partly because of the efficient Westinghouse air conditioner
mounted in the wall, partly because of the sense of oppressive
foreboding that permeated the rooms.

The man who had opened the door asked him to remove his
jacket. He did so. He was then searched, despite the fact that he
now wore only trousers and a shirt. The guard felt up the insides
of Sandingham's legs as far as his testicles and gently fingered
around his groin. He also checked inside his socks. Satisifed that
the visitor was unarmed, he opened a second door and Sandingham passed through it.

He found himself in a large room furnished in a curious
mixture of modern New York and ancient China. A steel writing
desk, bearing a black telephone and a vase of frangipani blossoms,
stood next to an antique bronze urn; a standard lamp with a
pendulous shade of garish green plastic hung over a wicker settle
covered with Thai silk cushions; a cocktail cabinet against one
wall was adjacent to a camphorwood chest with a relief depicting
dragons entwining on the front and lid. Through the hasp on the
chest, in place of the traditional lock, was a modern padlock with
a brass face, reinforced steel loop and a combination wheel. The
floor was covered by deep-piled Chinese carpets.

'Hello, Joseph.'

He turned round quickly.

'Hello, Mr Leung, how are you?'

'After all this time, you still don't call me Francis,' replied the
Chinese ironically. He had no trace of an accent: if anything,
there was a slight American twang to his words.

'Francis,' said Sandingham.

'Take a seat. Tell me how you've been keeping.'

Leung sat on the settle and studied him intently. His glances seemed to be merely passing over his visitor but they were far from being that shallow. He was a shrewd observer of all that he saw: to have survived in his world for as long as he had, he had been forced to be continually alert and aware.

For his part, as he spoke, Sandingham took in all that he could about Francis Leung. His fawn-coloured suit was smart and deliberately unostentatious. His tan shoes were hand-made but conservative in style and highly polished. He wore a dark brown silk necktie over a cream shirt. If Sandingham had seen him crossing Hong Kong harbour on the Star Ferry he would have assumed Leung to be one of the well-off Chinese middle class, a manager of a small firm, perhaps, or an executive in one of the European shipping offices where it was now becoming common practice to take on Chinese staff to other than menial positions. Leung was in his mid-thirties but still had the smooth skin of a young man.

'So things are not so good for you,' he commented as Sandingham came to the end of his statement of his current affairs. 'That is bad, very bad. Time you had a job.'

Leung laughed and Sandingham joined in, knowing that that was what he wanted. This Chinese had it in his power to give him employment, albeit part-time.

'I'm ready when you are,' he said, feigning humour, yet he meant it.

Leung became serious and leaned forward, elbows on knees, hands spread open. He looked like a Taoist priest about to give a benediction.

'Right now, I've nothing, but' – he saw a look of desperation sharpen Sandingham's eyes – 'there will be something in a few weeks. Have you ever been to Macau?'

'Not since before the war,' Sandingham answered.

'Well, maybe a trip there.' Leung leaned back. 'You will like it. It hasn't changed like Hong Kong has. It's still old-fashioned, like a bit of Europe transported to China four hundred years ago and left there. In the meantime, have you anything for me?'

This was Sandingham's cue, his opportunity. It had been like this in the old days, during the war. Leung had said it just that way then, too. Of course, at that time they had been equals.

'It's in my coat.'

Leung snapped his fingers and the door guard, who must have been awaiting the signal, entered carrying Sandingham's jacket. He did not return it to its owner, but went through the pockets himself, taking out a manilla envelope of the size used to send invoices through the post. He handed this to Leung who opened it and tipped out the contents: it was a lady's brooch. In the centre was a red stone and surrounding this were seven smaller, greeny-blue stones.

'A ruby and aquamarines,' said Sandingham, with what he hoped sounded like authority.

'Aquamarines, certainly,' replied Leung, twisting the piece in his fingers, noting that the catch was broken. 'But a ruby this size? I'm afraid not. If it was, it would be – what? – eight, maybe nine carats. No, Joseph, this is a garnet.' He spoke patronisingly with mock kindness, as if instructing a pupil in gemology. 'Nevertheless,' he added, 'it is a pretty brooch.'

He smiled expansively, passing the stone to and fro under the lamp.

'Where did you get it?' he asked after a pause.

'I found it,' said Sandingham. Leung chuckled at this. 'It's true,' he added quickly. 'It was on the vehicle deck of the Yaumati car ferry. It was in the scuppers.'

'Why did you not take it to the police? There might be a reward.'

Sandingham shrugged and tried a smile in return. Leung appreciated that: it was a sign that the European knew his place in this new world. He returned a grin and then, holding the brooch, his eyes hardened.

'Fifty-five dollars.' It was not an offer. It was a statement of fact.

Sandingham divided fifty-five by fourteen in his head – three pounds, eighteen shillings and four pence. His mental arithmetic translated the sum into three bottles of gin or fifteen hundred cigarettes.

'Seventy-five?' he questioned. He knew that, to buy such a brooch at one of the jewellery shops in Hankow Road, the owner must have had to pay at least four hundred dollars . . .

'You are the only man who would even try to dicker with me,' said Leung. He had picked that word up in San Francisco, too. 'Sixty-five is the best I'll go. And only for old time's sake.'

Considering himself lucky, Sandingham nodded. Without waiting to be asked, for he knew the routine, he stood up and turned his back to the camphorwood chest. The guard positioned himself so he could make sure Sandingham did not try to catch a glimpse of the combination. The tumblers fell very silently. When he heard the lock spin Sandingham turned around and Leung gave him sixty-five purple Hong Kong dollar bills bearing the head of George VI. They were in mint condition, although no such notes had been issued in recent years. Sandingham guessed they were from one of the hoards of currency Leung was rumoured to have accumulated during the immediate post-war years.

Carefully, he folded the notes into thin strips and tucked them into a hole in the waistband lining of his trousers. It was a trick he'd originally learnt from Francis Leung.

'Come and see me again, Joseph. In a few weeks,' said Leung as they parted. 'Yes, and one more thing.' He took a piece of paper from the henchman who had returned Sandingham's jacket. 'Take this. You know where. Ah Moy will see to you.'

'How can I thank you, Francis?' His voice was sincere and the Chinese knew it.

'It doesn't matter: don't even try. For old time's sake, Joseph. Take care.'

Leung turned and left the room without looking back. In this fashion Sandringham was dismissed and promptly shown out to the alley. It was humid outside after the comfort of the air conditioning within and he was sweating before he reached the guard. He walked slowly, with unconcern, but not too slowly. Leung's enemies were numerous, even in the closed criminal society of Kowloon City, and now they were certain to be Sandingham's enemies as well.

The guard remained in the shadows as he made his way towards the safety of Hong Kong proper. Within a few minutes, he was once more standing at a bus stop. A ragged queue formed behind him. Several old men joined the line, as well as two young women in cheong-sams and a few children who appeared to be unattached to any of the adults. They wore blue-and-white, sailor-type uniforms and carried school books under their arms. The bus was not long in coming.

As it pulled up to the kerb, the queue characteristically broke up and the people crowded around the two entrances of the vehicle. In the crush, Sandingham not so much felt as sensed a hand feeling along the waist lining of his trousers. He had been an expert enough lifter himself to know the touch of another past-master at the game. Without looking down, he expanded his stomach muscles to trap the exploring fingers. That, he thought, would discourage them. What happened next was most un-expected.

He was punched exceedingly hard between the shoulder-blades. The fingers thrust themselves into his trousers seeking not the money now but his private parts. That would mean a harsh crushing of his testicles, bending him into vulnerable agony.

Sandingham whipped around swiftly. His agility surprised his two attackers who had evidently thought that this skinny Euro-pean was an easy target.

One of the assailants was a youth in his early teens and it was his hand plunging down Sandingham's trousers. The other was one of the old men in the queue. He had delivered the two-handed blow and, had this man been in his prime, Sandingham thought, the punch would have laid him out.

It took him a split second to decide what to do and then his reflexes took control. With a sharp cut upwards, he sank his knee into the youth's stomach. He had aimed lower, but his attacker was too short for a solid crutch connection. The youth hissed and doubled up, his hand tearing free of Sandingham's clothing. At the same time, Sandingham swung his fist hard at the old man's shoulder. As he had anticipated the older attacker expected a blow to the head and ducked with the result that Sandingham's fist caught him on the cheek, just above the lower jaw. He felt one of the old man's teeth crack and heard a yelp like a dog having its tail stamped upon.

The bus began to move off. Sandingham jumped on to the step and tugged on the sliding bars of the passenger gate. It would not budge: the conductor, at the other door, had a foot on the upright and this controlled both the front and rear entrances. With a vicious thrust, Sandingham rammed the gate open and gained the upper step. The conductor swore vehemently in Cantonese down the aisle of the bus and then fell silent when he saw that it was a European who had bruised his foot. None of the passengers paid any attention.

Sandingham looked out the rear window. The youth was still doubled over, nursing his solar plexus; the old man had started after the bus but stopped when he realised it was gathering speed. He stood disconsolately in the gutter, shaking his fist. Tatooed on his forearm was a tortoise with Chinese characters in the segments of its shell. That meant the would-be pickpocket and his elderly accomplice were part of Francis Leung's band.

So Leung had tipped them off. No one else, except the guard at the door, knew he was carrying money and where it was hidden. So much for old time's sake, he thought. It would be better not to 'dicker' in future.

Sandingham slipped back into the hotel the same way he had left. He did not want to meet Heng.

Safe in his room, he locked the door behind him and checked that everything was all right. The opium was still in place; the cans of food were untouched; the tobacco tin had not been tampered with. More importantly, the bed had not been moved.

Very gently, so that he did not leave tell-tale scratch marks on the parquet floor, Sandingham shifted the bed a few inches to one side. Then, with his fingernail, he prised up the wooden tile which rested under one of the legs at the head of the bed. This tile hid a hollow he had scooped out in the concrete. It had taken him nearly four days working continuously with a sharpened spoon, stopping every few minutes to assure himself that he wasn't heard. The space was slightly smaller than the tile, two inches wide by three long and two deep. In this recess he kept his money, wrapped in a square of tar paper.

He took it out and counted it. Twenty-seven dollars. Plus sixty-five made ninety-two. He removed thirty and put these in his pocket before folding the remainder and replacing the floor tile.

It was approaching one o'clock. He felt thirsty and under-nourished so he breached a tin of the tomato juice and drank it by sucking through the holes made by the can opener. Contented with this, he flattened the can and hid it with the others, then lay back on the bed and dozed.

At first he was aware only of a slight pressure on his shoulder. This was followed by the shaking of his head in a room where Leung was handing him large wadges of dollar bills – and he was saying no, he did not want any money: he had enough. He was even wearing a lightweight tropical blue suit and matching shirt.

'Enough! I have enough!'

His words were slurred and Heng thought that the Englishman was saying he had had enough and so he stopped shaking him.

It was then that Sandingham awoke to find that he was dressed in his usual shabbiness and that Heng was standing over him.

The manager spoke clearly, in impeccable, if somewhat stilted, English. His phraseology recalled the pre-war schoolroom of a Catholic boys' school near Shanghai.

'I'm glad to have found you in, sir,' he said. There was not the slightest trace of irony in his voice. 'I had been hoping to catch you before you left this morning but I'm afraid I was detained in the hotel office.'

'What can I do for you?' Sandingham sat up: he knew perfectly well what was wanted.

'I'm sorry to bother you, Mr Sandingham, but it has been drawn to my attention by one of my clerks that you have overlooked settling your bill for the past month. As you know, I must request that clients of the hotel settle up monthly.' He paused then added, as if to give weight to his request and to show that he was not being biased, 'Even those who are staying here as the families of British service personnel are asked to pay their bills every month.'

'I paid last month,' said Sandingham, meekly. When in the face of authority it was always best to be subservient. It worked, as a general rule, in softening them. Afterwards one could hit them hard in subtle ways they might not notice . . . or better, might feel but not be able to pinpoint.

'How much?'

Heng made a show of taking a sheet of paper from his inside jacket pocket. By doing so, he momentarily delayed the demand he had to make. He did not like doing what he was now engaged upon: he had been a refugee, an outcast from his native country too, and he knew what Sandingham went through every day of his life and what he had suffered in the past. Indeed, it must have been worse for the European, because he had not only lost face in the eyes of his own kind but also in the sight of the Chinese. He was a pathetic figure and Heng knew only too well that, but for the whim of fate, the man on the bed might have been him. But he also knew that he could not afford to carry a free guest in the hotel. The owners would not stand for it. If Sandingham did not keep more or less up to date with his room rent Heng had instructions to evict him; after all, he knew from other managers in the trade that Sandingham had already been thrown out of at least three other hotels in Kowloon during the last twelve months.

'Three hundred and eighty-two dollars, sixty-seven cents,' said the manager. He held out the paper which bore the calculations. They were laid out neatly in a thin hand. The figure seven was crossed through in the continental manner.

Sandingham's face remained impassive.

'I'll have the money for you this evening,' he said.

'I would be most grateful if you would let me have it before you retire,' replied Heng. 'The owner of the hotel will be arriving in the morning and it is his custom to check through the books for the previous month.'

Sandingham allowed his head to drop slightly. He suddenly felt both tired and frightened.

'I'm sorry, Mr Sandingham, but I must obey the orders of my employers.'

'I do believe you are, Mr Heng,' replied Sandingham and he meant it. As the manager left the room, closing the door gently behind him, it occurred to Sandingham that, despite the gulf of difference between them, they understood one another very well.

One advantage of having spoken with Heng was that Sandingham could now leave the hotel by the front entrance instead of escaping by the back. And leave he had to, for he was obliged to find what was for him a fairly large sum of money by evening, and there was only one way to do that.

The sun had moved away from the front of the hotel by the time Sandingham walked through the lobby. The bar was closed and the glassware was dull, lacking the sparkle it had held earlier, or would again contain once evening arrived. Mid-afternoon in the hotel was always a slack time.

A small glass porch was beside the main entrance steps at the head of a set of stairs that led down to the garage. He stood by it, absorbing the heat of the day, and smelling the odour of warm gearbox and sump oil flow from the stairwell. It was a scent he knew from the past, reminding him of something he could not place.

As he turned right to descend the curving hotel drive, a movement on the front lawn caught his eye. Lying on the grass behind the low hedge was the young boy who had seen him attempt to cut down the papaya. The boy did not notice Sandingham: he was engrossed in playing with toy soldiers in the shadow of the tightly packed evergreen leaves. He had carved a network of tiny trenches in the dirt and, at the end of the hedge, in strategic positions, several khaki soldiers, one bravely emblazoned in the red tunic of a Grenadier, manned a machine-gun post in a salient. Behind them, tucked into the cover of the hedge roots, were a number of military vehicles – a small scout car, a five-ton Bedford truck, a jeep and a much-dented tank.

Sandingham watched the boy for at least a minute. His legs where they protruded from his navy-blue shorts were tanned and, as he lay on the grass, the shorts had worked their way up tighter around his groin, so that the tidemark of whiter skin showed higher up his thighs. The material had also wedged into the crack between his buttocks, accentuating their round firmness. His head was under the hedge, but even in the shade the sun caught his blond hair and gave it a golden sheen. It was the colour hair that Chinese, passing in the street, would touch for luck. Blond hair was lucky and Sandingham wished he, too, could stroke the boy's hair, for luck. He needed it as much as anyone.

Yet he could not bring himself to cross the concrete drive and do it. Touch it. It was not repulsion for the boy that prevented him, nor any morality such an action might contravene; quite the opposite. It was what the boy was doing: playing soldiers.

As he watched, he heard the child mouth a whee-ing noise as an imaginary shell hurtled from his finger into the dirt by the machine-gun post. Dirt flew as a pebble hit the dry soil and spurted it upward. The Grenadier's tunic coat grew dusty. These tiny details implanted themselves upon Sandingham's mind. When he had to, he could be exceptionally observant.

Another stone fell. It struck the scout car but did not turn it over. The boy flicked the vehicle over with his thumb, as easily as he might play a glass marble. He pursed his lips and blew his cheeks out to make a toy explosion.

In the shadow of the hotel porch, Sandingham winced. The burping bang in the boy's mouth took on the arcing screech and cumbering thump of a three-inch mortar. He looked up. The stone ceiling that was the main verandah looked safe, but the supporting pillars could easily give way. He decided it was best to get into the open. Standing under a building in a raid was not a sensible thing to do.

He stumbled down the steps of the hotel, pushing past the bellboy in his hurry. The youth laughed at him and shouted in Cantonese, 'Mok tau! Mok tau!'

Now Sandingham was screaming a high-pitched whistle like a rat held alive in a trap. He fled clumsily down the driveway and out into the sunlit street. Opposite, the bare earth of the steep hillside seemed to reverberate in the heat of the afternoon. He could see fountains of soil and stunted bushes funnelling upward and outward, falling as a slight rain of grit on him. He wiped it frantically away from his eyes and nose. As suddenly as it began, the attack stopped. He stood leaning on a silver metal lamp-post, sweat soaking through his short hair and running down his neck. He shook and hugged the metal to steady himself. It was almost too hot to touch but he ignored its temperature: it was something solid in an unstable universe.

Hearing voices he looked up, and saw the blond head of the English boy next to the black-haired head of the bellboy peering over the hotel wall.

'Who is he?' the fair boy was asking.

'He a c'azy man,' said the bellboy. 'He mok tau!' He laughed.

'What's his name?'

'He name? 'is man he cawld "Hiroshima Joe".'

Once again the bellboy laughed, this time uproariously.

At the southern end of Nathan Road the bus slowed to go right and drove by the impressive bulk of the grey façade of the Peninsular Hotel. Pulling away from the awning over the front was a huge black American car from the bonnet of which limply hung a Stars-'n'-Stripes, suspended on a chromium-plated rod. It was topped by a small silver-coloured eagle.

Sandingham watched the car as it drove away from the entrance. He could just discern, in the rear passenger seat, an elderly man with an Havana cigar protruding from his teeth. It had been a long time since he had noticed so grand a vehicle pull out from the Pen, and he shivered at the thought of his last view of such an event. Then it had been a 1938 Ford with large head-lamps on the mudguards: this, he guessed, was a Cadillac limousine.

By the low building that was the main Kowloon Post Office the bus swung into the terminus in front of the Hong Kong-Canton railway station. The standing passengers jostled for balance and Sandingham clung to a rail that ran along the ceiling. His equilibrium was not always good.

Soon he was standing on the hot pavement and looking up at the clock tower of the railway station. It was a famous landmark and had stood there a good many years. He had mixed feelings as he saw the time: three-fifteen. He could remember when it had been three-fifteen once before.

Once upon a time, he reflected, before war and revolution had split the world and sealed borders, one had been able to board a train here and step off at the Calais/Dover ferry. He had thought about that often. It had given him strength or depressed him immeasurably, depending on how he was feeling.

He took a ten-cent coin from his pocket. It was newly-minted and shone in his palm. He flicked it casually into the air, caught it just as George Raft had in pre-war movies, then walked towards the pay stile of the Star Ferry.

The ferry was the main passenger route across Hong Kong harbour. There were other ways to cross: the Yaumati ferry, for instance, the vehicular one upon which he had found the brooch, crossed from Jordan Road to Central District on the island of Hong Kong. But that was slightly more expensive and one seldom found Europeans travelling on it as ordinary passengers, for they usually stayed on the car and lorry deck with their saloons.

And there were other ferries run by the same company as the vehicular, but they plied between small jetties dotted here and there around the shores of Kowloon and were also expensive in comparison with the Star Ferry. There were wallah-wallah boats which operated between a quay by the railway station and Blake Pier next to the Star Ferry jetty on Hong Kong-side, but they were very expensive and usually found patronage among rich Europeans and Chinese, or sailors who had missed the last night ferry and needed to get back either to HMS *Tamar*, the Royal Naval dockyard on the island, or to warships lying at anchor. And finally there were sampans, slow tiny craft oared across by a woman or a young girl, and which were seldom used except as a last resort, for they took upwards of an hour to cross the mile of water and were more expensive than any other mode of water transport.

The cost of getting across the harbour mattered to Sandingham, but it was just as important to be seen travelling with his own kind, in his own eyes if not in theirs. He felt he owed it to himself to use the Star Ferry, as a mark of dignity. What is more, he would travel on the upper ten-cent deck, not on the lower five-cent one where the poor Chinese, the coolies and the amahs and the servants sat only a couple of feet above the waterline.

The turnstile chattered as he pushed through it. Once on the ferry pier, he followed the other passengers along a planking walk that was roofed over but open on one side. A ferry had just sailed from the jetty and he had to wait a few minutes for the next one to arrive. He reached the gate at the head of the wooden slope and stood just back from it, keeping slightly apart from the gathering group of other passengers. The platform at the base of the slope shifted a foot downwards as someone unseen operated the winch. The tide was ebbing. He could hear the metal hinges of the gate stretch and squeal.

He watched the crowd that was gathering at the gate. They were a mixed bag. Several Chinese dressed in short-sleeved shirts and slacks and carrying leather briefcases were chatting together: they were bank couriers making the last harbour crossing before public banking hours ceased. Two European women, one with a young child in hand, were talking about the merits of a tailor in Hanoi Road. A Chinese girl, in her early twenties stood reading a newspaper. Beside her stood two Royal Naval officers in white tropical uniform, their long white socks contrasting with their tanned knees. Their white shoes were scuffed but otherwise they looked smart and orderly; one held a document case to the side of his starched shorts. Two European businessmen stood apart watching for the ferry to come in while an elderly American tourist and his wife fiddled with their German camera, trying to insert a new film.

Looking down to avoid catching anyone's eye, Sandingham saw the deep blue of the sea lolling to and fro between the planks of the pier. Sunlight striped the wavelets. He wondered how many coins might be on the sea bed thirty feet below.

The ferry was nearing the side of the jetty. There was a fierce whirling of water and foam under the pier as the boat reversed its front propellers. Puffs of sooty smoke rose from the thin funnel, to be dissipated in the humid air. Passengers on the decks had stood up and were crowding around the top and bottom gangways, causing the vessel to list gently. A khaki-uniformed sailor threw cord lines on to the narrow parapet of the jetty where they were caught by another sailor who hauled in the thick mooring ropes and secured them round a bollard. The ferry edged into the side and finally bumped against the wooden piles, making the entire structure reverberate and rock slightly. At this, the child started to prattle with excitement.

Following the crowd, Sandingham went down the slope and stepped over the gangway on to the ferry's upper, covered deck. He sat on the open part of the deck, on one of the long, wooden-slat benches, first pushing the angled backrest over the seats. The seating was in this way reversable, so that everyone could face the direction of travel: the ferry had neither bow nor stern, being able to go in either direction without turning.

A crewman pulled the gangway up on a rope and secured it in place to act as a door. Then he peered over the side and signalled a comrade below who cast off and waved to the pilot in the lower deck steering cabin. The water surged at the end of the ferry as it glided away from the side of the pier.

Having cleared the shadow of the roof, the boat was bathed in brilliant sunlight but it was no longer hot. The movement of the ferry had caused a soft breeze to blow across the deck, which was

to Sandingham's advantage. He did not want to appear too
scruffy where he was heading, and sweat had a way of making
even the most scrupulous dresser look less than smart.

He regretted not owning sunglasses. He had once had a pair –
good ones, with Zeiss lenses – but had long since pawned or lost
or sold or exchanged them for a bowl of rice.

Now the sun scored into his eyes, as if seeking to burn his
retinas. He felt giddy and sick and put his hand on the painted rail
along the edge of the deck to give himself support. The feeling
passed, but it worried him. He had had such giddy attacks
increasingly of late.

Sandingham leaned over the rail, hoping the breeze would
drive away his sense of nausea. Before him lay the business centre
of Hong Kong: Central District, with its banks, merchant company and shipping line offices and its shops for the wealthy lining
the waterfront of Connaught Road.

As the ferry neared the Hong Kong-side pier he could see along
the low grey cliff of the quay rickshaws and cyclists amid the
traffic. Lorries, their tarpualin covers stretched tight over
bamboo frames above the truck beds so that they looked like
motorised prairie wagons, wove and steered between the cars and
pedestrians. Towards Sheung Wan the waterfront was crowded
with Chinese cargo junks, off-loading goods trans-shipped from
vessels swinging at anchor or buoys in the western section of the
harbour. All was bustle and maritime activity.

Lifting upwards, almost sheer from the business district, were
the slopes of Victoria Peak, one and a half thousand feet high,
with the residential Mid-levels crowded between its business
district and the steeper parts of the mountain. In the midst of this
Sandingham could clearly make out the central tower of Government House, the governor's residence, with its flat, pagoda-like
tiled roof.

Silhouetted along the skyline of The Peak, and the ridge
running eastward from it, were the blocks of flats and private
houses of the very rich or very fortunate, or an amalgam of the
two. He could see, creeping up the mountainside, the green and
cream-coloured car of the Peak Tram, the semi-alpine railway
that went from Garden Road to Victoria Gap, with a few precariously perched stations *en route*.

At the Hong Kong-side pier the ferry repeated the performance of docking. Sandingham remained in his seat, watching a few sampans drawn up on a thin strand of pebbly mud next to the ferry. On one flimsy craft was a Chinese infant, the seat of his trousers split open to avoid the inconvenience of nappies. His mother was sitting on the flat planking at the stern, eating melon seeds, delicately splitting them open with her fingernail before eating the kernels and flicking the husks over the side. A pipe dribbled sewage into the harbour by the sampan's prow.

At last the gangway was lowered and he disembarked, pausing only under the jetty's colonnaded front to purchase a copy of the day's paper from a news-vendor. He begrudged having to buy it, having hoped to find a copy on the ferry, but the seats must just have been cleaned for there was none to be had. He looked upon the purchase philosophically as an investment. At least it was cheaper than a magazine.

He crossed the road and walked up Ice House Street. At the junction with Chater Road he turned right and at the next junction of five roads he crossed again, dodging between two trams to reach the Gloucester Building: it was here that he planned to find the rent for the hotel.

The pavement of the building, which for the main part consisted of offices, led straight into the Dairy Farm restaurant. It was a large establishment, with waiter service, and its plate-glass windows were half-hung with curtains. These latter served his purpose well, for he could not be observed from the street outside.

He entered and sat at one of the tables. The place was busy. Shoppers – for the most part European women – were taking afternoon tea with their children around them. It was a scene of ordered chaos. Chinese waiters moved with speed between the tables, balancing trays laden with pots of tea, small cakes and buns, and ices or tall sundaes in glasses. One of the Chinese waiters approached him and he ordered iced lemon tea. The man did not give him a second glance: he was sufficiently well-dressed to be accepted.

The table next to him was vacated as he arrived, but it was soon re-occupied by a woman in her forties accompanied by three children, two of whom wore white school uniforms. One of the children was a morose-looking boy of about ten.

Sandingham listened to their conversation. With luck, they
would fit the bill – a harrassed mother, a pain-in-the-neck child
and two other offspring to offer distraction.

'What do you want, children?' the mother asked, in a voice
tired from traipsing around in the tropical heat.

'A coffee ice, a coffee ice!' chanted the youngest child, fighting
to be heard over his immediate superior's demand for a peach
melba, also repeated several times. Their voices jarred on Sandingham's nerves, but he managed to suppress his longing to shout
at them.

The sultry boy requested a strawberry ice, his words a near
monologue.

'You know you can't have an ice-cream, Jeremy,' the mother
retorted. 'It will hurt too much after the filling. Mr Bingham said
you shouldn't eat until the anaesthetic wears off and the filling
sets.'

Bingham: Sandingham knew a dentist by that name. He had
known him in times when there had been no supplies of pain-
numbing cocaine.

He had not seen Bingham for many years, but he knew the man
had a practice on Kowloon-side, near to the Star Ferry. As if in
tribute to the dentist, Sandingham pressed his tongue into a space
between his right lower molars. It had hurt like hell at the time,
but the abcess had been prevented from spreading. The resultant
blood poisoning might, in the circumstances, have killed him.

A waiter delivered Sandingham's iced tea, for which he deliberately and immediately paid. He sipped his drink, pretended to
read the newspaper and knew it was only a matter of time.

He was right. Five minutes into the tea, the morose boy stated
that he felt 'woozy'. He shifted from his seat to one next to his
mother. She, in turn, shifted her handbag from her lap on to the
back of her chair. It was an English-made bag of dark brown
leather with long handle-straps.

Choosing his moment carefully, and watching all around him
with a skilfully controlled series of glances, Sandingham lifted
the bag clear of the chair back, and at once put his newspaper
over it, ensuring that the straps did not show. Then he tucked
handbag and newspaper under his arm and rose to leave. Safely

outside, he turned left up Pedder Street, continued across several
junctions into narrower streets and soon arrived at Albany Road.
From there it was only a minute or two's walk into the Botanical
Gardens.

Seated on a bench, under the shade of a traveller's palm, he
unfolded the newspaper and, careful not to be observed, snapped
open the brass clasp on the handbag. He quickly rummaged
inside. A used handkerchief; two lipsticks; a base metal powder
compact that sprang open as he touched it, tipping fine talc over
him; a packet of State Express 555 cigarettes and a stainless steel
Ronson lighter, both of which he removed and pocketed; an
address book; a Hong Kong driving licence and a military pass
card – the woman was obviously a service wife, which accounted
(in his mind) for the fact that her children were unpleasant little
bastards; a diary; a batch of letters with British stamps on the
envelopes; a comb and a small mirror . . . one by one, he removed
these items of feminine clutter and tossed them into the thick leaf
debris at the base of the tree where fibrous leaves had fallen and
matted together. He even found a pair of sunglasses, but as they
were a lady's pair in faint blue plastic he could not wear them and
reluctantly tossed them into the undergrowth, too.

Finally, in a side flap, he discovered the purse.

The woman being a service wife had had him worried. They
weren't anywhere near as wealthy as the wives of local civil
servants or businessmen. But this woman must have been an
officer's spouse: in the purse was a lot of loose change – he
counted over five dollars before tipping it all into his jacket. In a
billfold within the purse was just over four hundred and fifty
Hong Kong dollars and eighteen pounds in sterling.

His hands shook as he transferred the money to the inner
pocket of his jacket and then rammed the handbag well down
into a low, thorny bush. It was a pity, because the bag itself would
have fetched a bit in a pawnshop; but a European man pawning a
European woman's handbag would have aroused suspicion, and
he was sure the police kept tabs on pawnshops here just as they
did in Britain. Now it would be some time before it was discovered, and by then the damp, the heat and the ants should have
reduced it to a state of fragile decomposition.

He knew that he had been very lucky. He had expected he

would have had to steal at least three such bags to make up his
rent, but at once he had enough and some to spare even without
cashing in the sterling. In comparison to what he had been two
hours before he was rich.

The green tram pulled up at an island stop in the middle
of Johnston Road near a playground which, every evening,
attracted hoards of ragamuffin children from the surrounding
sidestreets of Wan Chai. Sandingham stepped down and the
tram, with much grinding and howling of metal and humming of
static electricity, surged off along the sunken road rails towards
Causeway Bay and North Point.
   He negotiated his way through the heavy evening traffic,
crossed Hennessy Road and walked down a narrower street
consisting of overcrowded three- and four-storey buildings that
were of pre-war construction, and showed it. Their deeply-set
balconies provided the pavements with square-pillared arcades:
in them collected rubbish, small urchins and elderly Chinese men
who seemed to congregate always in twos and threes, seated
upon wicker chairs or wooden boxes, chattering and playing *tin
kau*.
   There were shops here, too, mostly selling food. The rice shops
displayed their wares in barrels or sacks open at the top, each
containing a different type of rice, long grain, short grain and, for
all Sandingham knew, thin grain and fat grain. To him food was
food, rice was rice; he had little time for variations. The vegetable
shops offered trays of water spinach, root ginger, Chinese
cabbage, yam-like tubers, spring onions and watercress. The fruit
shops sold mangoes and papayas, passion-fruit and oranges,
bananas and pomeloes. The lights were just coming on and
enhanced the exotic fruits with garish hues.
   But the shops were greatly outnumbered by the bars. Wan Chai
was the area of dives and brothels, cheap perfume, over-priced
drinks and whorehouses, each with a neon sign outside compet-
ing with its neighbour for brightness and variation. The area was
not far from the Royal Naval dockyard and was also near the
Gloucester Road pier where all American sailors landed when
coming ashore from warships on what was euphemistically
labelled 'R&R' – rest and recreation. Sandingham had always

been amused at this term for shore leave. They seldom rested and they often re-created.

He turned right into Lockhart Road. Just round the corner was the Vancouver Bar. He had been there often and was known slightly to the proprietor and well-known to the barman. The girls who sat in front of the plywood-panelled bar were a shifting population. They came and went as the mood, the proprietor or their pimps took them. He wondered if Lucy would be working the bar or if she had been moved on.

It was still early in the evening and the US sailors, whose ships were dry of alcohol, had not yet hit shore for a hard drinking night out; nor had Murray Barracks yet released its hoard of British squaddies for whatever dark-hour revelries were on offer: this would very likely include brawls with American crewmen. As he pushed through the bead curtain that separated the bar from the pavement Sandingham noticed the luminous hands of the clock over the drinks shelves. It was seven-fifteen.

The bar was in semi-darkness although it was still more or less daylight outside; the sun was well down over the hills of the distant western islands. In the centre of the large room was an area reserved for dancing, although this usually meant hanging around a bar-girl, hands pressing her buttocks, rather than obeying any musical impulse. This dance floor was in turn hemmed in by wooden and plastic-topped tables, at each of which was a set of metal chairs. The tables were round and bare; the floor was strewn with damp sawdust. In one corner, like a blurting electronic reptile with painted scales and hidden inner lights, was a much-abused jukebox. Overhead, four ceiling fans turned slowly in the half-light.

The rattling of the curtain beads caused a fluster of activity in a back room. The girls were still off duty, and the prospect of an early customer agitated them into action. The barman came out from another doorway, his face beaming in anticipation. He did not lose his smile when he saw Sandingham, even though he knew that this one was not a high-spending, high-rolling Yank from Ohio, hungry for a broad and a beer.

'Mr Sandin'am, you okay? Long time no see you Wan Chai-side. You go 'way?'

Sandingham leaned on the bar, rubbing the sole of his shoe on the brass rail that ran along the base on his side of the plywood. The dollar notes were uncomfortable under his instep.

'No,' he replied. 'I've not been away. Just busy on Kowloon-side.'

'You got job yet?' asked the barman with artful perspicacity. He added, 'It no good you got no job. Must have job fo' money. Fo' good money. No money, no d'ink, no eat, no livin'.'

It was good to be in the bar once more. Sandingham felt at ease here, as if he were released from the world and its cares, petty slights and dangers in the stink of eau de cologne and sawdust and spilt drink and sweat. Somehow they disguised his worries as effectively as the sanitary wicks killed the stench of stale flesh in his hotel room.

For a brief moment the squalor of it all came to him. It seemed as if he had been living in squalor, or on the ill-defined boundaries of it, for years. He had to admit it to himself, in all honesty. And it wasn't for lack of ready cash. It was simply a matter of habit. He had grown used to squalor. It suited him; it fitted him. He was disgusted with his world, but accepted it because it accepted him.

In earlier days, they had all sworn that it would not get to them. For many of them, it hadn't. He saw one or two of them, from time to time, from a distance and true to type they had reverted to wearing starched white shirts and old regimental or mercantile company ties. They wore polished brown shoes, had creases pressed into their trousers, drove Ford or Austin cars, and carried leather briefcases, and talked to their wives in the street. They had succeeded. He had not.

'Hey! You like beer, Johnny?'

Sandingham looked up. He had been staring at his shoe.

'This no' Johnny,' said the voice, not loudly yet as if broad-casting the news. 'This Joe. Hi, Joe! How you doin' now? Long time you no come.'

'Hello, Lucy.' He was glad to see her and it showed in his eyes. 'You're still here, then.'

She was of that indeterminate age between sixteen and thirty when it is hard to judge a Chinese woman's years. In fact, she was nineteen, but it would have been difficult to pin her down to an age or guess from her appearance. She was short and very slim, with small breasts and hip-bones that pushed hard against the tightness of her turquoise brocade cheong-sam. On her feet she wore a pair of soft cloth shoes and on her left wrist a cheap watch. She wore no other jewellery. Her hair was black, loose and long, reaching to her shoulder-blades. Her skin was sallow in colour and soft in texture; her cheekbones were not as high, and her eyes were rounder than many of her peers in the bar-world. Nevertheless she had the hard edge of the prostitute about her: a certain steeled look in her eyes, a distancing. Her voice could be raucous, and she could use her tongue with curt viciousness to put down any man that displeased her: but every bar-girl has a dream that one man will be unlike the rest, and Joe Sandingham was the one that inhabited her fantasies.

'I stiwl here. Where I got to go? You no tak' me out. You no buy me bar-girl champagne.'

He smiled because he liked her, and because the last word was the only one she had pronounced properly.

'Tonight, I buy you d'ink,' he teased.

This mild mockery pleased her for he often seemed so deep in sorrow, even in the easy atmosphere of the Vancouver Bar and her company. Most of the men she knew were happy enough, if only artificially so, prompted by gin, rum or rye whiskey. Joe was rarely in possession of even so much as a fragment of joy.

'Maybe buy me out one hour.' It wasn't a statement or a question, but a hybrid of the two.

The barman poured Sandingham a beer in a narrow tumbler and gave Lucy an innocuous-looking fizzy drink in a flat-bowl martini glass. It was faintly yellow and came out of a champagne bottle. The bottle was only for show and to allay the fears of any half-cut jack-tar who might question where the bubbly stuff came from: in fact, it was lemonade diluted with a little cold tea to give it colour.

The beer cost a dollar, the champagne one seventy-five – to a sailor. The barman winked at Sandingham and charged him one-fifty for the two. Even that price was well over the street value for the contents of both glasses.

Lucy took the drinks to a cubicle beside the jukebox. Sitting down, she gabbled something in rapid Cantonese to the barman, who nodded. Then, reaching behind the jukebox, she turned the volume down two notches and set a slow dance record into play.

It was close and dark in the cubicle. The bench seat faced outwards and was padded with simulated leather that stuck to the skin of the girl's thighs where they came into contact with it, through the slit in the side of her cheong-sam. The table in front of them bore a candle in a bottle which was lit but guttering from too long a wick. Sandingham took a long pull from the glass of beer. It was a local brew, made primarily from chemical additives. Lucy sipped her 'tart's tonic', as the sailors nicknamed it, her little finger crooked as if she were taking tea in the best rectory of the thirties' not far from Basingstoke or Oxford. Most men would have laughed at her. Sandingham did not. It was a part of her imagined world, and he acknowledged it as important to her. To him, even.

'How you bin, Joe? You no comin' here makin me ve'y sad.' Her brows rutted and she looked at him in the candlelight and glow from the jukebox.

'I've been all right. Very busy on Kowloon-side . . . '

'You no got job?' She was clearly incredulous but kept her voice low so that neither of them lost face with the other girls in the bar. It wouldn't do, for either of them, if the girls knew she had a boyfriend of slight means.

'No such luck.'

With her, as with no one else nowadays, he could be frank. Neither of them had any illusions about what they were and where they were fixed in the order of the universe. He was a tramp – or would have been had he lived in London – and she was a whore. His nemesis was poverty and his past: hers was fate and circumstance and an occasional dose of the clap. He counted himself lucky that he wasn't starving while she saw herself as fortunate that she hadn't contracted something worse.

'You know, Joe' – she sipped her drink again and pointed to it – 'champagne a lo'd of buwshit.'

He laughed loudly and she joined in, playfully smacking his arm, glad to see him happy. Often, in the lonely hours after the US Navy Shore Patrol or the British MPs had emptied the bars of drunks and besotted members of their respective armed forces, she wondered what life would be like if she were not a Chinese bar-girl and he were an executive with Butterfield and Swire, or the Hong Kong and Shanghai Bank; or manager of his own Wan

Chai bar. After all, a few of them were owned by Europeans or Australians, all of whom had Chinese wives or mistresses. But even in her dream she was unable to escape the image of the bars and he was unable to exorcise his past. She knew that the best she could wish for was that he would buy her out for an hour – or better, a whole night – and that they'd pretend.

Sandingham called out to the barman, 'Gin and tonic. With lemon.' He paused. 'And ice.'

The drink arrived, accompanied by another beer; the barman had seen that Sandingham's glass was empty. His initiative, as much as his clients' thirsts, sold drink.

'Joe, you ve'y good to me sometime.' Lucy's hand was on his knee and she moved it up his leg as she took her first sip of the real drink. Then, quietly, she asked him, 'You got money tonight, Joe?'

'Some,' he replied.

Even with Lucy he was cagey about finances.

'Enough? You got enough?'

He knew what enough was. Twenty-five dollars.

'Just.'

'Joe. You buy me out one hour. Please. I give you good time.'

Absent from her voice was the harshness of her profession. She wasn't looking to have him, but to love him, love being rare for a bar-girl.

By now, all the other girls had arrived and settled in the bar, standing or sitting about. They were all in their late teens or early twenties and they chatted, giggled and gibed each other. They did not interrupt Joe and his partner. They knew how she felt about him.

He was silent, thinking of her in his detached way. He wasn't looking at her, but at the candle. The flame was low now. It scorched the back of his eyes to look at it.

He had enough to take her out of the bar for an hour, or even for the entire night – it would cost him between eighty and one hundred dollars. His dilemma was whether or not he wanted her. He knew he desired her company, for she listened as he talked. But whether or not he desired her body was another matter.

'Okay,' he said finally.

She had been quiet, gently squeezing his thigh every now and again, avoiding the looks of the other girls who wondered why neither of them was talking.

'Okay? What you mean, okay, Joe?'

'I'll buy you out for one hour. No. Two hours.'

'You sure, Joe?'

He nodded. She left the cubicle and went to the barman who lifted the counter flap to let her behind the bar and out through a doorway in the rear. In a few minutes, she was back.

He drained his second beer.

The girls waved to Lucy as she left. She returned their waves. It was as if she wouldn't see them for days, yet she'd be back by ten. By then, the place would be packed out.

'It not far, Joe,' she said as she took his hand and guided him along the pavement. As they went, he cast a glance or two at his surroundings: he had not been this way before. She obviously had yet another room to which to take her clientele, and he assumed that her change of venue must mark a change of pimp or in the ownership of the bar.

They crossed the street, went down a dim alleyway between two other bars and climbed a set of echoing wooden stairs in a narrow well. At the top was a landing and, from it, three doors led off into rooms. A single, fifteen-watt bulb glowed overhead and from behind one of the doors came the familiar clatter of mahjong pieces and conversation. While Lucy took a key from a hidden pocket of her dress, Sandingham stood quite still, feeling his nerves shivering at the sound of the game through the door.

She beckoned him and he went behind her into a small, airless room. It contained an old mahogany wardrobe, badly scratched and dented, a wooden chair, a tiny table and a wide bed with blue cotton sheets on it. There was little space for anything else in the room. On the wall over the head of the bed was nailed a wooden box, painted bright pillar-box red and, in the centre of it, a gold and red varnished household god. In front of his fierce face a joss-stick holder sprouted two sticks of incense, both of them snubbed out halfway down. The room smelled of sandalwood. A lamp was by the bed and Lucy switched it on, at the same time reaching up to extinguish the centre light, a powerful bulb in a green plastic shade. The brightness flicked off and the room became gentler. The distempered walls looked less harsh in the yellow glow from the lamp.

She sat on the bed and took off her shoes. Then she stood and tugged the zip at the side slits of her cheong-sam upwards so that both her thighs were bare to the waist. She was wearing nothing under the dress. In the traditional style, the bodice of the dress was fastened up one side, to allow for the suckling of a child, had she had one. This she unbuttoned and let slip over her skin. Her breast beneath was as sallow as the rest of her body, and as soft. He reached for the brown ring around her nipple, but she brushed his hand aside and, slipping his jacket off, she undid his shirt. Bare to the waist, he sat on the bed removing his shoes and socks, careful at the same time to thrust both socks into one shoe to hide the money. She saw him do this and realised what his action meant. He did have money, a good deal of it, and it was in his right shoe, jammed into the toe.

'You wan' to taw'k fu'st?'

'I'm very tired,' he said. 'I've not been well these past weeks.'

He did not look as well as he had on his last visit to the bar. She saw that, even in the half-light. She did not know what was wrong with him but she made quite certain, by studying his features and actions, that it was not TB. A dose of VD was something she accepted with stoical resignation, a hazard of the job. But tuberculosis was something else altogether. Sulphur drugs and a course of injections would clear the clap, but months in a hospital out by Aberdeen harbour would be required to rid her of TB and the degeneration the disease caused would ruin her looks and therefore her livelihood. Her fears were allayed, however. He hadn't coughed, nor did he look empty enough of flesh and soul to be tubercular.

'You chase too many dragon,' she scolded him, taking his large, rough hand in both her smaller ones and tightening on it.

'It's not that,' he replied. 'I've not been to Ah Moy's for long while. Several weeks. It's not chasing dragons.'

'You shou'd see you doc-tor. He fix you up. My doc-tor fix me up okay last month.' She sensed he was thinking of this, and added, 'Right now, I clear pass. No clap.'

He laughed again, quietly.

She let his hand go and deftly unfastened his fly buttons, at the

same time gently rubbing his groin to help him desire her. He
pulled his trousers off and lifting the front flap of her cheong-sam
she lay back upon the bed. He could see her outlined against the
thin blue sheets as if on water. In the faint light of the room the
bush of hair just below her waist gleamed darkly and he moved
towards it as she let her hands slide around his neck. As her
fingers ran down his chest, she could feel every bump of his
sternum, every ridge of his ribs. On his stomach, just as she
started to delve her long fingers into the waistband of his underpants to pull them lower, she felt a rough, dry patch of skin the
size of a dollar bill. It puzzled her and she thought about it as he
moved to get himself inside her.

'How much?' he asked, as he dressed himself and she dried the
sweat off her legs with a towel.
    'Eight dollar.'
    He hadn't been any use on the bed, but that was not her reason
for cutting the price. Business was business where that was
concerned.
    He looked at his watch. It was a quarter to nine.
    'I thought it was twenty-five bucks an hour?'
    'Mistah Wong take eight dollar for one hour,' she told him.
'You just pay him money. I fuck you for free.'
    He regarded her in silence. It had been a long time since anyone
had given him anything. He tried to remember the last occasion,
and couldn't.
    With his foot, he pulled the shoe over and bent down. He knew
his money was safe for he hadn't let himself doze off. He thrust
two fingers into the toe and pulled out the wad of crumpled notes.
    'Where you get so much?'
    'I stole it,' he replied bluntly. 'There's more' – he patted the
lining of his jacket – 'but I need that to pay my rent at the –'
    He stopped. He didn't want her to know where he lived.
    'I go now,' she said, not noticing. 'You leave room. Jus' close
door and it lock okay.'
    Sandingham stood up and kissed her on the cheek. He thought
then how beautiful she was. He handed her twenty-five dollars
but she took only ten and gave the rest back to him. He saw, to his
astonishment, that she was crying. She stood up on tiptoe and

quickly kissed him back, like an innocent girl with her first love. Then she left and he heard her stepping quickly down the wooden stairway.

He finished dressing, put twenty dollars behind the joss-stick holder in front of the household god and left.

As he walked past the bar on the way to the tram stop he could hear the shouts of sailors inside. Soon, he knew, Lucy would be back in that tiny room, her legs spread out on that same bed with another man thumping his belly on hers.

As the tram juddered over a set of points at the bottom of Garden Road he thought to himself how much more bearable, somehow, life would have been in those bleak years, had he known that she was on the outside, waiting and thinking, counting the weeks off for him.

It was past ten when he reached the hotel. The manager was sitting on a stool at the far end of the green marbled bar with a milk shake before him. He was talking to a Chinese man several years his senior. Sandingham went up to them.

'Excuse me, Mr Heng. May I see you for a moment, please?'

'Good evening, Mr Sandingham. I trust you have had a good day?' Somehow he made the pleasantry sound genuine.

'I have your rent. Rather' – Sandingham saw the irony of the distinction – 'I have my rent.'

They went to the hotel desk and Sandingham took the money out of his pocket – he'd transferred it there from his shoe – and received a receipt for the full amount. He sensed Heng was curious.

'Gambling,' he lied. 'Wonderful people, the Chinese' – he spoke as if to a European – 'will gamble on anything. I won this on a cricket fight.'

'Really? Where?' Heng knew Sandingham was lying, but played along. He spoke as a European, too.

'North Point,' Sandingham said, 'or beyond. Near the tram terminus in Shau Kei Wan.'

'Sai Wan Ho,' said the manager. 'They do a lot of that there.'

He had not been through that part of Hong Kong Island in twelve months, but it was better to humour his guest. At least he now had the rent securely in the cash-box and would feel neither the wrath of the owners nor the acute embarrassment of having to evict Sandingham.

It was not a long walk to Ah Moy's hideaway in Mong Kok. On the way Sandingham stopped at a kerbside food stall to eat a bowl of fried rice with cubes of diced fish, peas and cabbage in it. It was inexpensive and nourishing and, laced with soya sauce, was tasty. He ate with the gusto of a Chinese, holding the rice bowl in his left hand and scooping the rice and watery gravy into his mouth with split bamboo chopsticks. A few passers-by noticed and gave him a second fleeting look, but most ignored him.

He was careful in his approach to Nam Tau Street. He leaned on the wall at the corner with Canton Road for over five minutes pretending to read from a street library. Such places, well patronised by people who could not afford to purchase books, always drew a crowd. On the windowless end wall of a building hung an array of Chinese paperback books and comics and, for a very small fee – five cents, perhaps – one could read a book for a set length of time. Every now and then the 'librarian' collected the fees. Even this late at night there was a throng of readers who provided Sandingham with the camouflage he needed.

Satisfied that he was not being watched, he walked slowly along the pavement, keeping close to the shop fronts and, at an appropriate moment, ducked into a doorway. A corridor ran down to a staircase.

At the head of the stairs was a door. He knocked on it seven times. In Cantonese, a voice asked for his name. He answered 'gweilo', a derogatory word for Europeans but the nickname by which he was known. He wasn't overly concerned by the rudeness of this password. He was the only European who visited here. Such a precaution was necessary.

Four bolts slid back and the door opened several inches on a chain. Reassured that the visitor was alone, the door-keeper removed the slider on the links, opening up so that Sandingham could quickly enter. As soon as he was in, the door was promptly slammed, chained and re-bolted.

In front of Sandingham stood a diminutive Chinese woman dressed in baggy black trousers and a white smock top. She looked like a child's amah in a well-to-do civil servant's house on The Peak.

She remained silent but held out her hand. Sandingham gave her Leung's piece of paper and thirty dollars. Still without speaking she led him into a room about twelve feet square. Along two walls, up to the ceiling, were rows of bunks without mattresses, eight in all. They were lined with base-boards, and each had a hessian pillow on it.

He lay on a bottom bunk noticing, as he did so, that three of the other bunks were occupied. The room was dark and he could see a glow at the edge of a top bunk.

The woman returned and gave Sandingham a small brass pipe, a little porcelain oil lamp with a tiny, smoky flame and a round ball of wax-like, brown opium the size of a child's marble. He pressed this into the pipe and got it melted and going over the flame. Soon it had burned away; he blew out the lamp and lay back. The pipe and lamp were removed by a young boy. He arranged the pillow under the back of his neck, knowing that this way would be most comfortable.

The sweetish odour of the opium clung to Sandingham's nostrils as he closed his eyes. He felt his arms grow heavy, then magically lighten. He heard Lucy say, quite clearly but as if from a great distance, 'This time I fuck you for free!' Laughter chimed and echoed round his head. Then he heard, as clearly as he heard Lucy, a voice say with considerable peeved annoyance, 'Well, fuck this for a laugh!'

It was an emaciated Englishman dressed in tattered shorts, with wooden sandals on his feet. He was standing by the bunk. His sleeve was torn and there was dry blood caked in the lines of his palms, and under his immaculately manicured fingernails.

PART TWO

Hong Kong: Christmas, 1941

THE FIRST FIFTY yards of Harlech Road were only just wide enough to allow passage for the Austin K30 truck. The private driving it had difficulty getting the vehicle round the corner, his problem compounded by the fact that the headlights were covered with black metal masks which stopped all but the flimsiest of beams from escaping. What was more, the officer in charge had instructed him to turn the corner as quickly as possible. As long as the lorry was at the junction it was visible as a tiny but significant silhouette: a shrewd observer over on Kowloon, equipped with a pair of powerful night binoculars and looking up at the mountain, would see the movement and note it down for further action in the morning. In his hurry to get into Harlech Road the driver had scraped the broad mudguard along the stone wall at the bottom of Mount Austin Road; the steel was bare along the deep scratch, and there was a white stripe like a flesh wound on the granite blocks.

The officer walked behind the truck. All he could see was the white disc attached to the rear axle, under the wooden-sided truck bed.

Where the road widened somewhat, the driver stopped the lorry and the officer worked his way around the nearside and got into the cab, his boot clicking on the running step.

'Been here before?'

'No, sir.'

'Then carry on but take it easy. The road stays narrow for some way – after a bit there's a passing place where you can pull off to the left and stop. I'll tell you when.' The officer paused, then added, 'When you do pull over, watch for rocks. Some of them stick up a bit. Certainly as high as the sump cover.'

'Yes, sir.'

The driver jarred the gears which slurred heavily together as he sought first: they moved off at dead slow speed. The faint lights showed virtually nothing in the shade of the trees that overhung the road.

'Go slower here.' Then, more urgently, 'Stop. Switch off the engine.'

The lorry halted. As soon as the motor was silent both men could hear water sluicing and tumbling in the night.

'There's a waterfall just in front, to the right of the roadway. I'll walk ahead and you follow me. It's on a corner. Tight bend left, iron railings on either side. Try not to decorate them with khaki . . . '

The driver nodded his understanding in the darkness and the officer got out, holding behind his back a sheet of message paper. The driver could see this as a white, indistinct blur. He started the engine once again.

The waterfall drew nearer and, walking ahead of the truck, the officer was freed from the incessant moan of the vehicle motor. He listened to the water.

It had a peace about it. No matter how powerful or surging the torrent, no matter how much threat it might hold, water always seemed peaceful. Perhaps that was why, Sandingham reasoned, the Chinese talked of the *fung shui*, the local gods, who were of water. *Shui* meant water. As the Romans had the lares, so the Chinese . . . There was a squeal. A mudguard met the railing. The lorry stopped.

'For Chrissake, driver!'

He walked smartly back to the arched bonnet of the truck.

'Sorry, sir. Can't see none too good.'

'Move aside. Let me do it.'

The driver slid into the passenger seat and Sandingham took the steering wheel. He deftly squared the lorry off and drove around the bend. Once through the difficulty of the corner, he drove on.

The trees thinned out and, in the starlight, both men could see the mountain climb sharply above them and drop away on their left to a reservoir far below. Beyond lay the sea and the end of Lamma Island.

Both men knew, though their difference in rank and the ever-important rules of morale prevented them from mentioning it outright, that Hong Kong had had it. It was only a matter of time now until annihilation or capitulation. The Imperial Japanese Army had not found it difficult to fight their way through the New Territories behind the Kowloon Hills. Resistance had been dogged and determined but the local garrison and volunteers had been vastly outnumbered. Now the Japanese occupied the entire colony except for Hong Kong Island: the last-ditch stand.

'I wonder if they've made that island yet, sir,' said the driver, thinking out loud and looking down the hillside.

Sandingham made no answer but, as if in reply, a light shone briefly on the island shore, then died out. A few moments later a muffled bump reverberated up from the valley beneath them.

Sandingham stopped the lorry and got out.

'Right,' he said, 'bring the torch and keep it angled very low. Very low, you understand?'

The private was young, not more than twenty. Sandingham was twenty-four and a fully-fledged man. He could see the soldier's face dimly in the light of the torch. A bloody boy. Newly arrived and still wet-arsed. Had it been summer, he'd have had sunburnt knees.

A large boulder loomed up in the darkness, blacker than the surrounding sandy soil. It had not rained recently and the ground was dusty. Scrubby grass grew where feet and heavy-duty tyres had not crushed or rubbed it out.

Once behind the boulder, Sandingham reached down for the field telephone relay box. It was military green in colour and the private could see that it had been lightly camouflaged with tufts of grass and twigs. These fell off as Sandingham lifted it on to the flattish top of the rock.

'Get the roll.'

The private went off with the torch and Sandingham stood up. He pressed his hands into the small of his back, stretching his muscles. The cloud cover was patchy and, through it, starlight coruscated upon the South China Sea. He turned to check that the torch wasn't showing.

'Here you are, sir.'

'Good. Hold the reel by the lugs on each side and run the line
out down to that tree there.' The stars were out now and the tree
came into ghostly view a hundred yards away. Now that their
eyes had grown accustomed to the night the headlamps on the
thirty-hundredweight truck were a help, too. 'When you get
there, put the reel down and come back at the double. Make sure
the wire is off the road – we don't want some clumsy-footed
infantryman tripping on it. Not even one of theirs.'

He trimmed the twin-core telegraph wire bare at the ends and
connected it to the terminals in the box. He couldn't see very well,
but he knew how to do it blindfold. He had wired up a set of three
boxes once in the pitch black of a broom cupboard, for a bet, in
Aldershot. Two and a half years before: it seemed more than a
lifetime away. They had drunk the five quid he won in the wager
in an old pub in Farnham, driving over there in Noel's Lagonda.
That was the night he'd first met Bob. He was wearing a cream
panama hat with a boating blazer and a Cambridge tie.

'I've done it, sir.'

'Fine. I'm done here. Now we work our way along this road for
about half a mile. You follow in the truck: don't pass me. I'll pay
out line and, when I reach the end of the roll, I'll wave to you and
you give me a connector. There's a box of them in the back
behind the cab. Under the canvas. Got it?'

He spoke sharply. There wasn't all that much left of the night.

'Sir!'

'Let's get on with it, then.' He looked up and across to the west.
Few of the clouds that were building appeared of any size. There
should be enough sky light to see by for a bit. 'Switch the lights
off. You'll see me better.'

The truck crept along at the slowest possible speed, the driver
keeping the revs low to prevent the sound of the vehicle travelling
unnecessarily down the mountainside.

On the way, the break in the line appeared where he was
informed it would: a shallow crater, ten feet across at the side of
the road, showed where an attempt had been made to sever the
communications that Harlech Road offered. He couldn't tell
from the scorched earth and stripped trees whether it had been
done by an air strike or fifth columnists.

The thought of the latter suddenly made him nervous. He reached into his holster and checked the revolver. He made sure it was loose in the leather, like a western gunfighter checking his draw would be rapid and smooth.

They reached the junction with Hatton and Lugard Roads within thirty minutes.

It was too risky at this point to allow the driver to switch the masked lights on again. Their intelligence was poor but the meeting of the three roads was visible from Stonecutters Island which they knew had fallen. It was necessary to get the truck down Hatton Road and this meant negotiating a bend at the start of the road and another, a hundred-and-eighty degree twist, halfway down.

'Move over once more, driver. I'll take it from here – it's a tricky stretch ahead.'

Indeed, it was not easy and, at the sharp corner before the hairpin, Sandingham wondered if he were up to it. He had been putting himself to the test a lot of late, usually just getting by. The bend was tight and he was forced to make a six-point turn to get round. Once the oversized tyres, intended for maximum cross-country purchase, scrabbled on the rim of the tarmac, scrubbing the earth for a grip. The young driver would certainly not have managed it.

Looking at the young man in the darkness, his face lit by the dashboard light, Sandingham could see he was petrified. God, he thought, if the boy's scared of the lorry slipping off the metalling, what will he be like when the show starts in earnest? He wanted to touch the boy, to pat his thigh or, just once, stroke his wrist. To reassure him. But he was an officer and that added even more barriers to their communicating.

The remainder of the downhill journey was easier and they soon reached the massive concrete gun emplacement, driving the Austin K30 into the central courtyard and tucking it in close to the wall for protection. A sentry had hailed them but no one else had been seen or heard. He sent the driver off to a room across the courtyard where the other ranks slept.

With tired arms, Sandingham yanked down on the iron door handle and struggled to get the steel door open. He entered the fortified position with a momentary sense of security. A weak electric light briefly shone its beam on to the outside stonework, but it would be impossible to see it except from the air or the top of The Peak. And no sorties were being flown at night. There were too many mountains around.

'You're the signaller wallah, are you?' asked a voice from the shadows cast by the dim bulb. 'Damn glad to have you here: been out since the afternoon. Get through now, can we? Heard a bit of jingling on the line.'

'It was me, sir,' replied Sandingham, saluting a major in his late forties, evidently Indian Army, possibly attached to the battalion of 5/7th Rajputs. He was grey-haired with a spruce, gingerish moustache. 'If I might try your phone now?'

He stood by the field telephone, picked up the receiver and wound the handle round several times, sharply. A voice answered his call.

'Give me Fortress HQ.' Pause. 'Captain Bellerby, please.' Pause again. 'I see. Can you tell him Captain Sandingham has re-established the line to the batteries on the Hill above Belcher's and High West? Yes . . . that's right. Can you give me a call back, please?' He put the phone down. It rang: the Fortress HQ operator. 'You are now through, sir.' He rang off.

'Grand stuff!' the major said, as Sandingham replaced the receiver, adding, 'Fancy a little snort for the road? Sit down, dear boy.'

Not waiting for a reply, he pulled a hand-stitched, leather-covered hip flask from his tunic pocket and unscrewed the silver top. He poured a generous tot into the cap and handed it across. Sandingham sat heavily into a folding armchair, took the cap and knocked the dark rum back in one.

He closed his eyes. They seemed more tired shut than open so he let his lids part gradually.

'Reckon it'll go on much longer?'

The major took a swig from the flask, refilled the cap and handed it back. He looked round the tiny room as if to check that no one was listening. It was a reflex action. The room was only just big enough for two.

'Frankly, no. A week, ten days at best. Won't be long before the little buggers get it into their heads to swim across or blow up their little rubber boats and row over. They'll do a bit more bombing and shooting first.' As if anticipating Sandingham's next question, he continued, 'Won't be to the south of the island. They're out there on Lamma Island, for sure – saw the flashes in the evening: they're shooting at some of our boys on Ap Lei Chau and from Kellet Bay round to Telegraph Bay. But they're not there in strength. Just nagging the lads. No: my guess would be they'll come at us either down there' – he pointed through the reinforced concrete wall in the direction of Kennedy Town and Sai Ying Pun – 'and fight through the houses, or land at North Point and head out to Stanley and along the waterfront of Causeway Bay and Wan Chai in a two-pronged attack. Head to control high ground. If I were them . . . '

There was a knock on the door. Sandingham looked up, startled. He realised he must have been dozing. A corporal entered. He looked haggard and tired. Even though it was winter, the armpits of his battle-dress were ringed with dark sweat stains. He smelt of cordite and brass.

'First light, sir.'

Sandingham had to go. He had been instructed to leave the truck and its driver at the battery and make his own way back to Fortress HQ. Quite how he hadn't been told. It would take him two hours to walk.

He explained his problem to the major.

'There's a motorbike in one of the storerooms,' offered the other. 'Brought up here by a despatch rider. Got a granite splinter in his arm two days ago. Why not take that?'

The major led Sandingham through a maze of stone-lined corridors. The motorbike was a heavy, olive-green BSA B30 with the typically masked front light and the rear bulb removed. He sat astride it, turned the ignition key and kicked the starting pedal down. The engine refused to fire at first, but finally it bucked into life and Sandingham took leave of the major after twisting his cap around so that its peak lay over the back of his neck.

'Take it easy, Captain. Remember what they say.'

'What do they say, sir?' he replied over the chattering of the motorcycle, but the major had turned and re-entered his concrete stronghold.

It was light enough not to need to use the shuttered headlamp. Sandingham stopped just outside the battery to ponder which route would be best. He could go back up to the top of The Peak then ride down the mountainside on the Peak Road, half of his journey out of sight of Kowloon, he could go down the steep Old Peak Road where he would be in view from the mainland for most of the way, or he could drive down to the Hong Kong University buildings below and then go through the western end of the city on Hong Kong Island. He chose the last way: although the road was cursed by many bends it took him through the wooded western slopes of the mountain.

It was going to be a dull day. While he had been sipping the major's rum and nodding off the sky had clouded and the stars had been extinguished. Now a light mist hovered above The Peak.

He rode slowly, careful to avoid the potholes caused by recent shelling, savouring the cool air upon his face, a welcome relief after the stuffiness of the battery office. The world had the silence and peacefulness of early morning and it was hard to believe that war was all around him, hiding in the air and the sea and the buildings across the harbour. Birds flitted through the branches of the trees and he thought he saw a monkey at a bend in the narrow road where it crossed a trickle of stream. Near the university, however, the illusion dissolved when he saw a Hillman pulled in by the side of the road, its window shattered.

He made for the waterfront, stopping short of Des Vouex Road West in the cover of the harbour-facing buildings. The streets which ran to the quays were blocked or sandbagged. Two soldiers were leaning on a table taken from a shop, their rifles propped against the wall though they both still had on their steel helmets. A brew-up was just ready and the sight of the small fire burning on the pavement made Sandingham realise how thirsty the rum had made him.

They had not expected an officer on a despatch rider's mount and at first didn't change their stance. As soon as they saw Sandingham's uniform, however, they jumped to their feet and saluted, simultaneously flicking their half-smoked cigarettes along the gutter into a puddle.

'Easy,' he said.

They relaxed and grinned sheepishly at him.

'Any action during the night?'

'We 'ad some chinkies come over, sir,' said one of the pair. 'Come in one of them sampans, like.' He spoke with a West Riding accent and it suddenly struck Sandingham as very odd to hear such a voice under a wooden, white-painted sign with red Chinese characters on it.

'We open' fire in t'dark,' continued the man, 'but they yell at us in English. Sergeant come up, says, "Stop firin', you dumb bastards. 'Em's friends." '

'We 'elp 'em up the steps,' said the other. 'It were lucky we didn't 'it any of 'em.'

They offered him a mug of tea and he readily accepted it, taking one of the soldier's billy cans while the soldier got hold of a rice bowl from under the table and drank from that. Sandingham took out a flat, yellow tin of State Express 555 and offered the cigarettes round. Both soldiers thanked him, took one each, and put them in their breast pockets. He lit one for himself from the fire.

The tea warmed him. He wanted to ask the two soldiers if they had any food but knew that would be tactless. Supplies were running low and their distribution growing more difficult by the day. The Chinese population were having to form long queues for rice and other staple foods and the soldiers and Hong Kong Police had been given the order to machine-gun looters.

After he had finished his cigarette, Sandingham walked down the short street to the quayside on Connaught Road, leaving the motorbike propped on the kerb out of sight of the harbour. There, tucked into the ground floor of a small godown, was a machine-gun nest manned by three soldiers. Even fifty yards from the tea-drinkers the atmosphere was completely altered. These men were alert and scanning the harbour across their entire arc of fire. They made to rise as he entered.

'Don't get up,' he said, as if he were a schoolmaster entering a room of studious boys whom he did not want to disturb.

The harbour surface was still dawn-grey. Nothing moved on it. The usual traffic of junks and sampans and small craft was totally absent. A grey slick against the hills was Stonecutters Island. From behind it a trickle of smoke was rising and spreading like a drop of paint in murky water.

'Nip ship,' said a lance-corporal whose task it was to feed the ammunition belt into the breach. He spoke with deliberately clipped syllables and his two mates quietly laughed at his joke.

Sandingham was amazed how three men, days if not hours away from their deaths, could be so blasé, so humorous. He felt a shiver pass up his spine; but he joined in with their laughter.

The room itself shared a sultry air of great weariness with its occupants. The clock on the gloss-painted wall by the door, like those usually found in rural railway station waiting-rooms, with large Roman numerals on a white-painted face, had stopped at ten minutes to two, though whether a.m. or p.m. no one either knew or cared. The maps pinned on the boards were smothered in red pencil lines, squiggles and arrows and the three tables were littered with signals, message pads, red- and blue-coloured pencils, cipher and encoding books, artillery manuals, rulers and set-squares, various bits of personal military issue and more maps, some folded, some opened, some torn and most out-of-date if only by hours. One of them seemed to sum it all up. It was a small-scale map of Hong Kong harbour. A wit had drawn a scarlet line down the centre of the water and drawn 'Them' over the mainland and 'Us' over the island. The nine hills of Kowloon had been roughly shaped with indelible pencil into a crude goal-mouth: a second was drawn on Wong Nai Chung Gap. Another hand had written below 'Japs 1: Diehards 0 – half-time score.'

At the biggest of the tables sat Sandingham. His chin was cupped in his hands and his eyelids were drooping. Even having shaved with cold water had not helped fight the fatigue that was seeping through him. Before him was an enamel plate on which was a thick slice of bread smeared with a sort of jam and next to that a cooling yellow mush. He had drunk the weak tea in one draught from a chipped white mug that matched the plate.

'I sometimes wonder if the British Army doesn't survive on tea, tinned jam and powdered eggs.'

He looked up. He had forgotten that Bob Bellerby was across the chaos of paper from him. He too had a plate of simulated scrambled egg in front of him and, similarly, his had not been eaten. He preferred to push the food round his plate with a fork, building it into small anaemic-coloured hills, dunes and bunkers.

'If it had a knob of butter on it . . . ' Sandingham said, looking woefully at the unappetising attempt at the breakfast that one of their brother officers had produced by balancing a saucepan on a one-man, solid-fuel field stove.

' . . . it would still be inedible,' answered Bob.

When the telephone rang on the table beneath the light, and the officer in charge went to answer it, Bob surreptitiously dumped his share of the food into the wastepaper-basket where it clung glutinously to the top of the discarded notes. He tore several sheets from a message pad, crumpled them then spread them over the remains.

An orderly came in to refill the mugs of tea. The officer for whom he had been batman had been killed in the first days of the Japanese advance over the border with China. He had died in a slit trench on Crest Hill, overlooking the railway line and the Lo Wu crossing point. He had been bayonetted. The batman had watched from higher up the hill, and had succeeded in turn in killing the enemy soldier. His shot had hit him in the neck. Even at forty yards he had seen the blood spurt out in a little spray from the severed jugular. Later, he had found the Japanese soldier's body further down the hill, his hand stuck to his neck by a massive, hardened clot. He had felt no emotion at all.

' 'Nother cup, sir? 'Fraid there's no sugar.'

His accent was south London, flat of tone and lifeless. Or perhaps, Sandingham thought, that was just the way it seemed. Most things seemed flat; dead or dying. He had to keep awake. He was still on duty. To give way to sleep now would lead to inefficiency, perhaps negligence. If he were negligent someone would be let down, possibly even killed: or he might let himself down and the chain of events in his life would be altered minutely in the present, magnifying as time passed until he, too, might be killed by this long-lost and forgotten moment of inattention. It was like stepping on a butterfly now and causing a bird to die far in the future. By allowing himself to sleep he might be initiating an act of suicide: a bizarre thought. He could kill himself by sleeping.

'Jay! We've got two hours.'

'What!'

He was jerked back to the present. Bob had placed his Sam Browne belt on the table and was checking his Webley .455 pistol. A box of bullets had been ripped apart and the little brass cases lay scattered about on the maps, looking like miniature fingers. Bob scooped up a handful and put them in his trouser pocket. The lieutenant-colonel from across the room came over and did likewise. Sandingham took the remainder.

'Time off. C'mon, let's go.'

The tea in the mug was brackish, the water over-chlorinated, but he drank it before they left the room. It somehow prepared him for the daylight, and there was no way of knowing when or if another cup would arrive.

He realised that increasingly he was pondering upon many of his most ordinary actions. Would this be the last time he would ever write his name, look at his watch, scratch his brow? In eternity? He could not accept such a concept even in the company of the dark angel. The chaplain at school had always warned him of that: beware the dark angel and be prepared for his visitation.

As they went outside it was still overcast. The cloudbase had risen a few thousand feet but the day was still grey and cheerless. There was no sound. No birds, crickets or cicadas were chirruping. No traffic was moving: or very little.

'It's like before a storm. Or an earthquake.' Sandingham sensed Bob was thinking the same. 'Where are we going?'

'I've a new billet. Secret.' Bob Bellerby grinned like a schoolboy who had a tree-house to which parents couldn't climb. 'How was Repulse Bay?'

'Paradisiacal.'

They had reached a parade ground around which a border of white-washed stones was arranged. Wherever the British soldier stayed more than a day, Sandingham thought, he inevitably painted stones white and arranged them in a square. Two thousand years from now an archaeologist digging in the rubble of history would find one of the stones and instantly assume with conviction that an army was once here and that army had fought a battle and . . .

They both saluted the major as he came up to them. He acknowledged them.

'Captain Sandingham, Bellerby: good morning, though' – he looked apprehensively upward at the sky – 'I can see little good about it.'

He rubbed his hands together to generate heat in the palms. Sandingham felt, by transference, the chill of the day.

'Nip in the air, sir?' asked Bob.

The major guffawed loudly and briefly.

'Very good, Bellerby! Not losing your touch for an apt remark. Keep it up! If your pecker stays aloft, your men's will.'

He turned on his heel and walked smartly across the diagonal of the parade ground.

There was a whistle – faint, like a dog call vibrating from far away, its note screwed just within the audible reaches of the human ear. Sandingham and Bob instinctively fell flat on the ground, covering their heads with their arms.

The shell did not explode with a bang, more of a thump, landing in a flower bed of wintering geraniums across the parade ground. A rush of warm air blew up Sandingham's back and both men were showered with fine grit, earth and pebbles.

'Run!' Bob Bellerby was up, tugging at Sandingham's elbow. He glanced in the direction of the major who was on his feet apparently unhurt, and brushing down his uniform with a show of indignant annoyance.

Sandingham clumsily rose to his feet and the two men sprinted uphill until they reached a long row of barrack huts which afforded some cover.

'Bombardment?'

'Not yet. Ranging shot. There'll be more.'

As if to prove the statement, another shell came in low and crashed into a vehicle-repair garage well down below them. A pall of rubber smoke began to escape from the rear of the building. A dark flame flickered in a window. The first shot was high. This one was low and to the left. The Japanese gunners, assuming Fortress HQ to be in the vicinity, were trying to centre their fire on the main parade ground square.

They ran on, but without the urgency they had mustered under direct fire. The barracks was situated on the lower slopes of The Peak. At its highest point, a tall brick wall topped with loops of barbed wire and broken glass formed the perimeter defence. This

had been breached by shell-fire some days before. At night a
sentry was posted near the gap but in daylight it was unattended.
No one had sought to rebuild it. There were more pressing duties.

Clambering over the heap of loose bricks was not difficult and,
once outside the confines of the barracks, they slowed to a walk,
heading westward along Kennedy Road.

'Paradisiacal,' said Sandingham.

'What was?'

'Repulse Bay. You asked about it. The hotel's set on a curving
sandy bay. Shade trees. Flowering bushes. A superb bar. Before
. . .'

He wanted to say 'before the war', but with it all around him he
couldn't. He didn't want to think of it. The less he accepted there
was a war on the less it might accept him as a part of it. Illogical,
he knew; but it was part of the escape mechanism he had built up
inside himself.

'Before . . . 1939, it must have been heaven. Film stars lying on
the beach, getting a tan. Not quite like that now, of course.
Packed out with civil servants and their families. Soldiers and
children and amahs. Refugees. Nurses and nuns.'

Another shell came over but they did not duck. Experience told
them that this was a wild aim and, sure enough, it burst four
hundred feet up the mountainside above them, harmlessly exploding in the steep wooded slopes.

'Know why nuns always go round in pairs?' asked Bob,
suddenly.

'No. Why do nuns always go round in pairs?'

The patter, the play-off of line against line: they could have
been in their school dormitory or in the mess near Salisbury,
sipping scotch and soda after a day's exercise out on the Plain.

'So one nun sees the other nun gets none.'

It was intended to be corny, and Sandingham laughed with
deliberate half-heartedness.

Just before reaching the Peak Tram line they turned left up a
stepped pathway through trees and low houses and blocks of
flats. Stray artillery fire had hit some of the buildings; the path
was strewn with debris and, at one point, a fallen tree. Halfway
up the pathway that led to Macdonnell Road, the next terrace-
like level of buildings on the mountainside, Bob stopped and

pushed open a door in the shrapnel-scarred wall of a block of flats. It was dark inside but he evidently knew the way; Sandingham followed him up the stairs. Three storeys up Bob stopped again. Another door was opened, this time with a key. Bob had fitted a padlock to the hasp.

They entered the apartment. It was still furnished but it had been looted for valuables.

'Wait here,' said Bob before disappearing into the kitchen and servants' quarters.

Looking around him, Sandingham saw that the owners of the flat had been wealthy. The furniture that remained was of the expensive cane variety. A set of shelves held porcelain ornaments and curios: some lay smashed on the floor. Everything made of ivory or jade had been removed but he could see from the dust circles where they once stood. Along a wall of the sitting room were bookshelves which the looters had ignored.

'Who owned this place?' he called.

'Somebody working for one of the big banks,' shouted Bob from a back room. 'They left a month before the Japs came in. Had a tip-off. Got windy. Who knows? Probably safe in Sussex by now, playing a round of golf on the nearby course.'

'Hardly.'

'Hardly what?'

'Hardly playing golf. It's the middle of the night in England. Besides, they're more likely to be in Calcutta or Bombay, swigging sundowners in the club and sorting out the finances of the local branch there.'

Sandingham had wandered into a bedroom. It was small and the single bed was covered with children's books. On the floor a clockwork train set was half laid out. He wound the locomotive up and set it on the track. It rushed forwards, left the rails where they ran out and trundled across the wooden floor until it hit the skirting board and fell on its side. The wheels spun and slowed to a halt.

He walked back to the main room and started to look through the books. Some were leather-bound and, even in the winter chill, had started to mark with mould.

He took down a copy of the 1777 edition of Young's *Night Thoughts* and, opening it at random, read to himself:

Absurd Longevity! More, more, it cries:
More Life, More Wealth, more Trash of ev'ry kind.

and

While Man is growing, Life is in Decrease;
And Cradles rock us nearer to the Tomb.
Our Birth is nothing but our Death begun;
As Tapers waste, that Instant they take Fire.

He stopped reading. Bob was standing in the doorway holding two fine china coffee cups and a full bottle of champagne cognac. He placed them gently on a table in front of a cane settle and poured out two large measures of the brandy.

'Just look at us, Jay,' he said. 'Dressed in dirty uniforms, in a ransacked flat on the coast of southern China with you reading eighteenth-century poetry out loud while I pour French cognac into Noritake coffee cups made by Japanese potters for the European market, while under howitzer fire from the aforesaid craftsmen. How bloody ironic!'

Sandingham picked up his cup and sniffed the scent of the liquid.

'I went to Cognac with my father once on business,' continued Bob idly. 'The smell of brandy was so strong in the streets that it made one heady just to breathe in the air. Wonderful!'

'You know, Bob, I think you sons of brewers could find a good bottle of hootch at a dried-up oasis.' He drank. 'And Arab countries ban booze.'

His cup refilled, Sandingham walked out on to the balcony. He was masked from view by a tree but could see through the leafless winter branches. As he looked at the tip of the Kowloon peninsula he saw a puff of smoke appear. Directly afterwards an explosion erupted near the naval dockyard. The Japanese had installed some of their artillery in the compound of the Tsim Sha Tsui police station that was on a rise behind the Star Ferry pier.

They sat together, side by side, on two of the cane chairs on the balcony. The cold breeze was abating, merely stirring the curtains in the glassless windows. They did not speak but drank slowly and meditatively.

Several more desultory puffs of smoke eddied or ringed out from the peninsula. The shells either hit the dockyard buildings or fell short into the harbour, sending up columns of grey spray.

They're trying to range their guns, to hit the defences on the shore, Sandingham thought, preliminaries to an inevitable assault on the island.

Bob was sitting stretched out, his feet pressing on the balcony rail and his head lolling against the bamboo chair-back. His eyes were lightly closed, the cognac balanced in his cupped hands just under his nostrils. Sandingham watched him breathe in the fumes and hold them before letting them escape from his lungs with a barely audible sigh. Every breath, he knew, was taking Bob away through the singing years to France and Italy, to Provence and Tuscany, to public houses he'd known as a boy, to leafy English lanes and Welsh hillsides, to illicit school drinking and weekend parties in his parents' country house, to private thoughts and secret dreams that Sandingham could not share.

In his turn, Sandingham shut his eyes and let the warmth of the cognac take him as far away as he could from the present; but he could not make the journey as far as his home. His dreams ended in Malaya with Bob.

One sight kept recurring, one wonderful sight. It was of a deep verandah-ed, colonial-style house with the fans of travellers' palms spread wide as green peacock tails on either side. A lawn led up to the building and the verandahs were in heavy shade. There was a slight and humid wind coming off the jungle. On the verandah stood Bob, bare to the waist, except for his identity tag, with a pristine white sarong lapping at his shins. As if projected on the screen of some cinema of the mind, the scene cut to a close-up of Bob grinning. He waved, and the motion of his hand disturbed a gekko flattened on the verandah railing.

Sandingham opened his eyes and looked about him like a man waking early. The balcony upon which they now sat had no gekkos on it anywhere.

When Bob had waved to him that day, from a house on the outskirts of Kuala Lumpur lent to him by friends of his parents away on home leave, Sandingham had parked the Morris beside one of the palms and entered the cool vault of the building. The ceiling fans rotated slowly and the plank floors glistened with polish between the rugs. Printed batik tapestries hung on the walls. Later, they had made love, not for the first time and yet, it now seemed, perhaps for the first time. Afterwards, it had rained in the typically Malayan manner, the drops huge and bouncing on the lawn, the noise like a vast hissing in the ears of the whole world. It had lasted an hour until, spent, the clouds had dispersed to reveal the sun shining so hotly that the steam rose not only from the jungles but also from their own skins. The houseboy, he remembered, had served them gin and lime from a jug surrounded by crushed ice.

After a while, Bob Bellerby broke their silence.

'Well?' he asked.

'It's all so bloody foolish,' replied Sandingham. 'We don't stand a monkey's chance. We'll hold out for another week or so, but the ammunition'll dwindle and then we'll be left with broom handles and saucepan lids.'

'Already has,' replied Bob. 'That box on the table was all that the sergeant could find.'

'So what now?'

'We fight. We try. We go down in the history books as the gallant defenders of a little bit of Empire. Names in lead on a monument erected on a traffic island. On a village green. Visited annually and otherwise ignored except by the publican's dog. Forgotten.' He swallowed another measure of cognac. 'Unmarked graves or a pile of dust. "Some corner of a foreign field that is forever England." Because we've fertilised it. Rupert Brooke was a stupid bastard. He got what he deserved – a lost grave on a Greek island. God save us from jingoistic poets.'

'Let's save some of the cognac. For a rainy day.'

As if to mock him, drizzle began to fall and the breeze drifted it on to their faces and hands. Bob rammed the cork back into the mouth of the bottle with the ball of his thumb.

'How much longer?'

Sandingham pulled back his cuff to see his watch and said, 'Have to report back in an hour and a bit. There's time.'

Bob hid the cognac in a large, cracked vase that had once served as an umbrella stand: no looter would be interested in a damaged antique.

The master bedroom was less disarranged. The wardrobes and

the airing room had been ransacked but not everything had been taken. Several fashionable lady's dresses lay across a chair and the drawers of lingerie and make-up were virtually undisturbed. The dressing-table set had vanished except for a silver-backed nail buffer. Without thinking, Sandingham put this in his pocket. It might come in useful. One day.

The bed had clean sheets on it. The blankets were smoothed and the silk tassles on the counterpane flickered in the air.

Both men stripped. Sandingham was so tired and his fingers ached so badly from wiring and rewiring, from steering trucks and writing curt signals, from pulling a trigger and gripping pliers, that he could not unclasp his belt. Bob helped him with it.

They got into the bed. It was blissful to feel the clean cotton against their skins. The cool material seemed to erase the grime and sweat that clung to them. Sandingham wished that they had been able to bath first, but there was no water or electricity with which to heat it.

Bob took Sandingham's hand in his and kissed it.

'I love you, Jay,' he said. 'God knows where we'll be a week from now, but never forget it. Wherever and whatever, I love you.'

'And I you, Bob. Regardless.'

He felt himself slipping into sleep. He wanted to stay awake, wanted desperately in his soul to make love but he couldn't gather the energy. The sheets were warming them both and the warmth was acting as a soporific. The cognac more than relaxed his brain. It numbed it and emptied it of all but love, an overwhelming desire to sleep and a distant fear from which he seemed now to be divorced yet with which he was still in touch.

Turning on to his side, he faced Bob.

'I'm sorry . . .' he said. 'I'm just so tired, so bloody knackered.'

'It's all right, Jay.'

He felt Bob nuzzle his lips into his neck and sensed his lover's hand slipping smoothly down his belly to work its way between his thighs.

And then he was asleep and in his dream two nuns came to him and told him the war was a game in which he must play up and score; a soldier with one arm served him real coffee with cream and he could smell bacon frying, hear it sizzling in a pan . . .

An hour later Bob woke him roughly, tugging hard on his shoulder. The first sound he heard after Bob's voice was the high hum of an engine straining against itself. He rolled over and faced the long bedroom windows. The first object he saw past Bob's strained face was a tall pillar of smoke rising from the waterfront near Causeway Bay. A line of dull flashes through Wan Chai explained Bob's urgent words.

'Wake up, Jay! Get up! Air raid.'

There was a heavy mist upon the mountains. It had come down silently in the early hours, filtering out sounds as effectively as a thick snowfall. The trees dripped eerily upon the winter carpet of dead leaves and on the road surface outside West Brigade headquarters at Wong Nai Chung Gap. As soon as any soldier walked out of the cover of the headquarters dewdrops clung to the hairs of the serge material of his khaki drill uniform and dampened it miserably.

The Brigadier was pleased. Without doubt, it would slow the Jap advance considerably. They had made good ground during the night and had promised to break through with the coming of dawn. Now the dense fog would hamper them. The Japanese, being on the offensive, would have to guard against attack at every bend in the road, every rock and bush and gully.

At five o'clock he had issued orders that a company of the Winnipeg Grenadiers should go up to Jardine's Lookout and, clearing it of any enemy troops who might have gained the advantage, should move on and consolidate a hold on Mount Butler. It was hoped that would hold up the Japanese movements westward along the high ground of the spine of island hills.

Sandingham was leaning on the rear mudguard of a Humber Snipe staff car. His driver was in the medical aid shelter thirty yards from the headquarters, obtaining a carton of field dressings. It was barely daylight. He was smoking a cigarette, the smoke exiting from his mouth and nostrils to disappear promptly into the damp air. The mist revived him to a point. He wiped his hand over his forehead and felt the sweat loosen and slip away. The dew was almost as good as a blanket wash.

'I'm ready, sir.'

He hadn't noticed the driver approach him. His mind had been on Bob Bellerby. They had not had another opportunity to be alone together since those two hours spent in the banker's apartment, and Sandingham was feeling the hollowness that absence causes.

'Right, Lance-corporal. Wait here, will you?'

He went into the headquarters where the Brigadier was studying a map spread across his knees and the lap of his intelligence officer. The sentry raised his rifle as Sandingham passed by. The Brigadier looked up expectantly.

'Captain Sandingham, grand! Now, this point here' – with a pencil, he pointed to a road on the map which wove its way down the wooded hillside towards the sea – 'by this driveway. Get down that far, with the car, if you can. No farther. Don't risk it. If you don't come under fire, go ahead to this bend here' – again he indicated the place on the map – 'and see what you can beyond it. Try not to engage the enemy. Then get back here and report.'

'What if I do draw fire, sir?' Sandingham asked.

'Don't bother to shoot back. Get out as fast as you can and head for home. We'll be on the lookout for you.' He turned to a company sergeant-major, adding, 'If you see the Humber coming towards you with its lights on, hold your fire. Pass that on.'

The CSM acknowledged the order with a salute and left.

'That all right, Captain? If you have any bother, let us know with the lights.'

The intelligence officer winked encouragement to Sandingham.

'*Bon chance*, Captain.'

As he left, he noticed the fog had become even denser while he was receiving his instructions.

'Lance-corporal Glass, we're off down to the seaside. Not all the way, so don't pack your trunks.'

'Bucket and spade in order, sir?' replied the driver as he handed his superior a few field dressings.

Sandingham forced them into his breast pockets and smiled. It was the kind of wisecrack Bob would have made.

They sat side by side in the Humber and Lance-corporal David Glass drove forwards in the direction of Repulse Bay. They had a mile or so to go to reach the Brigadier's selected point.

'Slow down and get the car into that entrance,' Sandingham ordered as they neared their destination. 'The driveway on the left. Tuck her well in behind that big tree.'

Thus far they had seen neither hide nor hair of the enemy. Possibly the Japanese had yet to advance so much to the west.

The lance-corporal swung the wheel and pressed hard on the brake pedal. The rear of the Humber Snipe slewed on the gravel that had been washed down the driveway and collected at the bottom. The front mudguard clanged on a stone culvert but did not arrest the progress of the car. Sandingham thanked his luck that he had a driver who knew his job.

'Get the car turned around, driver. Face up the hill. I'm going down to that corner to recce the road as far as the junction.'

'Right, sir. Want me to follow you down, sir?'

Sandingham considered this. Two pairs of eyes would be better than one, and if the Japs were breaking through over the ridge that ran south from Violet Hill then both they and the car were done for anyway.

'Anywhere you can hide the car? At least from view from above?'

Glass looked around. He scanned the building just up the driveway: it was a rich man's house, with a green pantiled roof and neatly arranged gardens along the walls, on which stood pots of flowers.

'Could get it under the shadow of the terrace wall, sir. The bushes should give it cover. Don't want to get it too near the house, though. If the Japs are coming down that slope then we don't want to afford them the house as a hidey-hole.'

'Do it. Then come after me. Can you hoot like an owl, Glass?'

His question sounded utterly banal, to the point of stupidity.

'Beg pardon, sir?'

'An owl, an owl. Hoot! Can you hoot?'

'I think so, sir.'

'Then if you approach me and I don't know it's you, do so. Like this.'

He made a cave of his hands and blew through the crack between his thumbs. A strangled squirting noise came out.

'Not much like an owl, if you don't mind my saying so, sir.'

Sandingham laughed very quietly. The lance-corporal grinned. Both of them stopped as they heard the stutter of small arms fire open up from the direction of Repulse Bay.

'I'd rather whistle "Tipperary", if it's all the same to you, sir.'

'Right,' he agreed, then said, 'but spare me all but a few bars.'

Sandingham got out of the car, putting his hand in his pocket as he did so. The bullets were there, warm from the proximity of his own flesh.

'Key in the usual place?'

Glass nodded, and reassured him by saying, 'Will be, sir.'

He gunned the six-cylinder motor and reversed the car into its hiding place. Glass stopped the engine and put the ignition key under the rear edge of the front off-side wheel, where he knew Sandingham would expect to find it in an emergency. That way, whichever of them got to the car would be able to drive it off. A dead man with the key in his pocket was no use.

In the meantime, Sandingham ran in a crouch down the left-hand side of the road, keeping himself in close to the cover. He reached a bend in the road and ducked into the bushes. Ahead of him, out of sight, he could hear someone muttering. It was a sound that the mist blunted, rendered indistinct yet did not silence.

Lance-corporal Glass appeared noiselessly at his side. Sandingham was glad that he had had the presence of mind not to whistle. He was carrying his Lee Enfield .303 rifle.

'What do you make of it?' Sandingham whispered.

Glass shrugged, then grimaced. Sandingham ordered him to slip into the trees above the road and work his way down to the top of a small bank from where the sound seemed to be emanating. If he saw anything he wasn't to shoot but to signal to Sandingham who would come along the road using the wide storm drain. They'd tackle the enemy together, as silently as possible.

Edging along the drain, Sandingham felt as if he were making enough racket to awaken a corpse. Dry twigs, deposited in the bottom of the watercourse, cracked and tweaked under his soles; he could ill afford to look down and check where he was stepping. As it was, he was bent double, with his head up, like a miner working his way through a gallery to the seam. In his hand was his revolver. The safety catch was off and he pointed it ahead.

The noise grew softer as he approached, but it didn't cease. He took the opportunity of the cover of a big lantana bush to stand up and check the lance-corporal's progress. The cover was not as thick as he had supposed when looking at it from the road, and he could make out his driver a little ahead of him and thirty yards higher up the hill.

The road began to turn left. As he cleared the lantana bush he heard a distinct, smooth click. It was the sound of a bolt going home into a breach. It was followed by another click as the bolt handle was pushed down. Someone was waiting for him.

His nerves were alive with the currents of fear. Every step counted now. He wondered abstractly if one felt much as a bullet entered the forehead and left by the cranium . . .

His finger tightened on the trigger of his revolver. He looked down. His knuckles were tense and white. The skin across the back of his hand was stringy: it reminded him of his grandfather's hand when the old man held a fan of cards. His bidding was so good. If he opened six no trumps, out of the blue, you shut up and he'd maybe make seven with a bit of luck or a slip on the part of his opponents.

His mind strayed to thoughts of summer-time peace, tea parties and bridge evenings in the old man's garden at Saxmundham. Meanwhile his body acted out the slow mime of war.

'It's all right, sir. I can see him. One of our lot. He's hurt.' His driver's voice was quiet but clear.

David Glass came quickly through the trees, ducking and weaving past the lower branches and making no pretence of silence. He kept his rifle at the ready, though, and Sandingham noticed that his bayonet had been fitted to the muzzle.

The wounded man was lying on the opposite side of the road, half his body out of sight down the slope. Only his head and shoulders were in view. He was muttering to himself. In front of him, on the kerbstones, lay his rifle.

'Stay down, driver,' Sandingham commanded quietly and then, to the wounded man, he called softly, 'Can you hear me?'

The muttering stopped and the man raised his head a few inches.

'Who's there?' he said hoarsely, his left hand scrabbling for his rifle. Twice his fingers touched its butt, but they seemed unable to grip it. All the effort he could muster had gone into sliding the bolt home. His second hand lay motionless.

'Signals officer,' said Sandingham. He stood, so that the wounded man could see him from the waist up, recognise his uniform and the cap from which Sandingham had unclipped his badge.

'I'm hurt bad,' said the man unnecessarily. His voice weakened with each word. 'Can't feel me legs. Can't move me fuckin' arm.'

He groaned and muttered something again. It could have been a prayer, Sandingham thought.

'Cover me, Glass.'

The lance-corporal rested his rifle in the notch of a sapling and faced downhill, the direction from which they expected any opposition to come. He adjusted his back sight to one hundred and fifty yards.

'Ready!'

Sandingham scuttled across the road and slid down beside the wounded man. He fumbled in his pocket for a field dressing.

Nothing happened; no hidden sniper opened fire. The lance-corporal rapidly crossed the road and knelt beside Sandingham, all the time looking up and down the road. Nothing moved except a bird which alighted in the middle of the road, sang a few shrill notes into the mist then took wing, to glide on to a branch overhead where it perched in silence.

The wounded man was a private in the Middlesex. He was wearing a battle-dress uniform with a webbing belt. His steel helmet was twenty feet down the slope. His right arm was without motion and felt clammy and cold. Around his shoulders was a dark patch that was not sweat, although it was warm. Where his left foot should have been was a ragged stump of flesh and bone with surprisingly little blood oozing from it. Stuck to the raw meat of the man's ankle were small twigs and dried leaves.

Sandingham ignored the soldier's legs. He undid the man's tunic and tore at the vest underneath. The shoulder wound did not look too bad. A piece of shrapnel was embedded in the tissue just beneath the collar-bone. He gripped it firmly and gave a sharp tug. The man grunted, muttered incoherently and fell silent. The shrapnel was out and the wound started to bleed again. Sandingham stuck the field dressing over it and lodged it in place with the vest. As he did so, he felt the dressing sink in the middle. The hole was larger than he had realised. He felt a hard lump beneath the dressing wad and tried to guess if it was collar-bone or another fragment of iron.

'If we're quick, sir, I can get the car down to this poor bugger. I can back along.'

'Do it!'

Glass disappeared. Within a minute, Sandingham heard the Humber revving up and then it careered around the bend, reversing dangerously at twenty miles an hour. The brakes locked and the car skidded to a stop. The lance-corporal had the back passenger door open. He left the driver's seat and helped Sandingham lift the private into the rear of the vehicle. The man collapsed on the seat, falling over sideways, blood from his back smearing the leather upholstery. Sandingham got in the front passenger seat and slammed the door. The lance-corporal moved quickly around the boot of the car to get in the driver's side. As he pulled the door handle down, three single shots rang out in quick succession. Glass spun about, his arms outstretched like a ballerina's. He hit the bonnet, his head denting the metal, and fell off. His forearm caught round the headlamp and the opening on his jacket snagged the sidelight on the top of the mudguard.

Sandingham knew he was dead. He had seen men pirouette like that before. He pushed himself into the driving seat and rammed the car into gear. It screeched and jolted foward. He pressed his foot hard on to the accelerator pedal. The Humber surged powerfully ahead.

A light machine weapon opened up. The pane in the rear window shattered and Sandingham felt small splinters of it hit the collar of his jacket.

The lance-corporal's body was hanging from the headlamp and sidelight. His boots trailed along the road, the metal toecaps sparking off the surface. For a quarter of a mile his body stayed in tow. Sandingham ignored it. Then the clothing tore and the body slumped, fell off and was gone. In the driving mirror Sandingham saw it rolling across the road. Around it, small calibre bullets were kicking up puffs of grit.

The machine-gun nests and pill-boxes at Wong Nai Chung Gap were half-expecting him. As he raced through the fog he kept his hand pressed hard upon the horn and it blared out in the sorrow of the mist. He had forgotten to switch on the lights.

Those dug in held their fire as he approached.

He did not stop at the medical aid shelter by the brigade headquarters but kept on going, easing up on the accelerator. Outside the headquarters was a pile of smouldering rubbish: it consisted of all non-essential documents.

As he passed some water treatment filter beds, to his horror, someone opened up on the Humber with a machine-gun. Their fire was inaccurate, but a few stray riccochets hit the nearside passenger door.

'You stupid bastards!' he screamed. 'You dumb, fucking useless, shitting, half-arsed bastards!'

His words gave vital release to the terror that was surging through him, a terror that had wanted to seek escape but which he had not dared let go free.

At the junction with Stubbs Road he passed a number of lorries speeding back the way he had just come. He hoped the gormless sods with the machine-gun would not fire on them as well.

Down at the racecourse in Happy Valley, the RAMC and the staff of a local hospital had established an emergency centre in the Royal Hong Kong Jockey Club building. He headed there and stopped the Humber outside the main entrance. A Chinese orderly ran out carrying a stretcher. A nurse in her mid-twenties followed him. They lifted the private out of the back seat and on to the stretcher. Sandingham helped carry him in.

Looking at the man, he knew the soldier was dead. His eyes were open and they seemed to be peering at the ceiling with an intelligent and studied gaze, but the skin around his jaw had sagged and his uninjured leg twitched like the rump of a cow bothered by flies. Lance-corporal Glass was dead, too. To save one he had lost one, and lost the saved as well. A shoddy bargain.

He picked up a civil telephone and dialled the military number. As luck would have it, Bob answered.

'It's Jay,' Sandingham said matter-of-factly. 'Can you get a message through to the West Brigade HQ at Wong Nai Chung? Enemy strength is through as far as a point half a mile north of the junction of Repulse Bay Road and Island Road. They are not motorised so far as I can tell but they are through in at least platoon strength.'

'We know,' replied Bob. 'They've broken through into that

area and are attempting to cut off the approach to Repulse Bay: those holding out in Eucliffe have been overrun.' His voice was distant down the line. 'Suggest you might have a go get – '

The line went out.

Sandingham wanted so desperately to say that he loved him. They had a code for that on the telephone. He had only to say, 'I and you'll . . . ', mix up the pronouns, get the grammar wrong and they would both know what it meant.

He left the makeshift hospital. It was crowded beyond its meagre capacity with injured Chinese civilians and Indians from the 5/7th Rajput who had suffered heavy casualties above North Point.

He started the Humber, aware of having no memory of having ever switched off the engine. Perhaps someone had done so for him. He was too tired to give a damn.

'They abandoned West Brigade HQ at ten hundred hours, sir. They were more or less surrounded when you came through. About the same time A Company of the Middlesex went up but came under heavy fire. Don't know what happened after that, sir.'

The soldier sat quietly after imparting the information. For such a large man he was remarkably serene.

It occurred to Sandingham that the machine-gun that had fired upon him had not been doing so in error. It had had a Japanese crew. He felt his neck prickle at the thought.

'What's your name, Sergeant-major?' he asked after a while. He took another bite out of the wedge of cheese. It was hard but delicious.

'CSM William Stewart, sir.'

'Bill or Billy?'

'Willy, sir. It's 'cause I put them up them, sir.' He saw the puzzled look on the captain's face: Sandingham was too exhausted to understand. 'The willies, sir. I put them up them.'

Looking at the CSM, Sandingham could see in his eyes a sparkle that even extreme tiredness could not extinguish. He was about to make a suitable retort when the door was flung open and a blunt head attached to the shoulders of another rank appeared around the jamb.

'All set! Let's go! Hands off cocks, on with socks!'

The hollering stopped abruptly to be followed by a profuse apology. The soldier looked sheepishly from the officer to the senior NCO.

'That's all right, Corporal. We're just on our way.'

It was with heavy limbs that Sandingham stood up and eased his feet back into his black leather boots, tucking his trousers into the webbing anklets. He could smell himself, the rank animal odour permeating his clothing. His mouth tasted sour and his teeth were sandy to the touch of his tongue. He lifted his hand to try and scrape off the smooth yellow film with his fingernail but saw his fingers ingrained with gun oil and dirt and decided against it. His peaked cap lay on the chair and he looked at it with unseeing eyes. He placed the olive-green steel helmet on his head and adjusted the strap tightly under his chin.

The CSM handed him a Sten gun and six hundred rounds of nine-millimetre ammunition packed ready into magazines. These he put in every pocket available, stuffing the last one into his shirt. The cold metal on his belly forced him to suck his breath in sharply. So equipped, Sandingham left Battalion headquarters.

Things had not been going well, to put it mildly. The Japanese had captured Wong Nai Chung Gap, were in command of Jardine's Lookout and held virtually all the rest of Hong Kong Island to the east. Stanley Peninsula was holding out under the control of the Middlesex and the Royal Rifles of Canada, but they were under increasing pressure and it was doubtful they would last for more than a few days, despite putting on a considerable defensive hold. East Brigade headquarters was long gone and now West had followed it, having been forced to withdraw. What had happened to the Brigadier no one knew and some wondered quietly amongst themselves if anyone cared. A replacement had not been named, and this left a hole in the command structure at a time when it was vital that there was seen to be cohesion in the upper echelons.

'Here are final orders. Gather round.'

The senior officer, a lieutenant-colonel, was standing in the centre of a group comprising all ranks. Around them, protecting them from being seen from the hillside, were the empty carcasses of tenement buildings. Sandingham joined in towards the front of the small crowd.

'Orders from Fortress HQ are as follows. We are to re-take Wong Nai Chung Gap. Intelligence has it that the area is now lightly defended and we should not meet with any fierce resistance. D Company – Captain Pinkerton; Captain Slater-Brown – will go straight up the main road towards the Gap and engage the enemy. C Company – Lieutenant Stanier – is to move up the valley to the left of the filter beds. There are paths there through the trees that should give adequate cover. Captain Ford and B Company are to go up to Wan Chai Gap and progress along Black's Link, through Middle Gap to the west of Mount Nicholson and come in to Wong Nai Chung Gap from the west and above. This will be a three-prong attack, a kind of pincer movement. Once we have secured Wong Nai Chung Gap we leave a holding force there and push on round to Jardine's Lookout. Any questions?'

'Do we have any artillery support, sir?' asked one of the D Company officers, a captain of about Sandingham's age. They'd never been introduced, but he had seen him at times in the mess. He was known as a good sort, a position of some standing in their confined social world.

'We have some field artillery promised. It's on its way now. Anything else?'

Sandingham wanted to ask what their chances were but that was definitely not the sort of question the lieutenant-colonel had in mind. It was not 'military' to try to assess one's chances of survival.

'All move out, then. B Company has the advantage on time and needs a head start. Good luck!'

Sandingham walked in a daze, his eyes cast at the feet of CSM Stewart who was ahead of him, carrying a Bren gun by its handle in one hand and under his other arm gripping half a dozen Bren magazines. He was so damned tired, so absolutely beaten out. His brain felt as if it had been newly forged and still remembered the smith's hammer. He was reacting to the events in the Humber, saw himself hanging from a moving car just as Glass had done. That was to be his fate, too, perhaps: to die dangling like a puppet from something. Someone invisible pulling the strings. At least, he thought with hurried conviction, it would be quick. Like killing a senile dog.

They reached the first of the Bren-gun carriers.

It never ceased to surprise Sandingham that the Bren-gun carrier (Carrier, Universal, Mark I [Ford] armoured, Bren gun, for the carrying of) was the ugliest vehicle he had ever seen or could imagine. It was squat, about twelve feet long and six wide and the sides came up to his chest. In the front, offset to the left, was a turret projecting forward on the side of which was a single headlamp. It had no roof but was armoured: for its size, the four-ton weight was excessive and made up mostly by the armour plating. A raucous eight-cylinder Ford engine drove it, and it was fully tracked. Not only was it particularly unbeautiful, it was also as noisy as the vents of hell. Driven over earth, it howled, bounced and thudded. Driven over a road, it howled, screeched, screamed, rolled and rattled all at once. The steel tracks were guaranteed to chew up tarmac.

Despite their hideous appearance, Sandingham had always enjoyed riding in these when they had been used in exercises. Sitting in one was the army equivalent of going for a spin in a sports car. They were exhilarating and had a good turn of speed. He found it less enjoyable to be standing beside one in these changed circumstances. They were a long way from the training ground at Chobham.

He climbed into the third of the three carriers lined up. The driver was in his seat and CSM Stewart was installing the Bren gun. Next to it were some magazines and a metal ammunition box, the lid of which was off. Sandingham could see that it was only half full.

'You're the jockey, are you?' he asked the driver. He had heard that term used in the tank corps and hoped it would be appreciated now. It was.

'Yes, sir,' replied the driver. He was a Royal Scot and his voice betrayed it. Glaswegian. 'And this is your mount, sir.'

Four other soldiers joined them and the CSM settled himself behind the Bren, checking it over and testing the action while he had the opportunity.

Two Albion three-ton tucks arrived. Everyone turned round: here was the first of the artillery. Only it wasn't. The lorries were transporting two Vickers machine-gun sections and some assorted equipment. They jumped out and the equipment was quickly off-loaded. D Company soldiers clambered into the trucks, after which everyone fell silent.

The waiting was always the worst. Thoughts had time to germinate, fears to escalate and expand. Sandingham wanted to light a cigarette, not for the sake of smoking but to give himself something to do. But the order was already out that no smoking was permitted. They were no longer at stand to.

Time passed very slowly until, at last, the command to start was given and the engines began to turn over. The increasing din rose to a crescendo, reverberating off the walls and deep balconies of the bomb-scarred buildings around them; thick black diesel fumes clogged the air.

If someone shouts 'Tally-ho!' he thought, I'll break into peels of uncontrollable giggling.

No one did; it was too serious for that. The odds that they would succeed were poor and everyone knew it. This was not a band of courageous warriors surging forward to victory but a group of determined fighters seeking to achieve something in the human scale of ordinary men's common lives. Quite what they could possibly achieve was beyond them just then.

They trundled through the streets and started to climb the lower section of Stubbs Road. When they reached the point at which it turned right, back upon itself, the Albions stopped and the troops disembarked. From here on they would follow behind the three Bren-gun carriers on foot.

Jesus, thought Sandingham, why don't we just send the Japs a signal or a runner? 'British troops advancing up Wong Nai Chung Gap Road; open fire at will.'

Their approach could have been anything but unexpected. With the Bren-gun carriers making their characteristic banshee scrawking and roaring they must have been audible three miles off.

Gradually, at walking pace so as to give front cover for the troops behind, the carriers went up the road. Several hundred yards ahead he could see a number of vehicles in the centre of the tarmac. As they drew nearer, he saw that they were all immovable, burnt-out hulks.

From behind him, over the noise of the engine and the tracks on the metalled road surface, Sandingham could hear one soldier comment to another, 'Campbell's A Company. Poor buggers . . .'

He checked his Sten. It was loaded and he cocked it. His actions caused each of the soldiers behind him to put a bullet up the spout of his own rifle. The CSM had aleady cocked the Bren.

As they neared the site where A Company had been ambushed still no one opened fire on them. The captain leading them and the Battalion intelligence officer, who were riding in the foremost Bren-gun carrier, had nearly reached the first of the ruined trucks.

Across the road lay strewn the bodies of A Company. It was obvious they had met with heavy machine-gun and mortar fire. Some bodies were partially burned and several were cut to shreds by crossfire. The uncharred ones lay in dark stains on the tarmac. It was strange how like spilt oil dried blood could appear.

Sandingham averted his eyes from the corpses around him. They did not smell: he noticed that consciously. The wind was clear and sweet; it seemed unjust that someone should have had to die on such an afternoon in winter.

Suddenly they were in the holocaust.

The leading Bren-gun carrier started to slew round and Sandingham's driver tried to do the same. Machine-gun rounds were bouncing off the road, off the derelict trucks, off the side of the carrier. He ducked below the armoured sides, twisting his head round to shout to his men to do likewise. It was unnecessary: they were all down low except for a ginger-haired youth who, as Sandingham turned, was hit in the chest. His battle-dress split and his torso opened in a horizontal tear, his lungs puffing outwards like pink sponge, only to disintegrate in the air. Red spots tattooed his hands and face, the force of the bullets lifting and carrying him over the side of the vehicle. It happened so quickly.

Behind them, an A Company truck tore open.

'Mortars!' someone screamed and, again, 'Mortars!'

Their own Bren carrier had by now turned and Sandingham, without knowing why, looked over his shoulder at the leading vehicle. It too was half-turned, side on to him, and he watched as it exploded. Against the flare he saw the two officers die: the good sort and the one who had winked to bolster his courage.

They went together, instantaneously and, to his mind, for no logical reason.

Without thinking, he opened fire with his Sten gun. The butt chattered against his shoulder but he didn't feel the bruising punches. He sprayed the trees uphill from the road, waving the barrel from side to side in a figure-eight pattern: then the magazine ran out.

Yet he did not crouch down again, nor did he insert a new magazine and recommence firing. He just stared at where they had been. The first carrier was burning furiously. Spilled petrol on the road had ignited, melting the tar which also caught fire. A soldier, his clothes alight, ran about demoniacally in front of the flames, his shrieks of pain an uncanny howling above the background rush of burning fuel and the stammer of gunfire. The burst of an automatic brought him down: it was not clear from which direction the bullets had come.

The second Bren-gun carrier was following his. He watched as it ran over the bodies of A Company men, its tracks flattening and rutting the dead, kicking up bits of their uniforms and their flesh behind it.

He did not feel sick, or sorry. He did not even feel tired. His mind was disengaged. Now he was not so much a man as an object that worked a gun which killed other objects that worked guns.

As soon as they were out of immediate mortar range they stopped and turned the Bren-gun carriers uphill once more, so that the weapons mounted on them were facing in roughly the right direction. Then they scrambled out into the ditches and scrub cover along the roadside. It took the Japanese less than a minute to find and correct their range.

He realised slowly that he might now be the senior officer.

'Open fire in your own time!' he yelled.

His voice attracted a fusilade of bullets and Sandingham flattened himself on the bottom of the shallow ditch. The Japanese were firing upon them from the safety of pill-boxes that had previously been held by Hong Kong volunteer force members. In addition, they had a heavy concentration of men dug in on Jardine's Lookout, and could snipe at them from both the south and the north-east. The only way to silence them was with mortars, hand grenades or field artillery fire.

A few yards to his left a soldier in his late teens was hunched down. His hands gripped his rifle and a blot of something wet stained his trouser legs. His face was bleached of blood, looking ethereally pale under the shadow of his helmet. His webbing equipment was awry and his bayonet and water bottle were missing.

Even in the midst of such terror Sandingham had a strong urge to hold him close and comfort him. He was so young, so out of place in this scheming, vicious world of men.

Sandingham started to work his body round, by lifting his hand and shoving against the rim of the ditch. The soil next to his thumb jumped and steamed.

'Whatever we do, they've got us.'

It was Willy Stewart's voice and it was not far away.

'Sergeant Stewart? Is that you?'

'Yes, sir. Above you, sir.'

He was lying behind a substantial boulder just beyond the ditch. His presence had a calming effect – not only on Sandingham but, it seemed, on the Japanese, for there was a lull in their firing. They were playing a cat-and-mouse game, thought Sandingham. It was pointless shooting at nothing. Much better to wait until something moved, then concentrate fire upon that spot.

Another voice said, 'Where the fuck's the artillery?'

'Sergeant, do you think we can get a messenger back down the hill? It's vital we have some big guns on the pill-boxes at least.'

'Not much of a chance before dark. Even then it'll be tricky. Besides, they must know what's what up here.'

There was a sudden blast of firing. It shook and swayed the branches over Sandingham's head as if a tornado were coursing through them. From the scrubby bushes opposite came a gurgling whimper, followed by the sound of something heavy tumbling through undergrowth.

'Think you can do it, lad?'

The CSM was talking to the boy in the ditch behind Sandingham.

'If you keep on your belly and work back with your toes, you'll make it down to the bend. Once you're out of sight you can stand and run. Tell them the strength is . . . Tell them what happened, son.'

The boy made no reply but started backwards down the ditch. Craning his neck, Sandingham could see him edging under an overhanging bush.

He had gone some way when, without warning, he was fired upon. It was plain that, at that point, the bottom of the ditch could be seen from above. The young lad, having come to the attention of the enemy, ought to have lain still and feigned death, biding his time. Instead, he jumped up impetuously and ran pell-mell down the side of the road. His progress was clumsy. His kit hung badly about him, knocking against his sides and un-balancing his flight. The machine-gun bullets followed him, striking off the kerbstones, and caught up with him. His body folded, skidded, then lay still.

The two other Bren-gun carriers had been rendered useless. One was alight while the other had lost the tracks from one side. There was no way out except on foot.

Sandingham knew he had to wait until nightfall. To move without the cover of at least twilight was to ask for immediate death.

As he lay motionless, he considered in a detached, almost impersonal manner the vagaries and mazes of warfare. A band of friends-in-arms a hundred strong could, within minutes, become two men shivering and pissing themselves in a ditch. And yet, an hour later, those two men could become comrades with new friends again and ride high on the successes of butchery. He began, without knowing why, to pretend he was a correspondent – for *The Times*, say, or the BBC – writing his despatch for a distant news editor.

'The Battle for The Gap; Joseph Sandingham reporting from war-torn Hong Kong,' he said out loud, forgetting himself for a minute. A bullet snickered by his shoulder and drilled a tiny, neat tunnel in the earth beside him, reminding him of his predicament.

As darkness fell, flames up in the Gap illuminated the carnage, giving it an infernal hue. The enemy, with the failing light, eased their fire and relied only on sniping at whatever they construed to be movement in order to keep their enemies' heads down. Later in the night, the Royal Scots received reinforcements from the depleted numbers held in reserve down in the town and, allying these to their survivors and a rag-tag bunch from an assortment of other units, re-grouped for a night attack back up the hillside. They pushed ahead and, just after midnight, recaptured Wong Nai Chung Gap. They did not hold it for long.

Furniture was wedged tightly into the corner shopfront and sandbags were in place three-high along the base of this barricade. The dull daylight pierced through the cracks and crannies. Sandingham had the Sten gun and two Canadians had the Bren. Across the floor from them, Bob Bellerby had another Sten. Through those cracks in their flimsy defence they could see along several hundred yards of Yee Wo Street. It was deserted. In several places, the tram lines had been wrecked during endless daylight bomb raids, the tracks twisting upward and curling back as if torn loose by some giant-sized sardine-tin key. A tram, gutted by fire, lay on its side halfway down the stretch under their surveillance. It was a major source of their attention, for its contorted steel frame and chassis bed provided more than adequate cover.

Their arc of fire was somewhat restricted by the building opposite, across Percival Street. Additionally, the curve of Yee Wo Street presented them with a blind spot in the longer, left-hand side of the bend. Similarly, they could not see round the bend beyond Jardine's Bazaar, but that didn't matter. No one could take much advantage of that, as the distance was too great.

Looking down Percival Street to their right they could just see the lower junction of Leighton Road below Leighton Hill, upon which there was a field artillery piece and several mortars. Each of the sideroads between themselves and the harbour wall had been conscientiously mined and barricaded with anything that was heavy and immovable. A few Indian troops were positioned to cover them as well, mostly armed with Webleys and .303 rifles.

Another Canadian came in from the door at the rear of the shop, stooping under the partially collapsed lintel. He was carrying a length of plywood upon which rested five mugs of tea.

'Awl rightee!' he said with relish. 'Here's th' god-dam' tea! It's Chinese but I guess tha' makes it none th' worse – after all, they invented th' god-dam' stuff.'

Bob and Sandingham exchanged glances as they helped themselves to a mug each. It was hot and scorched their tongues, but it was also strong, and there was milk in it that wasn't the powdered variety.

'Where did you get the milk?' asked Bob.

'No sweat!' The Canadian patted his water bottle. 'Got it out by Pok Fu Lam as we were pullin' back 'long th' south shore. They got dairy herds out there.' He pronounced it 'day-ree'. 'I got three pints of it. Milked by my own han's.'

'All we need now's some licker,' said the soldier lying behind the Bren and surveying the street down its sights.

Bob left the shop, propping his Sten against an empty rice barrel. His boots made no noise as he left, for they had covered the floor with old sacking, curtains and bolts of cloth from a bombed tailor's workshop. It made lying down much easier and it deadened not only their footsteps but also their voices. None of them was speaking loudly, but any precaution was worthwhile. It was almost snug in the shop.

Unless one knew the way it was hard to find the route through the bombed buildings of Wan Chai. Bob knew them, though. He had been the person to reconnoitre the shop gun nest the night before and the one to guide them to it. During the night they had thrown up their wall of furniture under his authority.

Sandingham silently followed Bob to give him cover. He forced his eyes to shift to and fro across the blank windows and doors, not so much guarding against but anticipating movement. Every corner was a possible rifle muzzle, every pile of debris a potential enemy.

They worked back to Tonnochy Street, crossed over Hennessy Road bent double, after first attracting the attention of the machine-gun nest that was covering it, and sprinted into Morrison Hill. There, parked under an overhanging balcony, was the Ford V8 that Bob had taken from the car section of the vehicle pound. The roof of the Ford was deeply dented in the centre, the windscreen was shattered and the lights were missing. Sandingham noticed that a tyre had gone flat, too. Folding down one of the tip-up seats in the back, Bob produced the cognac. The bottle was still a quarter full. He stuffed it inside his tunic and gave the thumbs-up to Sandingham. They were absent from their post for about ten minutes.

When they reached the shop, the others were tense and alert.

'What's up?'

'Mack here thought he saw some'un move down there,' said the taller of the three Canadians. He was looking through a slit in the defence, between a heavy butcher's chopping table and a tin hip bath that had been flattened by falling masonry.

'Are we sussed out?' Bob asked.

Sandingham quickly surveyed the scene then answered him, saying, 'I don't think so. Our camouflage in front'll be good enough.'

They had set up rubble and debris in front of the furniture and metal junk in order to disguise, as best they could, the fact that there were three automatic weapons hiding there.

The tea drunk, they emptied the leaves into a corner of the shop behind a broken till. The drawer had spilled out some small change on to the floor but no one had bothered to pick it up.

For twenty minutes each man watched as much as he could see within his arc of vision. Nothing moved at all except for a tabby cat that strolled nonchalantly across their field of fire. It did not turn its head but walked straight ahead, to disappear through a window on the ground floor of the derelict herbal pharmacy they were using as an imaginary distance marker for the Bren. Once passed, the sights were set: anything the near-side of the smashed front windows was in range and about to die.

'Th' cat ain't lookin' roun',' Mack said confidently from behind the Bren. He read this as a sign that no one was in the animal's vicinity.

'Cats're ornery buggers,' said one of the others. 'Got that feline, feminine knack of ignorin' what they dislike. They don't give a cuss fer wha's aroun' 'em. They jus' waulk . . . '

'There!'

It was Sandingham. His face was pressed to his viewing crack.

'Where?'

'Right-hand end of the tram, two o'clock. A balcony with a pole sticking out. Movement behind it — appears to be a man.'

His placing and commenting on the sight was so military, so correct, he grinned at himself. He, who was opposed to the whole bloody business, was talking as if he were a regular regular.

That had been a joke he and Bob had shared often.

'Are you a regular?'

'A regular what?'

'A regular lover. I'm a regular lover.'

'I'm a regular regular lover.'

The regular soldier. The one signed up for x many years, his soul sold to the regiment, the King's shilling taken and regretted and spent on beer, or fags, or a tart in Aden on the way out. How many soldiers, raw out of Southampton or Tilbury, lost their virginities to tarts in Aden? . . . At Malta they were still too shy, at Alexandria or Port Said they were still too scared, but Aden – by then they were fed up with what the lower deck called 'pulling their puddings' and they wanted the real thing, to prove that they were ready to screw and swear and die like men. And most of them under twenty-one had never been in love except to the girl in Bournemouth they'd met on their summer holidays in the early war years, or the girl from the next street, or the next village, or down the Locarno.

'I see it!'

Not him. It. Bob was not looking at a man through his field glasses but at an object that was hiding behind the collapsed end of a balcony where the tiling of the roof had caved in. It was wearing a soft cloth field cap with a matching peak and a brown leather strap. On the front of the cap above the peak was a small yellow star, which looked almost colourless in the dark shadows where its wearer lurked. As Bob watched, it raised a pair of binoculars to its eyes and started to scan the buildings above where their post was situated.

'It's a Nip officer. Infantry. He's spying out the land. Keep still, even in here.'

They all stood quite still as Bob kept his watch up. After some minutes, the 'it' disappeared into the depths of its own building. As it went, the ray-skin hilt of a Japanese officer's sword shone briefly.

'Stand easy. It's gone.'

'Reckon we can guess they'll move up now.'

'He'll have to get back and report, first. They're not going to march blindly up the street and chance it to luck.'

Sandingham rubbed his hand over his eyes. They ached with the tension of watching. He was certain that if there were a cockroach out there waving its antennae he'd spot it.

'Keep an eye open, Vale,' Bob ordered the taller Canadian, adding, 'Got a little surprise for you all.'

He tugged the cognac bottle clear of his clothing.

'Jee-zus Chris'!' exclaimed the tea boy. 'Milk's one thin', but real brandy's somethin' else! Where in hell's name you get tha'?'

'Ask not how you come thereby, but *when* you share in the bounties of the battlefield.'

Bob poured a tot into each man's mug. They drank as if it were the Blessed Sacrament. Vale sipped his without taking his eyes off the street.

'It's re-al gen'rous you sharin' it with us, sir,' he said as he rested his mug inside a battered crate by the side of his rifle.

'Another tot each sees it finished,' said Bob. 'Let's have your glasses, gents.'

He refilled their mugs.

'A toast,' he suggested.

'What we got t' drink to?' asked Vale.

'Christmas,' replied Bob. 'Christmas 1941.'

They raised their mugs, saying, 'Christmas 1941' in a quiet chorus.

'You know,' said Sandingham. 'I had forgotten it was Christmas Eve.'

They all fell silent then, drained their mugs and returned to the business of watching for 'its'.

Nothing was moving. The Japanese infantry officer did not reappear on the balcony and no cat recrossed the street.

Sandingham let his eyes scan the buildings but his mind was elsewhere. Keeping watch in this way was like driving a car while talking with a passenger – one could change gear, slow down or speed up, judge corners and junctions automatically while at the same time carrying out an involved conversation. The body was alert at its level, the brain engaged all the while on something completely different.

Christmas Eve. He cast his mind back to that same day in 1940, in 1939, 1938, '37 . . .

A year ago had seen him in officer-training school following the disaster of Dunkirk. The previous year, the war had been young and he had only been getting round to thinking of offering his services to it. His call-up papers hadn't come through: the army was large enough to rebuff the German advances. In 1938, he had been at the Great Missenden home of Charles Warrinder and his parents. They had had a twenty-foot-high tree set up in the main hallway of their house and it was decorated with fairy lights, cotton-wool snow and shiny glass baubles. Between the lights, at the outer reaches of the branches, candles in holders shed a soft light upon the Persian carpets and the paper chains hanging from the banisters and the minstrel-gallery rail. Their butler, Golding, was to die in the Blitz, serving with the ARP. That year – 1938 – was the year Sandingham had had his twenty-first birthday party and been thrown into the fountain in his grandfather's garden: his back had borne mauve bruises for days where he had hit and gone through the ice. The chill he caught had lasted three weeks.

The year before that had been 1937, the year of the sad Christmas. His mother had died at the end of September, in an earlier-than-usual autumn, and three months on he was still missing her more than he was prepared to admit even to himself, even now perhaps.

Now was Christmas 1941: a good moment to take stock of the past, prepare for what was to come. In a week's time, the new year would open. He would be twenty-five in 1942. If he saw the year out.

The goodwill, the warmth and the love, the *joie de vivre* that the season implied vanished. He felt nothing for those around him – except Bob. He looked across at the man he loved so deeply: Bob was standing with his hands thrust into his pockets, leaning his stomach on the rim of a wooden counter and looking down Percival Street. As Sandingham watched him, Bob took a hand out and scratched the two-day stubble on his chin. In the silence of their gun position, he could hear Bob's fingers rasping on his skin.

If, he thought, the two of them were to walk out of the shop now, stand in the middle of Yee Wo Street and shout, 'All right! We've all had enough. Let's stop now before this thing gets out of hand. Before we all start to regret it,' what would happen? Would the war stop? Would sanity prevail at last? Would a Japanese signals captain come out from the ruined pharmacy and say, 'Okay. You Blitish sodjyer woight. We stop now. We go home. You go home. Happy Chlistmas'? Thinking this, the accent in his head more Gilbert and Sullivan *Mikardo* than Tokyo pidgin, he realised he had never heard a Japanese speak in his own language, let alone in English, with the exception of the Jap who broadcast propaganda to them daily from a loudspeaker mounted by the railway station clock tower on Kowloon. And he spoke English without an accent. Or the loudspeaker distorted it too much for the telling.

Sandingham knew that if he did go out there and shout, little would happen or change. His voice would echo briefly. The officer in charge of the Vickers machine-gun section covering the western section of Hennessy Road might ask, 'What's that stupid blighter doing, Corporal?' 'Shouting out we ought to stop the war, sir.' 'Bloody ridiculous! Must've gone off his rocker.' Or else a hail of bullets would converge on him and he would die before the echoes did.

Soon he was going to have to poke the barrel of the utilitarian Sten through the crack in front of him and pull the trigger, emptying the oblong magazine into a man whom he had never heard speak, or sing, or laugh – indeed, whom he had never set eyes on before. And that man would die or live according to his luck. He might be someone skilled at painting portraits, or telling rude jokes, or mending broken toys. He might have a wife, children – a lover, even. His home might be a farmhouse surrounded by paddyfields. He might wake every day of his normal life to hear the quacks of his ducks and the bark of his dog; perhaps the sounds of his wife getting ready for her day's chores. Or he might get up to the sound of city traffic and go off to repair cars in a garage or count out money from behind a teller's window.

He would never know. Just moving his index finger a quarter of an inch towards his thumb would cause all that to come to a halt, irreversibly. With one tiny action, like a beckoning, Sandingham could erase for ever the farm, the loved ones, even the sky from one man's consciousness. Simultaneously he could make that mind itself instantly cease to be.

It seemed such a waste, so totally illogical, so utterly pointless; yet this was what he was supposed to do. On Christmas Eve.

'Phst!'

The Bren gun clicked from safe to automatic. Mack snuggled

the wood of the butt into his shoulder. Without knowing how it
came to be there, Sandingham found his Sten in his grip. His right
hand was evenly pulling the cocking lever back, the T-shaped
butt of his own weapon jabbing into his hip-bone.

'Back on the verandah! The Nip officer!' Bob was studying the
enemy through his binoculars. 'Can't see quite what he's at . . .
standing up. Out of sight – no, he's there. The shadow's deep.' He
fidgetted with the knurled focusing wheel. 'He's looking this
way. Now up the road. Got his glasses out of the case. Damn!
He's ducked out of sight again.'

Sandingham followed this running commentary through the
chink in their defences. He could only see the vague shifting of a
darker piece of shade.

The other two Canadians were preparing to fight. One was
checking his rifle while the other, Vale, was relieving himself
behind the door, in a rear room now roofless and open to the sky.
The stench of his urine wafted into their gun post, making Sandingham want to follow suit. When Vale re-entered the shop,
Sandingham went out.

He returned, trying not to stumble on the rubble. Any sound
they made now would echo alarmingly in the buildings.

The world appeared so silent, almost in awe of itself, as if
waiting for something it accepted unequivocally and inevitably.
He knew that if he were so much as to crack his knuckles it would
make an eruption of terrifying proportions. There was no defin-
able noise except their whisperings.

As Sandingham stepped on to the carpet, Bob was talking
quietly again, his voice so low that it had not managed to pass
through the doorway as the smell had done. Sandingham had
missed a development in the action of the Japanese officer.

'He's definitely got someone with him. Can't make out – yes,
it's an NCO. I can see his red collar patch. And his steel hat. Very
fancy knot under his chin . . . he's got down now. They both
have.'

'Do we open fire, sir?'

'No. Let them start it. We have the advantage so far as we're
quiet. I'm sure they don't know we're here.'

The next few minutes confirmed this, for the Japanese officer
was busy giving instructions in the setting up of a Type 11

machine-gun and was not too careful in keeping himself concealed. Sandingham could see the heavily ribbed barrel that
reminded him so much of the Hotchkiss on which the Japanese
weapon was mimicked. He thought at first they were positioning
the gun in order to cover an advance down Hennessy Road but it
became apparent that this was not so, for their arc of fire was too
limited. They were preparing for a stand at this point, consolidat-
ing a front-line hold on the area, readying for an offensive by their
enemies to the west. A machine-gun so placed could mow men
down as they came around the corner in the road and it would be
difficult to bring a field piece to bear on the verandah.

Sandingham suddenly understood, tossing up the odds for
their choice of position, that he was an enemy to them as they
were to him. The realisation shook him.

'What now?'

'We wait,' said Bob.

Sandingham looked at his watch: it was ten minutes to four.

No one spoke. The minutes were passing like hours. They just
watched the Japanese in the shadows. Keeping cavey on one spot
started to give Sandingham the stares. He had to keep shifting his
eyes to look at other things, nearer or farther away and, while
doing this, he saw it.

'Behind the tram!'

Bob turned his field glasses on the wrecked vehicle.

'To the left. Just above that projecting bit of the – '

'I see him!' cried Bob.

Mack wriggled his body a few inches to the right bringing the
Bren to bear on the left-hand side of the tram.

'I sure can see th' bastard, sir,' he drawled. 'Jus' th' top o' his
head.'

Not long, thought Sandingham. Twenty minutes, maybe. In
twenty minutes he would be dead. He looked at his watch again,
careful not to let go of the tubular barrel of the Sten gun. It was
three minutes past four now, and the light was beginning to fade
in the cover of the buildings.

Suddenly a loudhailer sounded from behind the tram, the
words bouncing off the sides of the empty buildings.

'This officah in Cowonel Shoji Regimen',' said the voice, with a
clipped officiousness. 'We know you in buiwding. You come ou',

hand up, we no shooting. You no come ou', we shooting.'

Sandingham said, quietly, 'Need we hold our fire any longer, Bob? They know we're here.'

'Not necessarily, Jay. It may be just a come-on, to winkle us out. They know we're tired.' He paused to see if he could spy the loudhailer then added, resignedly, 'But what the hell. We'll have a go. It's only a matter of time. Orders said to fire at will – '

His words were interrupted by an outbreak of rifle fire in the direction of the harbour wall.

'Right, Mack? Ready everyone? Good luck, and may your god be with you this day.'

Sandingham had never heard Bob say anything like that. So deep, so religious. He looked at him. He was not smiling. It was not a flippancy. Before Bob turned away, however, he caught Sandingham's eye and grinned, the grin of a boy about to scrump apples, or flick an ink pellet.

'I and you'll . . . ' he said, and left the sentence hanging in air.

Mack had pressed the trigger. The rattle of the Bren was amplified tenfold in the shop. He emptied the twenty-round magazine into the tram in under three seconds. The noise made Sandingham's ears ring and his head throbbed as if the sound were echoing within it.

Two arms were thrown up into the air behind the tram. Then silence. There was no fire returned, not even from the machine-gun on the verandah.

Judging his aim by looking through the simple sight and along the barrel of the Sten, Sandingham fired at the verandah shadows. He used half a magazine. The flickerings of flame from the mouth of the barrel tickled his retina – the poorly designed flash hider was ineffective in the darkening shop – but he could see plaster and concrete flaking off the stonework. It was as he was assessing the impact of his efforts that the Japanese machine-gun opened up.

'Down!'

They were all on the floor now, but the Japanese gunner was under the misapprehension that they were on the first-storey level, as he was himself, and he was riddling the rooms above them. Sandingham could hear the spent bullets bouncing around overhead.

Two squat figures ran, bent double, into the cover of the tram. One of the Canadians lifted his .303 through a hole in the barricade and pulled the bolt backwards, forwards and down.

'One up th' spout to shove up his ass!' he muttered.

A single bullet, followed by the crack of its report, slapped into the timber of the butcher's table. Another followed it, striking off the rubble.

'They know about us now,' said Bob with a matter-of-factness that momentarily scared Sandingham.

The .303 banged. He could see its owner's shoulder shake as it absorbed the recoil.

'Got him, the sod!'

A Japanese standard issue rifle slipped over the roof of the tram to clatter on to the road. They could hear it quite distinctly.

There was a shattering explosion on the street twenty feet in front of them. The front of their barricade was showered with debris and shards of stone; road surface and concrete spattered through their lookout holes. Black smoke billowed towards them and began to rise in a disintegrating pall.

Bob lifted his Sten and fired two magazines towards the verandah just as the machine-gun was opening up on them once more. They could see the flashes from its barrel: that meant they should be able to see the gunner. And then hit him. A bullet from the second magazine struck the Japanese officer in his chest. They watched as his body spun half round and he toppled sideways, to hang limply over the remains of the verandah wall.

With the officer dead, the Japanese mortar crew, who were hiding in Kai Chiu Road, had no one to spot for them. The next few bombs passed well over their intended target and into the remains of houses in Lockhart Road. It was not long, however, before the crew obtained another observer, and their aim grew increasingly more accurate.

In the meantime, the five behind the barricade kept up a steady fire and no one was injured until an enemy infantryman in the cover behind the tram lobbed a grenade at them. It exploded on the top of the wall and blew in a large slab of loose masonry which caught Mack in the small of his spine as he lay at the Bren.

He screamed once, a short, high-pitched curdle that Sandingham almost did not hear in the general din of gunfire. He looked down, as if by chance: Mack was already dead, his belly forced to the carpet and his arms flexing and tensing with all that was left of his life.

The magazine on the Sten was empty. Sandingham's finger depressed the trigger still, but nothing was happening. He turned to look at what was left of Mack: the hair, the flesh, the bones . . . He wondered if, by closing his eyes, he could not only end the war but return Mack to life, as if by shutting out the scene the slab of stonework would lift back to its position, the grenade fold back through the air and return, unprimed, to its thrower and the wrecked tram right itself and fill with passengers.

He thought this, yet he also knew it was impossible. What was done was done. The dark angel was around, had made this be. Just as the chaplain had warned.

'Dark angel!' he howled. 'Oh, God! Fuck the dark angel!'

Bob spun about at Sandingham's shouting. His face was taut.

'For Chrissake, Jay!' He glanced at Mack's prone body, then pointed with the barrel of his own weapon to what was left of the soldier, at the same instance inserting another magazine. 'Get him aside and use the bloody Bren. Use it!'

With the assistance of one of the others Sandingham shifted the stone block and together they dragged Mack to the rear of the shop. His body was pliable, fluid as if filled with water. The sickle-shaped magazines for the Bren were empty and he sat on a box and thumbed shells into them. He did not think as he did this, just loaded the curved steel boxes with ammunition and, when they were refilled, carried them the ten feet to the gun and rammed one into the square hole on the top of the breach. Having reloaded, he lay down on the carpeting and put his cheek to the wooden stock. It was still warm from Mack's face.

'The tram! Get the tram!'

Bob was watching the verandah, waiting for a chance.

With an ease that surprised him, for he had not used a Bren for any length of time except on the ranges at Aldershot, Sandingham found he was able to shoot quite accurately. With the Sten one sprayed the target but with this heavier weapon, with its front bipod to keep it level, it was possible to be far more exacting. The bipod did buck up but it was still a better piece.

Three enemy soldiers were shooting at them from the tram.

Two more were in the upper floor of what had been a bakery. The machine-gunner carried on intermittently, his weapon obviously jamming off and on. The mortar crew had not fired for several minutes.

Sandingham emptied half a magazine into the derelict tram. Another Japanese infantryman ran out towards it from the cover of the bakery, but one of the Canadians opened up and hit him in the groin. The infantryman crumpled up in full view of them and started to crawl to safety the way he had come.

Like an insect, thought Sandingham. It wasn't a man, or even an enemy, but a bug, a dull green thing that had to be exterminated.

He pulled the Bren-gun barrel left.

'Forget him. Draw a line on the LMG.'

He ignored Bob's order. This action had no military justification. This wasn't in the manuals of instruction, it wasn't for the sake of King, country or the pride of the regiment. It was because it had to be done.

Perhaps it was for Mack, he reasoned. Perhaps that was why he bawled, 'Shut it, Bob! This one's for Mack!' Yet he wasn't convinced.

He tightened the muscles in his finger. The butt shook against his cheek. The crawling man looked round just as the trigger reached the point of clicking. Sandingham saw him look up. The soldier seemed to know: he tried to stand. The stream of bullets from the little trumpet-shaped cowl on the front of the barrel of the Bren gun hit him in the chest, ripping his breast cage open. The force of it carried the dead man down the street. He folded over but the momentum of the shells kept him going along the tarmac like a piece of paper caught in a wind.

A feeling of satisfaction came over Sandingham. He could not understand it: he simply knew it was there.

He turned on his side, partly to bring the Bren gun to bear on the verandah, partly to reach for another magazine. As he did so, he found the front of his tunic soaked with blood and a chronic yellow, mucousy liquid.

His first thought was that he was hit. That somehow, without knowing it, he had been shot. Yet there was no pain. It was then he realised it was not his blood and bile, but Mack's.

He snapped in the magazine. The leaf sight had flattened itself; he lifted it back into place.

The light had nearly gone from the verandah now, and he could not differentiate the shadows of the collapsed roof from those of the men.

Still he waited.

There was a rush of staccato fire from the verandah. He aligned his sights on it, but it quickly stopped.

Deliberately, he reset the fire selector lever to single shot. Carefully aiming at where the last flash had come from, he pressed the trigger. Once. Twice. Pause. Thrice.

During a lull in the thunder of shooting, he heard a loud grunt. The floor of the verandah was on a tilt. Very gradually, the Japanese NCO and his gun slid forward and over the edge. They pitched out of sight behind a half-destroyed wall.

'Bloody fine shooting!' Bob yelled.

Then he was deaf.

An enormous explosion rocked the shop. Large fragments of plaster showered down on them. The barricade lifted several inches and resettled itself. The walls bulged. Dust fogged everything. Smoke wraithed about, marbling the air. Sandingham found himself choking. Choking on something wet and metallic and hot.

'Bob!'

Fear coursed through him. He could hear nothing, not even his own voice.

'Bob! Bob!'

It hurt him to move his jaw. He felt his teeth catch on something, he spat and skin flapped loose.

He looked to his left. Mack's corpse lay twisted over on itself, his body haphazardly decorated with the brass cartridge cases that had been ejected from the Bren. They shone dully in the uneven half-light caused by the beams, which had caught alight, and were now burning steadily.

Sandingham looked right. One of the Canadians had propped himself against the butcher's table. A long splinter of wood was sticking out from above his shredded ear. Blood was congealing in his hair and on his neck and collar. He was dead.

Behind was a sloping avalanche of assorted debris – glass,

mortar, bricks, concrete, wood, tiles, strips of cloth, carpet tatters. From out of the avalanche jutted a forearm. The pale hand on the end of the wrist dangled loose. It had no thumb. It was Bob's hand.

Sandingham looked at his own wrist. His eyes were numbed. His watch glass was broken and his watch had stopped. Four-thirty-two.

PART THREE

Hong Kong: Early Summer, 1952

TO STARBOARD WAS a solid floating wedge of lighters and cargo junks, barges, small launches and sampans. They bobbed gently against each other on the harbour swell, stirred by the passage of the Yaumati ferries past the jetty. The creaking of the wood, the slap of wavelets and the flap of rigging, sails, awnings and clothes drying on lines mingled with the calls of stevedores, the barking of dogs, the disgruntled puttering of marine engines and the self-satisfied clucking of hens. For the owners and crews of this armada the craft were not merely a means of earning a livelihood or a form of transport but an entire world – a home, a universe, a place for being born, courting, copulating and dying. Many seldom stepped on to the firmness of a dock or a beach. The children, even as toddlers barely able to walk, could guage the roll of the deck and stay upright. All could swim. They existed completely afloat, coming ashore only for certain after death: to be buried in water is to be eternally restless.

To port, in stark contrast to the mêlée of the other side of the ship, was the concrete pier. A double row of lorries was parked down the centre, one vehicle bumper to bumper with the next. The windscreens, grimy with salt from a long sea voyage, had forms stuck to the inner surfaces, while the doors and side windows were decorated with scrawled yellow chalk marks. On either side of the lorries was a clear area upon which coolies were working with the chaotic efficiency of ants. They received wooden crates that were slid down a gangway mounted with steel rollers, lifted these bodily off a pile of hessian mats placed at the foot to stop each crate from becoming damaged and man-

handled them into a neat wall beside the trucks. The crates had
incomprehensible black lettering stencilled on their sides: '1st
Div. Trans. U.: Veh. sps.', '5th. Arm. U.: Univ. Car. Engs. Pts. &
replts.' and '8th. Br. Gen. Eq. pts. & sps.' All that Sandingham
could understand with certainty were the words 'Top', 'Use Nets'
and 'Use No Hooks'.

Overhead, derricks mounted on to the superstructure of the
ship swung out over the dock and lowered one more lorry after
another, each held by ropes or chains passing under the front and
rear wheels. The booms and jibs whined and howled as they
gently lowered their burdens on to the dock where a special gang
of coolies pushed the vehicles into the line.

After an hour, two Europeans, stripped to the waist but wearing slouch-sided hats, arrived and commenced driving the lorries
away. As they passed him, Sandingham saw the tyre pressures
written in small white numbers over the wheel arches. He saw the
white discs bolted on to the rear axle differential casings, saw the
toggle-like hooks for tying down tarpaulins and noted the dun
colour of each vehicle. The make was in his knowledge, too. But
that didn't matter. They were army trucks.

Remaining by the Kowloon dock gates for the rest of the
afternoon, he saw more military equipment being landed and
removed. Some jeeps were driven out along with two low-loader
articulated lorries on which squatted massive crates, unblem-
ished by stencilled or painted markings. Consignments of NAAFI
ration boxes went by; so did cargoes under green tarpaulins, tied
down tightly and each truck with a motorcyclist riding escort. No
one could tell what was under the covers, but Sandingham knew:
ammunition boxes.

At around five o'clock in the afternoon, the activity started to
slow and eventually ceased. The dock gates, which had been
reserved for these military comings and goings, became clogged
once more with the familiar civilian traffic: one of the P&O
steamers – the *Canton*, heading for the United Kingdom – was
due to sail very early in the morning and the passengers were
mostly embarking the evening before. Taxis, rickshaws and
private cars arrived carrying passengers, their baggage, friends,
relatives and business associates. Cabin trunks and leather suitcases, circular hat and square uniform boxes, rattan baskets and

canvas bags gathered on the quay nearest to the Star Ferry jetty. Lascar deck-crew members scuttled to and fro with the luggage, and English stewards took in bowls and baskets of cellophane-wrapped flowers and fruits and other going-away gifts with all the readiness of acolyte priests accepting offerings to a great goddess.

The *Canton* herself lay moored alongside. Her newly-painted white hull, unstained by rust streaks, shimmered in the afternoon glare, almost too harsh to be looked at. The Plimsoll line was sunk well into the water now that she was loading fast. The cream-coloured funnel emitted a faint whisper of grey smoke and, from the ship's horn, a drift of steam wafted away into nothingness. At the head of the aft mast fluttered the flag of the line, quartered into garish diamonds, and from the foremast hung the Blue Peter. The portholes were all closed against pole-fishers.

It hurt Sandingham to watch the ship and her preparations for departure. Save for the mere necessity of cash for the ticket – and the rounds of drinks, and the bridge games at a penny a hundred points, and the raffles, and the tote of the ship's daily nautical mileage, and the keeping of face – he'd be aboard her. Often he had thought of the chances of stowing away. At his age, it seemed ridiculous, the kind of thing a wander-struck youth would do to see the world and find a bit of adventure.

It was ridiculous, too. He knew it. He'd be found out as soon as he had to give his cabin number to secure a seat for dinner. He wouldn't have a place allocated to him. At Singapore, they'd stick him ashore in the arms of the local police, then transport him back to Hong Kong in ignominy.

There were times when he considered himself a refugee from matters European, a man who had removed himself from the horrors of the shallowness and materialism and hypocrisy of the world in the West. He was a man purged of impurity, a man 'gone native', as the derogatory term had it. He saw himself as a pacifist Lord Jim. Conrad's Lord Jim. Except that in his case it would be Lord Joe. 'Tuan Joe.'

'Good morning, Tuan Joe,' they would say as he woke, looking out upon the virginity of the jungle and hearing the mynah birds calling and the parrots squawking; overhead would be the chattering of monkeys, and the calls of children would echo up

from the banks of the river where they would be swimming in the
freedom of glorious nakedness, the little girls unhaired by
puberty and the boys swimming hard into the current, diving for
mussels and raw opals polished by the grist of the sand. Each time
they dived he would see their firm buttocks rise above the surface
before disappearing in the foamy splash of their kicking legs.
After a minute, they would reappear and, holding their hands
high and treading water, would shout out, 'Tuan Joe! Tuan Joe!'
The sky would shake with their laughter. And his.

He would never lift a gun. There would always be food and the
love of the boys and the men, and the admiration of the girls and
the women, and no one would be there to censure him. There
would be waxy pink orchids hanging from the branches and the
milk of green coconuts to drink. There would be no gin or rum.
There would be opium, of course; that was natural.

In his heart of hearts, though, he knew that it wouldn't –
couldn't last. Some son of a bitch would come along with a need
to mine tin, plant ordered ranks of rubber trees, excavate the
opals with a dredger, fell the mahogany trees, shoot the monkeys
(for food, perhaps, as the Japanese had done in Hong Kong
during the war) or enslave the people with a desire for trousers,
nylon stockings, wristwatches.

At other times, he saw himself not as a willing and accepting
refugee, an acolyte of peace and simplicity, but as a castaway,
suffering the purgatory of deliberate rejection or cursory dis-
missal.

'Excuse me.'

Sandingham turned to one side.

'I say, excuse me.'

An Englishman dressed in tropical whites was struggling to lift
a heavy suitcase on to a rickshaw. The rickshaw-puller was
raising the shafts of his vehicle horizontal in the hope that that
might tilt the case backwards, but it was too heavy.

At first, Sandingham thought the man wanted him to move
along. That was not uncommon. Then he understood that, in this
instance, the man was actually asking for assistance.

'Could you help me in with this, do you think? God alone
knows what my wife's got in it – can't think! And I can't find a
free baggage coolie anywhere.'

Saying nothing, Sandingham took a firm grip on the underneath rim and hoisted it on to the seat of the rickshaw as the
owner of the case worked it from side to side. It took only a few
moments. He noticed the passenger's name on the 'Wanted on
Voyage' label: 'Grover – Mr & Mrs: Cabin B16.'

'Thank you so much,' said the man.

He did not offer a tip: Sandingham thought that, had he been
Chinese, the man would have dipped into his pocket for a ten-
cent coin. Because he was white, he didn't.

The rickshaw pulled away from the kerb and the European
settled himself into another in order to follow the luggage. Lifting
the case had made the man stickily hot and he removed his jacket.
Sandingham watched but said nothing. As the man went off,
Sandingham stooped quickly and picked up the paper that he had
seen slip from an inside pocket. He hoped it was a banknote,
possibly in sterling. That would have been more use than a Hong
Kong dollar. Although it looked too stiff, the colour of the ink
and size suggested that it might be a ten-shilling note. It wasn't. It
turned out to be much, much more valuable: a visitor's boarding
pass for the *Canton*.

There was only one way to exploit the pass and that would
require a change of clothes. Even as a European, he was not going
to get past a sharp-eyed P&O gangway officer, someone experienced in sorting out hangers-on from genuine sender-offers,
dressed as shabbily as he was at present. He took a number seven
bus travelling up Kowloon peninsula in the direction of the hotel,
quickly washed, shaved and changed into a jacket and fairly
well-ironed pair of trousers, then caught another bus back to Tsim
Sha Tsui. At the dock gate he flashed the flimsy card pass to the
policeman on duty and was waved through. At the head of the
gangway, he showed the pass to the ship's officer.

'Who are you seeing off, sir?'

'Mr and Mrs Grover. B16,' Sandingham answered, looking the
man full in the face.

The officer looked down his passenger list to check, then said,
'Thank you, sir. If you'll turn left at the head of the stairs and
follow the notice to B deck. Visitors will be required to go ashore
by eleven p.m., sir.'

It was cooler in the ship than on the dock where the stones and tarred wooden planks reverberated with the stored heat of the day. The lowering sun pierced the windows of the deck lounge as Sandingham walked out of the door and up the companionway to the starboard boat deck. A hot breeze soon removed from him the pleasant effects of the ship's blower system.

The boat deck gave him an elevated view of the panorama of Hong Kong which he knew so well from street level, but not from sixty feet up. Standing beneath one of the lifeboats, he watched the green Star Ferry craft plying across the harbour with their tall, thin funnels like stovepipe hats and their circular white lifebuoys hanging from the railings of the upper decks. There was a gentle swell on the surface of the sea that complemented the green slopes of Mid-Levels above Victoria. He found himself trying to pick out familiar buildings on Hong Kong-side – the Hong Kong and Shanghai and China Bank buildings were easy. So was Government House. The block of flats below Macdonnell Road was not so easy to place, even though he could see plainly the Peak Tram line, by which it stood, slicing up the mountainside: there had been another building erected in front of the one for which he was searching.

Descending by a different companionway, Sandingham walked slowly towards a first-class lounge and sat down at a small, highly-polished table in the middle of the room. He looked around.

As his eyes grew accustomed to the interior light, he saw that the lounge was sumptuously furnished with leather chairs and round card tables, the rims of which were raised in order to prevent objects from sliding off in choppy seas. There were carved wells for glasses at each of the four players' seats. The walls were panelled with walnut veneer sections and there were paintings screwed on to the wood. They were of a series depicting scenes from the various ports of call at which the ship stopped on her Far East run – Port Said, with gilli-gilli men producing eggs from passengers' ears; Bombay, and a snake charmer performing at the foot of the gangway; Singapore, and the ship surrounded by sampans selling curios; Hong Kong, and, inevitably, a portrait of the ship against the grandeur of The Peak at sunset.

A steward approached him.

'Can I get you a drink, sir?'

'Dry martini,' Sandingham ordered and the steward left, to return a very short time later with the cocktail on a silver tray.

'One and seven please, sir.'

'Can I sign for it?'

'It is policy to ask for drinks to be paid for in currency when alongside, sir.' He paused then added tactfully, 'It avoids later embarrassment. However . . . may I have your cabin number, sir?'

Sandingham gave it as B16. The steward left and Sandingham, to be on the safe side, moved to another table in a corner by a window from which he could note the steward's reactions when he came back in. Sandingham was experienced enough to be able to tell a man's mood by a mere glance at his face. He had had the best occupational training in the world for that: prisoner.

He need not have worried. The steward had checked the passenger list, being too busy to telephone the cabin and confirm the facts. He now simply asked him for his name and, on hearing it, allowed him to sign. After all, if this were one of the Grovers' spongeing friends, then they could accept paying for his drink.

The lounge was empty apart from Sandingham. Passengers and their guests came and went, but most were congregating to drink out on the deck, where the evening was growing cooler and balmier.

He stirred the green olive around in the martini. There was no hurry to drink the cocktail. And he could have another.

When the olive had soaked up as much as it could of the alcohol, he put it in his mouth on the end of the cocktail stick and sucked its sourness into his throat where it stung pleasantly. Sitting there, he could have been in another life in another place. His fingers twirled the tiny aluminium stick that was shaped like an arrow. In the flights were the initials 'P&O' and, on the other side, the name of the ship.

He ordered another drink and the steward served this without questioning the signing of the chit. He also put down before Sandingham two small glass bowls, one full of salted cashews and the other containing small, vinegared gherkins.

What heights of decadence, luxury even! It had been years since Sandingham had last tasted cashew nuts. They were never served in his hotel where the bar food consisted only of peanuts, over-salted and soggy with oil.

A plump European woman in her mid-sixties entered the lounge and sat down heavily at the table next to him. Sandingham watched her from the corner of his eye, studied her heavy make-up and loose-fitting blouse, the pink of her painted toenails sprouting through the openings of her high-heels and the faint blue rinse of her grey hair. The steward came in and she ordered a pink gin. Sandingham let his mind drift away from her, back into the luxuriousness of drinking in the evening, for free, in such cool comfort.

'Are you going all the way?' she suddenly asked in a scratchy voice, breaking into his reverie.

'What!' he exclaimed, surprised by her sudden words. He was accustomed to be being disregarded. Then, to be less conspicuous by his rudeness, he added, 'I beg your pardon?' somewhat brusquely, in keeping with his supposed class status.

'All the way. Are you going all the way?' She saw his incomprehension and added for clarity, 'All the way to UK. To Tilbury. Or are you getting off *en route*?'

'Port Said,' he answered, out of the blue. 'I'm getting off at Port Said.'

'Fascinating little town,' she commented, accepting his information in a patronisingly colonial manner. 'Quite fascinating. The first one sees of the East coming out, I think. I don't count Algiers and the Casbah, do you? After all, they speak French there. And as for Alex! Well, there they are positively bi-lingual. English and French. And Arabic, of course. Hardly a burnous to be seen these days. Most of them wear tropical suits!' She made a noise like a pony sneezing. 'Alexandria! My husband was there in '35 . . .'

Sandingham drank on. The martinis were making him drowsy and that was fatal. A sleeping drunk attracts attention; a drunk *compos mentis* does not; people ignore alert drunks. He strove to pay attention to the harridan's meanderings: they would keep him conscious if he concentrated. She could serve that purpose, at least.

'. . . Port Said in '45. And the Canal. Full of wrecks. Bombed boats. Awful. Took us hours. My husband said it would have been quicker on bloody camels.' She drank her gin and angustura bitters. 'Do you know Port Said well?'

'I'm in business there.'

'Really? How interesting! I love those urchins who dive for coins thrown overboard. They keep the money in their mouths, I'm told. Their mouths! I ask you. And the gilli-gilli men – how they pull live chicks and eggs from one's ears. And one doesn't feel a thing. Not a thing . . . '

Jesus, thought Sandingham, she actually thinks those yellow puffball chickens come from westerners' earholes. He wondered if she realised they could lift a purse or a passport from a pocket with just as much facility.

'What line are you in?'

'Curios, antiques, antiquities. That sort of thing.'

'In that case, I have something of interest to show you.'

He watched, dumbfounded by a mixture of her actions and the martini – the steward had served him with yet another – as she plunged her hand into the space between her sagging bosoms. As she tugged her blouse askew he noticed that her make-up ended just below the start of her cleavage: he felt an instant repulsion ripple through his flesh.

'Here it is,' she uttered finally, triumphantly, yanking a thin gold chain free of the frilly top of her slip.

She opened her hand to reveal a small, light blue, oval dot that at first he thought was a small aquamarine or turquoise, dirtied by contact with her talcumed flesh, then took to be a gawdy locket.

Beckoning his face closer, she held it out to him.

'What do you make of that?'

'It's a scarab,' said Sandingham, recognising the little beetle set in a gold clasp. 'Egyptian.'

'Scarab! Oh, really! You can't know much. It's not a scarab at all; it's a cowroid. Made of faience.'

'It seems scarab-like to me. But then I've left my close-up spectacles in my cabin.'

'It has a fine set of hieroglyphs on the reverse,' she boasted, reciting from memory, '*Suten but nub ankh*. "The King of Life is Gold." My husband bought it in Blanchard's Egyptian Museum in Cairo. Long before the war. Do you know Blanchard's?'

'He is my uncle. Was.' This untruth rolled out as fluently as the rest. He was an expert liar. He had had to be. He prayed that Blanchard, whoever he was, was dead. The past tense might give him away. Her next sentence calmed his fear.

'How fascinating! Well, I've other things I can show you on the voyage. While away the time.'

Sandingham could not take his eyes off the little Egyptian charm. He knew enough to be well aware that such things were sought after and collected: Francis Leung would pay well for it.

'Might I see it for a moment? It does seem a fine specimen. Rare these days. Cowroids.'

Without demure, she unhooked the catch of the chain and handed it to him. He looked at the jewel and tried to guess its worth.

The steward approached and requested Sandingham to sign for the last martini.

'Another, Mr Grover?'

'Please. And a pink gin for . . . '

'Mrs Forsyth,' she said, nodding her head to one side by way of introduction. 'Betty Forsyth. Cabin C76.'

Cheaper part of the ship, thought Sandingham. A lower deck. A widow in straitened circumstances going back to Britain to sponge off her son and daughter-in-law.

'Grover,' he said. 'B16.'

The drinks came and he continued to finger the talisman.

'The war is going rather well,' she said to change the subject, keeping conversation going.

'The war?'

'Korea. There was a most encouraging report in the *South China Morning Post* today and I heard it repeated in the BBC World Service at noon. A big push . . . '

'No war goes well,' Sandingham muttered, interrupting her. 'War is a foul thing, a disease upon the nature of men. A wart upon the cheek of humanity that we are forced to kiss as if we love it. War is a degradation of the spirit.' She was blushing slightly: he could tell by looking at the narrow pouches below her eyes where the sweat had worn thin her face cream and powder. 'War is an abomination, a stinking, filthy thing. It is a turd excreted by the anus of the human soul.'

'Well!' she sputtered. There was more she felt she could say on the subject by way of indignant retort and yet she was not eager to fall out with an obviously compliant audience so soon in the voyage. They had yet to cut free from the pier. 'I'm sure you're entitled to your opinion . . . '

'I watched the ammunition coming ashore this afternoon,' said Sandingham. 'Box after box of the death of young boys, sent by men who know no . . . '

He stopped. This was not the way to play it.

'I'm sorry. I get carried away at times,' he apologised. 'I was in the war. A prisoner.'

'I see,' she said. 'How awful. I am sorry.'

He knew she didn't understand, possibly didn't even care.

'Anyway,' he smiled, 'you are right. This is a cowroid and a very exceptional one. The inscription is most fine. Still very clear. Not worn at all. Might I examine it with a glass?'

She was pleased her little treasure was being appreciated, and by an expert.

'Certainly.'

He stood up, draining his martini. Was it the fourth? He had lost count.

'Will you be here in twenty minutes? I'd like to go down to my cabin: have a book there given to me by my uncle. Blanchard. Catalogue of finds. I might be able to trace it for you, where it was discovered and so on.'

Providence works in strange ways for some men. It had always struggled to do well for him, but that evening had been making amends. Before she could speak either way, a couple entered the lounge and, spying her, called out over-loudly, 'Betty! There you are. Been looking all over the blessed ship for you. All ready?'

They approached her. Sandingham took a step behind the newcomers, held up his hand with the chain dangling from it as if to show her he had it and pointed to his feet, indicating that he was going below. She just waved to him. Or to her friends. It might have been acceptance of his borrowing the piece or it might have been an affectation of welcome. Whichever: it did not matter.

In the corridor, he turned right and went into a small smoking room. From a writing desk that faced out on to the deck he took an envelope with the shipping line's badge on the flap. Dipping the pen into the inkwell, he addressed the envelope to himself at the hotel and slipped the cowroid on its chain inside, wrapping it first in several layers of ship's writing paper to give it protection. From there he went to the purser's office and purchased a Hong Kong postage stamp. There was still time to mail a letter: the ship's agent would take any last-minute letters ashore with him in just over half an hour. He slipped the envelope into the post box. Now it would not matter if he did meet the old witch again. As far as she was concerned the washed blue cowroid would be secure in his cabin, safe amidst the chaos of departure.

Avoiding the lounge, he went below decks to see what else he might release from its original owner. There were a few cabins left open and unattended but these were also unoccupied and offered nothing. Then on D deck, in the second-class, stern end of the ship, he came upon a baggage coolie knocking on the door of a cabin, trying the handle and getting a refusal of entry. The coolie replied through the door, received a curt answer and left a small leather suitcase in the corridor outside the cabin.

Someone shafting his lover for a last time, thought Sandingham.

He picked up the case and made his way towards one of the communal bathrooms on the other side of the ship. In a cubicle, he opened the case and rifled through the contents. Luckily, it was a man's. Some silk and woollen underpants took his fancy so he removed his trousers, took off his own grubby cotton shorts, and put on four pairs of luxury garments. Next he unbuttoned his shirt and tugged on three cotton vests. Then he exchanged his shirt for one hand-tailored in cream cotton and still in its tissue wrappings. He slipped seven handkerchiefs into his jacket pockets, then tried on the trousers lying folded in the bottom of the case. Far too big. Even with a belt, they would be loose and baggy. He had lost a lot of weight. The opium helped. Finally, he took an ivory-handled hair brush, two pairs of gilt cufflinks – he inwardly cursed because they were not hallmarked gold: Francis would know the difference – and a matching tie pin, three pairs of socks (one worn, two in his inner pockets); then paused. If he were caught he'd be in for the high jump so he left the brush and loose socks. No one would notice his surfeit of underwear. He flushed his own underpants and shirt down the toilet, rammed the case behind the pedestal and left, jamming the door of the cubicle closed with a square of lavatory paper so that it looked as if it were still occupied.

Without much hurry, he made his way through the ship to the second-class gangway and disembarked. He acted slightly drunker than he was and got away from the bottom gangway steps, but only just.

On the dock was a throng of people waving to a family on the boat deck. As he looked up to follow the gathering's gaze he saw Mrs Forsyth. For her part, she was looking down and directly at him. Then she saw him. He could not hear her, a fact for which he was not a little grateful; but he could see her.

She grabbed the arm of the elderly man standing next to her at the ship's rail, the same one who had mercifully interrupted her prattle. It was comical: he jumped at her grasp, dropping his glass. It toppled over on itself, spilling its contents, and fell to an inaudible splash in the water between the hull of the ship and the dock. She pointed towards Sandingham. He, to be friendly and in keeping with the mood of the occasion, waved back. He did this partly out of a sense of ironical humour and partly as an act of camouflage in the middle of the crowd. Swiftly, he walked the fifty yards to the dock gate and out into Canton Road. Breaking into a jog, he turned left then right into Peking Road. He was safely away. As he turned the corner, he looked back. At the dock gates stood the elderly man, a Chinese dock policeman by his side. They were hopelessly scanning the crowds.

The jeep was parked at the kerb outside the hotel when he returned from Francis Leung's house in Kowloon City.

In his pocket were two hundred and ninety dollars, obtained without any bargaining whatsoever. Either Leung had been feeling untypically generous or the cowroid really was worth more than he had suspected even in his more optimistic moments. What was certain was that Leung had not made a mistake; indeed, he had made Sandingham wait over an hour while a wizened Filipino with a gold-capped front tooth was sent for, who arrived and was able to judge the pendant's antiquity and attest to its being genuine.

The jeep was not painted in plain khaki, but was mottled with
olive green and brown in an attempt to disguise it in woodland;
break up its outline. The headlights were hooded, just as those on
the Humber had been long ago.

By the jeep, squatting on the pavement, were three of the
mechanics who serviced cars in the hotel garage. They were
playing *tin kau* with thin oblong cards. The stakes for the game
were under one of the player's feet for safekeeping.

'Whose is this?' Sandingham asked, jerking his thumb at the
vehicle.

'Tha' belong Ozzy sodjah. Lot of Ozzy sodjah in hotow'l.
Come 'is morning.'

The hotel lobby was busy. By the check-in desk stood an
officer. Sandingham recognised the pips on his shoulder as signifying a captain. From his belt hung a webbing holster, recently
blancoed and clean. The revolver in it was attached to a pristine
cord. The officer's trousers had neat creases in them, and the
brass of his uniform glistened from recent polishing. His boots
were black and shone like ebony. He was in his mid-twenties and
in full command of the situation bubbling around him.

By the hotel bar was a wall of army-issue kitbags, every one
bulging and tied tightly at the neck with thick twine. Black
lettering was painted on each and a brown cardboard label strung
through the draw holes named the owners. On the settle running
along the window was a pile of greatcoats that looked very much
out of place in a tropical hotel foyer. Sandingham knew that this
was typical of any army. If it looked like snow, issue shorts: if it
promised rain, withdraw the umbrella issue. The Japanese had
been just the same.

It was not until he reached the foot of the hotel stairs and
looked back that he spied what lay behind the kitbags. There he
saw, neatly lined up on the mock marble floor, battle packs: the
familiar rucksack affairs with an entrenching tool and a ground-
sheet rolled up on top of it, to one side a water bottle and the
other a gas mask – only that was not present here. In each pack he
knew what he would find if he were to go over and unbuckle one
– mess tin with cover, emergency rations, a bar of dark chocolate,
tin of jam, packets of tea and sugar, knife/fork/spoon, socks,
cardigan, water-purifying tablets. And a letter from a mother

sandwiched between three or four from a girlfriend full of phrases like, 'wish your hand was' and 'I can taste you now' and 'Take care, dearest: I love you.' Maybe a photo or two: self with dog on beach, self and Belinda at picnic near Lulworth. Except that in these packs, instead of Lulworth, would be substituted Brisbane or Adelaide or Whykickamoocow or some other weird-sounding aboriginal placename.

Guarding the equipment was a corporal in a slouch hat. On his upper arm was sewn a cloth badge with a kangaroo on it. In the corner of the bar, the potted palm had been moved to one side and in its place were stacked several dozen .303 rifles. Sandingham could smell the gun oil.

From the dining room came the hubbub of talk. He looked in. Every table was taken by four or six Australian soldiers. Although it was three in the afternoon they were all eating lunch – a ham salad with mayonnaised potatoes and pale tomatoes and lettuce hanging limp with the heat.

Once safely back in his room, Sandingham lay on his back on the narrow bed. He looked blankly at the off-white ceiling and cupped his hands behind his head. His sparse hair itched and, as he scratched, strands came away, caught in his fingernails. Pulling the hairs out, he felt them slice into the quick and he saw that his right thumbnail had purpled like a dense bruise again.

He felt lethargic, tired of breathing and being sad and living and watching and hurting deep in his soul. Physical pain was bearable, but what ached in him was not.

He started to cry. The tears welled out of his eyes and ran down his cheekbones, around his ears and soaked into his scalp or the sweat-stained pillow. He made no effort to rub them away. They were a part of memory, and he could not erase them any more than he could his thoughts. They were there and that was that. Who had said to be is to be? Nothing more, nothing less. I am what I am. I do not know what I do not know.

'Conversely, God fuck it, I know what I know.'

Speaking to himself again: of that he was conscious, and he immediately shut up. Talking to oneself was a sign of madness. Or just loneliness. Or both.

After dozing, he lit a cigarette and puffed at it, still lying on his back. The sun was warm on the door of his room and he could hear the metal crickling as it expanded in the late day's heat. Soon it would cool again, once the sun had set behind the school at the rear of the hotel, across the street. He could hear pupils playing basketball in the playground behind the high stone wall. The ball bounced hollowly upon the concrete court, echoing in the confines created by the wall.

Smoke rings wafted up from his mouth and did not disintegrate until they reached the plaster above his head. The door acted like a radiator, transferring its heat inwards.

He stood up and stripped himself bare. In the tiny bathroom, he turned on the shower and let it run before standing under it. The plumbing ran down the outside of the wall and the first few minutes of water would be piping hot from the sunlight.

Once beneath the cool jet, he reached for the carbolic soap he used. It was hard as pummice and just as gritty. With it, he scoured his body.

The area of his stomach was, he thought, rougher than when he had last washed. As the soap ground over it, flakes peeled off like sunburnt skin. Where it came away, it left a red blotch that was not raw but looked as if it should be. When the soapsuds wormed in under his fingernails, they stung like acid.

Refreshed, he put on the cream cotton shirt he'd stolen from the *Canton*, having saved it for several days and resisted the temptation to wear it. He had wanted to sport it that afternoon, to see Francis Leung, but thought better of it. If he saw Sandingham so nattily dressed, Leung might assume he didn't need the money so badly. Now he wore it not just because it was cool and smart but also because it gave him some self-esteem. He had been neglecting himself of late, he knew that. The opium did it, in part.

The first-floor lounge verandah was open and a temporary bar had been set up just inside the french doors. Two Australian officers, the captain and a lieutenant, were drinking beer and scotch chasers with a few of the other ranks downing glasses of local lager. Many of the troops in the hotel had gone off for the evening, most likely to see what delights the redder areas of Kowloon and Hong Kong-side might have on offer. A few younger ones with girls at home or a fear of a dose of the clap had stayed.

Sandingham took out a dollar bill and bought himself a beer.

With it, he went out on to the balcony and leaned on the parapet near but not too close to the two officers. They were talking about sheep rearing in voices that had the nasal drawl of the true-bred Aussie. At a lull in their talking, Sandingham broke into their conversation.

'Heading for Korea?' he asked, pointlessly. Where else would they be going? One could hardly hold full-scale manoeuvres in a British colony of three hundred and ninety-eight and a half square miles on the rim of a none-too-friendly Communist China.

'Reckon we are!' replied the captain. Then he said, 'You live here?'

'Since 1947,' answered Sandingham. 'Not all the time in this hotel, of course. I've moved about a bit.'

'You work out here?'

'I'm retired out here,' Sandingham said ambiguously. He was hardly of the age for a pension and he saw the captain throw an intimate, quizzical glance to his fellow officer and wondered if these two slept together. Probably not: Australians had too much of a masculine reputation to admit, even in private, that they were little queers like him. He let his eyes drop. Military uniforms were far better fitting in the fifties than they had been in the war and he noted with mixed emotions the tight fabric and firm, fleshy muscles beneath.

He must not have another beer: it would be a penance for allowing such thoughts to run in his head. He must not submit to the temptation. That was vital. It was also part of the excitement.

'What did you do out here before you retired?' the lieutenant asked, Sandingham catching the ironic twinge in his words that even a deep Australian accent could not cover.

'I was in the army. Then I was caught, taken prisoner. Of the Japanese.'

This changed the two officers' approach. Suddenly they were curious, interested, concerned for detail and truth about internees and their lives. They ordered three more beers and sat on the wall of the verandah between the pots of bushy chrysanthemums and pried into Sandingham's war years.

At first, he was pleased to tell them of the glory and the horror, the pain and the courage, the degradation and the spirituality and gut survival instinct of imprisonment. Within fifteen minutes, though, they were probing deeper and he was remembering, through the beer and the opium of the previous evening, what it had really been like.

'Is it true they tortured you just to get details about who kept a diary?' they asked.

The enquiry broke something in Sandingham's thoughts. He knew how a splinter of bamboo, a fragment of glowing charcoal or a ten-cent firecracker up your anus could feel.

'Wait a moment!' he burst out. 'Just hold on! Why do you want to know this? What is it to you? You'll not be facing this up in the hills around Panmunjong or wherever. You'll have comfy personnel carriers to kip down in and mobile hospitals ten minutes away by helicopter. There will be Coca-Cola and whiskey and fur-lined boots in the winter.

'You know what we had? A canvas sheet, a crumpled pack of field dressings and a clapped-out ambulance if we were lucky. Our Albion was seven years old, a stripped first gear, a non-existent clutch, rock-hard springs and bullet holes down the right side by the time . . . And we had stale water and sod-all booze except what we could scrounge or "liberate" and my boots were hard as wood. In the summer we sweated; in the winter we froze. And that was on active service. After being captured . . .

'You buggers haven't an idea. Not an inkling. And you never will have. Your war is a luxury battle alongside what mine was. You're all god-damn generals in cosy HQ billets by comparison.'

The lieutenant stood up slowly, easing his feet on to the ceramic tiles of the balcony. He put his beer down on the wall very gently, as if taking care not to spill a drop or even disturb the scanty froth. His friend put a restraining hand on his arm, but he shook it off with a quick jerk. He took a step towards Sandingham and stood close before him.

'You said it all, Pom? Enough? Anything else you want to add to that?'

Sandingham said nothing. Nor did he ready himself to flinch. Pain was nothing. The punch would come: it always did. What was the good of ducking?

'Leave him, Dave. The ORs'll see you.'

He spoke quietly so that the other ranks in the lounge wouldn't hear, but his words were to no avail.

The lieutenant turned his head halfway and stage-whispered, 'Stick it, Craig! Now,' he faced Sandingham again, 'let me remind you of something. You Poms and a few Canadians and some half-trained local volunteers lost this scrappy bit of China in eighteen days. Eighteen days! Christ! You couldn't even hold out against a bunch of bloody Japs for three weeks. Surrendered on Christmas Day. What an achievement, eh! What a fucking joke! I reckon the Indian troops you had must have fallen about with mirth at that one. The great Englishmen, the backbone of the British Raj – shot to fuck in eighteen days. Poms! Jesus!'

He stepped back and lifted himself on to the verandah wall again.

No punch came.

Sandingham said nothing. He held his glass and looked into it. It was shaking very slightly. Tiny ripples ringed in from the sides and met in a miniscule maelstrom in the centre.

In that little whirl of beer he saw Baz's face: Baz, whom he hadn't seen and who had been gone for years. It was looking up, but it was seeing nothing. There was sand in his hair. He could hear waves and voices screaming nothing and he saw the beer darken into blood.

He did not put his glass down. He simply let go of it. Before it smashed on the tiling, he was into the Australian's chest, fumbling at his tunic buttons, at the breast pockets. Slowed by the beer and chasers, the lieutenant lost his balance and toppled half backwards. One arm, flailing sideways for a grip, punched one of the big plant pots over the side. It hit the edge of a two-foot-wide sill, broke into three and shattered on the hotel drive below. A cacophany of Cantonese broke out from the ground floor and the bellboy, in his white uniform and pork-pie hat, came running into sight to look up at the cause of the crash.

The two Australians were grappling with Sandingham. Somehow, the junior officer had succeeded in getting one leg over the wall and was sitting astride it, his feet curved round, gripping the stonework like a polo player his pony. They had managed to get Sandingham into the centre of the verandah when, of a sudden, he went limp and ceased all resistance. This confused the officers

who let go of him He just stood there. He made no attempt to
leave or renew his attack. They edged round him cautiously, as if
expecting him to spring back to action: he might have been a bear
in a flimsy catch-net. Half a dozen ordinary soldiers stood watching. Not one had come forward to assist his superiors: rank and
file troops are people and officers are different, to be kept at arm's
length.

'All right! Back to your beers!' ordered the lieutenant. 'Show's
over.' Then, so that Sandingham couldn't hear, he added, 'And
leave the poor bastard alone.'

Together, they left the verandah in Sandingham's sole occu-
pancy.

It was some minutes before he moved. The veins in his neck
throbbed and his thumb was weeping from under the nail. Small
spatters of blood dotted the cream shirt. He stood at the verandah
wall and peered across the road to the hillside opposite. In the
fading evening light it appeared buff-brown and bleak. Torn
through it was a funnel-like fissure cut by centuries of tropical
rainwater.

Strung between bamboo poles bracketed to the side walls of the
flat roof of the hotel were run lines upon which the laundry
amahs hung the residents' washing. Wherever there were no
clothes hanging, the roof was taken up by rows and rows of
potted plants – geraniums, asters, chrysanthemums, small azalea
shrubs, miniature palms and kumquat bushes.

The plants were meticulously and jealously tended by the hotel
gardener who slept on the narrow landing at the head of Sandingham's backstairs escape route. He regarded all visitors to the roof
with suspicion, particularly the children of the European guests,
whom he abhorred. The gardener was a Communist who habitu-
ally wore the dark blue clothing so common over the border in
China. He tolerated Sandingham, but only barely. He often
watched him through the corner of his eye as he was bending
double over some plant or other, trussing it to a cane to guard it
against the ravages of a storm or, worse, a typhoon. It was not
that he was a man dedicated to his plants: they were merely the
way by which he kept his rice bowl full and his head dry in the wet
summers and warm in the cold of winter. Sandingham had learnt

not to trust the man, although when he at first moved into the hotel he had sought to be pleasant to him; after all, he had known Communists as friends and partisan allies.

Sandingham borrowed some clothes pegs from one of the amahs. She was a young girl, new to the staff of the hotel, who giggled shyly at him as he requested them in Cantonese. He smiled back at her but noticed, as he did so, the disapproval of the other, older amahs. Their washing drying in the warm wind of the heat-hazy afternoon, they took their young colleague aside and, under their breaths, lectured her to beware the Englishman whom they all called 'Hiroshima Joe'. He was a little touched in the head, they explained. A simpleton. That was the phrase they used. He overheard them, translated their words to himself and fully understood.

He had had to scrub hard to remove the blotchings of his blood from the weave of the cloth and now, with the cream cotton shirt flapping and billowing in the breeze, he was all but done in. He felt his arms aching from the exertion and he walked slowly to the parapet, nursing each elbow in his palms. Once there, he leaned casually over and surveyed the length of road at the front of the hotel. Distantly, he could hear a brass band playing and knew that it heralded a Chinese funeral procession making its way towards the public death-house unobtrusively tucked into the side of a hill down by Nathan Road.

Often he had passed the single-storey building with its tiled roof traditionally curled like a temple at the corners and ridge ends, smelling the soapy air that was made of bodies being boiled to the bone for the rapid burial of the poorer deceased. By cooking the tissue off, the bereaved did away with the need to own or buy an elaborate underground vault in which to allow the departed to rest for seven years, putrifying slowly in accordance with the divine laws of nature. Instead, the process of degeneration and, therefore, entry into the hereafter was greatly accelerated. The seven years disposed of in as many days, the mourners could return in a week or so for the bones, which they could then stash in the family bone pots. At least, that was what Sandingham had been told happened.

During the war years he had dreaded the place, often wondering how long it would be before he was reduced to a fatty scum on the surface of one of the boiling cauldrons. There had been times when such a finale to his life had seemed just hours, even minutes, away. On the rare occasions when he had been let out of the camp under escort, usually to be 'interrogated' – the Japanese euphemism for 'beaten' – he had been marched or driven past the place and had known what it was then. The interpreter had more than once pointed out the landmark. In his deepest nightmares, he was in there, alive yet forking his own body into the Irish stew of corpses.

The funeral parade drew nearer and began to pass the hotel. Two of the kitchen staff, resting on the roof in their white aprons and with their hands as blanched as a cadaver's from washing salad vegetables, sauntered across to gaze down on the spectacle.

It was not a grand funeral. The deceased had not been very wealthy but he had had enough put by to pay for seven floats, two bands and four professional mourners. Perhaps his investment in gold teeth had been the source of finance. His body was in a polished, ovalesque coffin built in cross-section rather like a four-leaf clover. It travelled in a lavish, sleek-black Studebaker with a hearse rear adaptation; behind walked the paid mourners, his immediate family and then his friends – not more than thirty in all – his closest of kin dressed in white and the rest with black silk ribbon tied around their arms or hanging as little flags from their jacket collars. The floats were fifteen-feet-high flats of flowers surrounding characters painted in scarlet, and each was propelled by a street-trader's tricycle wired to the back. To Sandingham they seemed for all the world like bizarre stage sets.

The bands wore white uniforms piped in dark blue and played in total disregard of each other. The foremost band was playing a slowed-down version of 'Yankee Doodle' on western brass instruments while the second ensemble, fifty yards behind, fluted out a haunting Chinese melody on traditional pipes and silver, elongated trumpets that held reeds rather than simple cupped mouthpieces. A man in a tattered T-shirt, baggy shorts and plimsoles carried a huge red paper orb, six feet in diameter, on the top of a vertical pole over his shoulder; from the interior of the globe a ladder projected upward through a hole in the top. This was for the devils to ascend – or the spirits. A framed photograph of the dead man was resting on a rack on the roof of the hearse.

The procession continued past for five minutes, then was lost to sight under the arch of the railway bridge.

Below on the front lawn was the boy. Sandingham had seen him as soon as he had settled himself on the parapet wall. He was not playing with his army toys but had in his hand a small crimson racing car which he had been sending careering down the rain gutter on the bank of the sloping hotel drive. Each time it reached the bottom it would crash into the metal grid over the outflow pipe, and the boy had been running beside the car, helter-skelter down the concrete in disregard of arriving taxis or the hotel shooting brake. The boy was standing on the stone wall in order to get a better view of the funeral, the car gleaming redly at his feet.

The high-pitched wail of the *sona*, a sort of Oriental oboe, had attracted several of the Australian troops out as well, curious to see what the noise was about. Now that the cortege had gone from sight they drifted back in ones and twos into the shade of the lobby, returning to their lagers and egg sandwiches. For most of the day so far they had been cleaning kit for inspection. A senior officer's presence was anticipated for the evening, when they were to be briefed in the hotel lounge from which, for an hour, the civilian residents had been told they had regretfully to be excluded.

One soldier had not re-entered the comfort of the building. He had stopped by the boy and was now, as Sandingham watched, holding the red racing car and commenting upon it. Even though he was three floors up, Sandingham could hear snatches of the soldier's conversation.

'That's a nice car you've got there.'

'It's an Alfa Romeo,' replied the boy.

'I had one of them once. And a blue BRM.'

'I've also got a Ferrari.'

A Kowloon bus went by and Sandingham lost the thread of their intercourse. Other traffic prevented him from hearing more but he continued to regard the pair with emotions that were a mixture of envy, hatred, love and yearning. The soldier, a private, could not have been more than nineteen, if that. He was tanned and muscular in the way that young men are who live physical lives: a healthiness glowing in him. He had short, mousey-brown hair but, from his elevated position, Sandingham could not see his face. His sleeves were rolled up tightly above the elbow as if he, too, had been doing his laundry. In his imagination, Sandingham could smell the young man – a mingling of Brasso and blanco, gun oil and leather polish, sweat and uniform.

The soldier was fumbling in his hip pocket. At last he drew out a wallet and flipped it open, showing something to the boy, who laughed, then ran into the hotel. The Australian soldier remained. In less than a minute, the boy was back with an envelope. He tipped its contents on to the wall and a breeze from the passing of a lorry blew the envelope down into the street. Sandingham could see a winged circle printed on the whitish-blue paper – it was a Pan American World Airlines envelope, filched by the lad from the rack in the lobby.

The boy and the soldier began to exchange objects which they appeared to pore over before putting them in their pockets. Sandingham felt his eyes sting. The tears were hot and the salt hurt: he rubbed at his cheek with his hand.

Through his tears he saw the Australian take a scrap of paper from his wallet and write on it with a general-issue army message pencil. He knew what the words, written in mauve indelible lead, would spell out – the information every soldier holds dear, regardless of his rank or his army or his nation. Name and number; unit address; home address for after the war. And the boy, for his part, with a scrawling childish hand, wrote his name and address on another square of paper which the soldier slid into his wallet for safe-keeping.

Tousling the boy's hair as a much older man might do, the soldier called to one of the bar waiters who came out and took his order: another lager and an ice-cold Coca-Cola in a sea-green bottle with a wax paper straw soon followed. They drank together, the boy-child and the near-man.

Sandingham left his vantage point and made his way slowly to his room. In the slot on the door in which, had he cared to do so, he could have put his card with his name printed on it, there was a message: he read it through smarting, tired eyes.

Mr Leung telephone you. He say you telephone to him. This evening. Half pass six oclok.

It was just after two a.m. when Sandingham reached the hotel back gate. He was in a sweat partly because he had had to walk so far in the humid mugginess of the night and partly because the opium had been a smaller dose than that to which he was accustomed. He was also suffering from cramps well before getting home. This was a comparatively new experience: he was not used to his muscles seizing up on him after a smoke.

In Dundas Street he had been stopped by a police foot patrol of two constables and an English-speaking sergeant. They had come upon him suddenly from the cover of a doorway and had badly surprised and consequently shaken him. The sergeant had harangued him in Cantonese for several minutes before Sandingham lifted his face and the officer saw that he was a European. He then asked if he were all right. Sandingham was taciturn. It was his only defence. If they had taken him in he would have been charged with possession, for he was carrying a quarter of an ounce.

The roomboy on night duty in charge of the floor was asleep, slumped in a cane chair behind his desk. A luridly illustrated Chinese paperback had slipped from his hand and lay on the floor, open at a picture of two lovers lying under pine trees on a bed of needles above a beach. Sandingham stood still observing this for a moment – for all its garishness it had a familiarity to it. He could hear the wavelets of an ebb tide meshing on sand and pebbles.

Quietly, he tore the page out, then replaced the book on the floor as he had found it. The picture he folded and kept.

By the desk was the guests' refrigerator, the white enamel door tempting him. Very carefully, for he knew that the catch had a loud click, Sandingham eased the door open and looked inside. The light came on and he moved so that his body shielded the roomboy's face.

In the top compartment was a block of ice-cream and, next to it, two trays of ice cubes. These he ignored. Below them, on the first shelf, was a row of bottles of beer, several bottles of quinine tonic and soda water and a package wrapped in greaseproof paper. Next down was a shelf with several pounds of butter in half-pound blocks, together with some slabs of cheese and a cardboard box of peaches. On the bottom shelf was a fresh lettuce, half a dozen smoked kippers that had been sent out by air mail, a pot of Cooper's chunky marmalade and five bars of Cadbury's Bournville chocolate.

He took one of the bottles of beer, a bar of chocolate and a peach, a large knob of butter and a half-eaten cheese square. He twice dipped his forefinger in the marmalade and sucked the skin clean. He also peeled off one of the kippers and, gently closing the fridge door, returned to his room where he ate everything, smearing the butter on the cold kipper with his fingers.

The ice-cold beer, which he drank last of all, lying on his bed, made his head swim. He stared hard at the central axle pin of the ceiling fan; it shifted to his right, then flicked back, only to sidle off once more. He tried to will it to stay in place, but couldn't.

PART FOUR

Sham Shui Po and Argyle Street PoW Camps, Kowloon (Hong Kong): 1942

HE WAS SQUATTING on his haunches, his hands loosely dangling from his wrists, his arms resting stiffly on his knees. The voice did not shout or call to him nor did it whisper: it simply spoke his name in a matter-of-fact, almost conversational tone from somewhere overhead. He looked aside from surveying his feet where one big toenail had turned a vague blue from being pinched in the pliers. His name was repeated. A hand then came into the line of his sight and between the finger and thumb, held as if it were a poisonous insect, was a thin, hand-rolled cigarette, the paper of which was clearly newsprint.

He took it thankfully, put it to his lips and drew in the sweetish smoke until he felt it scorching his lungs. A steadiness came into his head and settled somewhere in the centre. He turned his eyes up to see who his benefactor was but the man was standing with the late sun blazing behind him and Sandingham had quickly to face downwards again at the sandy earth between his feet.

He lifted his hand after he had taken a second deep drag, returning the cigarette. The voice said, 'Keep it. I got it for flies anyway. And I don't smoke.'

Slowly, painfully, Sandingham stood up. The man who was beside him was about his height but even thinner. He was one of those naturally wiry men to whom the first stages of starvation seemed to make little difference. Unable to stifle it, Sandingham grinned, then chuckled.

'I do look a bit – incongruous,' admitted the man.

He was wearing a white, tropical-issue, naval uniform shirt which was tucked into his *fandushi*, a sort of loincloth made of a

length of grey cotton. The shoulder-tabs on the shirt were button-
less and flapped like tiny wings. On his feet he wore a pair of
black brogues without socks. His head was close-shaven to the
skull and he wore a wristwatch on a leather strap and dark
sunglasses, the lenses of which were perfectly round and gave his
face a comically owl-like appearance. His skin was well tanned
but wherever it folded, in the elbows or behind the knees or in the
joints of the fingers, it was beginning to crack, and this made his
movements delicate, like those of a girl in a finishing school,
learning to balance her movements with graceful charm. He
joined in the chuckling.

'I saw you brought back early this afternoon,' he said. He let a
pause speak then for what he couldn't say. 'Did you see anything?
Of – um – value?'

They were together under a young pine tree that was one of the
smoking stands. The guards forbade smoking around the camp
except at certain designated places, partly to inconvenience the
prisoners, partly to ensure against fire and partly so that they
could keep an eye on informal groups. The soil was discoloured
by ash but there was not a single dog-end to be seen: they were
collected, broken up and recycled into new smokes.

It was a minute before Sandingham replied. His head still ached
badly and the foot was hurting so much that he leaned on the
roughish bark of the tree to alleviate the discomfort. He was
thankful Fujihara had concentrated on just his left leg.

'I was taken to the Kempetai HQ. I suppose it was, anyway.'

It was easier to go through the whole business than to pick out
bits at random: besides, to talk of it helped get it out of the mind.
With the memory purged, he could allow himself the luxury of
thinking just of the pain.

His fellow internee scraped his fingernail over an insect bite on
the side of his neck. It was not a wise thing to do, for infection
might set in, but he had not yet overcome the habit of scratching
an itch.

'The car was a big Ford,' Sandingham continued. 'We went
down to the HQ and I was bundled into an office. There was a
guard there – not one of ours, I think. The two who took me
stayed with the car. Anyway, Fujihara came in after a bit and sat
down behind the desk. He didn't say anything. Just looked and

looked at me, running his eyes up and down. Then Tsutada came in.'

A guard walked by near the perimeter fence and Sandingham used this interruption to draw once more on the cigarette. It was best not to say anything, just in case.

'What did they want to know?'

'About the escape.'

Three men had got out several nights before, one of them Willy Stewart, and the Japanese had been very edgy since then. They had thought the camp to be pretty well secure after the successful escapes in January and February of Colonel Ride's party of four and Captain Trevor and the other two. Apart from security, they thought the prisoners were now too weak or ill to try for a break-out. Every few hours they came into the large compound of the camp, grabbed someone and took him off to see if he could be made to divulge details. It was a very hit-and-miss process: out of four thousand four hundred prisoners they would be lucky to find by such random questioning even one in the know, and then he would most likely not talk. Few broke down under questioning or the accompanying beating.

'What did you say?'

'Nothing, naturally. I didn't know about it until afterwards, in any case. I said so. Did I know about the raft? What raft? I said. Where did they go? Out, I said. Fujihara hit me for that one. With the flat of his sword.'

The recollection of it caused a quick flick of agony to run through the weal across the small of his back. At the time, Sandingham had thought that his turn had come. If the blade had been edge on – and he had had no reason to suppose that it wasn't – it would have severed his spine; certainly split a vertebra.

'Were there any other escapes in the offing? I didn't know. Then they tried the pliers on my toe. The kind you use to shift rusted bolts.'

He spoke dispassionately of the tool, as if he were a plumber discussing a job with his apprentice.

'Not an electrician's pliers – ones with long handles for a better purchase. After that, I was returned here. Punchy had a go at me but it was a bit half-hearted. Just a slapping. Told me, "You no cheeky to Nippon." That sort of thing.'

'Did you see anything?' repeated his companion.

Sandingham suddenly weakened. A light-headed faintness flowed into him. His knees started to go. The bony arms of his fellow officer caught him under the armpits and lowered him on to the ground, leaning his shoulders against the tree trunk.

'Not a lot. There were some Chinese roped to the trees outside the barracks in Nathan Road. Their heads were in the gutter. The burnt-out truck is still at the junction with Jordan Road. Nothing of the escapers. Not a word. I think they must have made it.'

There was only one way to face up to it: optimistically. No breath without hope. Dream and you live, don't and you die. Either they would get away. Or be re-caught and tortured to within an inch of their lives, then thrown in solitary confinement and die there. Deep in himself he knew that was the way it went; yet he would not admit to it.

Chalky Stephens had gone because he had had no dreams. He was a schoolmaster before the war caught him up, a graduate in History from the University of Durham. Very grand. He had even been taken prisoner with his academic gown in his possession. He arrived in the camp with it and, at the searches, the Japanese guards had found the garment, unfolded it and been most curious. They chattered and giggled like schoolboys finding their first bra or knickers. They made him put it on and fingered it, twirling him round like a debutante. They could not understand what practical purpose it could possibly have served. It wasn't uniform. It wasn't camouflage. It didn't button up down the front, was not padded against the cold and, being black, couldn't be some piece of tropical kit. It wasn't a gas cape or a ground-sheet. In the end he had been allowed to keep it.

For the first few weeks he'd worn it every day, strolling about the camp as if pacing the grounds of his school on the lookout for miscreant students. Gradually, as his ordinary clothes grew tattier, he looked more and more ludicrous, for the gown was kept looking neat. He placed it carefully under the bed-boards at night to retain more or less the correct creases. He tried to form a few of the younger other ranks – corporals and below, a few of the bugle boys who were not much older than his former pupils – into a class. But he couldn't. What he wanted to teach them was not what they thought to be an important part of the prison camp basic curriculum. They didn't, as one of them put it to him so pointedly in broad Mancunian, '. . . give a fart for the Treaty of Wedmore, the Peasants Revolt or the Triple Alliance. What we want is how to make the daily three-ounce bun taste like a Lyons Corner House éclair.'

History is a lethal subject. It deals with facts, nothing but actualities that once were. And were no more. It is not a visionary subject but a collection of facts, one leading inexorably into another. History is a chain of events governed by the inevitability of truth. The more Chalky thought, the more he saw himself as a unit of history, unfolding day by day. He drew on his stock of precedents and saw what was to him unavoidable: that he would die, and soon, without a clear reason, in a god-forsaken, pre-war brick barrack. He would die of dysentery or pellagra, of cholera in the hot months or starvation in the cold. Despair took him over and, one morning, he lay down in his gown in the shadow of his barrack and rigor mortis had set in before they found him at the evening *tenko*. Within the hour he was buried and the stitching of his gown unpicked, the fabric being re-cut into *fandushis* or bandages.

Sandingham pinched the cigarette out and put the remaining stub in his pocket.

The spring was advancing now, the evenings staying light longer; soon they would be herded into the barracks for the night.

He made to get up once more. The other bent to help him.

'It's all right. I can manage.'

They walked slowly towards the hut. A single bird was piping in one of the pines, unanswered.

'Do you play bezique?'

'No,' answered Sandingham. 'Do you play canasta?'

'Not very well, but I'll give you a game. Do you have a second pack? We'll need one, of course . . .' His voice was tight with eager anticipation: another deck of cards would be an asset upon which to found a friendship. Then he said, 'You're Sandingham, aren't you?' It was unnecessary, for from his manner it was clear he knew. 'My name's Pedrick. RN.'

Sandingham's pack was short of the four of clubs. Whoever was to be dealt the last card had that as a ghost in his hand and stated he was playing it as he lay down nothing in thin air.

The lights flickered briefly and were extinguished just before nine.

He was woken at half-past four by the sentry whom they had nicknamed 'Cat-and-Dog' hammering on the barrack door. He was shouting hoarsely in Japanese. First light was shimmering behind Tai Sheung Tok, promising a hot day but the early morning air was clean and sharp with no shadows casting themselves on the dirt. He glanced out of the window to see Sally, the Pay Corps' black-and-white fox terrier, nosing around a patch of weeds; she was oblivious of a tabby-ish cat which was hunched up on the roof ridge of the building above her, watching her every move. Smoke was rising in a vertical plume from the kitchens: it did not disseminate for at least thirty feet, so tranquil and windless was the dawn hour.

Turning into the room once more, Sandingham saw Tom Pedrick bent studiously over a tin can covered with a scrap of grimy cloth. He had his hand in the can and was taking small dots out of it, placing them on a sheet of crumpled paper. He muttered as he did so.

'How many, Tom?' croaked an expectantly hopeful voice from the top of a three-tier bank of bunks.

'Two hundred and sixteen. But there's more to come. I've got three hundred and ninety-one from yesterday. Should make seven hundred . . . '

Leaning on his bunk, Sandingham grinned ruefully. British officers breeding bluebottles to swap for cigarettes – one fag per hundred flies. The idea was that the prisoners killed flies and thus cut down the risk of disease. The Japanese thought the flies were wild, did not realise that they were being factory-bred by enterprising prisoners on mouldy rice and a dead rat.

Cardiff Joe appeared suddenly at the barrack door but did not see the fly farm being shoved under a bunk. He was the best of the interpreters, a stocky and bow-legged figure who was helpful whenever he found his superiors looking the other way. He gained his monaker because he claimed he had a bank account in Cardiff.

'Eve'ybody up! Time to go to wuk! Fi'e minits! Fi'e minits!'

He moved on to rouse the next building. It was unusual for him to be about so early. He was normally not to be seen before seven-thirty. Tokunaga, the camp commandant, was obviously having one of his periodic tightenings-up.

The prisoners – eight hundred of them – formed lines at the kitchen and were each issued with the day's customary ration of a small bun and a clove of garlic. The first five hundred also got a third of a tin can of watery tea and a dollop of cold congealed rice and sweet potato. Sandingham missed this as he was last at the latrines and had to queue before balancing over the hole in the ground that served as a lavatory. As his loose turds fell into the slop containers below, which had not yet been emptied by the morning sanitary rota, he could hear the raucous buzzing of thousands of flies. His stomach was getting better: he had somehow managed to shake off the diarrhoea that had been bothering him for a fortnight. At least he was not a dysentery case. It had had him very worried.

The lines reformed for embarkation on to the ferry. The guards stood in ranks on either side and Cardiff Joe, after receiving the count, marched them off. The ferry took them down the Kowloon peninsula, round the tip by the Star Ferry pier and the landmark of the Kowloon-Canton railway station clock tower and up the other side to Kai Tak. Here they were disembarked and marched through some streets to the site of the airport. It was being extended to take Japanese aircraft.

As they paraded through the few streets between the ferry pier and the aerodrome the guards assumed the formation they had taken at the embarking point. They marched alongside the prisoners, rifles at the ready by their waists, bayonets fitted and their hands firmly grasping stock and barrel. The position each was obliged to take, half-facing inward to the labour column, made walking clumsy and the Japanese soldiers, for the best part short men, waddled and tripped rather than marched in a military fashion. It did not matter: no one dared laugh at the spectacle.

From a few shady shops and doorways, Chinese women and children gawped as the contingent passed. The Europeans – English, Canadians, Dutch, Portuguese – whom they had known as bank officials and businessmen, architects and dentists, police inspectors and customs officers, were now just coolies. This did not cause the onlookers any pleasure. It did not satisfy some obscure colonial rancour, settle any old scores. It shocked them that those who had made the world tick could be so reduced to such indignity, such obvious loss of face. They felt helpless sympathy for them.

Sandingham was put into a draft to dig a ditch. Pedrick, by chance, was in the same workforce.

At the site of the ditches they were issued with labourers' shovels with 'P.W.D.' painted on the handles, and common garden forks, and told in broken English to dig to a depth of eleven feet between the tied-out stakes about three feet apart. Some Chinese coolies were already at work in the ditch, clearing out what soil had fallen in during the night. Tom contrived to get next to Sandingham.

'I've not done this before,' Sandingham said, looking at the handle of his shovel and thinking of the twist of fate that gave him a government Public Works Department tool.

'We just dig,' said Tom. 'The coolies dig with us and we get them to shift the dirt out in those wicker baskets' – he pointed to a stack of them – ' . . . and we get a drink break of ten minutes mid-morning. Water. Half an hour at midday, while the guards and the coolies eat and then back as usual. What have you done in the past?'

'Moved explosives, piled up lorry tyres, mixed concrete, filled kerosene cans, that sort of thing. Tight supervision. Not like this.'

Casting casually about him, Sandingham saw only three guards for a work detail of at least one hundred PoWs and as may coolies. He started to tug his vest off.

'Don't do that. Keep it on,' advised Tom. 'It stops the dust from getting in the sores. I'm told the ground's a bit tetanus. After a bit, one of the coolies'll get a bucket of sea water. Wash in that. The salt does you good.'

They went into the trench, already thirty yards or more long. It was not a drainage ditch but a slit trench as cover against air attack. The first twenty-five yards were shored with rough-sawn timber, but the rest was not. Sandingham set to on the sandy, gritty earth with his shovel. It was hot going, but if he took it slowly it didn't tire him too quickly and, by mid-morning, he was in a routine.

'You no work too hard. Take it easy. We can do more instead of you.'

He had not been spoken to all morning, not even by Tom who was cutting planks and cross-members for the shoring. He started to twist himself round in the narrow passage of the trench.

'No. No see me. I standing behind you. Just listen. I can help you. You take this. Guards no can see. We too deep and my man watch out fo' us.'

Stopping digging, Sandingham was handed an oblong block of cooked fish about the size of a cigarette packet.

'Eat now!' ordered the Chinese voice with urgency.

He crammed the fish into his mouth and chewed on it. It was hard to swallow because his throat was dry, but he forced it down. It tasted good and had been poached in ginger. His lips ignored the sand on his fingers as he pulled the few bones out of his mouth, covering them with a shovelful of gravel.

'Thank you,' he said.

He recommenced digging. After a few minutes, a guard's shadow slid over the sheer side of the trench: he peered down to see nothing abnormal. He moved off and the lookout overhead tipped the Chinese the nod.

'You know you' senior officer?'

Sandingham replied in the affirmative.

'I got a message for him. You take it.'

The Chinese was still behind Sandingham and his hand reached round and bent Sandingham's arm behind his back. He pressed into the palm a minute square of paper, folded to the size of a postage stamp, and Sandingham deftly wrapped it into the creases of his loincloth where his vest tucked into the waistfold.

'What's your name? Who shall I say . . .?' he asked obliquely over his houlder.

'You just say Number 177. Very lucky number for Chinese. Nearly all sevens.'

'But your name? I can't give him a number alone.'

'He will understand. Tell him 177. For you, my name can be "Francis".'

The drink break arrived. Sandingham climbed out of the trench into full sunlight and the heat struck him. It was actually cooler in the bottom of the ditch. He squatted next to Tom

Pedrick and took a swig from the water jug. It was warm but refreshing.

As they doused their bodies with sea water from the buckets they spoke very quietly, their whispers disguised by the chattering of the coolies. The salt stung in their cuts, the cracks in their dry skin and their open sores, but it was a healthy sensation.

'I've got something for the CO,' Sandingham said bluntly. 'A note.'

Tom Pedrick seemed unperturbed, as if he expected such an occurrence. He didn't ask how Sandingham had come to obtain it.

'Put it under your balls if you get the chance,' said Tom. 'They won't search there and you'll not lose it because the material's tight around the crotch.'

Pretending to ease his testicles, Sandingham succeeded in getting the note shifted.

They returned to dig. At midday, the guards brought over half a petrol barrel filled with a thin soup containing some cabbage leaves and with bits of fatty tissue floating in it. The usual chrysanthemum leaves hung suspended in the liquid. The tissue was tasteless but someone said they believed it was dolphin: one had been found beached the day before by the detail working on the taxiway extension. They ate under an awning slung between four poles. A warm breeze flickered the hanging edges and the guy ropes.

One prisoner kept apart from the rest of them. He was slight of build with large ears that were exaggerated by his shaven head. His long fingers held his Chinese soup spoon very delicately, as if he were at a banquet. Sandingham studied him for some minutes. The man kept his eyes lowered and seemed to ponder his soup bowl with unnecessary concentration, sipping the liquid with a determined deliberation. Pedrick saw him watching the man.

'Who is he?' Sandingham enquired.

'Don't you know? He's – ' Pedrick answered, then he silenced himself.

Going mad, thought Sandingham. He's one of the ones who's going insane. Balmy. Off his rocker. Losing his marbles. He had been near to that himself in the first few months. He made to rise and go across to the man. Tom grabbed his wrist.

'Why on earth not? Look at him: he's cracking up. He's barely with us.'

'He's not with us at all. He's against us.' This puzzled Sandingham. Tom carried on, 'You know the hut by the kitchens, the one with the boarded-up window? He's in that hut.'

This did not solve the dilemma for Sandingham.

'Those two – the lance-corporal and his mate who were in that same hut – who were caught last month, trying to get out through the wire behind Jubilee Buildings? He' – Tom spat in order mainly to clean his mouth of the aftertaste of the soup that was tainted by the petrol formerly in the cooking drum, but also to show his dislike – 'ratted on them. To the Nips. Told Cardiff Joe. And that was it. Nabbed at the post. They've not been seen since. Second time it's happened, I'm told, but the first I only heard about umpteenth hand. This one I know of for sure. I was skivvying in the next room, mopping the floor. Heard him spill the beans. Now he's in Coventry. Will be for years if this bloody war goes on and on. And it will . . . ' His voice tailed off. That was defeatist, and Pedrick'd have none of it.

'What'll happen to him?'

'When we've won the war,' said Pedrick positively, 'and we're out of this, the fucker'll get court martialled. I do hope.'

His vehemence took Sandingham aback, but he understood it, shared in it to some extent. He could not avoid it.

The afternoon was spent digging monotonously. Tom and his partner on the two-man saw, a Merchant Seaman stoker with a tattooed moth on his chest, found the going heavy for the teeth were blunting. Eventually, the saw twanged and the nearest guard sauntered across to see what was wrong. In mime, they showed him that the teeth were not only blunt but breaking off. He ordered them to stop and sent a Chinese basket coolie as a runner to his superior. The coolie took his time and the supply of planking was held up. The digging did not cease, however, and soon there were twenty yards unshored.

Sandingham stopped and took the handles of one of the wicker baskets of soil. In the coolie's absence excavated earth was building up. He moved back through the trench to the nearest steps up. Here he put the basket on his hip and started to climb.

Off to his left was a rushing sound, like water running in a sluice. In a mill race in Suffolk: it made his thoughts cool to hear it. Then, funnelled on to him by the trench, there was a horrendous scream.

The sides were collapsing on to two coolies. The sandy soil had dried out in the heat of the day and now it just fell in. The two men were still screaming and then their scream was cut as if switched off. Dust eddied upward.

Everyone dropped tools and rushed forward. The guards unslung their rifles and hurried towards the scene, prepared for trouble. Several fixed their bayonets as they ran. Sandingham grabbed another man's shovel and he and Tom, a private from the Middlesex and several Chinese, started frantically to dig. A seven-or eight-yard section had gone. The eleven-foot-deep trench was now only a two-foot-shallow depression, ten feet across.

It was too late. Too much earth had fallen and over too great a length of the working. The guards moved in, hitting people aside with the butts of their rifles. A senior NCO came over and they talked together before the orders were changed. The trench was to be angled through forty-five degrees at the site of the cave-in.

As the prisoners lined up to board the ferry that was to take them back to the camp at Sham Shui Po, Sandingham saw Francis Number 177 glance at him. The Chinese winked once.

He wasn't sure what to expect of the agent and Sandingham's first view of him was perhaps a little disappointing. He didn't look like a secret agent, a spy for the Communist guerillas, the Nationalists or the British: one of those had to be his employer. He was stripped to the waist and his chest was slightly sunken at the sternum. He was tanned but not at all muscular. He wore baggy black pantaloon-like peasant's trousers, the waistband folded over, and rope sandals. His face was nondescript, commonplace Chinese.

They all look alike, thought Sandingham and he smiled to himself at the Europeans' cliché of ignorance. Number 177 smiled back quickly and turned away.

The harbour was smooth with a slight swell. Sandingham stood next to Tom at the rail. The guards knew no one would jump: they'd be shot or killed by sharks. The harbour, always rich with garbage and, now that it was wartime, an abundance of corpses as well, attracted them.

'Those poor bastards!' Sandingham remarked. 'God! What an awful way to die . . . '

'Any worse than being shot? Or bayonetted? Or dying of scurvy or cholera? At least it was quick.'

After a pause, Sandingham said, 'But to see it coming like that. A bullet – you never hear the bang. That's really quick. To see the earth falling on you, though . . . '

'No worse than seeing the bayonet plunge. Certainly no worse than seeing your stomach spewed up or your wound starting to smell gaseous. Be glad if your death's as rapid.'

They said no more at that.

As the craft passed the Peninsular Hotel Sandingham studied the large ground-floor windows. If he strained his ears he could almost hear a palm court ensemble playing a tea dance over the thud of the screw and the hissing of the waves gliding by below.

If he had had a blanket around his shoulders . . . if he had had a mug of steaming cocoa in his hand . . . if there had been a roaring fire in the grate before him . . . if his nose had been red . . . and if the room had smelt of roasted chestnuts . . . he could possibly have been at home on a winter's evening with a streaming cold. As it was, he had a temperature of one hundred and three degrees and stomach cramps and sat hunched over a battered tin basin with his feet in water that had been warmed by leaving it in a black bucket in full spring sunlight.

For several days Sandingham had been suffering from electric feet. It was painful and alike to permanent pins and needles, from the ankles down. The MO told him it was vitamin deficiency. A number of them were getting it. Soaking his feet in warm water relieved the pain for a while. His tongue was raw on one edge.

He had been standing for over two hours that afternoon in the 'operating theatre', assisting in holding down two officers while they each had a molar extracted without anaesthetic. Abscesses were becoming increasingly common, too. The operating table had seen better days taking the pink into the corner pocket off a cannon; but no one complained. It was so heavy it did not move, the baize surface was warmer than the cold slate beneath and the rims of the pockets could be used to anchor down particularly powerful and obstreperous patients.

Pushing his hands over his head in the luxury of a stretch, Sandingham looked about him. Some prisoners were playing an improvised game of bowls; a few were tending a very inadequate, dessicated vegetable plot while others were sitting or mooching or moving slowly about in groups of no more than three. Others still were gathered under the pine-tree smoking-stand. A sudden outbreak of masculine laughter rang across the compound.

'They can always laugh,' said de Souza. 'The British can always find humour in even the worst of their troubles.'

He was Portuguese, and had been an import-export broker before the Hong Kong volunteer force called upon his services to fight in the early weeks of December. His English was impeccable: he had attended a missionary school in Macau in the twenties. It had been his poor luck to be present at the massacre of the patients and the raping and subsequent murder of the nurses at St Stephen's College: he had seen the two doctors shot and bayonetted over and over on the ground. He had had a smashed hand which could still not grip well. That had been on Christmas Day.

Sandingham lifted his feet out of the water. As he did so, a prisoner came over to him with a kerosene can sliced in half and equipped with a short rope handle. He asked for some of the water and Sandingham gave him the lot, watching as he took it away to the steps of his barrack hut where he and three others stirred it with wood-ash and commenced to launder their clothes with the mixture. Soap was rare.

'It's a national trait, Suzie. We laugh at the terrible and take the light-hearted with deadly seriousness.'

'It's good, Joe. If you laugh at the awful it doesn't seem so bad. I can't do that. Sometimes I try – my mother was half-English, you know, and I've often hoped I've inherited some of her manners. But I haven't got that ability to find comic the essentially tragic. Like Shakespeare: who could write such funny, sad plays but an Englishman? *Romeo and Juliet* – dirty jokes and a lovers' death pact at the end.'

Carefully hoisting himself to his feet, Sandingham found that the pain had eased a bit from the soaking. With some difficulty, he managed to slip his feet into his new sandals, skilfully constructed from a webbing belt and an old car tyre. He hobbled off to the area between the two huts where there was what the prisoners called a 'pisaphone' – a galvanised steel funnel sunk into the earth, without screens, to serve as a urinal. The laughter followed him and came closer. Two officers whom he did not know drew up behind him, waiting their turn at the *pissoir*.

'Anyway,' said one, 'he's lucky in that he's the only person in here who's constipated. Still . . . he had another parcel yesterday from her. Just like the others, it came in a derelict perambulator! Passed straight through the guards. Not much in it. But they didn't search it too well. There was a tiny scrap of paper in it, of course. I saw it.'

Sandingham struggled to get his penis back into his *fandushi*: the skin of his fingers was so cracked at the joints he could not bend them enough to hook himself back into his clothing.

'What did it say?'

' "Darling Mickey," ' the officer quoted, giving the words their pidgin English pronounciation, ' – she could spell the "darling" all right! – "I got you sum vejtabul here – a litule cabag and some bens. I luv yuo. All so, I got you one more plam." '

They both chuckled.

'So what did he say?'

'Nothing! What could he say? Cat-and-Dog was right there. You can't talk to visitors. However, this morning he sees his Chinese piece going past the wire. Never mind the patrol, the bloody electrified wire, or even a good face slapping! He runs up as near as he can get to the fence and bawls out, "Hey, Gilly!" She looks his way, half-terrified to do so. "Hey!" he bellows again. "Not prams, Gilly. Not prams. Plums! Plums!" '

The laughter was the choking, chortling kind that always accompanies a good yarn. Sandingham smiled as he limped back to the step of his hut.

From inside, he could hear a French lesson in progress, a pupil repeating clumsily, 'Je ne suis par. Tu nay par. Il nay par . . .'

He rubbed his hand firmly along his shin. The ringworm was as brightly scarlet as a plague mark and pestering him again.

*

'It tastes fucking foul, if you don't mind my saying so, old boy.'

'I admit it's not Johnnie Walker, but I don't think it's that bad,' said Sandingham.

'You do better,' challenged Rodney Castleford, a tall, narrow young man who had been a steward in the Merchant Navy and was used to the wiles of the lower decks.

He was naturally thin when they arrived in the camp, marching in past the small, octagonal, pagoda-like guard-box. Now his thinness was accentuated by emaciation – behind his back, the others in his hut called him 'Tapeworm'. He had one of them, too. The papery, cream-coloured egg-segments passed out with his faeces. He could do nothing about it: they had no sulphur drugs. He called it 'Tony', after his headmaster at school, a man called Hill who had big ears, no sense of justice and was, in his estimation, 'a right shit'.

'What's it made of?'

'Rice, cabbage leaves and stalks, carrot tops, a few turnips and eleven ounces of sugar liberated from our Nipponese neighbours. Boiled up first on the ring.'

The ring was a home-made heating element powered by an illegal flex that was connected to the electrified fence. It worked well, if slowly, and all the huts abounding the perimeter fence had something like it. It had begun life as a form of primitive electric fire in February. Now, in April, it powered the fermentation bucket.

'It is rough,' admitted Sandingham after a second sip had burned his tongue.

'Rough? You could depilate sheep with it.' As a vet in civvy street, 'Black' Berry should have known.

'Well,' judged the medical officer, sampling a drop on the end of his finger, 'it won't make you blind but it might make you blind drunk. Anyone who can't stand their share can donate it to me and the sick bay. We can use it for sterilisation. Or cleansing cuts. And I'm not joking.'

'Better idea, doc,' suggested the vet. 'Keep it a few more hours to mature and use it as an anaesthetic.'

They all found that amusing.

'You!'

Sandingham stood as upright as he could, turned as smartly as he could, saluted as smartly as he could, then bowed from the waist as low as he could.

'When an officer in the Imperial Japanese Army comes by you, you salute immediately.'

'Yes, sir,' replied Sandingham to the dirt, upon which stood firmly planted a pair of highly polished leather boots.

'Stand up!'

He did so, pressing his hand into the small of his back to press the pain away. He had pulled a muscle badly while digging the trenches at Kai Tak the day before.

'Why is your hand not at your side? You stand to attention.'

He did so, but not fast enough. The slap across his jaw sent his head reeling to the right.

'Next time, you salute before the officer of the Imperial Japanese Army sees you and you hold that salute until he has passed from your sight.'

Afterwards, Pedrick asked, 'Who the hell was that?'

'I've no idea and I hope I don't have to find out.'

Sally was defecting. At the beginning, she had stayed with the Pay Corps sergeant but after a while she was to be seen offering her attentions more and more to the Japanese subaltern who was in charge of messing for the camp guards. Although their food rations were not exorbitant, they had considerably better quality food than the prisoners and there was a far greater quantity of it. Rice and fish or meat gravy, interspersed from time to time with pork or monkey scraps, was preferred by the bitch to her owner's skimpy servings of originally weak but further diluted soup and whatever she could catch for herself by way of rats, mice and the shining, brown-backed cockroaches that inhabited every crack and cranny of the buildings. The final sign that she was going over to the enemy occurred when, returning to the barrack hut late one night, she was noticed to be wearing a brand-new leather collar with metal studs mounted on it.

The sergeant scooped her up in his once-brawny arms. The dog, with a duplicity better suited to a feline, licked his face.

'You know, John,' said a fellow sergeant, 'I can't bear that soddin' animal. Watching it lick you reminds me of a whore. As she screws you, you wonder whose cock was up there last. The last chin that tongue slurped was probably Tokunaga's own.'

'Doubt it. The Imperial Japanese Commander of Saps Like Us, The High Honourable Colonel Tokunaga, Sir! would probably eat the poor little bugger. You can't blame the dog. She's hungry and finding 'er food best she can. Watchin' 'er operate makes me wish I was a little bitch like that. You got to admire 'er stayin' power.'

'What's more,' added another, 'she don't get diphtheria, she don't get scurvy and she don't get cholera. She do get mange . . .'

' . . . which is abou' the only bloody thing we ain't getting.'

He put Sally back down on her paws. She wriggled under one of the bunks and settled into a snug of crumpled paper she had fashioned into a PoW version of the bamboo wicker basket she had formerly occupied in the offices at Murray Barracks. Even dogs, one of the NCOs tersely commented, had to make sacrifices in a war.

For some days Sally continued to visit the guards for luxuries that would not have been refused by her rightful owners. On one occasion, in the manner dogs have, she returned with her breath smelling strongly of roasted chicken, much to the chagrin of the sergeant who had not seen a chicken since being captured, except for a solitary and scrawny cockerel that had mistakenly flown over the perimeter wire from the surrounding streets where, by April, there was none of its kin left crowing. The bird had quickly disappeared, almost before it had landed. A smearing of mouldy rice by the wire had assisted in convincing it that it should make the crossing of the no-man's-land of electrified fencing and the guard walks. Sally had, on that occasion, been presented with the parson's nose.

It was a sweltering day, even before the sun had reached the mid-morning angle. The prisoners who were on work draft had long since departed and would by now have been bathed in sweat at Kai Tak, the dusty soil powdering into their hair and ears, adhering to their skin like a thin pastry case. Some felt they might yet cook.

For Sandingham, it was his turn on the rota for general camp cleaning. A top-brass Japanese officer was expected to visit the camp in the evening and that meant everything had to be spruced up. The worst job was sweeping clear the dust that had settled on the concrete of the camp roads. The best job, after the sweeping was completed, was the washing down of the road. Whereas the British Army painted boulders white, the Japanese scrubbed roads: all armies do pointless things, Joe thought. Indeed, it was a job much sought after by the prisoners for it involved dowsing the hot roads with sea water and then sweeping it off into the gulleys, gutter-slots and earth. It was a chore that gave the prisoners two respites from their daily life – they could splash water about like errant schoolboys and, within the parameters of their life, 'enjoy' themselves; and the sea water was salty and beneficial to skin wounds.

It was a task to which Sandingham got himself and his small workforce of other ranks delegated. He took it upon himself to bring the water from the barrels mounted on the back of a lorry to the site of the operation as it worked its way along the camp roads. Chinese labourers were used to fill the barrels and they sometimes put small live fish into the tanks, knowing that the prisoners would capture these when the water levels dropped, and eat them. The fish were no larger than sardines and, when boiled gently, could be eaten whole with only the tail and head being cut off, for use later in the making of soup. The bones did not matter.

He stumbled as he picked up a bucket clear of the road surface: his arms were wearying sooner than usual which he attributed to the onset of the next stage of starvation. The bucket tipped on to its side but did not roll over and spill its contents. Instead, a small trickle meandered through the dirt to the side of the road. Looking up, he saw Sally heading back from the camp guards' quarters. She was trotting along with the boundless optimism dogs have when they are intent on doing something of which they are ignorant. As she drew level with Sandingham, something caught her eye towards the wire. She stopped and stood stock-still in the way fox terriers have, her pointed nose twitching slightly and her eyes and ears alert.

By the wire was a rat, standing in broad daylight. It was near a patch of ground used for the emptying of the night soil from the sanitation buckets, and it was engaged in eating something on the ground, pressing the hard brown object down with one of its hand-like forepaws that its teeth might get a better hold.

The terrier turned slowly. The rat, sensing it but not seeing it, stopped eating and looked up.

Sandingham said, 'No, Sally, no!' in a small voice but with what he hoped was an imperious tone.

The dog ignored him, the rat returned to its meal and the dog started to edge towards it. Even at forty feet, Sandingham could see the rat's grey fur glistening in the sun and could not help himself thinking that the rodent was in a far healthier condition than he was.

Speedy as her kind can be, Sally rocketed forwards, her pads grabbling for an initial purchase. Sandingham shouted for her to stop, heel, sit. The rat looked up, saw death closing rapidly upon it and abandoned its repast to flash towards the wire with the sensual fluidity of motion that rats can muster.

Eagerly, the terrier was after it. Sandingham was powerless.

The rat flicked through a run under the wire. The dog sped straight to the run and started to squeeze herself through after her quarry.

There was a hum, barely audible, like a bumble bee fondling a tower of lupin blossom. The dog jerked, her legs scrabbling once more on the ground without pattern to their movements. Then she was still. An alarm bell rang. A patrol of guards doubled at the ready along the road to where Sandingham was standing sadly. Their canvas and rubber boots slapped on the concrete. They could see no escapee.

Sally was dead. The power in the fence was momentarily switched off so that one of the guards could drag the dog clear by her hind leg. He carried her pendulously into the camp safety area and dropped her on the earth. She fell loosely, the bones and flesh already disconnected from the life.

The guards formed up in double file and marched back the way they had come. No one else moved.

'Willy's back.'

He heard the word passed secretly down the row of bunks in the twilight.

It was with an innocent and almost child-like joy that he anticipated the dusk every day. It was the only time when there would be no roll-call, no disturbance and no work, the ten

minutes when he let his fatigued body settle on to the bamboo
mat and the boards, his head resting on the firm pillow that was
stuffed with rice straw, leaves and torn shreds of cloth. Around
him would eddy a softened murmur of voices and, if he closed his
eyes and ignored the itching on his shins, he could transport
himself back to his school dormitory. The only effective means of
escape that they had was the one that took them into sleep.

The news that Willy Stewart had been recaptured and returned
to Sham Shui Po drove all thoughts of peacefulness from Sandingham's head. He said nothing but hoisted himself on to his
elbow and listened.

'Apparently, they caught him over a fortnight ago. Out on the
Sai Kung peninsula, in a village called Tai Mong Tsai. He was
living near there with Communist guerillas who were going to get
him over the border into China and up the lines to Chungking.
They were heading for the cove of Kau Tong Hau where there
was going to be a junk waiting. The partisans were ambushed,
though. Hell of a fight. Quite a number killed on both sides. Some
taken and executed there and then on the beach. Revenge killing.
Beheaded. By the sword, as usual. Willy was brought back.'

'Where's he been held since?'

'In the cells under the Supreme Court, I heard. Now he's in
solitary . . . Tsutada's been in on the questioning. And Cardiff
Joe. Fujihara, too.'

Sandingham lay back again. He wondered if Willy had put the
willies up Fujihara, and doubted it. Cigarette burns, dislocated
fingers and toes, deep bruising, loosened teeth with any cavities
fully explored with hot needles, slivers of bamboo and rifle butts:
all efficient means of stopping the willies being applied.

'He's to come back in here.'

'How do you know?'

'Senior Naval Officer told me. He got it passed in from some
agent. Seventy-seven mean anything?'

'All the sevens, seventy-seven. Anyone got a line yet?' hollered
a wit.

'Shut up, you dumb sod! The Nips can pick up waffle like that
and figure it out. You don't need to play Housey to get the
message.'

Silence from the caller of numbers ensued.

So 177 had been in on it. That must have been why he hadn't been seen of late by Sandingham in the Chinese work teams at Kai Tak.

The conversation changed to a new topic. No one wanted to dwell on the subject of CSM Stewart, for they all knew that when he was finally returned into the hands of his brother officers there would be little left for him save death by disease. He would be so weakened that anything minor, not to mention pellagra or beri-beri, would get under his reduced resistance and finish him off.

He was glad the number being bandied about was incorrect, albeit only slightly. It might protect the truth from reaching their gaolers' ears. There were a few prisoners who were willing stool-pigeons.

'You're very quiet at this time of the evening, aren't you? Everyone else shooting the bull.'

Sandingham stretched himself over the edge of his bunk and peered into the gloom of the one below. Their tier was against an end wall and farthest from a window. It had been warmest in the cold months but now, after a hot day, that part of the hut was the rankest and hottest.

'I like to think before sleeping.'

'So do I. What do you think of?'

The previous occupant of the bunk had died the week before. The newcomer was only recently moved in and was welcomed, but had yet to fit into the particular camaraderie of the hut that manifested itself at night, away from the tortures and ills of the day.

'How do you mean?' Sandingham rejoined warily. He did not even know the new arrival's name although they had worked together.

'Bingham,' the other man replied obliquely, feeling the suspicion implied by Sandingham's look in the failing light. 'Rob Bingham. I was transferred here from Stanley. I'm not services but a civilian. I'm a dentist, hence my arrival here. Dental surgeon. Formerly of Kowloon Hospital.'

Rob, thought Sandingham. Robert. Change the R to a B. All that was needed.

'I know. I was your table muscle the other day.' Bingham half-laughed at that, a short, stunted laugh that was unfunny before it began. 'Sandingham. Joseph Sandingham. Army. I'm called Joe.'

The dentist held his hand up and offered what looked in the semi-darkness like a hybrid between a pencil and a twig.

'What is it?'

'Ask no questions. Just chew the end until it frays and then rub your teeth with it. And don't throw it away afterwards. Re-use it. In lieu of tooth powder, it will do you a surprising service. Chinese use it. Herbal.'

With the delicacy of a man testing for poison, Sandingham did as he was bid. The stick tasted of mild licorice. He worked it over his teeth and, sure enough, it removed the furry scale to which he had grown unpleasantly accustomed. His tongue ran over his polished incisors. His mouth was fresher than for weeks.

'It's hell in Stanley,' Bingham volunteered. 'Mostly civilians. They've a lot of wives and children there, too. In the civilian prison. And Chinese. A lot of the guards are Indians. Mostly friendly, save the head man. He's called Ramdad. He's got it in for the British and gone over to the Japs. He's a right bastard, that one. Hardly any food. I saw one of our chaps – a Hong Kong Bank official who's not been drafted in to run the colony's economy – for God's sake! – for the occupying forces – baking a rat on a spade over a bonfire. Seems he's quite a chef de rat cuisine.' He chewed his own tooth stick meditatively before going on. 'Much illness. Deaths creeping up from diphtheria, children getting measles and one dead from it when I left. A Chinese commits suicide from time to time: they do it by shoving chopsticks down their throats. Seems to be a sort of traditional method. It's the loneliness. The most terrible thing is the loneliness. And the uncertainty. Some of the wives and girlfriends are lost. But even in there, romance raises its head in the prison grounds. The cemetery. The vegetable plots, so-called.'

'I think of romance,' admitted Sandingham. 'In the minutes before sleep.'

'I've a photo.'

The dentist moved his hand up and down the lining of his tropical-weight jacket, extracting a passport-sized picture of a woman in her middle age with a flower-print dress on, holding a

cocktail and smiling. Her hair was fashionably permed. He
passed it up to Sandingham.

'My wife. She's dead.' His voice dulled.

Offering a platitude, Sandingham hoped it sounded sincere. It
was hard to feel sincere about anything except the rigours of
being cooped up and the unholy bloodiness of camp life.

'One good thing, at least,' said Bingham. 'She died three
months before the . . . Well, before this. Cancer.'

From a specially fashioned pocket in his blanket, Sandingham
took out his photo and held it for Bingham to see but not take.
There was just enough light by which to see the inscription on it:
'Bob: Penang 1939'.

'Your brother?'

'No, not exactly.' Sandingham spoke cagily and Bingham
realised the under-meaning. 'More my brother officer. We were
very close. He was killed . . . '

Somewhere in the room, in the deepening shadows, he thought
he could hear a man say, 'I and you'll . . . I and you'll . . . '

'I understand, son.'

An outside light came on and Sandingham refocused his eyes
and was surprised to see that Bingham was an elderly-looking
man in his mid-fifties. He had not taken much notice of him as he
stood his turn levering molars free and disregarding the grunts
and mews of agony. His voice was younger than his years, but he
was not. He had thinning sandy hair that had not been cut to a
stubble, freckles around his liquid brown eyes which were
ready to laugh or show sadness. He could see that the man's
wrists were wiry and very strong, the ligaments standing out like
tensile steel straps under the skin.

Their fellow occupants of the surrounding bunks were at the
far end of the room where there was a game of cards in progress.

'There's nothing like company,' Bingham said. 'When I was a
young lad, about your age, in my last year of university, I had a
friendship like yours. Maybe not quite, but . . . Nothing like
having someone to talk to.'

'Is it true dentists are trained doctors?'

'Not quite. Why?'

'Do you keep professional confidences? Like priests? Is the
dentist's surgery sacrosanct like the doctor's?'

'If you like, yes. If I can help you.'

Sandingham suddenly, without demure, wanted to talk, to ask someone with potential knowledge about something that had been worrying him greatly.

In the camp, there was a young boy soldier. Indeed, there were a number of lads – bugle boys from regiments, young stewards on merchantmen or mess stewards from warships – but one had caught Sandingham's attention early on. He was a slight youth of about seventeen, blonde-haired with a very fair skin. He was ragged a good bit by his fellows and the other ranks in his barrack, but he had the strength of character to stand up to it and he gave as good as he received. From the start, Sandingham had fallen in love with him. At first, he thought of this merely as a reaction against Bob's death, but he found after a few weeks that this was not so, that there was more to it. He had not spoken to the boy, but he had wanted him. Several times, he had gone to the latrines when there were few about and masturbated, the boy in his mind, his velvet belly and soft neck against Sandingham's mouth. Every morning for days, he woke with his hand on himself and the boy in his waking thoughts. Now, he was still there as vividly as ever but Sandingham was unable to get an erection to go with the thoughts. This horrified and scared him.

'I can't get a hard on,' he said to the dentist. 'I used to . . . ' he reverted to the schoolboy idiom to make it easier to say ' . . . toss off when I was first in here. Just a few times. But now I can't.'

'It worries you?'

Sandingham nodded.

'Don't let it. You're not the only one, you know. I'll bet half the men in here can't get a grip on the old chopper.' He too used slang to save Sandingham's embarrassment. This wasn't a medical matter, anyway. It was a friend counselling a friend. 'It doesn't mean you're losing your manhood. It's a vitamin deficiency allied to tiredness and the circumstances of imprisonment. A mixture of all three. Cut out Vitamin E and that's one of the results.'

He slept restlessly after that, half-afraid that his confidence would be betrayed yet knowing simultaneously that it would not.

At morning *tenko* the next day, they were kept waiting after the count was taken. An atmosphere of apprehension hung over

them as they stood in the cool air, the sun deliciously warm on
their backs. The Japanese officer of the day kept them standing in
silence, in their rows, at ease but not standing easy.

A ten-year-old black Dodge saloon drove into the compound
and stopped before the assembled throng of PoWs. Tokunaga
climbed out of the front passenger door and, from the seat behind
him, two guards dragged Willy Stewart.

An audible short buzz sounded from the ranks of prisoners. It
was met with an immediate shouted order for silence.

Fujihara, the Kempetai officer, placed himself upon the low
dais that would have been a sort of saluting base had they had
passing out parades. He stood with his stocky legs apart, his
hands resting on his hips in a tyrannical pose.

'Prisoners! Pay attention! Colonel Tokunaga, commanding
officer of this camp, tell me to say to you that any prisoner who
escape from Sham Shui Po camp will be caught and severely
punished. The rules for prisoners of the Imperial Japanese Army
say that the offence of escaping and being caught is death and ten
years in prison.'

Pedrick said under his breath to Sandingham 'Does that sentence run consecutively or concurrently I wonder?'

'For a second offence of this kind, the rules say death and
twenty years in prison.'

A few PoWs, farthest from a guard, muttered ironically at this
piece of information.

'Prisoners in rows to right of staff car – attention!'

Sandingham jolted himself upright. As he did so he noticed that
only three rows of twenty or so men each were involved and this
worried him as it did the others.

'About turn! You march with Imperial Japanese Army
officer.'

A squad of Japanese infantry lined up alongside the block of
prisoners and the order was given to step out. They followed the
Japanese NCO through the camp to the main gate, out of it and
left in the direction of Lai Chi Kok. As they marched through the
last of the Kowloon streets, silent save for the sound of their feet
on the tarmac, local Chinese gathered on the pavements to watch
them pass.

Everyone was apprehensive.

'Stop!'

They stopped. A Japanese Army Isuzu TX40 truck passed them, followed by the Dodge.

'Go!'

The NCO in charge knew only three words in English and was known by them – Stop-Go-Fuck: it sounded more like a Chinese name pronounced in the Cantonese dialect.

They were marched on to a narrow sand-and-shingle beach. Across the water, a mile away, the olive drab smear of Stone-cutters Island hung in a developing heat haze.

Fujihara appeared from the far side of the Dodge.

'Line up in twos.'

They did.

'Attention!'

The sand shuffled as they brought their feet together. A cumulus cloud shifted over the sun and the glare off the sand lessened.

The Isuzu truck started up and moved off. It had hidden from their view a stout ten-foot breakwater post sunk into the shingle at the low-water mark. The tide was out. Seaweed had tangled round the foot of the post. Barnacles five feet up showed how far the high-tide reached.

Staked to the post was Willy Stewart. His feet were bound to the base. His hands were together, overlapping palm in palm, above his head and were nailed to the timber.

The Japanese troops divided into two groups. One, by far the larger, guarded the prisoners with bayonets fixed and muzzles pointing at them from hip height. The other, consisting of five men, were lined up under Fujihara's orders. They were the firing squad.

He shouted a string of curt commands in Japanese.

'Jesus Christ!'

Sandingham moved his head fractionally to the left. A captain from the Intelligence Corps stood there, his eyes wide. He could speak Japanese.

The rifles came up.

Another command.

Every shot deliberately missed, erupting tinily in the sea behind.

Another command and the rattle of bolts. Another oath from the linguist captain.

The second volley seemed to nick rather than hit him.

A third order. The captain said nothing. Tears were smearing the dust on his cheeks.

The bullets did not strike the head or the heart. They hit Willy Stewart in the thighs, in the lower abdomen, in the flesh of his biceps. He was far from dead.

Unable to turn away, Sandingham watched Willy gradually lift his head.

Discipline, he thought. Discipline. The maxim of the man they saw crucified before them: control yourself and you control the world.

His eyes were open and blood was dripping down his groin and legs.

Fujihara walked across the beach. The shingle sounded like an avalanche, the scrunch exaggerated by the gravity and squalor of the occasion.

He drew his sword, swung it back and struck at Willy's neck. He missed. Too high. The sergeant's jaw was severed.

He swung again.

Willy Stewart, who made no sound and shed no tears, died.

The sword, with its brown, red and white-woven braid over the ray-skin grip and its brass mountings, was wedged in the wooden stake. Fujihara tugged it loose.

Willy's head was sandy around the raw and jagged severing and the moist eyes were wide and vacant. It rested on its side against his feet, bedded in the seaweed. Blood fountained jerkily from the stump of his neck, blotching the sand.

They were about-turned and marched back. The body was left for the tide.

Sandingham felt nothing but an emptiness in his chest and an incomprehensible howl in his brain that could not get out. He had felt more obvious sorrow at the death of the dog.

The five hundred officers, selected by a seemingly random process beyond their powers of reason, were lined up at the main gate to the camp and would have presented a wryly amusing sight had it not been for the evidence of sickness, indignity and malnutrition in their ranks. They were accompanied by one hundred ordinary troops who were to serve as their batmen.

Most were dressed in the remains of their uniforms – khaki or white shirts, shorts, knee-high socks and peaked caps – but some wore less orthodox items of attire that would have shocked their officer-training sergeants into hoots of derision and sarcasm. One wore a Chinese Hakka woman's hat, a broad, flat top with an array of black, folded curtaining hanging six inches down all round; several others wore coolies' rattan hats with pointed cones like the roofs of pagodas. Chinese-style cotton jackets, singlets, a pair of cricketing trousers and a lightweight, once-cream cassock lent an amateur pantomine atmosphere to the occasion. Their baggage and loads were as curiously incongruous – some carried military kitbags or suitcases upon their shoulders, or in each hand. Some balanced large parcels tied with cord and wrapped in sheets upon their heads, like African washerwomen heading for the nearest waterhole with the village laundry. Others – those luckier or deemed weaker by their fellow prisoners – transported their meagre belongings in home-made hand-carts, a wooden Chinese barrow with a solid front wheel and a number of babies' prams.

The order was given in Japanese from the front and relayed back through the rows in English. With a large escort of guards, they marched out of the camp and headed off through the streets, watched surreptitiously by the local Chinese from the shadow of shop-fronts and balconies. Cyclists, a few cars and a convoy of military trucks passed them by. Children ran alongside them until seen off by the butts of the guards' rifles.

For three-quarters of an hour, the straggling parade stepped eastward until it reached its destination near the Kowloon Hospital. It was a camp previously constructed by the Hong Kong authorities to house Chinese soldiers who had deserted from their forces and who were fleeing from the advance of their enemy in the Sino-Japanese War.

One of the officers, walking near Sandingham with his possessions collected on a two-wheeled cartlet, said ruefully, 'Well, bugger me! I built this bloody place and now I'm in it. Make your own bed and lie in it. Well, I'm damned!'

As they entered the camp, it became obvious why they had

been moved. The number of successful or attempted escapes from the Sham Shui Po camp had annoyed the Japanese and caused them to lose face with their high command in Tokyo, the local Chinese and the prisoners themselves. There was a need to separate the officers from the men to discourage such escapades, and this new prison, Argyle Street camp, was set to segregate would-be offenders from those they led and so bring a stop to 'home runs'. The prisoners realised this at the moment of arrival.

The camp was not built in the Japanese manner, but with what was now construed a perverse British efficiency. Six guard towers surrounded the camp, each with a machine-gun and a searchlight mounted on it. There was a high fence all round the camp, and this was electrified. Walking out was impossible; so was crawling out, effectively: the ground was alternately too sandy or too stony for tunnelling. Once in, save for labour detail exeats, one stayed in.

Tokunaga arrived and addressed the prisoners. The gist of his words were to tell the assembled that this was a camp for those who were not exactly model prisoners. His speech was translated by an interpreter whom they had not seen before. He was of average height, with pointed ears and he wore a military cloak, highly polished boots and a good-quality wristwatch. He spoke with an American accent.

When Tokunaga had left in his Dodge staff car, the interpreter continued. The prisoners would have laughed had they dared.

'Right, youse guys,' he commenced, 'my name is Niimori Genichiro and I am the senior interpreter hereabouts. You got that?' He waited for a few nods. 'I was educated in the US of A, and I come from Chicago. That's my home town. So I know just what all you limey guys can get up to. So don' try nuttin'. Work rotas as before. You still go down to the ay-ro-drome. Others arrange general camp duties. Any of youse guys got questions for that?' None of the guys had. 'Right! Now this is one of my interpreters here.' He pointed to his left where there stood a Japanese officer of swarthier than normal appearance. He was unshaven, grinned in an uncouth manner and his uniform seemed a size or two too large for him. He stood as if to strut out at any moment. 'He is called Inouye Kanao. When you speak to us, you call us Mister or by our rank. Okay? No need to get too famil-ar but we want to get along with all youse guys. Got it?'

They got it.

Within hours, Niimori Genichiro was dubbed 'Panama Peter'. Inouye Kanao was 'Shat-in-Pants', for the seat of his trousers hung sack-like from his behind. Later, he was to be renamed 'Slap-Happy'. That was earned by his other, less amusing trait.

Once in the barrack assigned to him, Sandingham sensed depression hovering over him again, an invisible force pushing inward upon his most private thoughts: the march through comparative freedom had affected him in a manner he couldn't assimilate. The ferry trips to the Kai Tak workings, which he no longer took, had not deepened his awareness of imprisonment and yet the passage through streets, past shops and people had. The normality of it hurt him deeply. He sat morosely and miserably on his new bunk, the middle of three, and stared at the boards of the one above. Someone down the barrack was singing. The tune was 'Chicago, My Home Town'.

'Silver paper?'

'That's right. Lining of tea chests, cigarette wrapping . . . Anything. Silver foil of any sort. We need it. But it mustn't have a hole in it. And as creaseless as possible, please.'

'Why?' queried Sandingham. They were starving, dying of nutritional diseases and diphtheria, pellagra and hollow despair and this man wanted silver paper.

'Do you know how a radio works?'

'No. Not really. Just how to use one.'

'Well, the condenser is made of silver foil. Or so I'm told. And someone wants it.'

Silver paper reminded Sandingham of the bars of Cadbury's or Fry's chocolate that he had bought every Saturday with a penny from one of the red dispensing machines on the platform at Liverpool Street station. Gold lettering on a red wrapper? He tried hard to remember – such little things were becoming of considerable importance for him – but couldn't. Only the taste came back to him. He had always obeyed his mother. Screw up the wrapping and either put it in the ticket bin by the barrier or place it on the floor under the seat in the carriage so the cleaners could take it away. Garbage to one man is treasure to another: it was always so, and always would be. What one man threw away another could live off. Which meant, of course, that the first could, too. How much better to share and have no waste.

For several weeks he collected silver paper avidly. Then he was told they had enough. Then, a week later, it started again. One of the sheets must have had a pin-prick hole in it. The condenser didn't work. It had to be unwound and begun all over again.

'Owow!'

The bawled, meaningless exclamation shook Sandingham into standing to attention. He let the camp-made wooden hoe fall from his hand on to the dusty ground. A cloud of dry soil rose from it and hung in the humid air.

More shouting at him was accompanied by the slancing noise of a sword being drawn from the scabbard.

He attempted a salute. His hand was too heavy and hot to lift.

A string of Japanese words sprayed around him like flung grit. His head hammered. The sun had made the skin of his shaven scalp contract like a steel skull-cap. His shoulders burned. When he could gather his thoughts, he found them concentrating upon calomine lotion and cucumber rind.

'Kare wa netsu ga arimasu.' The accent was Australian.

The reply from the Japanese sergeant was rapid. Sandingham hung his head from exhaustion. He seemed to be suspended from a point between his shoulders.

'Atami ga itain desu. Atami ga itami desu.'

The sergeant said nothing. He turned and sauntered off in the direction of other gardeners. Every three steps, he swung his sword in an oblique, upwards and sideways slash. The blade audibly hummed in the air.

Just as he felt his knees begin to sag a steadying arm ran itself under his and held him tight. He was guided towards the luxurious coolness of the barrack hut, taken to his bunk and helped on to it.

'You want to watch Napoleon. He's a right bastard. Practises lopping off PoW heads with that sword of his.'

It was the same Australian voice, soft and burring. Sandingham was too weak to say anything.

A guard entered the room, pausing to allow his eyes to grow accustomed to the gloom before his boots clomped on the wooden floor. A verbal torrent of Japanese ensued.

'Kare wa netsu ga arimasu. Kare wa samuke ga shimasu, you fat and ugly little yellow cunt.'

This was spoken so politely that even Sandingham, in the stupor of heat-stroke, appreciated its grace and urbanity.

'Naze?'

'I don't know why, you greasy little turd,' the Australian replied, smiling broadly and raising his hands in mock puzzlement.

The guard beamed back, totally uncomprehending.

'You lie here, mate,' the Australian ordered Sandingham. 'Take it easy and keep out the flamin' sun. I'm going down to the khazi, do a bit of shoppin'.'

By the latrines, the Australian met with a lanky short-sighted youth, one of Panama Pete's junior staff, whose uniform was too small for him. With Shat-in-Pants, he could have made a comical variety-hall turn.

'I want some milk or milk powder. Can do?'

'Not sure. Maybe.'

'How much?'

He looked blankly through his thick-lensed spectacles and asked, 'What you say?'

'How much? Ikura desu ka?'

'Oh, yes. You got something? You got ring?'

'Yes.'

'I get you milk for one ring. Gold?'

'No, silver.'

'No milk.'

It was useless to argue with him.

The Australian returned to the barrack to talk with Sandingham.

'No luck. Sold out,' he reported. 'But I'll slip out later on and see if one of the other stores has had a delivery of charity. I'll let you know what happens.'

'Thank you,' Sandingham said weakly. His head spun.

'No need. We gotta muck in together.'

Later, the Australian saw one of the other interpreters walking through the camp and called to him. Kyoshi Watanabe had been a Lutheran minister before the war claimed him for its own religion, its own morbid theologies and dogma. He was kind to the prisoners when his superiors were not watching and he thought he could get away with it.

His was the nastiest dilemma of them all. He favoured his country yet loved his God. He dared not speak out or refuse military service for the sake of his kin, yet he abhorred the indignity and cruelty he was having to condone or often to enforce upon his fellow creatures. Prayer had not worked: no divine solution had come to him. He was therefore left to be human in his own way, as often as he could.

'Can you get me some milk, pastor?'

He knew that to address the officer in such a way struck hard into that personal dilemma. Or at least, he hoped it did.

The interpreter's smooth, blanched face peered back at him from the shadow cast by the barrack-hut wall.

'Yes. I can. How much do you want? I can't get a lot.'

'A pint. And a few eggs? I've nothing left but a silver ring but you're welcome to that.'

'There's no need to pay me. I see what I can do for you. Come here after *tenko* this evening. As soon as you are dismissed.'

The shadows were much longer and deeper when he returned. The Japanese was nowhere in sight. Beside a downpipe from the roof guttering was a small package wrapped in newspaper and tied with string. He hurried it into the hut. It contained a small medicine bottle full of milk, two eggs, a third of an apple and a tiny and dried raw fish.

He gave the eggs and fish to the first medical orderly he saw for him to smuggle into the sick bay. Sandingham drank the milk as he listened to the tale of its delivery. The apple pips stuck in the gaps between his own teeth that were increasing in width as the weeks passed.

'Priorities. Get out the copper wiring. That's the first thing, and it's vital. And the dynamo. Then see if you can get a bulb or two from the lamps, if they're still there. After that, any other bits – lead from the battery, for example. You can pour the acid out. Don't need that.'

Over the space of a fortnight the Baby Austin was systematically stripped. The guards who stood over them as they worked in
what was laughingly called the 'vegetable patch' did not notice as
the various parts disappeared. Eventually all that was left was the
chassis and wheels which were, with Panama Pete's permission,
adapted into a trolley that could be pulled to and fro, carrying
buckets of night soil for fertiliser, meagre vegetable produce –
and contraband. The copper wiring went into the entrails of the
radio that was kept hidden in a false garden plot in the camp. No
one who had built the car would ever have guessed that it would
one day be reconstructed as a receiving set and the only source of
life-supporting news from the BBC to six hundred men trapped
and dying in a prison camp of their own making.

Indeed, as Sandingham pointed out when he delivered the
speedometer, the garden had provided bugger-all by way of
sustenance for the body, but what it had given to feed the soul
was vast.

Number 177 suddenly appeared in the camp one day. He was
marched in with a group of Chinese labourers who were to build
a new prison building. The prisoners were either too weak or not
to be trusted with the tools that went with such a task. Within the
hour, Francis 177 had sought out Sandingham and accosted him
in the barrack.

'What you need?'

'Everything, Francis. Food, news, medicines and drugs, tools.
Guns.' The joke was appreciated and Number 177 chuckled.

'Got money or something?'

'Nothing. All I have left is this.'

From a hollowed-out cavity in the upright support of his bunk,
Sandingham produced the silver nail buffer he had taken from the
abandoned flat that last time he'd been with Bob. He had sworn
he'd never part with it, but that was before the unimaginable had
become reality.

'I can get you something for this. But not much. Not much
silver in this.'

'But it is English silver, not Chinese silver.'

Already, Sandingham was an authority on precious metals –
copper from vehicles, lead from batteries – and he knew that

Chinese silver had a high proportion of tin in it. And red gold was preferred to yellow gold.

'I see. Also you tell you' commander I can take message to Number 13. I come in every day for this week. For sure. Okay?'

Sandingham agreed and Francis 177 took the nail buffer. The next day he received two ounces of sulphur, three constipation pills and seven dried mushrooms which were chopped up finely and added to the evening's usual soup of rice, carrot- and turnip-tops and chrysanthemum leaves. The fungi gave a good flavour to the soup and, being so finely cut, everyone had a share of them; the guards didn't see that there was a luxury item in the ingredients.

'White Pig's made the headlines again.'

It was dark in the naval officers' hut towards the north end of the camp but on the table there stood a flickering lamp which provided just sufficient light by which to read or write.

On the front page of the *Hong Kong News* was a photograph of Tokunaga. Under it was a paragraph in which Tokunaga stated unequivocally that all prisoners-of-war in Hong Kong were now happy with their lot and grateful to be in the benevolent and honourable hands of the Imperial Japanese Army. He pointed out that fewer escapes were now happening – none for the past nine weeks, in fact – and this showed prisoners were more ready to remain safely in captivity. What was more, he claimed, illness that had been present was now dying out.

'For "present", read "rampant",' said Tom Pedrick, not looking up from his pencil. 'And if it is dying out it's because the carriers and victims are.'

'When this war's over,' commented a lieutenant-commander from the bottom bunk, where he reclined wearing a sarong-like skirt over his *fandushi*, 'Tokunaga and his cronies are going to get boiled in oil.'

'With luck, their own,' a third voice added.

The *Hong Kong News* was a paper printed and published by the Japanese for the prisoners and the local population. It carried news of the war, obviously slanted, and was a source of ribaldry and depression in equal doses. The radio counteracted its effects. After it had been read, it was useful in the latrines, although the ink was of inferior quality and often besmirched buttocks and hands. 'Black-arse', they called it.

A light draught caused the flame to dance and a figure in the gloom leaned over to cup it with his hands. If it were extinguished, not having any matches, they'd not be able to relight it until morning.

'Thanks, Steve. It's hell writing by this pathetic flame. Dim as a bloody NAAFI candle.'

'What are you going to do with that?'

'Bury it in a minute. What the hell do you think I'm going to do with it?'

'I mean in the long term.'

Pedrick looked up. The guttering flame added drama not only to his gaunt face but also to his words.

'If I live, it'll be a thing to read in the future, when I hit bad times. Nothing'll be this bad again. If I die, it'll be a testimony the bastards'll get their come-uppance by. And it'll show what we had to put up with. A bit of revenge and a bit of glory for us poor saps who hung too well on to the thread of living.'

'If that diary gets found, you'll be for the high jump.'

Putting down the stub of pencil, Pedrick shrugged.

He was neatly dressed in a grey tropical suit. His hands were clean. His hair was barber-cut and his shirt was ironed. The crease in his trousers was sharp except where the knee had pushed it out. He was clean-shaven and his sunglasses were unchipped. Upon his head was a panama hat. He wore a plain tie and his shoes were tightly laced in a bow knot. He carried a small briefcase and was walking with Tokunaga, Slap-Happy, several other top-brass Japanese officers and a Chinese clerk. His hand-shake was firm.

'Who is he?' whispered Sandingham.

The prisoners were standing round in groups, their work disregarded. The guards made no move to punch or slap them into activity.

'The barracks are clean, airy and sanitary,' Slap-Happy was saying, translating Tokunaga's words. 'The sick bay is well stocked with medicines – as well as our own, though you will understand that that is not all that we would want it to be.'

'He might be the local Red Cross representative,' explained Tom.

'Ask him where the Red Cross parcels are.'

'That's for the senior officer to do. I don't think we should say anything. The Japs'll pick it up and we'll be fucked if we speak the wrong words.'

'Food is plain, but good.' Slap-Happy was proferring a typed sheet folded into three. 'Colonel Tokunaga asks you to take this list of the day's foodstuffs as issued for the prisoners, for you to send with your report to Switzerland. As you will see, there is plenty.'

The party stopped by a group of internees. The Red Cross official spoke to the prisoner nearest to him.

'How is your health?'

His words were in impeccable English with a hardly noticeable French intonation.

'I'm fine, thank you. By and large. Some boils on my skin have cleared up.'

The man twisted his arm to show the inner, softer skin where red weals indicated recent infection. Some boils were still present. They were small by comparison with those vanished, but they oozed a little puss; the prisoner had been squeezing them to get them to weep on the off-chance that he might get an opportunity to show them.

As they spoke, Slap-Happy quietly translated every word into Japanese for Tokunaga and his staff.

'And your clothing?'

'We get by. We do need a few more items or more needles and thread, but we make do, just about.'

'How is your food?'

'Plain,' echoed the officer, wisely.

They walked on. As the representative passed by them, Pedrick made an obvious show of picking up a cigarette butt that he had deliberately dropped and putting it in his pocket.

The inspection party congregated around the 1938 Ford provided by the Kempetai as the Red Cross man's transport. Just then a plaintive voice from the back of the crowd of gathered prisoners shouted out. It was high-pitched and carried clearly in the hot afternoon air.

'Monsieur!' it called. 'Monsieur! Nous mourons de faim. Nous mourons de faim.'

Slap-Happy looked dazed. Tokunaga's face blackened. He asked what was being shouted. The interpreter said he didn't know. It wasn't English. Nor was the Red Cross visitor: he was Swiss. Tokunaga put two and two together.

The Ford drove off and the French-speaking officer was singled out by the guards and half-dragged, half-frog-marched away by Slap-Happy. Sandingham did not see him again.

In a light and edgy sleep he threshed and squirmed, waking twice in the early hours, a vagrant ghost of a worry circling in the outer reaches of his dreams.

The first time it was pitch dark and he could hear Shagrue, a captain in the Ordnance Corps, struggling to catch his breath in the humid cavern of the night. He was wheezing and his throat bubbled like a man gargling or preparing to hawk. Two of his friends stood by the sick man's bunk, one holding his hand and the other wiping his brow, from time to time, with what Sandingham thought must be the last surviving fragment of the academic gown. When he was lucid, Shagrue talked in a halting voice of his father's post office in a Herefordshire village. The name of the place was half-Welsh and half-English; it sounded like a mythical city from the Norse sagas as it slipped and stuttered off his tongue.

The second time he came to his senses, Sandingham heard first the shiftless murmur of men sleeping, living in other lives and other places. A few grunted in the love-making they were engaged upon with their wives, or lovers, or mistresses. One was talking softly, but the words were incomprehensible. Another was scratching himself hard in his sleep, the rake of his blunt nails rasping on the dessicated skin of his thigh. A mosquito whined in its typically lonely fashion in the dark over Sandingham's head.

He could not hear Shagrue clinging to the air and guessed that he was dead. In the morning, this was confirmed. His friends carried his body out before most of the barracks had escaped from sleep.

'Diphtheria,' Pedrick said matter-of-factly. 'What else? First the snuffles and a sore throat. Then the headaches and the grey membrane in the throat. Then death. There's a lot of it in the other camps. The Indians have it badly in Ma Tau Chung. That's not far away. Couple of hundred yards. Probably carry on the wind that short distance. Who's to know?'

They had just been dismissed from *tenko* and were making their way towards the kitchens, both picked for that duty roster. There was no differentiation between one cook team and the next, and there was no demand for even the simplest of culinary expertise. There is only one way to cook rice and scanty vegetables when the only equipment is a series of Chinese cooking vats and water.

'He's not our first, of course,' continued Pedrick. 'Allen died of it last week and there are two others down with it. Another possible four. By the end of the month, it'll have reached epidemic proportions.'

'Why don't the Nips act? They'll catch it as readily as we do. Isn't there a cure?'

'Not a certain cure. I've heard rumour that boils can be cleared up by eating mouldy bread, but I'm not so sure. Maybe that would do the trick. That piece of information came in with a message passed from another camp. God knows which one. It seems there are more camps than we at first realised.'

'There must be something, though.'

'There is, Joe.' Pedrick's short laugh announced the breaking out of his ironical wittiness. 'It's called a decent diet and preventative medicine. Rump steak could do as either, in my case.'

Sandingham arched his eyebrows in a show of resignation, before adding, 'With tomatoes, fried mushrooms and croquette potatoes.'

'At least the tomatoes. Grilled.'

Like a schoolboy keeping cave at a classroom door, Tom looked around him to ensure no one was within easy earshot.

'I've heard that there is food about, too. And drugs. It's just that we don't get it.'

'What do you mean?'

'I've been told of a bloke who worked for the China Light and Power Company before the war. Electrical installations – mostly factories and the like. Apparently, he was called in with a former

member of his Chinese staff to look at the wiring in Tokunaga's
quarters. When they got ... '

'Morning, youse guys!'

Panama Pete had come marching briskly around the corner of
the barrack hut ahead of them. He had in tow two Japanese
privates in fatigues, their torsos bare and their pantaloon trousers
tied under their knees with draw-tapes. On their heads were the
regulation-issue sun helmets.

The prisoners stood to attention, then bowed as low as they
could from the waist as Panama Pete walked by. The bending
hurt Sandingham's stomach muscles. He had been getting the
cramps in them of late. When they assessed that the interpreter
was out of sight, they straightened up and walked on, talking
more quietly.

'. . . got into the place, they found White Pig had a Chinese tart
installed, running the servants and no doubt serving the master's
desires. They inspected the wiring and were asked to make repairs
to a big American refrigerator that 'no longer he mek ice'. Ice!
Jesus! – what I'd give for a block of that.'

The sun was over the hills and the heat of the day was rising
into the eighties.

'Trouble is, I've nothing to give.'

They mockingly laughed at each other.

'And?'

'The Chinese tart seemed to get guilty thoughts, seeing her
fellow locals slaving for the Japs alongside the European. They're
still sure out there that the English'll return one day and thrash
the shit out of the Nips. That'll also mean them getting those who
turn collaborator and side with the enemy. So, to make amends –
an insurance for the day of victory – she gave them each an ounce
of coffee in a twist of paper.'

The two men entered the kitchens. Already, some other ranks
were lighting the fires under the cauldrons. Three officers were
coming in and out with buckets of water while another cleaned
dishes with the wettened ashes of the extinguished fires. The
morning bread ration had been given out before *tenko*.

'Coffee!'

'The CLP man asked her how she got it. The guard was out
having a leak or something. She took them into a former servant's

quarters room at the back of the pantry. Piled high with Red Cross parcels. Unopened, for the best part. Some breached, hence the coffee.'

A huge woven basket was carried in. Sandingham peered inside it to see what the contents were, though it was plain they would not have changed since the day before. Assorted greenery. Outer leaves from cabbages, turnip tops, nondescript leaves of a glossy, almost evergreen hue, peelings from other vegetables, particularly carrots. An onion.

The onion was unique. He knew that. There was only ever the one and it was always shoved down the side of the basket, about a foot in. He took the vegetable out, split it apart along the cut with his fingers and extracted the tight curl of paper. Then he tossed the two halves of the onion back into the basket.

'Coffee!' he repeated. 'Bugger me!'

'No thanks, my ole son,' answered Pedrick, grinning.

Sandingham guffawed and left with the message, saying over his shoulder, 'I'll be back in a tick to wash the aubergines and shell the peas.'

His remarks produced a groaning laugh from all: they rarely saw even pea pods.

The aviation fuel barrels had been piled into a circle in such a way that, in the centre, there was a space just big enough for two men to stand in. As the barrels were empty and piled high, awaiting refilling from a fuel lighter that came in to the beach every day, they were not well guarded.

The stink of the kerosene was overpowering in the afternoon sun, but it was better than the stench of death that hung over the other end of Kai Tak. The Indian PoWs in Ma Tau Chung were dropping like flies to diphtheria and cholera, the latter now running rife through the civilian population as well. The Japanese were trying hard to cope with the matter, but it was getting on top of them.

'Indian troops not very good,' explained Francis 177 in a hushed voice. 'They got no officers and they lose face over capture. They not wash, they lavatory in open gutters, they get much sickness. Some of them more senior try to stop this but many no care if he die or not.'

Sandingham said nothing. What could he say? He knew what it was like to be demoralised, to have the bottom kicked or slapped or punched or prised out of one's life. It was only nationalistic pride, he supposed, and a degree of stubborn determination that kept him alive and comparatively civilised.

'How do you keep going, Francis?'

'I am Communist. For now.' He smiled. 'Not all time though, Joe. Later, when war over, I go back. I be rich man then.'

There was, just for a fleeting second, a distant look in his narrow, almondy-coloured eyes and Sandingham saw that what kept him going was the desire to be wealthy and to hold the power that went with it.

'All Japanese dead. I get watches, rings, teeth. Japanese soldier go on patrol in New Territories. Go far into woods, up in hills behind Fei Ngo Shan, Ma On Shan, Kai Kwun Shan. Out where you' friend Stewart captured. We ambush them. Ambush?'

Sandingham nodded. 'Your English is improving.'

'Get bigger vocabulary.' Another smile. 'When we ambush, I get things and buy sell them to me for cheap money. Then I pay the money to the Communists. They buy foods, friends. Bribe Japanese soldiers. Get information on patrols. Go out and ambush patrols. And it go on and on. Like business. Buy, sell, create demand.'

It was Sandingham's turn to smile. He wanted to laugh, but the sound would have reverberated in the space inside the barrels and a guard might have grown suspicious. To Francis 177, war was business. He was more than an underground agent – he was a company agent, too.

'You got anything for me?'

'Only this,' replied Sandingham as he took from a fold in his loincloth a fountain pen.

'Not worth much,' said the temporary Communist. He unscrewed the cap. 'But nib is gold.' He studied it closely. 'Nine carat. I get you something for this? What you want?'

'Chocolate. Or a block of ice.'

'I see. Maybe can do, maybe not.'

An aircraft came into land, its piston engines throbbing in the sky overheard and its shadow flitting over the hiding place.

'You my friend,' said the Chinese. 'You no cheat me and, one day, I help you big time. One day, you want somet'ing, you call on Francis Le . . . Number 177. Lucky number.'

There was a 'psst' from the shadows.

'I go. You watch vegetables. See you, Joe.'

He was gone, disappearing with the rapidity and magic a gekko would have been proud of displaying.

The following day, right in the centre of the vegetable basket, wrapped in straw and newspaper, was a nine-inch square block of ice and a bar of chocolate, as rock solid and as cold.

In the mid-morning of 15 September, Sandingham was called to the guardhouse at a moment's notice. He went there at the double, for any order had to be carried out at speed for fear of reprisal.

In the room was a desk behind which sat Panama Pete. Sandingham stood to attention before him. He was not spoken to until Tom Pedrick entered.

'Right!' Panama Pete began, looking up from an army memo pad upon which was an obvious list of names in Japanese characters. Sandingham, who knew what his name looked like in its phonetic translation, tried to see it on the sheet.

'You two officers are to return to Sham Shui Po prisoner-of-war camp. At two o'clock, a lorry will come for you. You got that? You get your belongings together. You do not take food. You got that?'

'Yes, sir,' they replied in chorus.

Taking the risk, Tom asked, 'Can we be told why we are moving and no other officers are, sir?'

The 'sir' stuck in his craw but it beguiled the Japanese.

'You go to command some soldiers there. Dismiss!'

'Well, it would seem that at least we aren't going there for the chop,' commenting Pedrick as they made their way briskly through the camp.

'No.' Sandingham was apprehensive. 'But they must have a reason. I wonder . . . '

'Don't wonder. It'll happen if it's to happen. As for 177, which is what is on your mind: I'm sure they've not sussed him or you out.'

It did not take Sandingham long to pack his few belongings. It took him much longer, however, to say his goodbyes. Everyone accepted his farewells with a mixture of blessing, curiosity and fear, all emotions which he himself churned over in his mind.

'Suzie' da Souza gave him his usual piece of advice: 'Remember, Joe. Laugh. Laugh at the awful and the terrible comes easier.'

Rob Bingham gave him six tooth-cleaning sticks: how he maintained his supply puzzled Sandingham.

From the senior officer, he received three messages to be passed to his opposite number in Sham Shui Po. Sandingham hid these in a slit in the sole of his rubber-tyre sandal.

On the dot of two, he and Tom Pedrick climbed into the lorry with their escort and were driven out of the camp.

'What's it all about?' Tom said.

'It's like this. At least, I think this is their reasoning.' Sandingham had been talking to those officers in Sham Shui Po who had not been moved to Argyle Street. 'A week or so ago, a draft of prisoners was cobbled together and shipped off to Japan. It seems they want to use PoWs in factories and the like in the Nip homeland: so much for the Geneva Convention. But this is rather encouraging, as it suggests that things are getting tight for them at home. Anyway, this lot went off. That left an under-staffing ratio of officers to ORs, in their eyes. So we've been brought in. Suppose because we're of the comparatively healthy few.'

'Do you think we are heading for the Land of the Rising Sun?' was Tom's next sentence.

Ten days later, on 25 September, their speculation was satisfied.

'Attention!'

The ranks came to some semblance of order.

'This officah,' Cardiff Joe shouted out, indicating the man at his side on the platform, 'is Lieutenant Hideo Wada of the Imperial Japanese Army. He has a message for you all. Pay attention to his words and listen. It ve'y good news.'

They listened. The lieutenant talked of Japan, how it was an ancient land, a beautiful land of calm where 'all is green and prisoners will be cared for by the Imperial Japanese Armed Forces who look after their prisoners very well and treat them as worthy and honourable opponents.' He told them how he was to be in command of a draft of one thousand eight hundred prisoners who were to go to Japan in a few days upon a ship called the *Lisbon Maru*. By going to Japan, he assured them, they would escape the diphtheria outbreak. In Japan, it appeared, disease was all but unknown.

The following day, Sandingham and Pedrick spent some hours in a queue for innoculations, the first they had had since the fall of Hong Kong. They had no idea against what they were being immunised. Evidently only healthy foreigners would be allowed to enter the homeland. After the innoculation, every prisoner was forced to bend over while a glass tube was inserted up his anus and a Japanese doctor studied his rectum. It was quick but thorough, impersonal and painful. Some prisoners were weeded out, but the majority passed. As Pedrick said, the Japanese standard of health must be considerably lower than that of the British; few of the men were really well enough to make the trip by sea. Some even had diphtheria and not one was anywhere near fair health.

From the radio in Argyle Street, Sandingham knew that American naval activity against the Japanese in the South China Sea and western Pacific area was on the increase, and this worried him. He voiced this concern to the senior officers who debated the issue and managed as a result to get a message out of the camp through partisans, with instructions to tell the British consul in the neighbouring neutral Portuguese colony of Macau that a Japanese ship was about to leave loaded with a human cargo of prisoners-of-war. He, in turn, could pass this on by radio to the American naval authorities.

Perhaps the agent was delayed: perhaps he was stopped and searched and had to clear himself. Maybe the ferry was held up with a breakdown and did not sail. Whatever the reason, the message was never to arrive.

PART FIVE

Po Lin Monastery, Lantau Island
(Hong Kong): Summer, 1952

HE LOOKED UPWARD. The looming mountain peaks, suddenly appearing then vanishing into the clouds, reminded him of those others he had known in similar weather, the skies thick and gun-grey and the wind gradually rising by the hour. A tropical storm was on the way and the air carried its threatening message in a close and humid anger. The ferry crossing from Castle Peak had been choppy and he was still unsteady on his feet, even after walking half a mile along the promontory from the jetty and across the stout wooden bridge to the village, through the little streets and over the paddyfields behind.

He had halted once to buy some sticks of sugar cane. Biting strips off and sucking the sweetness into his throat before spitting the woody fibre on to the path ahead would give him the strength he required to climb the fifteen hundred feet ahead of him. The shopkeeper had been surprised, though he had managed to hide most of his amazement, to see a European in his small store. Although they occasionally passed through the village *en route* for the mountain, they seldom if ever stopped to make a purchase, and they certainly never came in the summer. It was too hot for them to face the mountain paths in the middle months of the year: they generally arrived in February or March.

The shop was made of charcoal-grey bricks, as if it were solidified from the dull sky overhead. Across the front and under the canvas awning that was flapping and tensing in the wind hung several strands of fish and squid, drying in the air. He had asked after the price, but they were too expensive for him. That, too, had surprised the shopkeeper – that he should have been asked, then have the European refuse after counting through his loose change. Strange behaviour for a *gweilo*.

A cube-shaped rattan basket blew over the stone-slabbed platform below the awning as Sandingham left. A girl not yet in her teens, with an infant sister strapped in place on her back by a brightly-coloured cloth that criss-crossed her childish breasts like a gawdy parachute harness, came out and prevented it from bowling away towards the river.

The paddyfields he took to after leaving the village were dark emerald with tall, near-ripe rice although the colour was muted by the dull weather. The heads of grain hung over and swished together in the wind like a million distant cicadas.

On the path stood an old man who was watching the crop with a worried frown. It was not ready for gathering and he knew that if the eye of the storm hit the island with accuracy, as was forecast, then by morning most of the grain would be levelled to the dense, muddy water in which it was rooted. A peasant woman wearing baggy black trousers, the legs rolled up to her knees to display her muscled calves, was taking no chances. She was approaching along the path, a bamboo pole over her left shoulder with an overloaded basket of cabbages and assorted greens hanging from each end. The old man stepped on to a paddy wall to give her passage and they muttered incoherently together as they reached each other. To let her by, Sandingham stood aside upon a stone balanced over an irrigation channel.

The rain began. At first it was a meagre drizzle but this cleared, to be followed shortly afterwards by large drops that were warm and heavy and hit the top of his cropped head with a firmness that was so definite he could count the impacts until they grew too numerous. It was then he knew he would have to find shelter.

Ahead were a few houses, but they lacked awnings. The windowless front walls were punctuated only by single doors, beside each of which, pasted to the stone doorposts, hung red paper scrolls bearing prayers in black characters, faded by the sun. The eves were typically shallow, and water cascaded from them – for there was no guttering – pitting the soil beneath.

Just before the houses was a ruined fort. Sandingham made for that.

He pushed the overhang of branches aside and sat down in the doorway of a collapsed room. While the rain fell he chewed upon the cane and listened to the water's clamour on the leaves. When it ceased, he stood and went up the crumbling steps to the battlement. Several rusting cannons poked their snouts over the low balustrade and into the top foliage of the trees. He sat upon one of them. From there, he had a good view over the fields towards Ma Wan Chung, a panorama that had been studied previously by Chinese soldiers serving in the Opium Wars of the early nineteenth century and, before that, Portuguese soldiers trying to prevent the scourge of pirate junks from raiding the fertile valley.

He spoke out loud to no one. The wind whipped the words away. He tried to remember who had said it to him, and when.

'History is now. War is all the time. There is always a fight going on somewhere. It's all a part of human activity. Common as buying and selling.'

Beyond the fort the path skirted a wooded slope before crossing another expanse of flat fields prior to rising up the first foothill. He adjusted the army pack on his back, altering the brass buckles so that they did not bite into his shoulders or chafe his collar-bone. The knapsack was not a left-over from the war years, a relic treasured for its associations with memory. He wished it were: he could have done with it then. In fact it had been stolen from a soldier in transit through the hotel.

The ascent was gradual as far as the temple but, shortly after that, it increased sharply. The path narrowed as it wound through a belt of pine trees, then ran up a valley beside a gushing, splattering brook. The rain-swollen torrent, plunging down from the upper slopes of the mountain, was undermining the roots of the saplings by the path and, from place to place, was gouging out the pathway itself.

After an hour's climb, he reached the first gate to the Buddhist nunnery. Here he paused and sat upon a rock, looking back over the route he had just taken. The drizzle had set in below him, and he could only see as far as the start of the valley.

With the wind tossing the trees, he set off once more, the path following the contours of the bleak sides of Lantau Peak. Short grass clung to the steep slope and he had to brace himself against the wind which tugged at him with no motive beyond a primitive desire to point out his human weakness to him.

As soon as he had reached the gap below the summit he paused once more. He sat down under a ceremonial archway, mist swirling around him and drops of dew collecting on his clothing. He was hot from the climb but not uncomfortably so.

Through the gap was a plateau and the mist lifted sufficiently for him to see the neatly planned fields of the monastery. Ten minutes later he was within the precinct and standing by a door. He banged with the palm of his hand upon the wooden panelling.

The wind was flinging grit up from the forecourt to the temple. It rattled upon his shoes. By and by, the door was opened by a shaven-headed monk in a dark habit.

'Tso shan,' Sandingham said, although he knew by now it was mid-afternoon. 'Seung tso fong. Saam yat.'

The monk beckoned for him to enter, and closed the door against the weather.

'Okay', he replied. 'Three night okay. Welcome to Po Lin Buddhis' Monastery. Follow me. I show you to our gues' dormitory.'

The monk's English pronunciation was better than most Chinese could manage, and Sandingham felt he had lost face in speaking in pidgin Cantonese to him. He also knew that he need not worry. Face did not concern the inmates of Po Lin.

The two men passed through a bare room containing only a table and several chairs, pausing for Sandingham to write his name and address – he non-commitally wrote 'Waterloo Road, Kowloon' – in a visitors' book. It had all the formality of a hotel. The monk watched over his shoulder as he wrote.

They left through a rear door and went down a narrow alley-way towards a two-storey, stone building. The monk pushed at the door with his hand. It stuck, then swung open suddenly, helped by the wind funnelling along the passage. Sandingham was ushered inside.

It was dark in the building but he could see a long table with forms to either side running down the centre of the room that constituted the entire ground floor. At the far end, by the only window, there was an open wooden staircase with no railing.

'M koi – thank you.'

The monk told him what time the evening meal was and then

asked, 'You wan' to eat here or wi' monks?'

It would be easier for him to eat with the community. He was certain that he was the only guest, and to dine alone would seem churlish. He replied that he would eat with the monks.

'T'ank you,' said the monk and turned away, only to stop on the way to the door. 'You been to Po Lin before?'

'Yes. Last year.'

'Tha' righ'. I remember you.' He paused. 'You wan' see abbot again?'

'Yes,' replied Sandingham, not a little surprised that the man should recall him.

'Okay. Can do.'

Sandingham had first learned of the monastery when he overheard two Europeans discussing it on the Star Ferry. One of them had visited it as a weekend trip, taking a long hike to what he obviously considered, in a patronising way, to be a typically Chinese – he implied 'native' from his tone – and yet movingly strange and wonderful place. He had gone simply as a tripper and, although he had not really regarded his visit as anything more than a curiosity call, Po Lin monastery had left its mark on him.

'Anyway. This monastery's a quiet spot and no mistake. Buddhist. No cars, no phones. No electricity, either. Or hot water: had to shave in a trough fed by a stream. Just the monks muttering prayers about the place and one old boy ringing a damn great bell all the time. Must be bloody freezing in mid-winter as it's a fair way up the mountain. Still, they like a bit of ascetic discomfort, don't they? Purges their souls!'

Both men chuckled magnanimously.

'Cost you much?'

'Ferry fare. And the pain of undiscovered muscles. But staying in the place is buckshee. The monks are bound by an oath of hospitality. Can't turn you away. Naturally, you drop a bit in the old box before you leave, but how much is up to you.' The ferry slowed as it approached the pierhead: the man looked at his watch and continued, 'The food's bloody good. All vegetarian, of course.'

For the rest of that day, as he sought tourists to filch from, the thought of the monastery lingered in Sandingham's mind. Such a place might do him good. He wanted such peace so very badly.

The monk left and Sandingham went up the stairs.

The upper floor was made of bare planks. Along all four walls were two-tiered bunks. It had the familiar security of a dormitory, the certainty of comrades, the safety of numbers. Over each bunk hung a mosquito net tied into a suspended knot, and at the foot of each was a thin cotton quilt. In lieu of a pillow was a chocolate-brown lacquered box shaped to fit the neck. There were no mattresses but instead there were dun-coloured blankets.

He looked out of the window. The wind was risen higher still and the force of it had dispersed the mist. The storm was coming. He placed his knapsack on the bunk nearest the window and, going downstairs, left the monastery to walk south through the adjoining fields. Ahead of him was a low rise on the sides of which were pagoda-like vaults, fifteen feet high, the tombs of former monks. He walked up to one, looked uncomprehendingly at the characters engraved upon the stone, then topped the rise. There was a boulder there that was shaped like a crude seat: the abbots sometimes went to sit upon it and meditate.

Sandingham looked down over a deep, wide valley beyond which was a thin strip of beach and the open South China Sea. The swell was heavy and crashing in spray upon the sand and the rocky outcrops nearly two thousand feet below. The village that was halfway across the base of the valley seemed to be cowering from the imminent storm. Each breath he took was a struggle to snatch from the howling wind. When the rain started once more, rising vertically up the hillside towards him, he left the boulder and returned to the monastery where he lay down on his bunk and let his limbs slacken.

The dull bell boomed against the wind. It was not a continuous ringing, such as one might hear from a church belfry, but a deep, broken knell that came every ninety seconds exactly. The monk in charge of the bell rang it daily, for hours on end, and his blood was attuned to the sound and the timespan for each impact of the log-like hammer that hung from two points on a rafter over his head.

Sandingham could hear it as he shaved in a basin of cold water he had collected for himself from a trough outside the dormitory.

A small mirror was screwed on to the wall near the stairs and, by the light of a paraffin lamp, he was able to do a fair job of his toilet. He washed under his armpits and sluiced his chest. The water refreshed and renewed him.

'We eating in t'irty minutes,' the monk said who had come to tell him. He was ready; even his shirt was clean – he had rinsed the one he had worn for the climb in the overflow from the trough.

The wind was vicious but warm and the rain had eased off as he opened the door to the dormitory, turned left and made his way through a round moon-gate into a tidy garden in which shrubs were flourishing in porcelain pots under the shade of Chinese willow and plum trees. Faint lamplight from the windows cast a waxy pallor on to the swaying boughs.

A row of twenty-three monks was filing in through a rear doorway as he entered the refectory. They chanted as they moved and the sound that issued from them was more like the wind's than a man's voice. The guestmaster pointed to the place at which Sandingham was to sit.

There was no table. The monks squatted along the walls of the room on child-size stools. A rice bowl, china spoon and chopsticks were laid on a woven reed matting before each setting.

The abbot sat at the head of the gathering, coming in last. He made no acknowledgement of Sandingham's presence. Nor did any of his brethren.

A monk worked his way round the oblong of monks with a ladle and cauldron. From this, he filled each bowl with a thin soup in which small yellowish leaves floated. Sandingham did not eat. He watched what the others did. In their turn, they prayed, intoned and murmured, sipping at the soup between verses or prayers. Sandingham could not understand – could hardly hear – a word of their speech. It was so low that even the simplest words escaped him. He was even doubtful they were speaking in Cantonese. Slowly, so as not to appear in a rush, he drank.

Over the space of an hour other courses followed. Each was served by the same monk. They consisted of dishes made with vegetables, milk, eggs and cheese, bean curd and rice flour. Several looked like meat and tasted like meat but Sandingham knew that they were not. It was against the Buddha's teaching to kill flesh.

When the last of the meal was eaten, tea was served in smaller bowls. When the tea arrived the monks stopped their incantations, but they did not start to speak.

A moment was reached when, as if by an invisible signal, all the monks rose to their feet, their dark robes swishing on the ground, and left the room.

Sandingham was alone.

The serving monk then came in and began to collect up the bowls, stacking them on a broad wooden tray. Sandingham voluntarily helped him. The man spoke no word of thanks, but smiled warmly at this Englishman who was staying at his monastery in the wrong month of the year.

As Sandingham made his way through the garden, the storm now raging on the mountain and across the plateau, another monk appeared and beckoned for him to accompany him as he led the way down a pathway on the right and into a building.

The abbot was seated on a plain metal chair at a deal table with a covering of sticky-backed plastic. It seemed most out of place in the monastery – more suited to a cheap Kowloon restaurant for coolies. Another upright chair was before it. A paraffin lamp gave a cosy hue to the room. A Chinese pot of jasmine tea was to one side of the lamp and there was a pair of bowls already poured. The guestmaster was seated in the shadows beyond the lamplight, to act as interpreter.

'Mr Sandingham, I am glad to see you back at Po Lin. How are you?' the abbot asked through his acolyte.

He indicated the chair and Sandingham took it nearer to the table before sitting.

'I am well enough, Abbot. Not too well, but well enough.' He spoke in English, preferring to use the services of the guestmaster, as his Cantonese was not up to a good conversational standard.

'You still smoke a pipe of opium?' enquired the abbot.

Sandingham nodded. He knew that he must not smoke in the monastery buildings. It was forbidden.

They sipped at the mild-flavoured tea. A limp jasmine blossom was spreading its petals just below the surface in Sandingham's cup. It reminded him of the bloom in one of those glass domes filled with dessicated coconut snowflakes which, when agitated, vanished in a tiny artificial blizzard. The liquid in which it floated was the straw-colour of plasma and piping hot.

'And how are you in yourself?'

The abbot knew of Sandingham's anxieties. They had talked of them long into the night during his last visit. From their meeting then, again conducted through the translator, Sandingham had gained some solace, though it had evaporated as soon as he returned to his everyday living.

There were times when he wished that he were a monk, care-free except for a study of prayers and texts and the observance of a rule, regardless of what the world was doing outside the encompassing barricades of belief. If he were to be a monk, he'd become a Trappist, take the vow of everlasting silence and close his inner as well as his outer eyes to the world, facing only the wall of himself, his religion and his cell. But then he knew that that was what he did now – face only matters in the confines of his world, his personal universe.

'I am still troubled.'

'By what?'

'The same as I was before. The futility of it all.'

The abbot twisted the cog-wheel on the lamp and lowered the flame which was beginning to smoke. His steady hands were smooth, untanned and the skin was uncrumpled.

'Once there was an ant,' he said, speaking quickly. 'It discovered a dead hornet on a dusty pathway and tried to tug it to its nest. It knew that hornets kill and eat ants, but this one was dead. The ant could not move it for the insect was too large. Instead, it returned to the nest and waved its feelers about, sending its word to the worker ants with which it lived. "I have a dead hornet! Follow me." "Are you sure it is dead?" the other ants asked, warily. He assured them it was. There could be no harm from it. They marched from the nest to the hornet. It certainly seemed dead and they rejoiced. They scattered around its corpse, testing it with their feelers, assuring themselves it was truly dead. Once convinced, they joined their jaws upon it and started to move it off the path. Once in the nest, they would scissor it up and consume it. It dragged in the dust. It was snared by stones. It jarred on twigs fallen on the pathway. In their tugging, a leg broke loose. The ant, wanting the leg, returned to the centre of the path to fetch it. There, a man too busy looking upward for rain stood upon the ant, killing it.'

He looked at Sandingham's face while the guestmaster's version in English caught up.

'You are like the ant,' he continued, sucking the hot tea in with his lips. 'It had its life to live. It shared with others its fortune. It met its fate. So it is for us all. We find goodness in wickedness, we turn it to our use, we live with it. We die. As the ant did. That is all.' He put his fingertips together pensively.

'The abbot says it is not a good story,' translated the guestmaster. 'He is sorry . . .'

Sandingham enjoyed the abbot's parables. He saw his present situation in them, even if they were allegorical: they showed him his predicament all too clearly.

'It is a very good story,' he replied, politely. 'Yet how does it relate to me? I cannot turn evil into good. My hornet cannot succour others.'

A bell sounded in another room. The abbot heard it and glanced at the interpreter.

'You use your hornet to be alive, as did the ant. Even if it is the evilest of things. It is food for you. In it lies your reason. The more you know of it, the more it helps you see men. It is sad you see them badly. Often they are so. But you see some who are good through it, too. You are good, for you know what it is. It makes you good.'

The conundrum puzzled him and, putting his cup down, Sandingham said, 'I am not good. I – '

'No!' interrupted the abbot. 'You are good. You are good because you care. For life. About the hornet that buzzes in you. The evil you know makes you concerned. That is the view of a good man.'

Sandingham was about to reply, to prove his wrongness, but the guestmaster pointed out that the abbot had to go to prayers.

'Before you go for tonight,' Sandingham spoke quickly. 'What can I do about my hornet anyway? The ant's was dead. Mine's alive, and flexing its sting.'

The monk had trouble with the word 'flexing', having to request that Sandingham give an alternative. He did.

Standing up, the abbot answered, 'Avoid the sting. Teach others to avoid it.'

'How can I? I am but a small man.'

'Was the ant not small, one of a larger mass? He stood still and passed on his message. So must you.'

The abbot bowed slightly. He asked how long Sandingham would be staying and the guestmaster told his superior, adding to Sandingham, 'You shall talk together again. Tomorrow. Now the abbot says goodnight for you.'

Lying on his back in the bunk, with the quilt pulled up to his chin and the lamp guttering as the oil thinned in the tin reservoir beneath the wick, Sandingham gazed at the rafters. They jittered as the flame bucked. Rain beat upon the louvred slats of the shutter. There was no glass in the window itself, just wire mosquito mesh. The blast penetrated it with ease.

He was not good. He wanted to be, but he couldn't be. He wanted to act, but was unable to. He had let people down. Himself, too. He smoked opium and was addicted to it. He drank too much and that was also necessary to him. He stole. He had killed. He lustfully desired men: was that not a mortal sin?

He drove himself into sleep on these thoughts and, during the night and his dreaming, cried.

The sky was still smothered and grey but less foreboding. He stood at the stone trough and emptied a wooden dipper over his head, rubbing the yellow flakes from his eyelids. The iciness of the water made him see stars, as if he had been clubbed by the flow.

During the night, the eye of the storm had passed and now the wind, though still strong, was lessened and blowing from the opposite direction. A drift of green leaves, torn from their stems, floated in the corner of the trough, held in place by the fist of the wind. It flagged at his open shirt.

Back in the dormitory, he saw that someone had placed a pot of tea and two sweetish buns on the table while he had been outside washing. He sat and ate this meagre breakfast in silence. The monks had long since broken their fast and were now going about their daily duties. Some swept the monastery and did domestic work. Others were out in the fields picking crops for the day's meals or repairing storm damage. Still others prayed in the seclusion of their rooms.

Fortified by the tea, Sandingham tidied his bunk, put on his jacket and went to the monastery temple, entering it from a back door that gave on to the alleyway.

It was dark inside and he had to move slowly around the side of the large room to the front where the doors, facing south, were still closed against the wind. He could hear it whining through chinks in the panelling.

The altar was set to the rear and the image of the god was higher than the level of his face. No one looks down upon their god, he thought. Before it was a table covered by a gold brocade cloth, upon which was embroidered a pattern of pine boughs, flowers, clouds and white cranes, their black beaks thinly angled against the rich yellow background. On this table was an assortment of white vases, earthenware pots and bowls of fruit and sweetmeats. In the centre was a silver-plated basin filled with sand in which were stuck many joss-sticks, all of them alight. Candles on bamboo sticks flickered with them. The blue smoke marbled the air above and wafted into the roof beams. Behind the table was a crimson fence like an altar railing in a Christian church. Beyond this was the high altar, surrounded on either side by small silver statues of the Lord Buddha, of animals and more incense-burning vessels. Two red oil lamps swung gently from the rafters, glowing hotly.

The main figure of Buddha was set in a dark cupboard-like recess in the centre of the altar, draped on either side by deep green curtains. The shutter doors were open but might be closed upon the god. He was constructed of wood and was at least four feet high. The entire surface of the wood was burnished with leaf and sheet gold, which glimmered secretively. The idol was seated in the lotus position, one hand resting palm upward in its lap, the other holding its finger in a delicate formation before its chest.

This was not the Buddha of the tourist curio shops in Tsim Sha Tsui – a gawdily painted china figurine with a jovial face, pot belly and twinkling eyes. This was a serene and dignified man with an expression of calm and saintliness upon his face. He was strangely non-racial – not Chinese, not Indian, not European but an amalgam of all three.

Above the Buddha's head was another red light. It had a thin flame, unlike the other lamps, yet it gave out much more illumination than might have been expected. The only other source of light in the temple came from two slit windows high on the wall over the south door.

The pungent scent of joss tickled Sandingham's nose and he was obliged to rub at his nostrils to clear them.

He felt both ill at ease and fully at peace. If this had been a church with Christ on his crucifix he would have know what to do – genuflect before the altar, cross himself or simply bow. Yet the monks of Buddha did nothing like this of which he knew. In reverence he dipped his head and, taking a handful of joss-sticks from a side-shelf, he held them in the flame of one of the candles until they were alight. He then blew the flames out that the joss might ember and smoke and shoved the red-slivered ends into the sand in the silver basin.

On the floor were what he took to be kneeling cushions. He lowered himself on to one of these with painful difficulty: the joints in his legs were stiff from the previous day's long hike up the mountainside.

Holding his hands together as if he were a recumbent figure on a medieval tomb in an English cathedral, he tried to pray. From his fingers he could smell the dust of the sandalwood incense.

It was difficult. On his last visit, he had considered praying but had not made the attempt. Now, facing the task of opening his heart to a god, he struggled. For half an hour, he strained to talk to the immovable, inscrutable face of the idol. It was not that he could not speak: he could. Yet the words he uttered were false, unconvincing even to himself. If they sounded so fake to him, how must they appear to Buddha?

At mid-morning, he opened the south door and walked on to the temple forecourt. The wind had dropped to a sharp breeze and the sun was striving to penetrate the clouds. Every now and then a diluted ray succeeded. Another mountain path, other than the one he had taken to arrive at the monastery, meandered through the farm fields and tea plantation before disappearing around the corner of the low hill where he had sat the previous evening.

He set off down this path, and within a few minutes was out of sight of the monastery.

For half an hour, he continued downwards. The descent was gradual and he did not stop until he came to a section of the path where it narrowed considerably, with an upward slope to the left and a sheer drop of several hundreds of feet to the right. Here he halted, leaned against the rock face and looked westward.

The sun was patchy upon the sea. The first post-storm fishing junks were making for the open ocean around the Fan Lau peninsula, far over Shek Pik village. The sails of the vessels looked like the spread wings of bats hovering upon the dying swell.

He moved his toe against a stone the size of a football. With no effort, he flicked it over the drop. It bounced twice before tumbling into the trees far below. He pushed another stone after the first. It bounced only once.

It would be so easy. He had only to take two steps and death would rush towards him in the shape of a boulder halfway down the side of Lantau Peak, and the trees under it.

He sat with his feet over the chasm of the valley, swinging them to and fro as he had when perched upon his uncle's garden wall above the GWR line near Wellington. He closed his eyes and the steam thump from the locomotive hauling the Exeter/London express from the black maw of the tunnel under White Ball Hill rumbled in his head. He could see the plume of steamy smoke through the branches of the huge cherry tree that stood in the meadow between the house and main line. If he tipped forward, as he had never dared, he could drop five feet into the lane; or five hundred.

Opening his eyes, he found himself leaning forward; he balanced back on to his buttocks, and got to his feet.

Walking slowly back to the monastery he knew why, all those years ago, he had not jumped into the lane. Or just now into the valley. It was a matter of courage.

'Can I help?' Sandingham offered.

'Okay. You go with him.' The monk in charge of the monastic farm pointed to a novice in his late teens. 'He will show you what to pick.'

Three hundred yards away was a field irrigated by a stream

flowing from the hillside by the past abbots' tombs. The water glistened and rattled musically in the bright, washed morning sunlight.

The novice gave Sandingham a short knife with a worn black handle and showed him how to cut long-leafed lettuce off cleanly, near to the soil. Having passed on the instruction he moved to a nearby patch and spent half an hour plucking runner beans from their tendrils.

To work in the fields as if he were a fellow monk gave Sandingham a satisfaction he had not felt for many years. This was not hard toiling merely to keep a miserable life going, but a simple act, as basic and wholesome as breathing the mountain air. It had no ulterior motive. That was what was so rewarding about it. There was nothing else in his life that could be so regarded.

Sandingham felt the damp, warm earth on his hands. The black mountain soil grimed his fingerprint whorls and nails. The sun was luxurious on his back. He stripped off his shirt to take advantage of it. This was like that other time: picking vegetables. Only then there had been snow in the air and the freedom of the Po Lin fields had not existed. Perhaps never had.

'You see,' said the guestmaster, translating for the abbot, 'how these tiny fish live in their pool? What do you call them in English?'

They were standing by a shallow depression in a rocky burn at the end of the plateau. Glass-clear water from a nearby spring was splashing through it. Minute fish darted in the currents.

'Minnows.'

'Minnows.' The monk repeated the word and passed it on to the abbot who grinned at the ludicrousness of the name, and echoed it to himself. Soon he spoke again.

'You see how they live? Halfway up a mountain, far from the big rivers or the sea, they thrive. They think not of where the water comes from, nor where it is going. As we do not think of the source of the wind or where it blows. They accept it as a right and they exist in it.'

He placed his hand on the surface and the fish, after taking to cover under pebbles, ventured out and inquisitively inspected his fingertips, nibbling at them.

'My hand could kill them,' he said. 'It could close in on them and crush them. They know that, and are always ready to take flight. Yet my hand does not.' He stood upright and the movement of his fingers scared them into hiding once more. 'My religion demands I must not kill them. They do not know that my hand will hold back. They have to accept that it will, or will not.

'So must you take your destiny. Fate will use you as it will. A great hand controls you. You cannot resist it.'

A bird flew up quickly from the brown grass. It rose and hovered in the air, shrilly fluting.

'The abbot says think well on what he tells you.'

Sandingham looked into the guestmaster's eyes. He was a shrewd man with a deep human wisdom apparent in his face, mingled with much humour and understanding. His gaze, before he politely lowered it, bored into Sandingham as if it were vital the visitor should heed well his abbot's lesson.

They turned to walk back towards the monastery. Crickets were chirruping in the grass and, in a lone pine tree by the path, a cicada was grating its call.

'Do you know, Mr Sandingham,' the abbot said after a few paces, 'that the cicada lives as a – how do you say, "not formed into adult"?'

'A grub? Chrysalis?'

'A chrysalis – yes, that is the word. I remember,' the guestmaster interpolated before continuing. 'The cicada lives as a chrysalis for fifteen years, changes into an adult and dies within a day of its hatching – yes? You may think that a waste of life. But it is not. The day of the cicada is a hundred years long. It sings because it lives. You must do that.'

As they approached the tree, the insect ceased its noise.

'It stops that we might not see it. But look.'

The abbot pointed to a spot on the flaking bark below the ragged jumble of branches. At first Sandingham saw nothing but then, suddenly, he saw the creature. It was as big as one of the joints of his thumb, and perfectly camouflaged.

'You did not see it at first.' They walked on, and the insect, gauging their departure, began again its metallic sound. 'The cicada is like the truth. Always there, but not so easy to be seen.'

The late sunlight turned the heat-scorched side of Lantau Peak into a saffron cloth. The eastern sky was turning azure as the night advanced. Overhead, the air itself seemed blue.

The three men did not speak again until they reached the forecourt to the temple. The maroon colouring of the building was made richer by the light, the sun now down behind the hills.

'I leave tomorrow, Abbot,' Sandingham said. 'Shall I see you before I leave?'

'The abbot cannot see you in the morning,' stated the guestmaster without passing on the words or asking the abbot's reply.

'Tell the abbot I have been very happy here.'

The reply came, 'He knows that. He says you must take the peace with you wherever you go.'

'Tell him I shall try.'

As he said it, Sandingham knew he was lying: each step down the mountain would shed the calm of Po Lin Monastery.

The abbot entered his quarters and was gone. He did not say goodbye.

'Can I pay you for my stay? Something towards my food?'

'That is not necessary,' replied the guestmaster. 'A Buddhist monastery has to obey a rule of hospitality.'

Sandingham knew that was the case; he also knew that it was done to offer payment.

'Please take this,' he said, pulling from his pocket twelve one-dollar bills rolled in a rubber band.

'Thank you. But the abbot says I take no money from you. He knows you need this. You are not like the other Europeans who come here. He tells me to say that you must not pay but instead remember him. Your memory will be your payment. And do not forget the little fishes that accept the will of Buddha, or the cicada who is the truth, or the ant.'

From the deck of the ferry returning to Hong Kong, Sandingham looked back at the peak of the island. It was shrouded in afternoon summer mist. All during his four-hour walk along the spine of the hills he had thought over the words, the parables, the advice given so obliquely. By the time he reached the pier at Silver Mine Bay he had decided. He would try to teach, to warn others of the terror in his life and in their own.

*

PART SIX

On board SS Lisbon Maru *off the Chinese coast and Japan:* 1 – 15 October, 1942

THE LAMP-BULBS in the bulkhead mountings, fitted into sockets behind waterproof glass domes in turn protected by stout wire grills, were of a low wattage and, because the glass coverings were grimy, only a jaundiced glimmer emanated from them. This lent the hold an added appearance of being an antechamber to some pit for sinners and their benighted disciples.

As if in witness to such an image one man, lying on the sloping steel cover over a bilge pump housing, kept crying out, 'What have we done to warrant this? What have we done? What have I done? What have I done? What have I done?'

His words took on a childish incantation as if he enjoyed the experiment of repeating them, the sounds soon rolling into one as he grew increasingly delirious.

'Wotvidun . . . Wotvidun . . . Wotvidun . . . '

'For Christ's sake, shove it! We ain't done nuffing. We jus' go' done, tha's all.'

'He can't help it, man,' came another voice from the area of the moaner's perch, the words clipped with a distinctly upper-crust accent. 'Just ignore him. He'll be asleep soon.'

By morning, thought Sandingham, the man would be dead anyway and then they'd not have to listen to his rantings.

The air was fetid and noxious with the reek of male urine and liquid human faeces. Those with dysentery were unable to make it in time to the wooden latrines that had been constructed on deck, overhanging the sides of the ship like the amenities at the rear of a traditional Chinese junk. They squatted apologetically in the scuppers along the lowest level of the hold, dropping their pants or *fandushis* over the oily swill of sea water that lapped from side to side in the bulkhead channels. The air was hot and the stench rose to permeate every level of the ship's living cargo. For those who could contain themselves and get on deck with the next exercise group, it was not so bad. Their excrement merely smeared down the side of the ship or fell sheer to the gliding waves.

'There are eighteen hundred of us,' said Tom Pedrick, carrying on the muted tones that the sick man's ravings had broken into: all talk was kept to whispers or quietened mutterings, not because the Japanese wanted silence but because it seemed indecent to speak loudly in such squalid conditions.

'The officer in charge,' he went on, 'is that prat with the talk about Japan being the land of milk and honey. Name of Hideo Wada. A lieutenant in the army. The ship's called the *Lisbon Maru* – got that from a bloke in the Royal Artillery who saw it on a life raft – they're in Number Three hold at the stern. Number One, in the bows, has the RN boys in it. God knows why I'm stuck in here with you lot. Bloody cheek, billetting a tar with scum like yourself.' He grinned, elaborately looking Sandingham up and down as if eyeing a girl in the Savoy Grill. 'The ship's captain is called Kyoda Shigeru. The crew's Nip and there are eight hundred IJA troops on board as well.'

There was a rumbling overhead and some hold planks were lifted aside. A Japanese voice shouted out an order and one of the translators near the top bawled, 'Next shift on deck. Thirty minutes.'

Pedrick and Sandingham climbed on to the metal framework of the companionway and began to clamber up the ladder. It was difficult, pulling one's body up with the arms as well as pushing from below with the legs. Sandingham was stiff from sitting on the hold shelving and his neck had a crick in it. For those who had electric feet, that permanent torment of pins-and-needles brought on by vitamin deficiency, the climb was agonising.

It was a warm, soft tropical night into which they rose. The sky was clear and the stars miriad. They lined up at the makeshift latrines and took their turn to balance precariously over the side of the boat. Privacy was non-existent and there was nothing upon which to wipe themselves clean. A standpipe had been erected by the side of the ship and many simply wiped their anuses with their hands which they then rubbed under the brass nozzle of the tap.

Once finished with their crude ablutions, the prisoners sat on the deck or leaned against the superstructure of the bridge. The few who had tobacco smoked it. A member of the crew, wearing baggy Oriental trousers and a vest, made his way through the hundred or so prisoners handing out an aluminium mug of water to each from a wooden bucket with a rope handle, snatching the mug back as soon as it was drained. The water was cool but brackish. Another distributed three-ounce hunks of coarse bread, which he broke off by hand from larger, sand-coloured loaves, and rigid strips of dried, salted fish. Every prisoner ate slowly to make the food last longer.

The ship was darkened for security, and showed no lights. The starlight, however, was so intense that the men lounging or walking to and fro on the deck could see quite clearly for some miles.

'Is that land?' Sandingham asked Pedrick as he looked over the port side, spying a narrow black smudge on the horizon.

Tom, with his trained seaman's eyes, had already recognised that it was not cloud.

'Mmmm,' he said. 'Chinese coast. We've been in closer and will get in closer again. I think that's an estuary or a sound. We're crossing the mouth of a river or something. They're keeping to the coast for protection from the Yanks.'

'Whereabouts do you think we are?'

'Can't be sure. With an educated guess, I'd say about halfway up the coast towards Shanghai. That's probably where we're heading. Re-fuel there, pick up an escort or something, then cut across to Japan.'

After twenty minutes or so the coast loomed nearer. The offshore breeze carried with it the inviting scents of land. They could see the outline of hills silhouetted against the starlight.

Sandingham lay on his back, his spine flat against the deck, looking up at the stars. A meteor jagged briefly across the expanse of lights, expending itself as quick as a spark from a cheap toy gun.

'Did you see that?'

'What?' Tom asked, leaning over on his elbow. He had been

surveying the sea, studying it with intense concentration.

'A shooting star. Up there by that very bright one. Went across to the Milky Way and fizzled out.'

'The bright one's Aldebaran; magnitude one-plus,' Tom said. 'Funny to think you can see it from St James's Park . . . '

The ship rolled gently in a slight swell and the motion set Sandingham dozing. It was the only restful sleep he was to snatch that night, and it was soon rudely curtailed by Pedrick digging him in the ribs and saying, 'Time to go downstairs.'

The guards hassled them towards the hatch.

'Second sitting for supper in the First-Class dining room. The fancy dress ball commences at midnight on the recreation deck forward of the bridge. If you have no costume, come as you are,' announced a wit, formerly a senior steward on P&O.

Another retaliated, 'I'll go as a shagged-out PoW.'

In the hold, to those returning from the night outside, the atmosphere appeared worse than it had before. As Sandingham went lower down the ladder the stink grew increasingly foul until, upon arriving at his allotted shelf, he felt he would vomit. Only common reason stopped him. If he threw up he'd lose the food and water he'd recently been given and it would be a long while before he was to receive another issue. He lay uncomfortably on his side, facing the steel plates of the ship, and concentrated on the rivetting in an attempt to shut out his surroundings and get back into sleep.

'Sandingham?'

A hand was shaking his arm.

'Sir!'

He sat up, remembering just in time not to hit his head on the girder. When one's hair is cut short – and Sandingham's scalp was all but shaved, to keep down the lice – such an impact is worse than when there is hair to act as a shock absorber.

'Give a hand here, will you?'

The moaning man was dead. Three privates from the Royal Scots were lifting his corpse up the companionway towards a door halfway up the side of the hold. The door was open, which it had not been previously, and Sandingham, looking up, saw framed by a light from the passageway beyond a Japanese NCO with a dim torch. The three men had insufficient strength on their own to lift their dead comrade up the vertical height to the door.

Going ahead up the steps, Sandingham reached down and grabbed the dead man by his shirt collar. The man's stubbly crop of hair itched against Sandingham's arm. He heaved upward and the others lifted and levered from below. At last they got to the door. The Japanese officer indicated that Sandingham and one of the shovers-from-beneath should carry the dead man on to the deck. They gripped the body by the ankles and shoulders and struggled with him to the ship's rail. There, without ceremony, they humped him over the side and watched as he splashed into the spume churning aft from the bow wave.

Sandingham's helper crossed himself.

'Say a prayer for the poor fucker when we get below, mate,' he suggested.

Nodding, Sandingham said he would. Yet he didn't. What was the use?

Daylight was seeping through cracks between the hatch covers when the prisoners in Number Two hold heard a pumping thump from the centre of the ship. It was as if a damp fist had slapped the bulkhead wall. The lights went out, then came on again.

The hatch covers, open to allow the emptying of night-soil buckets, most of them dripping on to those lifting them up, were slid shut and the planks dropped home. A lance-corporal in the Middlesex, who was on deck tipping the fetid contents of the buckets overboard, was hastily bundled below.

'What about the sodding pails?' complained a peeved voice in vain.

There was a clamour of annoyance but this was cut by the lance-corporal's shouting, 'I think we bin torpedoed.'

'Bollocks!'

'What does he know? Bloody burke in the Pay Corps . . .'

'Who'd do it? The Japs sink their own tub?'

'Hell of a pricey way of doing for PoWs.'

A loud hubbub of speculation ensured.

'Quiet everyone!' It was an officer's command and a sergeant-major relayed it somewhat more exactingly.

'SI-LENCE!'

The racket died.

The ship's screws had stopped turning. The familiar, accepted throb of the propeller shaft and the undercurrent of hum was still.

'She's stopped engines,' Tom observed, 'but I can't hear pumps.'

There was a clatter of leather, *tabi*-clad feet across the deck high over their heads. Screamed orders in Japanese were just discernable.

'Bit of a panic up there. Reckon they . . .'

The sentence was cut short by the opening up of machine-gun fire from above.

The prisoners were hushed. In many of their minds the expectation of a US Navy destroyer or frigate coming upon the scene was building. Liberation might be but a landing party away. On the other hand, they might be gunned down in the holds before the landing party could board. Would the Nips dare do that? It would mean a slow and steady death at the hands of the American sailors: not one of them would want that. Or would such a death be glorious in the eyes of the Emperor? Might it ensure their smooth transportation to the Heaven of the Rising Sun? Or would they believe the magic cloths they wore round their stomachs, with a thousand magical stitches in them, would protect them?

The 6.5 mm machine-gun bursts were joined by rifle fire. Then, quite clearly, pistols came into play as well.

There was another explosion. It was loud and below the water-line and it vibrated through the fabric of the ship.

'Another hit?'

Sandingham could sense the skin on his face tighten.

'I don't think so. Sounded as if it were short. I think they've bagged a torpedo on the run. Got it short of the ship.'

The firing ceased. An aircraft could be heard, followed shortly afterwards by far-off explosions. Tom explained to Sandingham in a whisper that he was sure they had been hit by a single torpedo, very possibly two, and that the submarine that had fired them was now being depth-charged from the air.

The senior officer climbed the companionway and shouted through the hatch covers for the attention of a Japanese officer who might fetch his opposite number.

'Lieutenant Hideo Wada o yonde kudasai! Lieutenant Hideo Wada o yonde kudasai!'

There was no reply. Instead, the prisoners could hear the tarpaulins being dragged over the hatch covers.

'Jesus! We'll suffocate!'

Everyone started to slap their hands on any metal surface that they could reach. It was to no avail. Soon they stopped and sat in a desultory murmur of anxious, afraid mutterings.

As the hours went by that day, two changes gradually occurred. At first they were so slight that no one noticed them, but by mid-afternoon they were obvious. One was that the smell in the hold was verging on the unbearable. The buckets were overflowing across the floor – more than half had not been emptied from the night before – and excrement was making it slippery. The other was that the ship was now listing at least five degress to port. Everyone was breathing raspily and one man had died from suffocation exacerbated by claustrophobia. No one spoke now.

Late in the afternoon they heard a ship drawing near. There was shouting on deck and the prisoners could hear rope ladders being thrown over the side. Much scrabbling down the sides of the hull followed, accompanied by the thuds and clangs of small boats coming alongside and bobbing there.

'They're abandoning ship,' someone whispered hoarsely.

No one answered, but a few people started banging on the bulkheads again. It was futile.

The temperature in the hold was well into the nineties. Sandingham felt his sweat seeping his strength and will from him.

Some time in the evening Tom nudged him.

'Listen. Feel! We're moving . . . '

The ship was in motion. Still listing, she was nevertheless definitely under way.

'We must be in tow.'

The movement kept up for half an hour. Then there was a distant thonging noise and she stopped. Tom interpreted this as the tow-line parting.

The heat increased and with it came a sense of light-headedness that at first worried Sandingham and then brought him an air of mental distancing as he might have felt in the first stages of getting well-and-truly plastered at a good mess night.

The mutterings and moanings of the men around him trans-
formed themselves into far-off music played on an organ. The
sluicing of water in the bilges became the chiming of glasses and
bottles. He heard a champagne cork pop and tasted the bitter-
sweet and sharp bubbles on his cracked lips.

Suddenly, he was alert and alive. He looked around himself
with a critical and observing eye, at the prone and huddled figures
in the half-light contorted by awkward postures in vain attempts
to find sleep. He saw the protruding shoulder-blades of a man at
his feet, the crooked blood vessels standing out on another's
skull, the drawn tendons on the back of a third man's talon-like
hand. He studied the shrinking muscles on his own arms but
concluded, quite objectively, that his body wasn't as bad as some
of those about him.

Quite why he wasn't so emaciated as some of his comrades he
could not understand. Perhaps, he reasoned, with inappropriate
logic, his metabolism was different. Certainly, he'd not been
eating rare beef while they'd had roast rat. And, peering into the
gloom, he could see a few others in better condition than the
majority. If they were dogs and being readied for a show, he
thought, he'd stand a good chance of winning top of breed. Coat
in fair shape – he rubbed the stubble on his chin appreciatively –
nose not running, no waste flesh: lean and hungry-looking, like a
whippet. Hungry, anyway. He drew his lips back in a snarl.
Someone patted him. He turned to lick their hand but it was only
another prisoner, shifting his position, accidentally nudging
Sandingham with his foot.

All that night, the men lay in the hold and wondered. At about
two o'clock Sandingham fell into a dazed sleep.

'You've been able to sleep. Can you lend a hand up top?' Captain
Buzzard, affectionately nicknamed Baz by all ranks who came
across him in Sham Shui Po and a man noted for his sense of dry
humour, was tapping his shoulder. 'We've got to get some fresh
air in here. Some of us are going to try and penetrate the hatch
covers.'

'What with?' Sandingham replied, incredulous.

It transpired that Baz and another officer had found a tool

box and sawed four angled metal struts off the cargo shelving units.

Balancing on the top of the ladders, they started to hack at the planking. Splinters started to rain down. The wood, however, was inches thick and their work was at first unsuccessful. After a rest, they renewed their attack on the covers and a hole was made under the tarpaulin. This was enlarged until a length of plank could be cut free.

'We're through, sir!' Baz called down.

'Potter!' instructed the senior officer, 'you go up and try to talk with the Japs. Get to their CO if you can. Tell them we'll all die down here if we don't get air.'

The canvas was ripped apart and Lieutenant Potter, once an officer in the St John's Ambulance Brigade and a Japanese linguist, lifted himself through, promptly followed by Sandingham, Pedrick, Baz and several others.

Potter stood on the deck and raised his hands.

'Tasukete!' he shouted, although he could not see a single Japanese. 'Tasukete!'

A soldier appeared on the bridge.

'Tomatte kudasai! Kiite kudasai!'

Another soldier on the wing of the bridge aimed and fired. A man climbing from the hatch was hit, fell back into the hold. Another shot sounded and Potter crumpled forward on to the deck.

'Cover!' yelled Pedrick and the men scattered.

Bullets bounced and whined around them. Some soldiers from the Royal Artillery had managed to breach the planking on Number Three hold and were coming out to meet a crossfire from the bridge and the sterncastle. They stopped in the safety of the bridge superstructure.

Sandingham looked around him. With a clarity that surprised him he found himself taking in every fine detail of the day . . .

It was a beautiful October morning. Brilliant sunshine coruscated off the waves and spray that were decorating a running four-foot swell. High, fair-weather clouds scudded over the Chinese mainland and some rocky islands a few miles off. In the same instant he was aware that several Imperial Japanese Navy gunboats were hove to off the starboard beam.

'We've got to get the bastards overhead,' Baz yelled from the cover of a deck winch housing.

Crouching low and weaving to and fro, Sandingham joined him: they were safely out of view of the bridge.

Tom Pedrick was lost from sight round a ventilator shaft inlet.

'Let's go!' Baz hollered in Sandingham's ear.

Jumping clear of the winch, Sandingham entered the body of the ship through a varnished wooden door and ran down a corridor, expecting at any minute to be shot. He met no one. By what appeared to be the officers' mess, he halted and cautiously looked in. Not a soul in sight. By the door was a fire cupboard. He opened it. Hanging from hooks were a long-handled axe and a hatchet in a holster on a belt. He put this on, took the axe and began to go up a set of stairs.

The chartroom behind the bridge was empty. The wide drawers of the storage cupboards had semi-opened and spewed their contents. Maps and navigational instruments, fallen from the chart table, littered the floor. Mariners' almanacs, tide tables and a military code book were splayed open on an upturned chair, their broad spines cracked. He was careful so that he might not be heard stepping on the crisp paper.

Through the door to the bridge, he could see, by the ship's wheel, a Japanese private. He was loading his carbine from an ammunition pouch at his waist.

There was a snapping sound. The soldier lifted his head and looked sharply across the bridge but not in Sandingham's direction.

For a split moment, Sandingham knew what was registering in the enemy soldier's eye: he could see beyond him and through a far door. A prisoner was creeping up on the Japanese who was standing on the wing concentrating, down the sights of a light machine-gun, on the expanse of ship below him. The private was fumbling in his loading of brass cartridges into the carbine's breach. In his haste, he dropped two and the sound camouflaged Sandingham's movement.

Sandingham watched him, bemused. In a second or two, the man was going to die. He, Joseph Sandingham, was going to kill him. This wasn't a shadowy figure in a building over the other side of the road, gliding about like some player in a magic-lantern show. This was a human being, a real living, working unit: flesh and blood existing in harmony to pump a heart, fill lungs with air, fight disease, digest food, flex muscles, spit and swallow, talk and laugh

'Ki o tsuke ro!'

The soldier at the machine-gun abruptly turned. The prisoner behind him, whom Sandingham did not recognise, had in his hands a large can of bully beef. He swung it down at the guard's head. It struck the Japanese heavily on the crown and he fell. His machine-gun overbalanced and toppled on to its side on the deck.

Sandingham now lifted the fire axe. He swung it at his guard in the wheel house. The pointed spike of the reverse blade hit the Japanese on the shoulder, deflected upwards and struck him just above the ear. His skull cracked open with the crisp click of a ripe apple being divided by strong fingers. Pinkish-grey slush oozed through the split sutures. The man's body slumped across the compass podium and collapsed on to the wooden flooring.

The machine-gunner was dead as well. He had struck his neck on a projecting bracket as he had gone down and his head was angled back into the shoulders, the skin of his throat stretched and bruised. The soldier who had killed him had disappeared.

An uncontrollable urge rose within Sandingham until it took over his whole being. It was like the mountain of emotion he had always felt at the moment of love-making, a terrible madness at once orgiastic and all-wonderful.

He ran over to the dead soldier on the deck and turned the unconscious form on to its back. Knowing nothing, his brain blank of all but a primal desire, a sort of lust he could not understand or assimilate, he buried the hatchet deeply four times into the corpse's sternum. Its legs jerked as each incision interrupted the closing-down of the circuits of the nerves.

'Let's get off this sodding liner!' Baz's voiced shouted from somewhere distant. 'I've had enough of cruising.'

As if to encourage him, the *Lisbon Maru* took a shuddering lurch and Sandingham half-slipped, half-rolled across the bridge. He clamped his fingers on to the chartroom door.

'She's going over! Jump!'

Baz was at the end of the bridge. It was only thirty feet to the water.

Dropping the blood-smeared hatchet, Sandingham, standing up at a crazy angle, looked over his shoulder, his eyes ranging backwards and forwards over the bridge. There was his own personal murder in a puddle of brain tissue, bone splinters and blood. His own shattered handiwork. He looked away from the body and his eyes searched for Tom Pedrick. He wanted to call out for him, but the words would not shape in his mouth.

'Get a move on! Another five minutes and you'll be listed missing on active service. Jump, for the love of God!'

Baz waved his arm, beckoning to Sandingham. In doing so, he lost his equilibrium and fell towards the sea, changing his clumsy pitching into a dive on the way.

The deck slewed a bit further. Spent cartridge cases clattered down the slope.

Suddenly, Sandingham's mind cleared. The power that had gripped his soul evaporated as rapidly as it had begun. He felt utterly emptied. If a man could change into a base animal and then return to human shape these would be his feelings.

'Fuck!' he screamed, unable to command another oath. 'What for? God, what the hell for?'

In his anguish, he swung the fire axe across the bridge. It arched through the air and shattered the circular glass of the ship's engine-room telegraph. The brass handles protruding upwards bent awry.

He scrambled down the deck. The angle was increasing and the surface of the sea was nearer now. Baz was in the water some yards off, waving to him again. He raised himself on to the rail, crouched, hugged his legs and let himself roll.

When he hit it, his knees bunched to his chest and held close by his arms, the water was not as cold as Sandingham had prepared himself to expect. Had he been able to look at himself he'd have been hard put not to have laughed. There is little more foolish than seeing an unmanly man trying to act the hero but playing the clown.

Yet he had just killed another being, and this was what gods did. Now he was a god, for all his scrawny flesh and blotchy, sore-covered skin.

As he surfaced, he heard Baz's voice from nearby.

'Over here, Joe. Paddle over here.'

There was a swell running and the up-and-down motion made Sandingham dizzy for a few minutes before he could gather his senses. The ship was not so badly affected by the swell: it was obvious that the stern, now well submerged, had come to rest on a reef or sand bar. It was also just as obvious that no one in the stern hold could now be alive.

'This way, Joe! Joe? Can you hear me? Where the fuck are you? Joe? Joe?'

It was Baz's voice again, but fainter. Sandingham wondered, in the bright, warm sunshine, if this was so because he was drifting away or because Baz was drowning.

This made him strike out in the direction of the voice. He did not call out in return. What was the use of that in the circumstances? he thought. A voice gives nothing except comfort, and he had no comfort to give.

The sound of Baz's voice disappeared, lost in the hills and valleys of the ocean.

The saltiness of the sea upon his many sores jerked Sandingham alert. The sting was not unbearable: more a prod to his senses than a power-sapping ache. The occasional spray off the swell tops brought tears to his eyes. In a moment of coherent thought he realised how lucky he was, in that there was no oil slick on the surface. Oil inhaled to the lungs or swallowed into the guts was a sure, slow and steady killer. That had been the fate of sailors in the Atlantic on convoys: he'd heard so from a tar he'd met in Hong Kong who had come east for some 'sex, sun and fun far away from the sodding convoy patrols' of the war in the west.

Suddenly, thinking of this, Sandingham realised that the sailor had been one of the bodies he'd seen sprawled on the roadway at Wong Nai Chung Gap. How strange, he considered, that he remembered that now months (or was it years?) later, when at the time it had not registered on his brain at all. Or was this an illusion? Perhaps he was drowning and this was the first act in the last replay of his life that all dying men see . . .

'Wake up!' He spoke aloud.

'I am awake,' he answered himself.

'Then don't drop off. Stay alert. Where there's life . . . '

He chuckled.

Someone else laughed.

' . . . there's hope. What a time for a cliché, dear boy.'

He looked around. Halfway up a four-foot-high wall of swell was a head. It was bearing down on him. On it was a naval officer's peaked cap. The crown and anchor badge glimmered in the reflected sun. It was a dress-uniform cap, not one to be worn on deck in action.

'Didn't Nelson wear dress uniform at Trafalgar?' asked Sandingham as the current took him towards this apparition.

'Trafalgar?' The head pronounced it 'Tra-fal-gar', breaking the syllables up. 'I believe he did. But I swore when they took me I'd not be parted from this cap. Besides,' the head added, 'I've yet to pay for it. Got the bill in the post the other week, believe it or not. "Gieve, Matthews & Seagrove, Ltd, 21, George St, Hanover Square, W. and all major ports." Marvellously efficient! Why don't you climb aboard?'

Sandingham noticed that the officer was hugging the side of a large crate-like box bound with iron hoops, his head and cap bobbing above his jacket wafting horizontally just underneath the surface. Sandingham reached the side of the crate and, in fumbling for a hold, discovered a handle.

'I've the hinges here. Grab hold of the catch, but for Pete's sake don't open the door. I'm sure the air inside is all that's keeping it bouyant.'

'What is it?'

'A cold-box.'

After a time, they could hear the distant throb of marine diesels. They seemed to be getting nearer, but the swell was such that neither man could see a craft, even when on the summit of a wave. All around them in the sea drifted other prisoners. Some clung to flotsam – wood planks, furniture, deck equipment. A very few had life-jackets, and one had a life-preserver on. It hadn't lived up to its name. As he drifted by, Sandingham saw that the man was dead. His arms moved with the water as though he were feebly attempting to swim, but his mouth was open and water slewed into it and out again.

The diesels came closer.

'We'll be picked up now,' said the officer. Sandingham did not think to ask his name. He spoke with the sure conviction of a master mariner of years of sea-going experience who knows the ways of men afloat.

'Listen!' Sandingham blurted, his mouth filling with sea water.

Both men twisted their heads. A mile away there was a dim explosion, the sound muffled by the water and the swell. They rose on the next crest. The *Lisbon Maru* was stern down, bow up in the water. Her list to port was more pronounced. Dust was thrusting out of her straight funnel in gouts, like a locomotive shuffling to leave a station. The Japanese troops' laundry, which had been hanging out to dry on some of the jib wires and mast stays, flapped merrily in the breeze. The fo'c'sle and fore deck were smothered with mobile dots.

'They're men!'

'No,' replied the officer. 'They're dead men.'

The swell carried them down into a trough. A small wavelet on the side trickled over Sandingham's head, cool and refreshing where the sun had tightened his scalp. It was as if the sea were nursing him. They rose on the next run of water.

The surface was empty. The ship had gone.

Sandingham spun his head from side to side.

'Dead men. They were dead men,' the officer repeated. He took off his gold braid cap. The skin on his fingers was wrinkled from the water.

'God have mercy on their souls,' he said with genuine reverence.

He replaced the cap.

'Now,' he spoke clearly with the defiance of a determined survivor, 'to be rescued.'

The marine engines came nearer. From a swell ridge, they caught sight of a Japanese gunboat. From the stern fluttered the *hi-no-maru*, the white flag with the vermilion sun disc at the centre. The sides of the boat were manned. The men were holding what looked from that distance like short boat-hooks.

The craft came nearer. It was not slowing.

'My God!' said the officer. His words were incredulous, like a man seeing a miracle performed personally for him. 'It can't be! They'd never!'

The bow ploughed through the first group of prisoners. The undertow sucked some into the hull, took them down and under the keel and along and through the propellers. The sea pinked, then returned to jade green.

The gunboat turned about and returned to the area of the sea in which the prisoners were treading water, waving, shouting for attention – for saving, for mercy. Some merely shouted. There was a chatter of rifle fire. Some men dived, others jumped in the water. Others still merely rolled over and faced down to the sea bottom thirty fathoms below, viewing with their sightless eyes the way of their going.

So taken was Sandingham by this vista of carnage that he failed to see a second gunboat approaching their cold-box. The first he knew of it was a pumping vibration in the water around him. He turned his head and there it was. The grey sides of the hull loomed above him. Japanese soldiers were peering over the rail: many had their rifles to their shoulders. A command shrilled out over a loudhailer. Sandingham thrust his body downward behind the cold-box. He felt the box shiver as the bullets struck it, then died in the water. They hissed for a second as they sank.

Sandingham surfaced. The gunboat was past, but the officer was gone. Upon the sea floated his peak cap, the right way up. Had not Nelson been shot because a sniper had spied his gold-threaded uniform from the enemy rigging? he thought. The irony of pride, the courage of conviction: and all that was left to show for it was an unpaid invoice in a London clerk's ledger.

Sandingham stared at the cap as it drifted away, slowly turning about and about as the wind took it.

He was being carried on a fast current towards some islands. Other men were travelling in this direction with him. Some were dead, some were weak and some were strong. A number were dying. Others were stubbornly holding death at bay.

Some were going to land on the islands. It was obvious even to Sandingham at surface level that they were heading towards the shorelines. Many of them, he feared, might be smashed to pulp on the rocks he could distantly hear being pounded and thudded by the sea. Some would be whisked past such a fate only to drown, later that night, far out in the lonely vastness of the sea, slipping slowly into death. A few would be more fortunate.

Dusk fell.

Upon and within the sea, like glow-worms hovering in the night of the water, phosphorescence shone on and off. Every wave-break, every fragment of spray, every movement Sandingham made – though he made few now, being tired to the point of exhaustion, his arms numb from the gripping of the cold-box – glowed radium green. The magic of the sea took him. It was like a fantastic dream.

Gradually the dream became a reality. Brighter and whiter lights appeared, bobbing and pitching on the swell.

With all the strength he could muster, Sandingham threshed his feet and tried to steer the cold-box towards the nearest of the lights. For all he knew, they could be some weird marine *ignis fatuus*, a *doppelgänger*, a mirage of dying, the last cruel trick of the day.

It was a sampan. In it stood two Chinese fishermen, their wet torsos glistening in the lamplight. Each had hold of one end of a net. Sandingham was soon snared in it, like an ugly, brown fish. Had he gill slits, he'd have torn them on the mesh. Instead, it was the flesh of his fingers, bloated from his time in the sea, that were cut, and cut badly.

He was too tired to speak much. He just muttered to them, 'Yan . . . Yan . . . Ts'ing . . . T'sing . . . '

Cantonese not being spoken so far north up the coast, they didn't understand him, but they dragged him over the wooden gunwhale of their sampan and laid him on the deck. Around him, sardines and anchovies flapped their last.

'M koi nei,' he gasped, but the two men just grinned and studied him before fumbling with his wrists and fingers, stroking his neck in the light of the hurricane lantern by which they were fishing; a strange series of actions, like the preliminaries to a primitive ritual of love-making.

He realised they were looking for a watch, a ring, a St Christopher. When they found nothing, he feared they would throw him back, a worthless fish, inedible and unsaleable. Then he remembered next to his testicles was the small, waterproof pouch

he had made from inner-tube rubber and fat. In it was nothing of
value – a rolled-up photo, a pinch of tobacco, three matches . . .
He prayed they'd not find it. They didn't and, having found
nothing else either, seemed to decide to help him.

Sandingham had ruined their nets, but they did not seem
angered. They gave him a mouthful of fresh water and propped
him against the bow board while they dropped their catch into
wooden pails of water. This done, they hoisted their sail and set
off in the direction of the nearest island. It was now near midnight.

Sliding in and out of consciousness, Sandingham heard others
calling from the sea. He paid no heed and, in his half-wakening
state, hated himself for his selfishness. He was safe.

A lighthouse blinked from the shore of the island and the
fishermen headed for a bay to the leeward of the light. The swell
was less and they sailed into the calmer water, to run softly
aground on a shingle beach. Sandingham was helped ashore,
half-carried and half-dragged to a line of trees and bushes, then
sat down against a rock protruding from the sand. It was light
enough to see by, though whether moon- or starlight he knew
not.

The fishermen disappeared and Sandingham fell into a deep
and comatose sleep.

He was hot. Hot as in Hades where, for all he could know or care,
he could now be roasting. He was burning. He could see his blood
running in his veins. He opened his eyes. It hurt, so he closed
them. Grey light came over him. He opened his eyes again.
Someone or something was kneeling over him. Hands like claws
were shaking his arms. Water was running down his chest. He
flexed his fingers to make a fist. The pain shouted at him. Then it
intensified to unbearable levels. He whimpered, not being able to
find the urge or energy to scream.

Fujihara must have got him back. Somehow. He couldn't
figure out how, but that must be it. Perhaps it was Tsutada.
Tokunaga, The White Pig himself, had managed to swim to land
as well and get hold of him. He was even at this moment dis-
locating every finger joint of Sandingham's he could grip with his
pair of electrician's pliers.

An acrid stench hit his nostrils.

An English voice made him jerk with surprise as much as the pain did.

'Keep still! They've got iodine.'

Crouched by his side was an old man. He had a wispy mandarin's beard and colourless pupils in the middle of porcelain-white eyes. His cheeks were made of yellow parchment. Sandingham drew back.

'Don't worry. He's all right. He's for us.'

The back of the old man's hand was scarred and one of his fingernails was three inches long and horny as a toad's lips.

As Sandingham's sight grew accustomed to the morning light he scanned the beach. In a group around about him were seven or eight other prisoners. He did not recognise any of them. Like himself, they were all dressed in baggy black Chinese trousers and loose jackets that shone like cheap, tarred silk. He realised that, in his sleep, he had been dressed.

His hand slid quickly to his groin.

'It's okay. I've got it here for you.'

A prisoner with a pencil-thin moustache handed Sandingham his packet.

'If there's money in that, we'd like to give it to them.'

'There isn't.'

However, Sandingham opened the package, partly to ensure that the contents were dry, and handed the tobacco to the prisoner who gave it to the Chinese. The old man grimaced his thanks and took the package carefully as if it were the sacrament, wrapping it in a twist of paper he pulled from the folded-over top of his own, similar trousers.

A china bowl was placed in Sandingham's lap. In it was a small heap of cold rice, three dried fish and a spoonful of berries.

'Eat slowly. You've swallowed a lot of sea water.'

He obeyed without questioning this wisdom.

His arms and legs itched badly. All those rescued had been profusely bitten by insects during the early hours.

When he had eaten, Sandingham walked to the water's edge, took off his newly-acquired clothes and soaked his body in the warm sea. The salt eased the aggravation of the mosquito bumps.

Sitting in the water up to his chest, Sandingham watched the

Chinese who had, he presumed, saved them as any mariner might rescue another in distress. Certainly, they were sea-going fishermen and knew only too well the dangers and fickleness of the ocean.

The islanders had, Sandingham knew, suffered at the hands of the Japanese for centuries, though not as cruelly as their fellow countrymen on the Chinese mainland had in recent years. For the fishermen, a passing Japanese ship might loot some food, the crew indulging in a bit of roughing-up for sport but nothing more. On the nearby coast and inland atrocities of a greater nature were more common.

By the line of bushes at the head of the beach, where a path wound through the branches, Sandingham spied a little girl. She was wearing a loose-fitting pair of black trousers and a matching vest-like top. Her jet-black hair was woven into little pigtails on either side of her head, the ends tied with cord. She had a quizzical look on her face.

Sandingham smiled and beckoned to her. Hesitantly, she came to the water's edge and looked at him with much the same expression as a man might view a mermaid. She tipped her head from side to side to get a better view of the man with the pinky-red skin.

'Hello,' Sandingham said rather pointlessly, 'what's your name?'

She studied him for a moment, made no reply and then, with an adult composure, turned on her heel and marched up the beach, her arms swinging jauntily and her feet kicking up a small fountain of sand with each step.

The Chinese, who were now collecting up their food bowls to wash them clean, started to jabber together in an incomprehensible dialect. Swiftly, they ran into the undergrowth. The little girl was the last to go, taking a final sidelong glance at the strange men from the sea before following her elders.

Sandingham turned to look out to sea. He had neither heard nor seen anything to cause alarm.

A Japanese launch was turning into the bay.

'Not bloody likely!' The words came from nearby with a quiet, unemotional assurance. 'Not bloody twice!'

Sandingham watched as two prisoners rolled into the bushes.

He heard their passage through the branches, the scuffle of leaves in the undergrowth fading to silence. He wanted to join them, to escape the rigours of re-captivity. He wanted to be rid of *fandushis* and beatings and insufficient food and the ever-present smell of his own dung and fears. Yet an utterly uncompromising resignation seemed to be in command of his soul, an all-accepting lethargy that reasoned that this was not so bad. He was alive, at least. In a manner of speaking.

They were not allowed to retain the clothing the Chinese from the fishing village had given to them. As soon as they boarded the destroyer they were ordered to remove the black trousers and jackets and throw them overboard. In their place, they were issued with odds and ends of Japanese uniforms and articles of clothing donated by the crew. Those prisoners who were ill or sick from ingesting too much salt water were moved below, but everyone else remained in the open air. Plentiful food was served twice that day, cigarettes were forthcoming, fresh water was in good supply and, as night fell, hot cocoa made with milk powder was given to the prisoners in rice bowls.

The sea was smooth. Sandingham slept on deck against a bulkhead, on the other side of which was some piece of machinery that kept the metal plating warm throughout the night. By morning he would have cramp in his left arm and leg but at least he had slept and not woken up time and again shivering, as some of the others had.

On 5 October they arrived in Shanghai, everyone agreeing that the Imperial Japanese Navy had treated them fairly. The dead officer with the dress cap had been right after all. No matter what the nationality or the circumstance, sailors take pity on those being claimed or seduced by their joint enemy, the deceptive and deceitful sea.

As soon as they disembarked the situation altered drastically. A Japanese Army officer, carrying a briefcase and followed by two minions, strode across the dockside, stepping carefully over the sunken railway lines and avoiding with military precision the various crates and boxes, drums and bales that littered the area. He marched up the gangway and, on seeing the prisoners sitting or standing and chatting in groups on the open deck, barked a shrill string of invective at them before rattling his boots up a companionway in the direction of the bridge.

Ten minutes later, a Japanese officer appeared on the dock. His uniform was neat and crisply laundered and his stance erect and also military.

At first, Sandingham did not recognise him: then it dawned on him. This was Lieutenant Hideo Wada, the officer in charge of the guards on the *Lisbon Maru*. He was accompanied on the dock by a merchant marine captain whom some of the prisoners thought they recognised as Kyoda Shigeru, the master of their ill-fated prison ship. He too boarded the destroyer and made his way up to the officers' quarters.

Forty minutes later, a contingent of IJA troops were marched on to the wharf. Some formed a semi-circular cordon around the bottom of the gangway while others came aboard the warship and lined the rails, guarded the doors and, having herded the prisoners together and brought up the wounded from below, patrolled the deck with fixed bayonets.

Leaning against a warm galley bulkhead, from a porthole in which issued the tantalising scents of frying rice, Sandingham watched the sentries going past him. Beside him was a group of other prisoners. A few spoke in subdued voices.

'Shaggin' Koreans!' suddenly grumbled the man next to Sandingham, who had not spoken at all so far. 'Right little bastards they is, sir. Worse than th' soddin' Nippos.'

With that observation he relapsed once more into morose silence.

Sandingham looked at the man through the corner of his eye. He was dressed in Japanese Army general issue pantaloons that were loose below the knee rather than tied by a cord. That was now absent. His chest was bare and his hair was a gingery stubble, matching that on his chin. On his feet he wore a pair of Japanese naval rating's deck shoes, a cross between a slipper and a plimsole. His skin was yellowish, as if he had suffered recently from jaundice. Sandingham thought that if he rubbed the man with his sleeve the frost on his skin would clear as from a window and he would be able to see the interior of the man, all the parts working or waiting to be used, like a factory. Nothing showed his rank.

Other men were in command of them. Not special men. Just men like themselves. Shorter, thin-eyed, small-limbed maybe, but nevertheless men. They were just as equal too, in the face of natural order. A small advantage here, a twist of fate there. Kismet. Chance. The spin of the wheel. That was the only difference.

And 'sir': the man had said 'sir'. Even in odd clothes he thought he knew his place. Sandingham wanted to correct him, to point out that he was not a 'sir' but just another human in the same state. He opened his mouth to speak.

'Kike!'

The officer with the briefcase was standing stiffly at the rail of the next deck up. His arms pokered out from his shoulders and his hands gripped the wooden railing top. He gabbled out a long chain of commands.

By the depth charge mountings, a prisoner spoke up loudly.

'Motto yukkuri hanashite kudasai? Wakarimasen.'

A statement was brusquely made. This was followed by an evident question, asked by the Japanese officer, to which the interpreting prisoner did a quick mental calculation, finally replying, 'Ha-ppyaku – and, um – yon-ju-san.'

Sandingham understood numbers: either eight hunded and forty-three of them had died, or the same number had survived. Whichever way, it was roughly half those who had set off from Sham Shui Po.

The initial commands were repeated more slowly, after which the prisoner addressed his fellows.

'We are to go on to Japan.' He spoke loudly and without emotion. Experience told him that to imply something by tone could lead to a thrashing.

'First,' he continued, 'we are to sit down.' Those who were standing sat as instructed. 'Now, take off all your clothes.' Looks were exchanged, but the order obeyed. 'Pass all clothing to the right. You two men by the capstan, pile them up.'

When stark naked, they were made to stand and form a file of two. The Korean guards earned their reputation by rifle-butting, punching and kicking them into line, making sure the boot or the wood hit a vital place: the kidneys seemed a favoured spot. Once assembled, the prisoners were marched off down the gangway,

across the dock, through an empty and echoing warehouse, out
of the dockyard gates, down a mile of streets lined by silent and
blankly staring Chinese, in through another gate and there,
ahead of them, were congregated the remaining survivors who
had been rescued by other warships.

He was surprised with himself. Walking through the
streets, bare-footed and bare-arsed, his sagging balls banging
against the insides of his scraggy thighs and his cock wob-
bling limply, Sandingham felt no shame. It came – somehow –
naturally.

Now, squatting on his haunches on another quayside, he
realised that he could go no lower, could be debased no further.
There was nothing left he could lose, except the rolled-up photograph in its bit of rubber, lying sideways across the inside of his
mouth.

He had, with a difficult sleight of hand, succeeded in transferring this when they had been ordered to undress. Now it was
between his tongue and the roof of his mouth, it was uncomfortable. He could have folded it, but he'd had neither the time nor
the desire to crease the picture further. He looked as if he had an
abscess developing.

A prisoner who had been a medical orderly asked him if there
were something he might do – look at it for him – but he
mumbled a reply and turned his face away, tears of shame and
embarrassment at last filling his eyes: whatever the Japs did now,
he thought, it had to be on the up.

They were formed into squads of forty prisoners and chivvied
towards the gangplank of another cargo vessel. The hold was
better equipped than that in the *Lisbon Maru*: there they had had
only a few litters, being accommodated upon Japanese-style bed
platforms, but here there were hammocks and stretcher-like beds
of canvas. What shelving there was had been covered with thin,
kapok- and straw-filled palliasses.

It was to his good fortune that Sandingham was in one of the
first drafts to board. He had the pick of a pile of clothes that were
heaped in the centre of each hold. Some of the clothing was
European or American.

As the hold filled up with its living cargo, he climbed to the
second tier and claimed a hammock for himself. Settling into it,

he noticed some faded lettering stencilled upon the canvas stays. They read 'USN'.

All that Sandingham noticed as they were disembarked was that it was night and the docks alongside which they had tied up were sparsely lit. A fleet of Toyota KB trucks stood in the shadow of the godowns and the prisoners were pushed towards these and told to climb over the tailgates. Canvas flaps were then tied down on both the inside and the out, two guards positioning themselves in each truck with their charges who were made to kneel, squat or sit cross-legged on the floor.

The trucks moved out at what Sandingham reckoned was just after midnight. They drove through the dark hours, unable to sleep or even nod off because of the twisting and bucking of the vehicle and the road upon which it was travelling. The guards prevented anyone from standing up. By the time the trucks halted, every prisoner on board them was stiff and aching.

The canvas flap of Sandingham's vehicle was untied and tugged to one side. A cold air brisked into the truck. Sandingham shivered, though from the drop in temperature or as a premonition he could not judge.

In the vague promise of light from an imminent dawn he saw that they were in a compound. Before them were wooden barrack buildings, along the fronts of which ran arcades supporting over-hanging roofs on wooden pillars. The windows were a pale creamy colour, though not because of illumination from within: they were made of paper.

More clothes were issued, all of them the civilian Japanese khaki drill garments of the factory workers. Split-toed canvas and rubber *gomugutsu* were handed out, along with one thin cotton-and-fibre blanket for each prisoner. Finally, each man was given a creosote pill and told to swallow it. The idea was that this would cure any disease they might have brought with them.

A camp guard counted them off into unequal groups and they were led away by a sentry to their allotted building.

Behind the newer barracks were older buildings. Some had been small warehouses, others civilian quarters for the workers of a local factory. As at the docks hours before, the lighting was minimal.

Another guard with a key wired to a carved wooden block appeared from the shadows, shone a dim torch across their faces and counted them quickly prior to unlocking a door in the overhang of an arcade. A warm air billowed out and wrapped Sandingham in its arms, driving off the chill of the wind that was now rising in readiness for daylight.

He was pushed inside, ahead of the others. The rest of his group followed and the door was slammed shut. They were in utter darkness.

'Right, here we are,' someone commented in the darkness. 'The Land of the Rising Sun.'

As if to mock his irony still further, a very weak, peanut oil flame spurted into life far down the room.

'Well the hell!' said a dozy voice from the vicinity of the flicker. 'If it ain't limeys!'

PART SEVEN

On board SS Takshing en route *to Macau and Hong Kong: September, 1952*

'I NOW HAVE that little job I mentioned some months ago for you to do,' Francis Leung had said.

He had not called Sandingham to the building in Kowloon City, for that might have attracted the attention of the police; instead, he had had him summoned to a small but very comfortable house set in pine trees above the Castle Peak Road just beyond the eleventh milestone.

Alighting from the bus, Sandingham had followed the directions he had been given over the telephone – he had received the call at a specified hour on a telephone in the rear of an apothecary's shop by the railway bridge in Waterloo Road – and found himself at a pair of wrought-iron gates hung on stone pillars and leading on to a curving concrete driveway set with pebbles. It had rained in the night and water was sluicing down the culvert to the side of the gate. The pebbles shone.

In a tin box screwed to the left-hand pillar was a button. He pressed it. What he supposed from his dress to be a gardener came to the gate and asked him his name. He gave it. The man surveyed the world outside and Sandingham realised that the gate was so constructed as to give a good one-hundred-and-seventy-degree view of the Castle Peak Road along which afternoon traffic was steadily flowing. From the beach off to the left came the sounds of children splashing and playing. In a layby was parked a Royal Naval bus: obviously, the beach was a regular favourite with service families. All seeming clear, the gardener opened the gate and admitted him. Sandingham, on the watch for such things, noticed the man was carrying an automatic pistol, tucked well into the top of his earth-soiled trousers.

Tea was served in tiny cups without handles.

'What do you want me to do?'

Leung's attitude towards Sandingham had changed in recent months. He had become more distant, more deliberate in his statements and less inclined to accept items Sandingham had filched or otherwise 'acquired', as he put it. Sandingham could not understand Leung's changing relationship with him; in truth, Leung was rising fast in the crime circles in which he moved, but there was no way Sandingham could have discovered this for himself. The Chinese organised crime world was far removed from that of even the European gangster.

'Collect something for me. From Macau. Do you have a good set of clothing, Joseph?'

'Not really.'

'Then we must get you a suit. You'll be staying in a good hotel once you get there.'

He snapped his fingers and one of his men detached himself from the shadows of the living room and appeared at Leung's side holding a fat manilla envelope. Leung passed this to Sandingham.

'In here is enough money to buy a lightweight suit, some new shirts and a pair of better shoes.' He looked at Sandingham's feet where his present shoes were worn at the heel and scuffed. 'It should leave some spending money – about a hundred Hong Kong dollars. Also in here is your ticket to Macau. Return. Your hotel bill will be settled by my – my representative. You are booked out on the *Takshing* on the morning of the twenty-fifth. Be sure you catch the sailing, Joseph. Tickets are non-transferable.'

He might have been a tour guide. In a way, he was. The trip, however, was his own.

'When you get to Macau you will be met and taken to your hotel. The Bella Vista. One of the best.' He laughed shortly. 'Maybe the only one. I never go to Macau . . . '

Leung looked pensive for a few moments. It was rare for him to let his feelings show so.

'What do I collect?'

'You'll be told. Just a package. Not very big. About one chek . . . fourteen inches long and – about as big as a building brick. It will reach you. Don't worry. It's not too heavy. Four cattys. About five and a half pounds. All you must do is get it back to Hong Kong.'

'Why don't you have one of your men collect this parcel?'

'That is not possible. Not this time,' Leung replied with a surprising candour that he was quick to disguise by looking hard at Sandingham as if to discourage further enquiries in that area.

'Where do I take it?' Sandingham asked, to change the subject.

'Nowhere. It will be taken from you.'

'How do I know it will be the right man I give it to?'

'It will be,' Leung answered, with quiet emphasis.

Sandingham sensed that he was expected to leave and stood up. He did not ask how much he was to receive. He knew better.

'Do you not want to know how much you will be paid?'

'Yes.'

'Five hundred Hong Kong dollars. A lot of money for a messenger boy.'

Sandingham looked Francis Leung straight in the eye. Just for a split second. He seldom did that. In the man's pupils lived a demon of malice. It flitted by and Sandingham knew then that this was not a favour for an old friend from the war, an old compatriot from the trenches of Kai Tak. This was business. This was the post-war Leung, patronising capitalist, currency hoarder, Triad secret society boss, gangster, smuggler and who knew what else. Sandingham deferentially lowered his eyes again.

'One more thing,' Leung said. 'Don't try anything, as they say in cinema films.' He laughed drily. 'And don't go to the whore called Lucy any more. She belongs to me now, not the bar owner. She is going to be more up-class.'

From the tray on the bamboo table, Leung picked up Sandingham's tiny tea cup and dropped it on to the marble slabs of the patio. It clinked as it hit the ground, rolled over and split in two. Fragments, sharp and thin splinters of china, flicked out.

It wasn't a rice bowl and it wasn't full of the blood of a cockerel or whatever it was that Triad members shattered in their ceremonies, but it didn't have to be.

He left the hotel with his case at six o'clock, hailing a rickshaw to take him to Ah Moy's. It was a bit of a risk going there in daylight,

but he had to take it. There was no way he could face going to
Macau without having a pipe first to calm his nerves: set him up
for the trip.

He was well aware that whatever it was he was doing for
Francis Leung it was not carrying an oblong moon festival cake
through the Hong Kong customs. From the description Leung
had given him he knew what he was bringing back. Size of a
brick; five pounds in weight. Five hundred bucks for doing it. It
was raw opium he was to carry. Obviously, Leung's pet carriers
were being watched. Few narcotics squad or customs officers
would suspect an Englishman of running opium.

It was a risk. Like going to Ah Moy's. Like dodging bullets.
One got hit or one did not. It was up to the gods.

Later, lying on the planks of the bed, he did not dream as
vividly as he was wont to do. Some flowers insisted on pressing
themselves upon him. Bob appeared once and sang a sea-shanty,
of all things. Or it might have been a psalm. It didn't matter.

He left the opium den after dark and caught a bus to the Jordan
Road vehicular ferry pier. This would take him to within walking
distance of the Hong Kong-Macau ferry berth on Hong Kong-
side.

He had bought himself a tropical-weight suit as Leung had
ordered, with two cream cotton shirts, at a small tailor's shop
near the Alhambra cinema in Nathan Road. It was an off-the-
peg, light brown suit originally made as a window display to
entice passing sailors in to buy more expensive made-to-measure
garments. The material was slightly faded from the sunlight, but
this allowed him to buy it cheaply and therefore have a little extra
left over to spend at Ah Moy's. His new shoes were polished tan
and matched his clothes. He felt strangely and unusually dignified. Just as a European should.

As the ferry steered its way through cargo ships lying at buoys
in the harbour, Sandingham sat on one of the passenger deck
benches and pondered his mission. He had seen blocks of opium
before – not often, but memorably so. They were indeed brick-
sized, hard and dull brown. Often they had trademarks imprinted
upon them just like real bricks. He recalled one that had stamped
upon its surface 'THREE AAA BRAND' and, below it in smaller
lettering 'Bewar of imitaations'. It had reminded him of an ingot

of silver he had once seen in a jeweller's shop in Nathan Road.

He reached the SS *Takshing* with plenty of time to spare. Across the side of her superstructure, under the bridge, was emblazoned a huge Union Jack. The flag was illuminated both by the lights of the Macau ferry dock and a spotlamp mounted on the ship herself.

'Passpor' an' ticke', plees.'

Sandingham handed them over the desk top to the Hong Kong immigration official, noticing as he did so that there were two European police inspectors standing in the background with several Chinese constables, one of whom, unusually, was holding a rifle.

'What you reason for goin' to Macau, sir?'

'Holiday. I've not been there for many years. Maybe' – he added to give a more genuine-sounding answer, make a joke of it – 'to gamble.'

The official showed no sign of acknowledging this standard cause for Europeans' journeys to the neighbouring Portuguese colony across the other side of the mouth of the Zhu Jiang.

'W'ere you stay in Macau?'

'Bella Vista.'

'You lugg-age?'

'Just this case. I'm only going for a few days.'

As he spoke, he felt rather than saw the police inspectors look at him, absorb his details.

He was waved through and climbed the steep ramp of the gangway. The tide was high and slopped against the waterline. At the top of the gangway a steward took his ticket and ushered him towards a cabin on the next deck up. The cabin door was of varnished wood with highly polished brass handles and, in place of a window, there was a fixed series of angled slats. The steward unlocked the door. Sandingham entered, took the key and handed him a tip. He felt very good, giving a tip. When the steward had gone, closing the door quietly behind him, Sanding-ham dropped his case on the floor and, removing his new jacket and trousers and sleek new shoes, lay back on the bunk. The white sheets smelled clean and the air was sharp with the tang of polish. The wash-basin was pristine, as if it had never been used and, on the shelf over it, a tumbler stood upended in a greaseproof-paper wrapper declaring it to be 'sterilised for personal use and hygiene'. From the vent over the bunk issued a current of cool air slightly tinged with the odour of fuel oil. He fell asleep, to be woken several hours later by the ship getting under way.

He put on his trousers and left the cabin, to stand on the edge of the deck and watch the western approaches to Hong Kong Island glide by. His bare feet were warmed by the scrubbed planking.

It was still dark. The street lights of Connaught Road West slid by. Up the hill, he could vaguely make out the main tower of the university building. Higher still, against the night sky, he could see the flat top by the Hill above Belcher's. He felt the euphoric calm and good from the pipe still easing through him.

A voice spoke to him from close by.

'You're the signaller wallah, aren't you?' it said.

'What?'

He turned. There was no one at hand: he had the deck entirely to himself. The shadows from the rigging, the rails, the companionways and uprights shifted slightly as the ship moved. The dull yellow of the lights behind their storm glasses shone softly upon everything. The warm night breeze wafted over his face and ruffled his hair.

'Fancy a little snort for the road?'

No one.

From across the water, he could hear an Austin truck change gear noisily. Someone coughed throatily, they might have been hawking or choking.

'Remember what they say.'

'What do they say?' Sandingham asked.

But there was no answer to that.

A Chinese deckhand appeared from a door and walked by, carrying a mop in a bucket of warm, sudsy water. He stopped by the firepoint at the far end of the deck and began to swab the planking. Sandingham turned his attention to the shore again.

There it is, he thought. I can see it. By the steps.

He was no longer standing on the *Takshing* but in the sidestreet that was now slipping silently by in what had once been a night rife with terror . . . He could scent the tobacco smoke from the 555s, see the lapping flames of the fire and the billy on the boil. The tea would soon be brewed. And he could hear, quite clearly, coming to him from across the two hundred yards of water, the voice of the long-dead soldier saying, 'We 'elp 'em up the steps . . . We 'elp 'em up the steps . . . We 'elp 'em up the steps.'

It was gone. Kennedy Town came along the shoreline, followed by the two islands that formed the westernmost edge of the harbour. Clear of Green Island, the ferry swung to port and on to a south-westerly course which would take her clear of Lantau. As she made her turn the deck moved at an imperceptible angle. A list. Sandingham's fingers mechanically clenched on a stanchion.

He returned to his cabin and, from his case, took a bottle of bourbon, purchased before he left the hotel that afternoon. Half of it was already consumed. He finished it off and lay back once more on the bunk, screwing the ventilator to the fully open position and directing the blast of night air on to his face. He was sweating heavily. The rush of air cooled his sweat and dried the tears as they fell on to his cheeks. The luxury of sleeping in a bunk, in a cabin that was rightfully his and already paid for, lulled him into a rich sleep. His last conscious action was to ease off his shoes with his toes, allowing them to tumble to the cabin floor. To do this hurt at the joints of his knees, but he didn't give a damn.

He awoke swiftly with an urgency that only his subconscious comprehended. Something was amiss. Someone was waving a football rattle. The ship was no longer under way. He glanced at his watch and cursed. It had wound down, had stopped at four-fifteen.

He struggled into his jacket and put on his shoes, without caring to untie the laces, treading down the heels. Knocking the empty whiskey bottle over in his haste, he twisted the door handle and let in the daylight that was, of its own accord, already finding its way through the slats. The cold morning air made him realise that his flies were unbuttoned, so he slammed the door shut and fumbled to do them up.

A few passengers were lining the rail and looking out to sea. The lounge steward was hurrying along the deck, talking quickly.

'Pleese. Eve'yone into they-ah cabin. Or into salon. Thank you.'

Few made any effort to move and he started to touch people's elbows.

'Pleese,' the steward repeated, more loudly and more insistently, the tone of his voice drawing attention by its unfamiliar directness. 'Into cabins or to salon. Pleese. Eve'yone go insi'.'

'What's going on?' Sandingham asked as the passengers began to drift away from the ship's rail. 'Why have we stopped?'

'Communis' Chinees Navy,' the steward replied tersely.

Sandingham had not been paying particular attention to the man's face, but was instead scanning the horizon, waiting for his eyes to adjust from the gloom of his cabin. Now his gaze fastened on the Chinese steward and he saw that the man was terrified. The steward's skin, normally tan-golden in the delicate way the southern Chinese have, was pale and blotched. His hair seemed greyer than normal for his race. His hand, where it touched Sandingham's elbow, shook electrically: it reminded him of the feeling he had once had on holding a newly-shot rabbit.

'You don't need to worry,' Sandingham said, though the man's fear was transferring itself to him and he was feeling his own shoulders tighten and his nerve-ends fray with the first pangs of uncontrollable alarm. It was like the encroaching well-being of opium, but in reverse: in place of peace was turmoil.

The steward made no reply.

'You're not an illegal immigrant to Hong Kong, are you? You didn't get in on a night junk or swim the Sham Chun River?'

The man shook his head.

'And you've got a Hong Kong passport, or identity card or something?'

The steward nodded.

'Then there is no need to be afraid.'

He took the steward firmly by the arm and gripped him encouragingly.

It was ridiculous and Sandingham knew it. Here he was comforting a man who was going through the same crisis as he had gone through time and again and which he knew he was about to meet with once more. He had no right to comfort him, had had no right to comfort others in the past, as he had done. He was a mute cripple trying to cure a deaf invalid: the blind leadeth the blind unto blissful ignorance, he thought. There was nothing he could do if it came to the crunch. And it might: the steward's next words confirmed the possibility, his English pronunciation deteriorating pro rata to his escalating anxieties.

'We in inte-nashunor watar.'

That much Sandingham understood. International waters. Anything can happen in international waters. You can be pirated, murdered, plundered, blown off course, torpedoed . . .

It hadn't been a football rattle. He knew that now, had probably known it all along, but some inner valve had kept the fact from his awareness. The rattle was a concentrated burst of machine-gun fire.

An emptiness opened up in the pit of Sandingham's stomach and grew until it was a huge void that contained him like a vast bubble. He fought against its sides, but it was rubberised and gave and stretched at his touch. Nor had he any means with which to puncture it, no means of escaping the claustrophobia of all-enveloping fright. He had to accept it, and did.

The steward entered the salon to listen to one of the officers who was addressing the passengers.

So far as Sandingham could see, there was no sign of the Chinese Navy lying off the *Takshing*. Perhaps it was a false alarm.

The ship's engines started. He leaned over the side. The propellers were churning the sea and the waves were beginning to shift past the hull. They were steering off the course to Macau.

His talk over, the officer left the salon just as Sandingham entered it. He had a frown on his face. The steward, in order to drive away his fear, was busying himself with pots of coffee. Everyone was chattering. Sandingham joined a group of English husbands and wives who were going to Macau for a break from the routine of Hong Kong's social whirl.

'What is going on?' he asked. They looked at him somewhat askance, as if he were arriving late for a Government House cocktail party, after the Governor. 'I was sleeping in my cabin,' he continued by way of excuse.

His question was taken up by a man in his mid-fifties dressed in a white suit and a pale blue, open-necked shirt. He wore a gold Rolex watch and his shoes were evidently hand-made and squeaked as he changed his weight from one foot to the other.

'Weren't you here?' he started unnecessarily, ignoring Sandingham's excuse. 'Well: it seems the Reds want to ask us a lot of questions. God knows what about! There will be hell to pay after this, I can assure you. And the Bank'll have something to say, for certain. The minute we get to Macau, I'm ringing the Chief Accountant and the Colonial Secretary.'

'It won't be long before the RN get here,' added another passenger. 'They've been radio-ed.'

'We aren't going to Macau,' Sandingham pointed out. 'We're steering in another direction.'

'Apparently,' said the first man's wife, a pretty brunette in a flowery print dress, at least fifteen years her husband's junior, 'we've been ordered to go to Lap Sap Mei Island.'

'Why?'

No one could proffer an adequate answer to that query, but at this point the steward appeared at their side with a tray of coffee, interrupting their conversation.

'Toas'?' the steward enquired.

'Yes. With ginger marmalade,' ordered the wife.

Only the British, the real British, Sandingham thought, could specify the type of marmalade to be served in a critical predicament. She would ask for demerara sugar next for the coffee.

'And brown sugar, please, steward.'

Sandingham laughed loudly. It wasn't a laugh of humour but one mingled with fear, a laugh that wasn't meant to be jolly but to release tension.

'Look,' said the man with the gold Rolex, realising how Sandingham was feeling and lowering his voice, 'you don't need to show it. Damn it! We're all a bit flustered but nothing will happen. Not to us.'

Not to us, thought Sandingham. No: we're as invulnerable as the vaults in the Hong Kong and Shanghai Bank. No one can touch us, the Europeans, the colonial pushers and shovers, the controllers of the lives and fates of others. We're as right as rain. Safe as houses. But the steward, the deckhand with the mop, the poor bastard with the mooring hawser, the engine-room artificer, the baggage coolies, the Chinese passengers on the cheaper deck with all their meagre worldly possessions tied in blue cloth bundles or tucked into rattan baskets. They were the ones who were defenceless.

The ship slowed and stopped. The officer returned to the salon.

'Ladies and gentlemen. Please be sure you have your passports ready. The Chinese naval forces of the Central People's Government' – there was more than a trace of sarcasm in his words – 'are going to board the ship and search it. Please do not hinder them in the course of their duty. I can additionally let you know in confidence that two of Her Majesty's vessels are on their way from Hong Kong in response to the captain's radio alert for assistance. There is no need to be concerned. Personally speaking, I think that this is just a muscle-flexing exercise on the part of the Communist Chinese. The captain suggests that you either remain in the salon or go to your cabins. The most important thing is that we are not seen to be disrupting or hampering the boarding party in any way. Our instructions for such circumstances are that co-operation is better than confrontation.'

Sandingham, looking out of one of the salon windows, saw a grey gunboat coming alongside. A group of armed men in uniform was assembled on its deck and he could hear a ladder being lowered down the hull of the *Takshing*. He noticed that the steward was still ashen-faced: he was concentrating on collecting or refilling the coffee cups. Another steward who was obviously as worried as his colleague was handing out toast. They were doing everything possible to contrive that they remained in the salon with the European passengers.

It was not difficult for Sandingham to understand their motives. He had often seen men, who would otherwise have shunned one another's company, cling together for mutual safety and protection.

There was a clatter of metal on metal and the salon door to the deck opened. Two Communist Chinese soldiers entered. They said nothing. The sub-machine-guns at their hips spoke volumes. After they had positioned themselves by the door, an NCO came in and started to look around the room. He did not request passports, nor did he search personal belongings. He looked instead under chairs, into cupboards and into the faces of the stewards. To each of the two Chinese he drew his own face close and studied them. It was as if he were filing away their features for future reference or searching their countenances now for some clue that would trigger off in his mind's eye a visage from a

wanted poster or a dossier shelved somehwere in the police and
military archives in Canton. Both stewards looked straight back
at him but neither moved so much as a cheek muscle.

Satisfied with his search, the NCO left in the company of one of
the guards. The other remained, covering the passengers with his
weapon. For their part, the passengers spoke quietly or not at all.
The stewards, like figures in a film that has been stopped and then
restarted on a projector that takes a few minutes to regain its
former speed, carried on with their coffee-and-toast routine.

Sandingham lowered himself heavily into a chair in the corner
of the salon and gazed at his feet. He had escaped once more. The
threat was gone, removed more by chance than design.

It was ever so with him: there was nothing he could do to alter
the shape of destiny, his own or that of others. Events happened
to him, and he observed them and recorded them much as a
mother might record the growth of her children through the years
in a photograph album. And, from time to time, he reviewed
them, just as the mother opens the album. The difference was that
with her she saw love developing, saw the expansion and life of
the flesh of her own body coming to fruition and her joy and pride
increased with them. For him, it was a reassessment of failures
and lost loves and the destruction of himself and those whom he,
in his turn, loved or knew well.

The salon door burst open. Even the remaining guard jumped.
Quite clearly, Sandingham heard the safety catch on the guard's
sub-machine-gun snap into the 'fire' position. His head swam
hazily.

A Chinese officer marched in and barked out a command. No
one moved. He barked it out again.

Through a marbling mist, Sandingham was certain he could see
Tokunaga standing there. He was looking at him, pointing to
him, his hand on the hilt of his sword. He could smell the steel.
Though he knew The White Pig had been dead for many years, he
nevertheless stood up slowly.

The officer beckoned to Sandingham who followed him; the
passengers' eyes traced his progress to the door.

He was led down the deck to his cabin. Inside, a Communist
soldier had emptied Sandingham's suitcase on to the bunk. He
was sifting through the contents with his hands, shaking out the

clothing and running his fingers over the linings and seams.

Another indecipherable command was spoken and, at this moment, the ship's officer who had addressed the assembled passengers in the salon arrived on the scene, fetched by another of the boarding party.

'He wants to know your name. There is nothing in your case with it written on.'

Sandingham thrust his hands into his pockets and clenched his fists in an unsuccessful attempt to stop his shaking with fear. He prayed the soldier would not notice his shivering.

'Sandingham. Joseph.'

He almost added his rank and number, long since forgotten or, more accurately, pushed back into a recess in the catalogue of non-successes and hurt he carried, so well indexed, within himself.

'He wants to know where you live.'

'In Kowloon. Waterloo Road.'

There was a discussion between the searcher and his superior. The ship's officer was spoken to again.

'He wants to know if you are going to Macau at the order of a man called Leung Ping-kin.'

'Tell him I'm not,' said Sandingham, his brain active with fear and, simultaneously, considerable curiosity. 'I'm going to have a few days' holiday and to do some gambling. I've not been able to go to Macau since before the war.'

This was conveyed to the Chinese officer who demanded Sandingham's passport, scrutinised it and returned it. He gave another curt order and the guard left the suitcase and they both quit the cabin.

Sandingham felt his knees buckle. The ship's officer caught him and helped him on to his bunk, clearing aside his clothes with a free hand.

'Are you all right?'

'I'm fine, thank you,' replied Sandingham, trying to show that he had regained his composure.

'They'll be gone soon. I suggest you remain here in your cabin.'

His mind was a chaos of confusion. How they had conceivably known his mission was beyond him. He tried to guess what Francis Leung's dealings with the Communists could be that he should be sought by them. He had no idea. Opium smuggling could hardly be the cause of their searches: if they had wanted that they'd have stopped the returning ferry, not the outward-bound sailing. But anyway nobody exported opium from Hong Kong to Macau. And the drugs were seldom smuggled into China: usually, it was the other way around. Perhaps it was all a mistake, a Communist cock-up: he struggled to remember if Leung's Chinese name was Ping-kin.

There was a commotion on the deck. Against his better judgement Sandingham went out to see what it was, joining the other passengers at the rail.

Below them and slightly to their aft was the Communist gun-boat. Most of the boarding party had returned to it. Now they were bundling on board its foredeck a Chinese passenger. He looked quite ordinary. He was dressed unmemorably and non-descriptly. As soon as he reached the gunboat he was hustled inside the bridge; Sandingham could see him being forced below.

A scapegoat, he thought. They didn't find whom they were after – or what they were after – and they didn't dare return empty-handed, so that poor beggar got it. There was always one.

The *Takshing* quickly got under way again, and no sooner had she turned than two Royal Naval craft appeared on the scene. The White Ensigns flapping at their sterns gave Sandingham an inner strength, a lifting of an intense oppression. He was liberated once again. He smiled to himself.

'We not goin' to Macau,' he was told by the steward who came to his cabin as he was repacking his case. 'We go bac' Hong Kong.'

'Thank you,' said Sandingham. Then he added, 'Are you okay, steward?'

'Yes, t'ank you, sir.' the man grinned expansively.

Sandingham tipped him a dollar bill, though neither of them were sure why, and enquired, 'Why did they take that man off?'

'He mek money.'

'What do you mean, he makes money? Everyone makes money.'

'No. He mek money. At him home. He mek silwer coins and sen' it to his family in Canton. They spen' it.'

'You mean he is a counterfeiter?'

'Tha' wha' guard say.'

Sandingham wondered, after the steward had gone, if that was another of Francis Leung's games. Coining. Corrupt the body with opium, the soul with evil and the wallet with tin yuan.

There was a crump. It came from outside the window, to be followed by a liquid spouting noise.

From the salon he could hear shouts and a single, high-pitched scream that was short and sharp and sounded like a steel pin being dragged across glass.

Out of the cabin window he could see Lap Sap Mei Island. On its shore was a flick of light. He automatically counted out loud, like a child waiting for thunder after the lightning.

'. . . five, six, sev –'

Another crump. A pillar of water rose three hundred yards short of the *Takshing*.

'Christ!' he said, though there was nobody near to hear him. 'They're shelling us!'

As he spoke, one of the Royal Navy craft returned fire. The boom was loud, making the air and the wooden slats on the cabin door vibrate. A billow of grey smoke issued from her gun, the final cords of smoke stringing out on the wind like some deadly ectoplasm. Another shot was fired.

Seated in the salon once more, Sandingham ignored the jingoistic, complaining talk that hummed around him. He ordered a large whiskey from the steward. Now that they were well and truly safe in Hong Kong territorial waters he could let himself go. His hands shook. His eyelid twitched. He could not sit still. The drink would calm him. A pipe could, too, but he was without his emergency supply, which was still folded up behind the cistern in his hotel room.

The *Takshing* shuddered as her engines were run to their limits.

That afternoon, Sandingham was summoned back to the house on the Castle Peak Road, the message given to him by a rickshaw coolie at the Macau ferry dock. Presumably, had he reached Macau and collected the opium brick, this coolie would have been his drop on his return.

'So you could not help it. I know that. Never mind,' Leung said.

'What will you do? Shall I go again?'

'You know what you were to carry for me?'

He nodded. He knew Leung knew he knew. There was nothing to be gained by pretence.

'Right. And no, you do not need to go. I've had a friend bring it in. Another friend,' he added obviously.

'If another job crops up . . . '

He had not told Leung that the Communists had known something about him. That would perhaps be to know too much. It was best he kept this to himself. In any case, Leung was probably aware of the facts already.

'Not for a long time, Joseph.'

Leung looked at his watch. Sandingham noticed that it was a new Patek Phillipe in silver – no: it would be white gold or platinum – on a black leather strap. He had seen such watches in the window of a high-class jewellery store in one of the expensive shopping arcades in Central District. This was definitely not a watch from one of the jewellers' shops in Hankow Road.

'Your bus will be along in less than ten minutes,' Leung stated pointedly. 'You'd best get down to the stop by the beach steps.'

As Sandingham was about to step off the patio, Leung said, 'One thing more, Joseph. As you did not complete the assignment, I shall need back the money you spent on clothes for the trip.'

It came out of the blue. The hair on the back of Sandingham's neck rose against his collar.

'I haven't that kind of money. I do have some left over from expenses.'

It sounded so trite, like an office boy accounting for the petty cash to his manager.

He took out about thirty dollars from his jacket pocket.

Leung accepted this, folding the notes before passing them to a henchman who counted them, then continued, 'That's the down payment. I shall need the rest back. A fortnight?'

'It's impossible. I can't even steal that much that quickly.'

He could not afford to lose his temper, but he wanted to.

'You'll be able.'

'What if I can't?'

'You will. If not . . . Ah Moy will be a customer short, will she not?'

At the bus stop, Sandingham raged within himself. His anger took on no firm shape; no definite actions occurred to him. He just stood there in the hot afternoon sun and cursed himself, his luck and the world. And Leung.

Just as the bus pulled away from the dusty kerb he saw, down on the beach, the boy from the hotel. He was playing with another child near the water's edge. They were guiding toy tanks over a corrugated battlefield. As he watched, the second child hit the boy's tank with a handful of damp sand. It knocked it over and half-buried it. They both jumped up at the fun of it and, abandoning their toys, ran splashing into the sea.

PART EIGHT

Japan: 1943 — 1945

THE SOUP WAS watery and faintly mauve. Small bits of blanched fibre floated in it along with strips of parchment-like material and some shreds of potato peelings that had not been added for the cooking but later, as an afterthought to nutritional requirements.

Tentatively dipping his metal spoon into the soup, Sandingham made every effort to avoid noticing its colour.

'Purple death,' said Norb. 'You ain't had it before?'

Sandingham shook his head and asked if it were as poisonous as it appeared.

'No – does you no harm. Probably does you no good, too. We have it about once a month. Takes its colour from water-lily stems. Them's the stringy bits.'

Norbert Heybler occupied the *tatame* above Sandingham's own. He was a tall and thin New Yorker who had worked for the city transportation department before the war; upon the destruction of Pearl Harbour he had been drafted into the US Navy as an officer in charge of vehicles at a shore base in southern California. After that he had been sent to sea, been sunk off the Philippines, captured in the fall of Manila and since then had done the rounds of five camps – one in the Philippines, one in Formosa, one in Okinawa, one near Osaka and now here. Sandingham had known all this within the first quarter of an hour of meeting him. Like all Americans, it seemed, Norb had told his life story right at the start. If it was a national trait it was one that Sandingham liked: it promoted friendship.

'It ain't so bad when you've gotten used to it,' he encouraged Sandingham, seeing that the Englishman was not overly keen to sample the delights of the soup. 'Think of it just as a food colour. We colour things in the States – you get canned pears that are emerald green. How I could eat a pear right now! You know what I mean?'

Sandingham knew exactly what he meant.

'You married?'

'No. Had a broad once. Hung around with her, but she went off with this insurance salesman from Schenectady. I'd known her from high school, too. Still. Just as well. I'm alive and he bought it near Syracuse.'

'Fighting?'

For a moment, Norb had to think; no one fought there. Then he realised.

'Hell, no. Syracuse, up-state New York. Icy road and this car of his slips off the carriageway and rolls down a bank. Clouts a wall, flips over. Hits the river. Cracks the ice – early winter, see? Not too thick as yet. Goes straight through. Freezes over on top. Didn't find him till the level dropped in the summer and the wheels of the car showed through the surface.' He chuckled. 'If I'd have married her, it might have been me.'

The logic of this study of potential destiny confounded Sandingham who concentrated instead on the consumption of his purple death.

With his soup swallowed, Sandingham hunched forwards and considered Norb's attitude to life. Skinny and starving, with ulcers on his back and pains in his swollen joints, he could sit in a prison camp in Japan and cogitate upon how unlucky he might have been to have wed a certain girl in the States and wind up as an insurance representative at the bottom of a frozen river. If that was poor fortune avoided in the past then, conversely, he must think of himself now to be better off. At best, luckier than dead. He was alive and, by his reckoning, he was better off than some: he had no tax affairs to settle with the IRS, no mortgage owed to the First City Bank of Where-he-lived, no wife to worry over (either how she was coping without him or, in his own words, who she was balling in the 'big brass bridal bed'), no kids to put through college, no accountant or attorney to subsidise, no Blue Cross Plan to pay out. That he now had no doctor to treat the sores on his spine or dentist to extract his rotten molar, nor sufficient food to keep illness and hunger at bay was neither here nor there.

Had Sandingham drawn his attention to these facts he would have been quick to point out that they did have a doctor and a dentist – they did not have drugs, anaesthetics, medicinal supplies and bandages or surgical instruments, but that wasn't the point. For example, the wagon-train masters hadn't any of those things either and they had successfully taken their folk over the prairies and the Rockies to the Promised Land, through disease, drought, starvation, Apaches and 'other hostiles', flood and vicious mid-continental winters. Norb could quote in detail the stories of Jack London, plot by plot – *Tales of The Klondike* – and what about the man in *To Build A Fire* who died frozen to death through his own stupidity? There was always one somewhere worse off than oneself. Sandingham doubted it but marvelled at the pioneer spirit and the optimism of his comrade-in-barbed-wire.

The mention of ice and a north American winter brought back to him the condition of his own surroundings. It might have been warmer in the insurance salesman's car after the accident. Certainly, it would have been in the old man's cabin at Sulphur Creek.

He was seated by the *hibachi*, a small brazier at the end of the barrack room. The Japanese camp commandant had just conceded that it was indeed now winter, the day being 3 January, and had issued them with some fuel. This consisted of three one-hundredweight bags of very small coal particles that had been swept up from the concrete platform where coal was unloaded at the railway station three miles away. Much of the contents of the bags was coal dust and the prisoners who were too sick to go to work had spent the day forming this into balls by mixing it with water and a little clay. The quantity of clay had to be exact – too little and the balls fell apart, too much and they wouldn't burn. It was an acquired art that only the longer-term inmates had mastered.

The *hibachi* gave out little heat. To stave off the cold, Sandingham was wearing all his clothes – a *fandushi*, a pair of trousers, three vests, his two shirts, a padded jacket, his blanket, two pairs of Japanese socks and his clompers. Over his lap he had draped two hessian sacks that he had obtained from the lumber yard. He had been fortunate to be issued with the padded jacket, for only

half the prisoners had such a garment and even then the lucky
ones were forbidden to wear it outside the camp. He had got his
because he was without his own uniform jacket. His clompers
were of his own manufacture: they were made from a block of
wood shaped to his foot and instep and had as uppers three sheets
of hessian and a band of rubber tyre nailed to the soles. He had
also been issued with a pair of *tabi*, but these were too insub-
stantial to wear in the bitter cold of winter and he had so far only
used them in his few first weeks in the camp.

The forty-watt light-bulb dimmed, a guard's hand somewhere
in the camp closing down the power. With several others, Sandingham stood up and left the barrack room. It was dark outside
and the wind was blowing down from the hills. It carried tiny
flecks of white upon its back.

'Jezuz! Is it gonna snow tonight.'

They walked down some steps cut into a bank and entered a
long covered way. At the midway point to the end barracks they
turned left into the latrines. The *benjo* was simple. There were no
urinals or cubicles but just a wall against which one urinated
down into a gutter-pipe sunk into cement, and a row of timber,
box-like water-closets but with no flushing water. Anything
dropped into them fell on to a wide trough and lay there until the
civilian cesspit collectors, known euphemistically as 'the honey
bees', hosed the troughs down into barrels. They were then carted
off to the fields, drawn by plodding oxen, emaciated donkeys or
equally emaciated children and old folk.

By the time they had completed their toilet it was thinly snowing big flakes that settled on the ground.

'Hey, Joe – you humping tonight?' Norb asked Sandingham.

'All right. Yes.'

'Your place or mine?'

'Mine,' another voice suggested. 'Foursome is better than a
twosome. Reminds me of this high-class knocking shop in
Wahiawa. Twelve miles from Pearl. Officers only. Very select.
One of them Go-gan paintings on the wall of some Tahitian
broad with her bra off.'

'Okay, Bill. Your place.'

If he had not been a prisoner, Sandingham would have baulked
at the close physical company of such men. To be close to them

would have aroused him and it would only have taken one of them to wake in the night and sense his rigid penis against his back or thigh, or his hand on someone's shoulder or arm, for them to have known and subsequently ostracised him. But now there was no fear of that. Had not been for nearly a year.

Nearly a year. He was three days into 1943. It was over a year since the fall of Hong Kong, and Bob's death and the end of normality. He forced himself not to think of what the past twelve months had brought him – and brought him to in its own vicious manner.

They collected their blankets together – Bill's was of Australian Army issue and thick with wool: the guards had yet to discover it – and squeezed on to Bill's *tatame*, a planked bunk, one of which was designated to each prisoner. To share the meagre supply of bedding and bodily warmth, they had been sleeping in groups since the week before the Christmas they none of them had celebrated except with whispered prayers after the lights had been switched off.

Despite the hardness of the bunk and the fact that Sandingham was second in from the edge – it could have been worse: he could have picked the shortest cotton – he was soon asleep.

The last words he heard were from the man on the outside who muttered, 'C'mon, guys! Shift in a bit. Share your lice.'

The snow had lain for more than a week, added to every night by a fresh fall of, at the least, a few inches. It was not the snow that was so bad, however: it was the frost. By day, the temperature barely rose above freezing. If it did, a slight thaw set in, but it only melted the top crust which then iced like glass at nightfall when the air dropped to well below freezing. Walking was treacherous, for one's bare feet were liable to adhere to the black ice, each step peeling off a layer of skin from the ball of the heel. *Taiso* was even worse.

Every dawn there was a roll call. After *tenko*, the prisoners were subjected to half an hour's *taiso*, a cruel joke the fates played upon them. The Japanese, believing the best way to keep their PoW workers hale and hearty was to keep them fit, forced physical exercise upon them. The prisoners thus stood in their ranks as for *tenko* and jumped on the spot, swung their arms, touched their knees – few could make it to their shins, let alone their toes – twisted their hips and, if Pluto was in charge, did twenty press-ups, their hands and toes on the night's fall of snow, their fingers slipping on the ice and turning blue.

After *taiso* they were given breakfast. This was usually a bowl of rice-mill sweepings. One had to be careful eating it in case there were small stones in the mix. A shard of gravel could kill if one's stomach lining was badly shrunk and weakened.

With their fast broken, as the Dutch padre put it without losing sight of the irony, they formed up on the parade ground in their work squads. Sandingham was in Number Two *shotai*. His group was employed in the timber yards about four miles away on the outskirts of the city. Their work-gang boss, the *shotai-cho*, was Captain Alex Ryder of the REME who had been shipped to Japan from the camp at Changi, just outside Singapore.

On some days they were marched to the yards, on other days they were taken in a semi-derelict lorry, more rust than steel. With the icy roads slowing their marching rate down, and therefore reducing their working hours, the lorry had been prevalent of late.

On the way nobody spoke. In the late autumn they had joked or chatted quietly, but now there was nothing left. It was more important to bunch down low, reduce the body's surface area and retain the warmth as much as they could, and for as long as possible. Talking expended heat. They just sat on the floor of the truck bed and moved with the motion of the vehicle as it rocked, slewed, crabbed and skidded along the road.

By the time they left the camp the sky was creamy-grey, with the promise of more snow. As they pulled into the timber yard compound the promise was fulfilled and the snow began to fall, rapidly becoming heavy. They jumped from the truck and were directed into the nearest of the three sawing sheds. In there was gathered the civilian workforce, standing in a huddle by the stove.

'Wuk wun are!' shouted the *hancho*, the foreman of the saw-mill. This he then translated into Japanese for the benefit of the workers and the three guards who remained at the yard with the prisoners.

Sandingham was amused to note that the order should have come in English first.

Without question or any evident animosity, the Japanese workers made way for the prisoners to join them around the stove. The tarpaulin that served as a door over the entrance to the shed was lowered and the three bare light-bulbs that hung from the roof on flex were switched on. It was almost cosy.

'We should be singing "Ten Green Bottles" or "Green Grow the Rushes-O",' said Alex adding, 'I was a boy scout once.'

'With steaming mugs of chocolate and marshmallows on the ends of willow sticks,' Sandingham mused.

They spent the next few minutes explaining this ritual to the American second lieutenant who was in charge of sawdust. Once he understood, he left the group and swept up more shavings for the stove. With these put on the flames, the smoke thickened and puffed out of a crack in the galvanised tin chimney halfway to the roof. Sandingham watched the puffs, mesmerised by them.

This rest from work was more than welcome. It was, moreover, very rare. The *hancho* had not given them such a respite before. His decision now was forced upon him by circumstance, for the men had cleared the shed the evening before and they were unable to bring in new timber for sawing because the frost had locked the trunks and rough-cut planks together by freezing the sap. He was banking on the snow ceasing and either a thaw setting in or his requisition for more crowbars arriving from the central stores.

The wind buckled the tarpaulin and whipped across the floor, the iciness hitting their ankles. Everyone, Japanese and European alike, moved in closer to the fire, sitting on planks balanced on logs. Alex stood up to help with the next load of shavings and Sandingham found himself sitting between a couple of locals. The two races seldom spoke to each other except from necessity prompted by their common labours. Even then, they spoke in monosyllabic Japanese. The prisoners were fearful of reprisals if they spoke to the locals and assumed that the locals were afraid of being seen to consort with the enemies of their Emperor.

Glancing from side to side, Sandingham smiled at the two civilians like a man joining strangers on a bench before the departures board at Paddington station. All they lacked, he reflected, was a loudspeaker announcing the time and platform number of the next train to Bristol.

On his left was a man whom Sandingham guessed to be in his

late thirties, perhaps slightly older. He was unhealthily lean and his face was so drawn that his already narrowed eyes seemed thinner still, mere slits behind which pin-pricks of light glimmered. His hands were calloused and one of them shook. In fact his whole body shivered intermittently, his teeth clicking inside his opened mouth which amplified the chatter.

On Sandingham's right was a much younger man. He was about eighteen. He did not shiver but sat stolidly facing the stove. Every so often, he lifted his hands up to its hot sides and rubbed them together with a washing action. His face was as drawn as the man's and his ears were white with the cold.

Casting his gaze around the entire assembly, Sandingham noticed that every person present had a common denominator: his headgear. Everyone, from the guards to the boy at his side, was wearing a *boshi*, a little peaked cap.

'What is a marsh-mullow?'

Sandingham turned to the man on his left.

'I'm sorry.'

He was so surprised that the Japanese had spoken to him that he was unable to find an answer straight away.

'What is a marsh-mullow?' the man repeated, 'You said just now you would like a "marsh-mullow" on a stick.'

'It's a sort of sweet,' Sandingham explained. 'You cook them over a fire. Make them warm and eat them.'

He could almost taste one, feel the soft, liquid sugar slide over his teeth, sticking to the roof of his mouth as the crisp hot shell rubbed and stung his tongue. It was a sensation as sensual as any he could imagine at that moment.

' 'ank you,' said the Japanese, and he returned to shivering.

From outside came the sounds of a lorry pulling up. The driver's door was slammed shut and voices were heard dimly calling across the yard, the words deadened by the snow.

It had not occurred to Sandingham that any of his fellow labourers could speak English. Now it dawned on him that everything they had said about the Japanese, none of it very complimentary, had most likely been fully understood by at least one of them. And possibly passed on. But then, if it had been reported, where were the beatings, the reductions in food, the removal of fuel allowances, the restrictions on what tiny liberties

they occasionally received? Obviously, it hadn't. Their lives had
carried on with each face-slapping having an obvious, if unjust,
reason. Food was as scanty as ever.

'What is your name?' he ventured.

It came so naturally. The man had spoken to him. This was
next in the common course of communication between one
human and another.

'Mishima. My name is Mishima. Mr Mishima. Mishima–san,
we say. And you?'

'Sandingham. Joseph Sandingham.'

'Where do you live? I mean in England, not in Japan.' He
half-smiled. 'We all know where you live in Japan.'

'Near London. My family live near London. I have no home of
my own at present.'

He hadn't, and the fact hadn't occurred to him before. He was
homeless. Unless he counted the *tatame* in the barrack at the top
of the bank, up the steps, past the latrines and ablutions. Second
tatame down from the *hibachi* on the left of the room as you
entered it.

'I live two miles away. In a suburb,' Mishima offered. 'This is
my son. His name is Katsuo.'

The youth next to Sandingham said, 'Hajimemashite.'

Sandingham was about to reply incorrectly, 'Genki desu. O-
kage sama de,' but the father interrupted.

'In English. In English.'

'How you do?' Katsuo enquired sheepishly.

Mishima shrugged the shrug of every father the world over
who has his patience tried by a teenage son.

'How do you come to speak such good English?' Sandingham
asked him.

'I am a high school master. I teach English. Or I was before the
war. Now my school is closed and we must all work . . . '

'Wuk! Wuk!'

The tarpaulin was dragged aside. It had stopped snowing and
the crowbars had arrived. Sandingham was detailed to prise
planks apart. Alex Ryder started up the circular saw. Soon, the
blades were screeching and howling through the wood.

From time to time, the *hancho* allowed the prisoners to take away from the timber yard sacks of sawdust and shavings which were utilised in the camp in the making of the fuel balls. Mixed with coal dust, the wood made for easier lighting and longer burning. It also emitted greater heat than the other variety of clay and coal mix. What was more, it gave the barrack rooms a scent of pine sap as it burnt and the prisoners were not slow to discover that if one inhaled the perfume of wood shavings boiled in water it cleared catarrh and eased coughs. The smoke that leaked into the room also seemed to cut down on the bedbugs, although Sandingham believed that this was a myth put about by those who sought continually to boost morale.

When the cold weather began to abate and give way to a lukewarm early spring, the senior officer in the camp was successful in persuading the commandant to allow for the continued burning of wood dust: it was, he said, in the interests of the Japanese, as well as the unworthy prisoners, to allow for the continuation on the grounds that the prisoners were healthier for it and it would make cooking cheaper and easier. Additionally, the smoke would keep at bay the mosquitoes that were beginning to invade the camp from the surrounding fields. A single bite from one of these voracious insects was quick to suppurate and they most likely carried malaria as well, although most of the prisoners already had that from previous camps in south-east Asia. He was careful not to say that such an action would make the prisoners happier. That would be a sure way to have the sawdust stopped. In truth, being allowed to keep the supply running did boost morale considerably: such a small concession meant so much to men in the dire circumstance of imprisonment.

Mr Mishima and his son were absent from the timber yard for some weeks but, early in April, they reappeared.

Standing by the banshee-whining of the planing machine on their first day back, Mishima made sure he was hidden from the foreman by the protective cowling over the top of the band-saw housing. Pulling off a heavy work-glove, he nodded minutely to Sandingham and, receiving the all-clear, approached him in order to speak to him.

'My mother has been very ill,' Mishima explained. 'I had to go to Tokyo to be with her.'

'I hope she is all right now?'

The planing machine completed drawing its latest plank through and the whine dropped suddenly to a hum as the wood cleared the spinning blades. Sandingham, with an expertise born of practice, let his voice drop the instant the whine ceased.

'She is dead.'

It was so bluntly put the announcement took Sandingham off guard. In England, the bereaved would have been so much more gradual in his statement.

'I am sorry. How . . . ?'

'Tuberculosis. There is no medicine in Japan now.'

A guard came into view around the stack of planks, his rifle slung over his shoulder but ready to be slipped down into his hands. Their conversation was curtailed.

Later in the afternoon, Mishima spoke again to Sandingham, but this time his words were muted, for they were standing in the centre of the yard, close to the lorry.

As he handed Sandingham a sack of shavings to be loaded into the vehicle, he said, 'Note this sack.' His hand surreptitiously patted a character painted on the sacking in red. 'This letter is *kome*. Rice. Be sure you take this sack back to your camp.'

He turned away as the guard came towards them, shouting for Sandingham to hoist the sack up.

All through the remainder of the day Sandingham was curious to know why he should have that specific sack. Obviously, there was something in it. But what? Mishima could hardly risk giving him anything. His punishment for such a thing, if he were caught, was likely to be even more severe than one levelled at the prisoners themselves. He would not only be seen to be degrading and debasing himself by associating with beaten enemies, but also treacherous. He would be tortured, then killed, and his family would live in perpetual shame.

Once in the comparative safety of the barrack hut, Sandingham untied the neck of the sack and rummaged inside. The contents appeared to consist entirely of shavings from the plank planer which had been Mishima's responsibility that day. Only hidden right in the centre of the shavings, was a small parcel. Sandingham removed it and lay on his bunk, facing the wall as he removed the plain paper wrapping. It was as well to take such precautions, just in case there was a stool-pigeon in the camp. He did not think there was one, but there had been in Sham Shui Po and the risk was ever-present.

The package contained a bottle with a cork rammed in the top. Around it was a piece of paper. Smoothing this out, Sandingham read it to himself:

Today is 8 April, Buddha's Birthday. In the bottle is a traditional tea for this day. It is made with liquorice. Drink it and think of the Buddha, a man of peace. The tea kills stomach worms. Rub it on your bed pillars: it will stop insects climbing. Last week, Tokyo was bombed by Amerikans. Please destroy this paper.

The handwriting was sloping and cursive, typical of the script taught with regularity in all Japanese schools. He smiled slightly to himself at the mis-spelling of just one vital word.

He drank as much of the liquid as he could in one swallow. It tasted utterly foul. He rubbed what was left on the legs of the table. That way, he hoped, it would serve to keep ants from the food that was sometimes left there. In the latrines, as he gratingly coughed as loudly as he could, he smashed the bottle on to the concrete floor and dropped the pieces down into the half-full troughs. No one would find them there. The shredded wrapping paper followed it and he urinated on that to make sure it was well embedded in the filth.

There was still time before the evening meal was ready. Sandingham walked through the camp towards the kitchen, the note rolled as tightly as possible, and pushed into the folds of his *fandushi*. The senior officer, a major in the Royal Artillery, was standing by a large cauldron, stirring the glue-some ingredients with a pole.

'When I was a lad, Joe, I had a nanny. My parents had a number of staff. Our washer-woman – "laundress", to give her her correct domestic title – whenever I returned from school for the holidays or an exeat, used to get my games kit from the nanny and stir it in the copper boiler in our laundryroom in much the same way as I now prepare a repast for my men. Pity,' he remarked solemnly, half in thought, 'we can't get a weekend exeat.'

'Can I have a private and urgent word, sir?'

'Wilkins, see if you can keep this from congealing while I have a word with Captain Sandingham here.'

The kitchen orderly, who was let off work duty as he had only two fingers on his right hand, took over the agitation of the soup. Sandingham and the major went into a corner.

'Yes.'

'I got this today, sir. From a friendly Nip at my work place.'

It made him uneasy to call Mishima a Nip.

The major read the note quickly.

'Where's the liquid?'

'I drank a bit, sir – tasted like Jeyes Fluid smells – and rubbed the rest on our table. I didn't like to be seen with the bottle.'

'Where is it now?'

He told him as they returned to the soup.

The major loosely crushed the note up and slipped it on to the glowing fire under the cauldron. Sandingham watched it char, then briefly flare.

'I'll spread the word in the usual manner,' the major informed him. 'Grand news. Tokyo bombed. Japan is within the range of USAF aircraft. Maybe even carrier-borne . . .'

Wilkins relinquished the stirring pole. The soup had turned more glutinous than before but could not be thinned. There was no water to spare.

Later, as they sat around their hut table slurping the soup with china spoons, one of the Americans commented, 'What the hell is that goddam vile stink? It ain' the soup here. It seems to be coming out of the very woodwork. I didn' notice it before. Some kind of Jap secret weapon.'

Sandingham kept mum.

By morning, the word was about in the camp. Tokyo had been bombed.

Due to the collapse of one of the supporting poles for the awning over the lorry, assisted by rusting and the artful manipulative bending of the private who contrived to sit by it every day, the tarpaulin cover was dispensed with in the early spring. Although it meant a cold ride to the timber yard in the early morning, it did mean that the countryside was now open to their view. The sight of the local Japanese peasants going about their domestic and agricultural chores gave the prisoners' lives some new if passing interest.

Any thoughts of escape over the sides of the truck were ludicrous and inevitably doomed to failure. The islands of Japan were a secure prison in themselves. Rumours circulated from time to time that some prisoners had escaped from a camp in Kyushu and were living rough in the mountains, from which they conducted lightning commando raids upon Japanese military establishments, but these were inventions of fancy.

At first, Sandingham had believed in them: they were vaguely plausible. But soon the stories took on the hints of fiction more commonly found in *The Boys' Own* and he disbelieved them totally after he heard whispers to the effect that this band, now grown to forty strong, had succeeded in destroying an armaments convoy heading to the naval base at Kobe. They had mined two bridges, so the story went, trapped the trucks between the explosions and mown the occupants down with heavy machine-gun fire. That Kobe was in Honshu and the prisoners were reputed to live in the hills of an island south of Nagasaki, three hundred and fifty miles away across Japan's most southerly island, the well-patrolled straits at Shimonoseki and the Inland Sea, only proved the lie. The more ignorant of the prisoners, though – those of the other ranks, who had no inkling of the geography of their temporary host nation – believed in the fantasy and Sandingham was inclined not to disabuse them.

Sandingham rested his head on his folded arms and peered over the woodwork of the lorry. The two guards that morning were crouched in the lea of the cab, sitting close together to avoid the cut of the wind. The snow had been thawed for a fortnight but there was still a frost at night at least once a week and the wind coming down from the hills was raw and sharp. His eyes filled with tears from the cold and his nose ran but he wiped neither. There seemed no point. He would wait until they reached the timber yard then blow his nose in the oriental fashion, pinching his nostrils between his thumb and index finger and squirting it clean on to the hard ground. In the meantime, he sniffed.

There was a military commander inspecting infantry units in the area at the time and his staff car, with its accompanying bevy of vehicles, appeared ahead of their truck on the narrow road. Their driver pulled in to the approach lane to a small farm to let the saloon cars by. Once they had passed, he put the truck into gear and pressed the accelerator. The engine roared and the gears squealed; then there was a grunt from the engine, as if it were fed up, and all sounds of activity within it ceased. The driver attempted to restart it but with no result other than a gravelly grinding of the starter motor.

The guards sprang into action, jumped over the tailboard and positioned themselves so that they had a clear view of the rear and sides of the truck. The prisoners were ordered to stay put. Two guards were not sufficient to march them all the remaining three miles to the timber yards or back to the camp. The driver and the warders discussed the matter in muted tones and the former then set off to find a telephone. With a degree of shouting, gesticulation, gabbled English and one face-slapping, the prisoners were made to sit on the floor of the lorry facing outwards. They shuffled themselves into position, trying to get closer to each other for warmth as they moved. Finally satisifed with the seating arrangements, the guards stood easy but kept their rifles at the ready in both hands, bayonets fixed.

As if to bless the little gathering of men in dire need, the clouds broke open and the first of the warm spring sunshine that they were to know in the few brief weeks between winter and the heat of summer bathed them. The light was weak but soft and penetrating, and as it shone the men grew chatty and whispered amongst themselves. Their guards ordered them to speak, not whisper: a whispering man can be plotting subterfuge while logic demands that a talker cannot. It made little difference, for neither of the guards could understand textbook English, let alone the idiomatic prisoner-slang that was used to confound or confuse the captors.

Not bothering to join in the conversation, Sandingham let his mind wander across the view before him. Immediately below the bank of the road was a paddyfield, the earth in it hard and dry and as yet unplanted. A tree was growing on the path between this field and the next, and from it he could hear the song of a bird he did not recognise. It was a shrill pip-pi-pip call, and was repeated three times, then four times, then twice before going back to thrice again. Between each call was a brief pause and, every time the thrice call was reached, there was a longer break.

In the camp, he now realised, he seldom heard birds. He tried hard to recall when it was he had last listened to a morning song like this but he couldn't remember. It must have been in Hong Kong. With Bob.

Bob. Long-dead Bob. The ultimate escaper. Not for him the home run through Chungking and the underground, the dream of liberation. He was already liberated, and gone wherever dead men go. Probably, Sandingham reasoned, a dark void where there is nothing. Nothing was preferable to the something he knew. In nothing there is no starvation, no sickness, no pain, no punishment, no work. There was no *hancho*, no *taiso*, no *tenko*, no *hochotore* each time he passed the camp guardhouse, his feet hurting at the ridiculous goose-stepping march; no *benjo* full of shit.

He still loved Bob. Sometimes, when he was exhausted or working like an automaton in the timber yard doing a job that required no thought, like sweeping up or sawing through a log, he daydreamed about their meeting after the war. He would be wearing a well-tailored blazer and slacks and Bob would be dressed in a light summer suit and they'd be walking along the banks of the Cherwell in the University Parks. Through the trees the spires of Oxford would point to God and the block of Magdalen College would dent the distance. Young men in punts would glide by through his mind like swans on still waters.

The song stopped. Sandingham watched. A dull brown bird dropped from the branches of the tree and disappeared into some rank weeds by the paddy wall.

Damn! he thought. He could not dredge the memory back. From the University Parks, was it possible to see the tower of Magdalen? Or did other buildings get in the way? Weren't there a lot of houses across the river from St Catherine's that blocked the view?

He bothered this over in his mind, seeing nothing of interest from the lorry until a pig waddled into the far end of the field and began to rout about in the damper earth by an irrigation channel.

The sight of the pig took away his thoughts of Oxford. Instead he watched the animal scrabbling with its trotters and teeth and pictured a large joint, the skin crisped with oil and crackling in his mouth and the roast onions and potatoes browned with Bisto gravy. And broad beans. He accepted that this was what he was reduced to: a pig could erase his memories of home and his love for another human.

This realisation pushed itself upon him and immeasurably depressed him. To match his thoughts, a large cloud blew over the sun, obscuring it and causing him to feel once again the chill air.

There is no hope. He knew that now. No chance for liberation except in death. No chance for resurrection from the pit of prisonership.

The farm buildings, two hundred yards away behind the row of willows, were dark and low. The slight pitch of the roof and the blackness of their wooden construction made them particularly un-European. Looking at them, Sandingham had driven into him even more forcibly the fact that he was an alien in an alien land, unnecessary and insignificant.

The cloud shifted. The wind had picked up and hurried it along. Sandingham watched the progress of its receding shadow hasten across the brown fields towards him. There was warmth again on his skin.

The farmstead shook with life. The sun shimmied upon the trees to the left of the pig sty. The pink-white fluff caught the sun and translated it into beauty.

'Cherry blossom!'

'What's that, mate? Sir . . . '

'Cherry blossom, Wilkins. Over there. Nine o'clock from the farm . . . '

Wilkins screwed up his eyes. He was suffering badly from conjunctivitis, his eyelids red and bruised, his pupils bloodshot and itchily painful.

It was with considerable disgust that Sandingham perceived that he had used the army field-spotting method to point out the blossom. It was an insult to nature.

'Can't see it, sir.'

'By the buildings, man. To the left by that low shed. There are two trees – leafless. See the pink haze?' He had become agitated with the excitement of his discovery. 'It's cherry blossom.'

Wilkins squinted.

'Think so, sir. Is it important?'

Sandingham thought then said, 'No. Not really.'

Yes, it was. In all pain there is beauty; in all strife there is peace; in all sorrow there is laughter. Maybe hope, even. One just had to find it. To do so he stared at the distant blooming tree.

A van arrived. The two mechanics lifted a heavy toolbox from the rear, opened the bonnet of the lorry and started to tinker with its engine. Fifteen minutes passed. They could not get it to do more than turn over on the starter.

The guards, the driver and the mechanics held a conference. The mechanics left in their van. Twenty minutes later, another lorry arrived. It appeared to be as delapidated as the one that was broken down. Nevertheless the prisoners were transferred to the second vehicle and driven off to the timber yard.

As the transport edged out of the farm lane Sandingham, watching the cherry blossom, saw a movement closer by. It drew his attention. He looked at the patch of scrub into which the songbird had dropped. There it was. A small boy, four or five years old, was hiding in the cover and surveying the prisoners. His eyes were wide with the curiosity of the ignorant and the innocent. Sandingham gave the boy a broad smile and he smiled shyly back.

The fever subsided after a week, during which time Sandingham had tossed and twisted in the bunk allocated to him in the sick bay, a somewhat fanciful title given to the smallest building in the camp, situated the other side of the latrines and, due to the prevailing wind, usually immersed in its doubtful perfumes.

The weather was humid and close for most of his illness. The Dutch doctor, a highly qualified eye surgeon from Java, could do little for him. There was no way for him to regulate his patient's temperature except by keeping his sheet soaking wet in the noon-day heat and dry and close to his skin at night. The Dutchman's main intent, as with all his patients, was not necessarily to save Sandingham from death, but from being carted off to the *byoin*, the 'hospital' camp situated twenty-five miles up the coast. Any *byonin* who were transported there seldom returned. It was deemed better to die in the hands of the prisoners than at the

hands of the hospital camp staff. They were not noted for their
sympathy, which was as lacking as their medical skill was wanting.

Sandingham's chances of surviving his fever, which the doctor
at first feared the herald of an outbreak of diphtheria or cholera,
but which turned out to be neither – though what it was he was
not able to guess without a microscope and a slide – looked slim
from the outset. On the first three mornings of his sickness the
corporal who was in charge of deducing who was fit for work and
who was not, decided in Sandingham's favour and excused him.

Known variously as 'Top-Hat-and-Tails', 'The Wreathman' or
'Coffin Charlie', the corporal stepped into the sick bay on the first
morning and sauntered down the row of bunks and *tatami*, as
usual tapping ill prisoners' feet with a short cane. Those who
made no or little response to his tickling or prodding gained his
standard prognosis.

'No wurk. You for box.'

Each day, as the *gocho* left the building, he would detail the
first three prisoners he spied, release them from their chores and
order them to chop kindling for the cremation.

Upon Coffin Charlie's departure from the sick bay the old
sergeant, a *gunso* from the Kwantung Army, would come in and
sooth any doomed man's brow and say, rather ineptly, 'You no
sweat. We get you OK-A1. No box for you. No box for you.'

He would assist the Dutch doctor all he could and was kind,
sympathetic and never brutal. He was nicknamed 'No-box.'

Towards the end of his fever, when he was able to remain lucid
for more than an hour at a time, Sandingham appreciated the old
gunso's kindness and, like the man who promises to his god that
he will be good and pray after the current crisis is ended, he swore
he'd do something for him after the war. Buy him a wristwatch.
The *gunso* had one and still wore it, but it never told the time,
having lost both its hands.

'Keireishiro!'

Sandingham snapped to attention, saluted then bowed low
from the waist. He was not quick enough. The butt of the Arisaka
rifle struck him in the ribs and he tottered sideways.

'Keireishiro! Isoge!'

Again he bowed, lower. He could feel the blood rush to his head and his ears rang. He was dizzy and unable to stand still.

'Keireishiro! Isoge!'

'Watashi wa memai ga shimasu,' Sandingham pleaded. He should have known better, but the dizziness affected his reason.

A backhand hit him on the side of his head and knocked him to the ground. A boot hit him hard on the shins, then wedged its toes under his groin to turn him over.

He rolled with it and saw against the scorching disc of the sun a group of Japanese soldiers standing in a semi-circle round him. One was a little way back from the rest.

'Yu! Up! Up!'

He did not attempt even to sit. A rifle was raised.

'Kamawanai de kudasai!' he yelled.

The words came out at a high pitch, barely human.

'Yamenai to okina koe o dashimasu yo!'

The rifle butt smashed on his shoulder. The pain wavered and jolted through his dizziness.

'Yamero!'

The ring of soldiers edged back slightly and the single figure moved in. Another order in Japanese snapped out. A *heicho* stepped forward and grabbed Sandingham under the arm. A private assisted him. They dragged him towards his barrack, one of his *tabi* coming off on the way as his feet ploughed through the dust.

'You fucked that one good and proper,' stated a voice in the red glare beyond his sight. 'The visiting commander. God forbid they decide to do us for it.'

'I'm . . . I'm sorry,' Sandingham stuttered.

'Can't be helped,' replied the voice. 'Here. Help me get Joe's shirt off. Jesus! Look at the bruise.'

He'd been out of the sick bay nine days. This was his first rest day from the timber yard.

It had no front cover, back cover, title page or fly and was smutted and dusty and smelt of old wood and bone glue, which reminded him of the secondhand shop near the chemists in Saffron Walden. More than half the contents were missing. Where the pages were torn, sawdust had slid in between the leaves and every time he opened it a tiny fall of dust trickled on to his sheet and meant he had to take it up and shake it out of doors. Sawdust, Sandingham knew, was worse than biscuit crumbs. Or so he supposed. It had been a very long time since he had last had the unbelievable luxury of being able to eat a biscuit in bed.

The book had come from Mr Mishima in the usual way, following intermittent deliveries of miniature packets of tea, dessicated fish heads, dried lentils and once, memorably, three aspirin. The sack on this occasion had not had the Japanese figure for rice on the side but the five characters that meant peas. It had not been used for a long time. Snuggled in the centre was what was left of a guide book to Japan and her customs.

At first, Sandingham read it from boredom. He had nothing else, for books were very scarce indeed: there were whole weeks that went by in which he did not see a single English word printed on paper. Even the Holy Bible did the rounds as fiction or non-fiction or a mixture of both, depending on the reader's interpretation of the life of Christ. After a while he started to find the book of interest. It gave him phrases that might be useful, though not in his present circumstance. There was little scope for '*Donna toriryori ga arimasu ka?*' ('What poultry dishes do you serve?'), '*Koko wa kaze ga arimasu hoka no teburuo o-negai shimasu?*' ('There's a draught here; could you give us another table?') and '*Konohen ni dansu horu ga arimasu ka?*' ('Is there a dance hall anywhere here?') The book also contained a section on Japanese festivals, another on dress and a third on religion, much of which was missing.

He read it all with interest and, in the moments that they could snatch together, he talked about what he had discovered with Mishima who, in his turn, explained things further.

A few of the other prisoners took to the book as well. Word spread that it existed but no one accused Sandingham of being a Nip-lover, a Nip-scholar or a Nipper: if he had had *Mein Kampf* or *Das Kapital* tucked into his hidey-hole they'd have begged a read of those as well. Certainly, those who greatly missed books would have done so.

His hiding place was skilfully contrived. With care and considerable patience, he had started to manufacture it – 'sculpt' would be more appropriate – just after the arrival of the liquorice tea. He had found a loose strip of wood on one of the barrack hut beams and had removed this and carved out a deep cavity behind it. In this he kept the book. From time to time he removed it and buried it under the earth beneath the floorboards, but only when the beam was needed for something else.

Most of the prisoners had their own secret niches. Some broke the vital law by keeping stamp-sized diaries in them, the writing almost microscopic. When snap searches, known as *kensa*, occurred, the guards were usually not interested in delving too deeply. They were generally searching for stolen food, radio receivers or English-language newsheets. They never found a thing. There was no radio as there had been in Hong Kong, any food was generally consumed within twenty minutes of the theft and there was no newspaper-boy, newsagent or *Times* correspondent within two thousand miles.

News did filter through to them from time to time, however, in Japanese newspapers. These reached the prisoners in a number of ways. Food for the kitchens was wrapped in them, it was issued in strips as toilet paper, it was handed out to get fires started, it was flattened and lacquered for use in windows and walls, it was sent in shredded to be used as a basis for papier mâché that was employed to fill draught cracks in the barracks and, on a good day, it blew in from outside, winging over the wire like a drunk flock of birds.

To everyone's surprise, it was never censored. The camp authorities knew that there were Japanese-speakers and readers amongst the prisoners, but seemed not to worry. News from Europe was reported with surprising candour and the prisoners were, considering their position, reasonably cognizant with the situation on the Western Front. The Pacific theatre, of course, was carefully monitored and censored before publication, victories being announced but defeats ignored. However, by careful study of the news articles by a group of prisoners assigned the task it was possible to chart the progress of the war by listing omissions from week to week, rather than by noting admissions. In this way the prisoners learnt of the advance across the Pacific, of the eventual recapture of Corregidor and the Battle of Midway.

Two events occurred in the mid-summer of 1943 that gave the prisoners a release from the humdrum work-slave-sleep-work routine into which they had gradually and almost unconsciously slithered.

Both took place in the timber yard and happened in extended midday breaks, stretched from one to two hours.

The first was the celebration of *Doyo no Iri*, the First of the Dog Days. The *hancho* came into the shed and switched the power off at the junction box by the entrance. The grinding and howling were quickly replaced by silence. The prisoners looked at each other in bewilderment and anxious expectation. Someone must have done something.

Whenever the unexpected came about, even if it were a small matter like a guard bawling at him as he boarded the truck, Sandingham grew agitated. It was surely only a matter of time before somebody caught him and Mishima out: what might then happen did not bear thinking about.

The workers were herded together outside in brilliant sunlight. The sky was a harsh blue and the clouds were fine weather cumuli blowing in from the sea.

The *hancho*, who had gone into the yard office, reappeared accompanied by an unusually tall Japanese man in his forties, dressed smartly in a cream kimono with a narrow red obi into which was tucked a *yatate*, a container for a pen and ink pad. On his feet he wore white *tabi* socks and a pair of straw *zori*. On his nose perched a pair of steel-rimmed spectacles and behind him stood two servants holding between them a rattan basket.

All the workers bowed low to this man who might have come from another planet, such a contrast did he make with the labourers.

A long speech was given. One of the prisoners who understood Japanese was allowed to stand up straight and translate as the speech was made: everyone else remained in the bowed position.

'This man is Mr Kumisada. He owns the timber yard. He owns many timber yards. He is from an ancient samurai family. He wishes his workers a good summer. Today is a festival. He wishes to share with his workers the fruits of their labours on this auspicious day.'

Facing the parched earth, Sandingham gave a wry grin. It could not be seen.

For a minute the speech continued without translation, then the prisoner interjected, 'The gist of that is that Mr Kumisada is thankful – rather than grateful – that we have contributed so much to the glory of the Emperor and the war effort. Obviously,' he added, knowing that no one present in authority spoke English, 'Mr Kumisada is in blissful and convenient ignorance of the articles of the Geneva Convention.'

The servants came forward and placed the basket on the ground. The lid was removed and the prisoners and Japanese labourers were chivvied into a line, the PoWs at the rear. As they moved forward to the basket, each man bowed as low as he could to Mr Kumisada and received a small cake which he broke open and ate in pieces. The Japanese muttered, 'domo, domo' as they passed.

Sandingham accepted his cake and went into the shade to taste it. It was crumbly and sweet, the surface pastry soft and sticky with sugar. He swallowed it slowly, to make it last, and noticed as he did so that the Japanese were doing likewise.

It was then that it occurred to him that the local population were hungry. Food was getting scarce for them as well as for the prisoners, and he felt the nagging fear that if things became really bad for the Japanese then what might it become for their unwilling guests?

The translator stood up and went into the centre of the yard. Mr Kumisada was seated on a stool in the shadow of the office. He too was eating one of the cakes.

Tact was an easily acquired and much-practised art with the prisoners, and this one knew it.

'Mr Kumisada,' he began in Japanese, addressing the owner in what he hoped were formal tones, 'I stand to thank you on behalf of the unworthy prisoners present who have the honour to work in your timber yard. It is with deep gratitude that we accept your kind gift of cakes to celebrate your festival. We apologise for being unable to repay your hospitality and generosity save in renewing our efforts on the behalf of your company.'

He then saluted, bowed, turned about and marched back to his place with the others. Mr Kumisada nodded to them all in the way benefactors have.

That afternoon, the translator got hold of a hammer and a four-inch nail, knocked it deeply into a pine trunk and then put the timber through the circular saw. The nail stripped over fifty teeth off the blade and rendered it inoperable for a fortnight.

The second event came a few days after the new circular saw blade was delivered.

An emaciated mule pulling a cart arrived in the timber yard compound on a sweltering afternoon early in August. There was a tropical storm on the way and the heat was unbearable, the discomfort compounded by the appearance of storm flies, small midges that settled on everything and itched furiously, especially on the prisoners' near-bald heads. It was time for the mid-afternoon rest period, a ten-minute break that allowed the prisoners and their co-workers to relieve themselves, have a quick smoke and then fill up on water to replace that lost in the urine and the day's sweat.

The carter called to the *hancho*. The *hancho* called to the *shotai-cho*, the work squad leaders. They returned to their units and passed on the message.

'Mr Kumisada sends his regards,' reported the translator, 'and instructs that we have a three-quarters-of-an-hour break this afternoon. He has sent refreshments in the cart.'

They stopped work and congregated at the door of the shed.

'You know what I'd like now, boyo?' commented a Welsh lance-corporal who had only recently been drafted to the camp. Nobody answered him so he continued his soliloquy. 'I'd like a cold pint of fresh milk in a glass bottle.'

'Not a hope in Christendom,' replied Sandingham. 'If it's fresh water that's not sat in the sun for hours we'll be more than bloody lucky.'

But they were.

Pulling aside some layers of straw, the carter produced a crate of Japanese bottled beer. It was handed out, one bottle between two men. It was warm but not hot and they cracked the tops off by prising them loose on the edge of the platform of the planer.

The prisoners drank with a sense of wonderment. They'd not had real alcohol since their capture. They lay on the ground in the shade, ignored the storm flies and the gathering heat and let the beer ease its way through them like a drug. Soma could not have had a more magical effect.

When they returned to the camp that night they kept their mouths shut about their good fortune. It would have been too cruel to let on about their beer and extra lay-off to those who worked all day under the clenched-fisted, often whip-holding, hand of the *hancho* at the lime kiln works nearer the city.

That night, the storm struck. Inside the camp the power failed and the guards off duty were rousted out to assist in patrolling the perimeter with those on the sentry roster. The roof lifted off the kitchen and took days to repair. By morning, the hills were misted in grey, miserable clouds and the guards were in a foul mood. It was as if the gods were doling out punishment.

At Christmas, they were each given a postcard and were told they could write home if they wished.

Sandingham borrowed a pencil and wrote on his card, 'Dear Pa, Am well and in a prison camp. Life is not too hard. Wish you were here! Love, your son Joseph.' To write more would be to invite the censor's red pencil and a refusal to mail the card.

As he walked through the camp, Sandingham gazed at the oblong of pasteboard in his hands. He rubbed his fingers hard on the edges, soiling them slightly with grime. If, he thought, he pressed hard enough, some minute shards of himself – flakes of skin or smears of sweat – would come off and, as his father picked the card up from the bristled doormat in the porch, they would perhaps somehow transfer themselves to his hands. His father would peer first over his half-spectacles at the stamp and then read the message. He tried to imagine him reading the card out loud over the breakfast table as he knew the old man would. After that, he would grunt as he always did and return his attention to the morning edition of the *Manchester Guardian*.

He posted it in the wooden box by the guardhouse, tears in his eyes. It was the only letter he had posted since before the fall of Hong Kong.

It was delivered five months later, though he did not know it at the time, the day after his father's death.

While Pluto stood guard over them with his cartoon-character

sagging jowls and soulful eyes – by which he had earned his
nickname – they dug over the soil and lifted the small hard
potatoes from the clods of earth shivering and blinking in the first
light shower of snow. The foliage of the plants was dried and
browned on the surface and they were careful to harvest that as
well, for it was crisp as tinder and burned easily.

The wind had dropped and the snow flurries ceased by the time
the four of them reached the end of the row and had filled the two
baskets with potatoes.

'Spuds,' Wilkins said laconically. 'Chip 'em and fry 'em wi'
cod. "Two cod and six penn'orth o' chips, missus. Sorry, dear:
cod's off. Got a nice bit o' skate, though. All right. Ta. Two skate
and six penn'orth. That'll be one an' ten." ' He mimicked each
voice. 'Vinegar chained to the coun'er. Salt chained to the
coun'er. Rain pissin' down outsi'. Fat hissin' in the frier. Steam on
th' winders. Number Fourteen going by. To Peckham.' He
looked up at the snow-laden sky. 'Four'een go to Peckham? I
can' bloody remember. Use to get it every day t' school.'

Sandingham hoisted the bamboo pole on to his shoulder and
slid the notched ends into the ropes on the baskets.

'Sure you can manage, Joe?'

'No. But I'll do it. If you hear anything crack, it's not the pole.
It's me.'

'You make a dandy coolie, Joe.'

'And you make a dandy spectator, Phil,' he answered and they
all staggered off, guard and guarded, to the camp gateway under
their load of potatoes, oncoming winter and imprisonment.

Sandingham dropped his cargo in the kitchen and was about to
collapse into a corner when the day's cook asked him to split
some wood. He picked up the axe from beside the door and went
back out into the cold. It was getting dark but the camp lights
were on, casting their morbid rays across the woodpile heaped at
the rear of the next-door barrack.

He picked up a large log to use as a block, then balanced
another upon it. He rubbed his hands on his trousers to give them
a grip on the axe handle and swung the blade over his head.

Sandingham could not recall when he had last been so tired.
Not even since being taken prisoner: not even in the days
immediately before his capture. He did not want to chop wood.

He did not want to eat. He did not want to talk, or read or dream. He wanted simply to sleep. The longer the better. Forever, if possible.

The blade struck the log, was embedded in it and came free. The wood did not break open. He lifted the axe and tried again. This time the axe merely dented the up-ended log. He took aim a third time. The axe penetrated the wood and there was a ripping sound.

He picked up another log. It rejected the blade on the first swing but peeled open easily on the second. He started on a third.

This was not a log, though. It was the skull of the soldier on the bridge of the *Lisbon Maru*. It was the chest of the machine-gunner on the deck outside. It was the round moon-face of Emperor Hirohito. It was the glowering visage of Winston Churchill. It was Stalin's head. It was Roosevelt's. Hitler's. It was Goering's head. It was Shat-in-Pants' head. It was everyone he hated. It was everything he hated. It was the god Mars and Vulcan and all the warring deities of the Oriental pantheon.

'For the love of Pete, what are you doing, Joe? We've all had our food. Where the hell were you?'

Phil, the duty cook for their barrack, was standing by the corner of the building with his arms on his bony hips and an amazed expression.

Sandingham said nothing. He just lowered the axe and rested the blade on the ground by his foot. He let go of the handle and watched as it toppled over on to the chopped wood. He was surrounded by sheared logs: he had broken up half the month's firewood supply. It was dark and it was snowing heavily. He was covered with snow and heaving and smoking like a horse after a frosty morning canter. Phil caught him as he fell.

The winter lasted as long as life itself, or so it seemed in that second year of captivity. The anniversary of his being taken was not something Sandingham recognised now. The months became a monotony of drudgery and working at the timber yard. He pondered, one day early in 1944, how many planks he had planed, trees he had cut or logs cracked. He tried to guess how many tons of sawdust he had swept up and bagged, how many miles of curling shavings he had peeled off, how many balls of

pine sap he had rubbed into his sores, his insect bites and the rims
of his nostrils.

Seated within the arc of feeble heat the *hibachi* offered to them,
Sandingham and his hut comrades talked through a rest day that
was forced upon them by a blizzard raging outside. It was so
fierce that even walking to the latrines was a struggle, never mind
journeying to the timber yard.

'If this were Blighty now, we'd be sitting round the fire in the
front room roasting chestnuts. What I'd give for a roast chestnut.
Lick it first and dip it in the salt.'

'For God's sake, mun, shut your bloody mouth,' protested a
Geordie voice from the darkness outside the glow of the *hibachi*
and the dim bulb. 'The more you t'ak about it, the worse it is.'

'Pipe down, Wallsend! It's memories that keep us going.'

'Mem-or-ees are made of this,' sang a dis-harmonious third
voice.

Silence ensued before one of the Americans said, 'In Oklahoma
right now, the snow'll be highern the barn on the farm. You can
climb up in winter and toboggan from the ridge of the barn to the
drift by the creek.' He pronounced it 'crick'.

'Crick in the neck?'

Laughter.

'Only if you hit the guttering on the way down.'

More laughter.

'I haven't seen the snapshot yet. Anybody got it?'

There was a rummaging in a bunk and a photo was produced.
It was a large black and white print, eight by ten inches, taken by a
Japanese photographer on Boxing Day. Of course, it was posed.

Quite why the commandant had ordered it be taken wasn't
sure, but the general idea was that the prisoners should indicate
how happy they were as the shutter snapped and the old-
fashioned magnesium powder plopped on its little metal platform. Speculation had it that this was a sign that the commandant
was lining his nest against accusations after the war was won by
the Allies that he had mistreated his charges. This in turn gave rise
to the hope that the war was indeed drawing to a close. Certainly
things seemed to be on the turn in Europe.

Sandingham held the photograph under the dim light. It
showed the inhabitants of his hut ranked down the central aisle

between the bunks and *tatami*. They were all dressed in their best articles of clothing – at least, those to the forefront were – some of which had been borrowed under orders from fellow PoWs in other barracks. No one was smiling. A few looked blankly at the camera while the rest attempted not to show malice for what was so obviously a put-up job. Any hint of disagreement or obvious displeasure would be certain to warrant a beating after the shutter had revealed its secrets.

Before them, his back to the camera, was the commandant. He was saluting. The prisoners were standing to attention, but each held in his hands either a book or a bowl within which was piled what appeared to be food. It wasn't. It was sawdust. To add realism, one of two of them had real buns beside their sawdust 'rice'; but these were taken away after the silver chloride plate was exposed.

'One day, I'm going to get out of this shit-hole and tell the truth about that picture.'

'Don't be so optimistic, Taff. You'll have to find a senior officer to tell the tale to. How many would believe it?'

'Someone will believe,' Sandingham said quietly. 'One day, the story will get out and there will be people who will believe. There will be doubters and pooh-poohers and there will be those who will listen and exaggerate the stories for their own ends. There will be others who will believe it but will play it down just as there will be others who'll listen and believe but ignore it all. What they won't believe is the kindness of some of the Japs. Most of them – the whole damn nation, probably – will be branded for decades as mean-minded, sadistic little yellow sods. Nips. Narrow-minded little cunts, as quick with the rifle butt to the ribs as with the cigarette butt to the cheeks of your arse and the skin of your balls. We'll remember them for that. We'll forget the rest.'

Nobody answered him until Foster did. He was a prisoner who before the war had been an engineer for a tin mine up-country from Kuala Lumpur. He was thin on capture, and was now so near to death from starvation that his skin was tight across every surface bone of his body. His wrists looked as brittle as matches and his face was like a skull with eyes. His chapped lips were drawn to bloodless pencil lines. He had suffered worse than most from the deficient diet as he was allergic to some of the starchy root vegetables they were fed: if he ate them, he threw them up soon afterwards, losing not only what he could not eat but also what he had been able to swallow and could normally retain.

'Joe's right. We shall forget the kindnesses. Once we're liberated, we'll overlook the good things and recall only the bad. Joe's man in the timber yard; the sympathetic *hancho* at the docks; Phil's Private Higashino from Camp Seventeen; Natch's two lady-friends at the railway marshalling yard . . . We'll forget them. We'll remember the bastards – Coffin Charlie, Pluto . . . '

'Napoleon, Wada, White Pig, Fujihara . . . '

Sandingham stopped listening to the catalogue. He had his own index of horrors: Willy Stewart's crucifixion, Baz's voice drifting out to sea, the floating peak cap . . . Bob's death and the ambush at Wong Nai Chung Gap. Enough was enough.

As for liberation – that was the ultimate in pipe-dreams.

There was a sound of loud, repetitive hammering in the early light, but no one took any notice of it until the prisoners began to stir for the day's work.

'This you've gotta see. You'd not believe it . . . '

Sandingham and two others of his *shotai* were heading for the parade ground where the lorry was due to arrive at any minute.

'What is it?'

'New school rools nailed up by the Headmaster him-self,' replied the US naval rating. 'You ain't gonna believe it.' He did not speak too loudly in case there was an interpreter about, out of sight around a corner.

A board, four feet square, had been nailed to the wall of the barrack that overlooked the square. The paint was new and the lettering was English, but also quaintly Japanese. Sandingham stood close to read it, his eyes smarting in the cold.

1. It no allow kill commandent:
Punished – life imprison & shooted to death
2. It no allow damage commandent:
Punished – life imprison & punished with shoot
3. It no allow think kill commandent:
Punished – shooted to death & imprison
4. It no allow steal Imprieal Japanese Army:

Punished – big punish & death may be
5. It no allow rude to Japanese Imprieal Army
solder
Punished – ordinary punish & keep life
6. It no allow escap

'Apropos Number Three,' asked Foster, 'do you think you're
shot before or after life in prison?'
'Yes,' answered Sandingham. 'And in Number Four, who the
hell would want to steal the IJA?'
The American rating looked about him. The nearest guard was
seventy-five feet away, staring out through the wire.
'I sure know. Gen'ral MacArthur sure would!'
'I wonder,' Sandingham pointed out in the lorry, just as it was
about to leave, 'how they'd prove Number Three.'
'They wouldn't. They just do it and fuck you, Jack.'

It was evening, the first week of March. The sun was set, the sky a
light, flesh pink and Sandingham was sitting on the steps to the
kitchen building cleaning the woks that had been used to prepare
the evening food. As chemical cleaners were short to the point of
invisibility, he was using a mixture of grit, wood-ash and water to
remove the smears of food from the metal.
Foster appeared and sat next to him on the bottom step. He
had a cigarette in his right hand, the fingers now so bony it looked
as if he were clawing at the tobacco rather than holding it
between two digits. He lifted it to his lips and sucked noisily on it.
He had had trouble getting his lips to meet and air eked in at the
corners. He had been off sick from the *shotai* for more than a
fortnight and had spent his days with two other seriously ill men
down at the beach, under the single gaze of a guard who had lost
an eye fighting in China. He was a member of the *gunzoku*, the
corps of disabled servicemen from all ranks who had been in-
valided into the prison camps to release fitter men for active
service.
Every morning, they were marched – 'walked' would be more
accurate, for they no longer had the strength to march in the rigid
goosestep of the Japanese Army style – to the sandy beaches two
miles away where they spent the day seeking out the tiny white

crabs that inhabited the littoral zones. The crabs were no bigger than a half-crown coin, even when fully grown, and they were found in burrows in the sand from which they carried out sorties to establish their own territories against others of their own kind, searched for any organic material washed up and left behind on the tidemark and ran to the waters' edge to wet their gill filaments. If one were careful, one could waylay them on their route back from the sea to their burrow, for under no circumstance would they entertain hiding in another crab's tunnel.

These crabs, with winkles, small shore clams and mussels, tiny fish trapped in rock pools and edible seaweed were stirred into the evening meal, giving it a gritty texture but adding valuable protein in the process. On occasion, the three prisoners would discover sea birds' nests and steal the eggs. If they were particularly hungry, and if they were sure the fragile linings to their stomachs could accommodate it, they ate some of the shellfish raw. More often they would eat the gulls' eggs by drinking the yolk and sticky albumen from a sliced eggshell.

'Do you know what happened today, Joe?'

Sandingham shook his head and grunted, his hands swilling and grinding the grey mixture in the utensils.

'Our *gunzoku* – Cyclops – was mounting guard on us at the beach when we found a gull's nest by the spring in the rocks. Four eggs in it, bluey-whitish colour. Big as a bantam's. He saw us find it from where he was squatting on the first dune and shouted something to us. We thought we were in for it for wandering too far from him, but instead he gets up from his dune and walks over to us, leaving his rifle in the grass.'

'Why didn't you grab it?' was Sandingham's automatic response.

'What's the use?'

He nodded in agreement.

'Anyway, when he got to us,' Foster carried on, 'he pointed to the eggs. We'd not touched them. He signals to pick them up, so I do. Then what?' He drew on his cigarette and waited until he had exhaled before speaking again. 'He takes one, cuts off the top with a little jack-knife he had in his pocket, gives it to Brackenby. Takes another from me, slices it open and hands it to Alan. Takes a third. Tops it. Gives it to me. Takes the fourth, removes the top, says, "Jabber-jabber onzarokku" and drinks it back in one, just like any old *shogoto*. What do you make of that?'

He thought: if the guard was prepared to share a raw egg with a PoW, this meant either that the egg was a rare local delicacy or the captor was as hungry as his captives. The latter seemed the most likely explanation, and Sandingham said so.

'I never thought of that,' said Foster. 'Poor bastards . . .'

Leaning against the door jamb of the kitchen building, he pulled again on the cigarette. Sandingham heard his hiss of breath above the swishing sounds of his chore.

The woks were finished. He stood up, tipped out the filthy water, piled them into each other and lifted them into the kitchen. The rice cauldron was next. He lifted this off the floor by the big stove, slopped some clean water in it from the storage barrel, dropped some ashes on the water and tipped in a handful of sand. Carrying the cauldron outside, he put it down by the step and started to rub the inside clean.

'I think they're starving. The Japs. I think things are getting pretty bloody tight for them, too. The raids have increased, the USN's semi-blockading Japan and their own navy's getting thrashed to hell.'

Sandingham looked to the ground by the cauldron where something thin and white caught his attention. It was a half-smoked cigarette, the flame still feebly glowing.

Foster was dead. His head was tilted to one side and his mouth was shut. His eyes were open and blank and his hands were loose on his lap. Sandingham touched him and he was already cold. It couldn't have been three minutes.

Looking in the direction of the dead man's eyes, he saw what he had been looking at last. It was the side of a barrack hut, the dust whipping in an evening breeze. It was the typical panorama of captivity. The last of the sunlight was dimmer now.

'Poor bastard,' he whispered to Foster, unaware that he was quoting the man's last words. 'You poor bastard.'

There was nothing else to do. He left the cauldron and went in search of the senior officer who would act as priest. The Dutchman had been dead for less than a month.

The summer of 1944 inexorably moved along. News of the

successes in Europe filtered through, partly via the study group
and partly through the good offices of Mr Mishima who was
able, on rare occasions, to receive the BBC or the Americans on
his radio. He did this late at night, without anyone knowing.

He wasn't a turncoat. Nor a traitor. He explained it all to
Sandingham one midday break.

'You see, I know Japan is finished. We are an island and we
cannot fight. We live under Bushido and Bushido is old-fashioned
now. The laws of Bushido, of honour, of that kind of patriotism,
are out of date. We must move into the new era. *How* is the
question.'

It was not defeatist but realist talk, and both men knew it.

'See there.'

Mishima pointed to an ant nest under a pile of bark chippings
and debris.

'See the ants? There are red ants and there are black ants. The
black ants eat tree juice and the red ants eat meat. They eat dead
moths and grasshoppers, dead mice and rotten things like that.
Now the black ants are in the red ant world. They are fighting.'

Sandingham looked closer. Sure enough, the red and black ants
were going at each other hammer and tongs. The battle was fierce
and many black ants were dying. Many more than the red ones.

'Watch.'

A few minutes later, there was a distinct pause in the fighting.
The black ants surged forwards, collected up their dead and
retreated with them, heaping them under a large roof of bark.
Then the battle recommenced.

'They have a truce to collect their dead. Now they fight. All
over again.'

Three times a truce was invisibly, inaudibly ordered. Finally,
the black ants came forward and there was much feeler waving
with the red ants; then the black ants retreated and the red ants,
after a final assault, won the day. They did not follow the black
ants to their nests, but left them to retreat – ignored them. Even
so, the black ants had decisively lost.

'Japan is the army of black ants,' Mishima said. 'They could
not win. But still they fought until it was hopeless. Too many
were dying. Then they ask for peace and the red ants give it after
showing for a last time how strong they are.' He shifted to keep

himself in the shade. 'Men are like ants. If you were a Buddhist teacher you would know. Watch ants and you see the world of men in tiny.'

'Miniature,' Sandingham corrected him.

Mishima smiled and thanked him for the putting right, before saying, 'But you and I? Are we black or red? We are neither. It doesn't matter. So long as we live and do not fight amongst ourselves. Perhaps we are Buddhist ants.' The *hancho* was getting up from his chair in the shadow of the office. 'Best we are no colour. Just be ants.'

That afternoon, as they strove at the saws and planers, Sandingham thought to himself that Mishima was wrong. At least, he was partly so. Ants accept when they are beaten or winners and then they stop. Men don't do that: they go on and on until the bitter, attritious end.

Arriving back in the camp that evening, Sandingham was met by an uproar of excitement amongst the prisoners. An IJA vehicle convoy had visited them during the day and delivered thirty-seven prisoners. They were all American sailors and they were billetted in the hut by the latrines, everyone originally in there having been moved out and distributed to the other barracks, to step into dead men's places.

'What are they from?' asked Sandingham as he helped in the kitchen.

'A destroyer. Sunk by air action,' Phil explained. 'We've only had a chance to talk to a few. They were captured a fortnight ago and the Kempetai's been at them. Some of them are in pretty ropey shape. The boss is in with the commandant now, asking if we can mix with them. Since they arrived, they've been under guard in their hut.'

He jerked his thumb at the window and Sandingham looked out. By the door of the barrack was a pair of guards: three or four others walked around the building, ascertaining that no one peered out of the windows. Or in.

'A couple are in the *eiso*.'

That stopped speculation. The guardhouse punishment cells were terrible. Each was six feet square with a threadbare blanket and a bucket. Without light and without air, proofed against sound, they were the worse form of solitary confinement the

Japanese could invent. The loneliness was regularly punctuated by brutal beatings described as interrogations.

The senior officer entered the kitchens. He looked grim.

'We can't see them today. Maybe tomorrow. We can take them in food and those who take it in can stay while it is eaten in order to bring out the dishes. They eat after we do. Joe: go to the stores. The QM's going to issue three pounds of bean curd for them. We can water down the soup a bit and give them that, too. What's in it?'

'Purple death, some carrot tops, some crabs from the beach, water, a fish, eight potatoes and three and a half pounds of rice millings. Also a couple of daikon. And, of course, there are soya beans in it too, sir.'

'Good. Do your best.'

Sandingham was one of those chosen to deliver the food to the new inmates. After swallowing his own meal, he set off with some others for the barrack. The guards pulled the bolts and opened the door.

Inside it was dark. The guards had switched off the electricity. Sandingham lit a peanut oil lamp he had brought with him. Others lit similar lamps.

The Americans were lying around on the *tatami* rows, or sitting of the edges of the bunk and at or on the two tables.

There was not a word spoken until one of them, not seeing clearly who had entered, warned, 'More goddam Nips, guys. Get yerselves orf yer asses.'

A shuffling of feet followed a desultory straightening of limbs.

'I'm English, actually,' stated Sandingham – the last word, which he did not usually use in such a context, somehow comically capping his introduction in his mind.

'Limey?'

The enquirer was incredulous.

'Yes. We've brought you some food. Not very good, but what we usually have here.'

This information was greeted with a low hubbub of consternation.

Sandingham and the rest of those from the kitchen set the food on the table and began to pour it into bowls. Spoons were handed round. The Americans said nothing, but lined up to collect their servings, then sat down to consume them. Still there was no conversation.

As they collected in the empty bowls an American by Sandingham, who was wearing the remnants of an officer's khaki naval uniform, took him by the arm.

'Hey, Joe. We owe ya. Okay?'

Sandingham laughed and, in the dull light, the Americans looked at him with a renewed puzzlement.

'You got my name right. Joe Sandingham. British Army, captured at the fall of Hong Kong.'

'Jesus H. Christ!' replied the American. 'You been prisoner for two and a half years . . . '

'Right,' Sandingham admitted. 'Is there anything else you need?'

'Last month, I was in San Diego with my . . . ' The American realised the tactlessness of what he was about to say and Sandingham ignored his words in preparation for the noun that didn't come – wife, or lover, or mother.

'Yeah. There is something we need. We got a young seaman here who's hurt bad. You got a doctor?'

'We have, but we've no drugs – or anything else, really – to go with him. But I'll see what I can do.'

It took the senior officer more than an hour's humbling discussion with the commandant to get permission for the doctor to enter the barrack. When he did treat the young man he found his main injuries were several broken ribs, a twice-fractured arm, severe contusions and lacerations and a number of burn marks. None of the injuries was typical of those obtained in a sinking ship. The burns were caused by red-hot iron rather than floating, ignited fuel oil.

Three days later, the Americans were allowed to join the remainder of the prisoners and were integrated into work squads and issued with their bango tags, numbers on toughened card discs that had to be worn at all times. Once they were in with the rest the stories started to circulate.

Their destroyer, which for obvious reasons wasn't named, had been sunk in the most bizarre fashion. At first, many of the prisoners found it hard to believe.

'What happened was this. We were cruising about four hun-

dred miles east-south-east of Okinawa, about due south of
Kyushu. Anti-sub. patrol. Catch them two days outa Kobe.
Hadn't seen anything for several days. Suddenly, the klaxon goes.
All hands to 'Action stations' quick as hell. Our captain was real
tight on drilling us for this. Radar picked up hostile aircraft. No
sweat.

'AA guns manned, loaded, ready. Bearings given. Then we see
the planes. Three of them. They run by us, too close to be clever
and at about eight hundred feet. For'ard guns open up. Hit one.
He nose-dives. Hell of an explosion. Other two peel off.'

There was nothing unusual in this narrative, Sandingham
thought. They'd heard it all before, over and over. Some had
experienced it.

'The two that peel off. They bank up high, real high. Five
thousand feet. Maybe more. Too high for a torpedo or bomb run.
"Those bastards are gonna spray us!" says the aimer. I gott' agree
– it'll be tracer shell. Down they start to come, near as dammit
vertical. Their range is greater than ours. We wait to open fire.
But they don't first. They jus' come on down. 'Wotthehell!' I
heard some guy say. We open up now. Fire fast as hell, aiming
quick as hell. Hit one. He trails black smoke for about three
hundred feet then – Wham! – one hell of a fireball. Through my
mind goes this one thought: how come the guy's got so much fuel
after flying so goddam far from base? We knew there weren't no
carriers out. And since when does fuel ignite like that . . .

'The other one's still comin' on down. He's weaving.'

The listeners were with him, in the picture, the fighter coming
at the ship, waiting to open fire at the last moment in order to get
a good hit on the bridge. Demolish the steering and then go in for
a bomb or torpedo run when the ship's out of control.

'Then I get it. The bastard's trying to crash into us. That's what
it was, too. We hit him a coupla times, I'm sure as God knows we
did. But it di'n't stop the plane. Maybe by now the pilot's dead.
The plane ain't. It comes straight down and hits the ship aft of the
funnel. I was up in the bows. Ship shakes on the impact. Count
three and then there is one god-awful explosion. The plane was a
flying bomb with a poor sonovabitch guy in it guiding it in . . . No
parachute showed.'

It transpired that rumours had been about in the US Navy of

the Japanese planning suicide missions, kamikaze pilots who dedicated themselves to their gods and their Emperor and, after a special service in a temple, then set off on a one-way flight, their flimsy plywood aircraft loaded with explosives and insufficient fuel for a return to base. Some of the aircraft were said to drop their undercarriages at take-off, leaving the wheels on the ground to be re-used.

'What do you make of it, Norb?' Sandingham asked his pal amongst the long-term Yanks.

'I guess it's true,' the other answered. 'And I reckon it shows that the Nips are getting pretty damn desperate.'

'It is true,' confirmed Mr Mishima, the next day.

'How do you know?'

'We have had it in the newspaper and my neighbour, who is called Mr Hoshigima, has his son gone to be one.'

He looked glum and Sandingham guessed why.

'And your son?'

'He is on a list for going. Already, he has his cloth – *hachimaki* – to wind around his head. A white cloth . . . '

For a moment, he watched the boy carrying planks out to a waiting lorry; not wanting to press the point, Sandingham turned back to the planer.

'You know what they say for the pilots?' Mishima stared at the spray of sawdust fanning on to the floor. 'It is an old poem in Japanese. In English it says,

> Death is lighter than a feather,
> Duty higher than a mountain.

But what use is that to me if my son dies? I have only one son and why should I give him when the war is lost for Japan? If I have no son, my family name dies.' A plank was slewing awry and he pressed the stop switch on the saw. 'You know what "*hagakure*" means?' Sandingham shook his head. 'It is the code of honour of samurai. It says, "The Way of the Samurai is Death." All Japanese think of this now.'

The following week they were excused the Thursday from working in the timber yards. It was not a festival or a holy day,

nor even a rest day. Whatever the reason, they made the most of
it. On returning on the Friday they found a new and large
machine installed in the shed. The planer had been moved to one
side and the saw shifted.

'What's it for?' Sandingham questioned the *hancho*.

He replied through the interpreter that it was a machine for
making and shaping plywood.

Garry had been the officers' mess steward. Nineteen years old, he
heralded from Saginaw, seventy miles north-west of Detroit. He
had been drafted into the Navy from a set life as a chef in a diner
on Interstate 75 at Bridgeport and a keen fisherman in Lake
Huron. He knew all the best spots to catch walleyes, blue gills and
crappies from Whites Beach round to Caseville. His skin was
tanned, his young flesh firmly trim, his blonde hair close-cropped
in a crew-cut and his stomach badly bruised from the repeated
kickings he had received at the hands of the Kempetai who were
particularly vicious in their treatment of US personnel in the light
of the increased air raids upon the major cities.

When he slept, he chattered with fear but when he was awake
he affected a brave face. Sandingham befriended him when he
was placed in charge of his well-being and convalescence – the lad
was assigned to duties in the timber yard, sweeping up and
sharpening the teeth of the band-saw with a shaped file.

It was difficult for Sandingham to watch over the lad. He was
unbowed by the bloodiness of his treatment at the hands of the
Kempetai and he exhibited an open hostility to their captors. He
declined to speak to a Japanese and flatly refused to obey orders
unless they were translated for him, feigning ignorance of the
most obvious sign language or pidgin-English instructions. This
was taken as arrogance by the more hostile guards, especially the
Koreans, and he suffered many a slap or punch for his insub-
ordination.

Without success, Sandingham tried to introduce him to Mr
Mishima, but it was to no avail.

'Joe,' the boy told him quite categorically, 'I like you. You're
straight down the line. But I don' give a shit how good a guy he
may be. He's a goddam Jap and the only good Jap's a dead Jap.'

'He's not like all the other Nips – or what you take them to be.

Many of them aren't, as a matter of fact. They don't want the war and they know they've lost it.'

'Then let 'em surrender. MacArthur's ready for 'em.'

'It's not that simple, Garry. They can't just jack it in.'

'Too bad.'

Garry shrugged his shoulders and lifted the broad wooden shovel of sawdust, tipping it into the hessian sack hanging from two nails by the entrance.

His wounds were healing, but in Sandingham's view he should not have been sent to labouring work so soon. The fractures were mended but the bruises were prolonged by the continued use of the muscles. After ten days Garry suddenly let out a groaning yell and doubled up on the floor of the timber shed. Sandingham and Mishima ran to his aid before the guard arrived.

'What's wrong?'

'My stomach!' He was choking on the words. 'It's like awful cramp. Right across it.'

O God, thought Sandingham, he's got appendicitis. It was a killer, for there was no way to operate. The expression on Sandingham's face told the lad more than words.

'No,' he divined, 'I've not got appendix trouble. It's been took out.'

Maybe a hernia, Sandingham said to himself.

They lifted him on to the pile of sawdust sacks waiting to be taken to the camp with the prisoners at the end of the day's work. Garry lay there on his side in an embryonic crouch while Mishima explained the problem to the two guards and the *hancho*. They agreed to let him stay there as he was.

That evening, the doctor having diagnosed acute cramp, Sandingham squatted by the steward's *tatame* and massaged the young man's solar plexus, gently kneading the muscles loose. His fingers pried and smoothed the flesh as his patient lay awkwardly and painfully naked upon his back. They were alone in the barrack. The evening *tenko* was over and the prisoners were left to their own devices. Many were sitting on the parade ground in the last of the sunlight.

'If we were back in the States,' Garry murmured, 'I'd let you do that to me any time.'

'Relaxes you?'

It being so long, Sandingham suspected nothing.

'Sure does. And if it didn't hurt so much, I guess you'd see other muscles tighten.'

His words gripped Sandingham's mind. Garry was at one with him. An overpowering feeling of companionship came over him, the comradeship that springs between two men who belong to the same freemasonry of sexual attraction. He carried on pressing gently on the youth's stomach.

After a while, Garry wished him to stop and, with difficulty, tried to raise himself on to one elbow. It stung him deep in the gut and he grimaced. Sandingham put his arm under Garry's shoulders to help him up.

'Thanks,' Garry muttered.

He eased himself round so he could face Sandingham, lifted his right arm and put it around Sandingham's neck, drawing him down and kissing him on the mouth. His tongue briefly slipped wetly across Sandingham's lips. For his part, Sandingham made no response. He was altogether too surprised, and moved, and confused.

'C'mon, Joe. I know you like it and you're one of us. I can tell by your touch.'

'It's not that easy. You're right to recognise me – I'm like you and you are like me, but . . . '

'They ain't gonna see us.' Garry spoke with all the adolescent thrill at a clandestine sexual encounter. 'We can be quick here. It's almost dark.'

'You don't understand. I . . . '

'They're not gonna label you and me. And if they do, who cares? We're in the crap too deep in this camp to get people worried about two queens like us. And we ain't alone. We all got too much to be concerned with.' He giggled, then stopped, for it ached his belly muscles.

Sandingham drew back.

'You're new to the camp. New to Japan and being a prisoner. Look at your body and then look at mine.'

Garry smiled tenderly and interjected, 'I'm not worried about your skinniness. I ain't put off it. I just want the warmth we can make. I just want the love; if you can, I can.'

'My last friend was killed with me in Hong Kong,' Sandingham confided. 'I've not had anyone since, and now I'm just not able to.'

'You shouldn't let memories screw you up.'

'The memories don't. I've got over them now. God knows, it's been long enough since then. A year here is a decade elsewhere. But I've been on a meagre diet for thirty odd months now. I haven't . . . ' He tried to remember what Bingham had said when he had fallen for the boy in the camp in Hong Kong: he'd forgotten that boy until now. 'I mean, I can't get horny. Can't get a stand. It's because the diet here has no vitamin E in it. I'm too run down for sex. Even at the sight of your . . . '

His eyes wandered over Garry's torso. Between the scars and bruises the young man's skin glowed with health.

Garry beckoned Sandingham nearer. He leaned over and Garry kissed him delicately on the side of his neck.

'We'll be close,' said Sandingham. 'Be sure of it. But we can't be lovers. You can, but I can't. I'll be your lover, but you can't be mine.'

Lowering himself back on to the *tatame*, Garry said, 'No, Joe. That's no deal. Just stay put while I get to sleep.'

When he was asleep, and the other men had entered the barrack, Sandingham left, and walked quickly – for the guards would soon be locking up – through the twilight to his own barrack. On his own *tatami*, he curled up under the cotton sheet and tried to sleep himself. He could not. He so wanted to love and be loved, but he just could not.

Lying awake, he let his fears grow and multiply: what if he were now incapable of love? Not just the sexual kind but the spiritual too?

Over the next few weeks, the friendship between the two men evolved into a kind of love and Sandingham was comforted by this: his body might be beyond even a hint of consummation but his mind was certainly not. He discovered an unfamiliar peace descended upon him when he was alone – or as alone as was possible in the circumstances – with Garry. If they were preparing food in the kitchens together Garry would deliberately brush his hand against Sandingham's arm and wink surreptitiously to him. In the latrines, Garry would hand him the block of communal soap after rubbing it on his thighs. In the timber works, the younger man would draw quick erotic shapes in the sawdust and then rapidly blow them away. He was cheeky and funny and lively.

In quieter moments, he would talk of his home without any concern that he might never see it again. He dealt with the past in a matter-of-fact manner: it had happened, so why not think about it? It was the future he did not consider, partly out of a horribly rational fear and partly, he admitted, out of a super-stitious belief that, if he thought optimistically, he ruined the unborn chance-to-be.

At night, they did not sleep together. That would have been asking for censure, and was out of the question. Yet Sandingham would lie so that he faced the general direction of Garry's *tatame*, although it was in another barrack, and he was somehow deeply cheered by the thought that Garry was facing him through the darkness and over the prone, groaning, shifting mass of their fellow sufferers' bodies. Sleep came more easily to him now than at any time since he had been taken captive.

One puzzle did kept him awake on some nights, however. Now that he was in contact with human love once more, albeit only in thought rather than deed, he found himself wondering in the darkness as to why he was still alive. The odds were against him. They were against them all. The longer one was held prisoner, the less one's chances had to be. It was merely statistics. He tried not to think of this, accepting Garry's assumption that to think of death meant death. Yet his continuing survival continued to surprise him.

'Listen!'

They were lying back in the sun. The guards on the ground were strolling to and fro by the wire while those in the towers were fanning themselves.

'I can't hear anything,' said Sandingham.

'I'd swear I can – there it is.'

It was very far off, very high up: a dull droning.

'So?'

'It's a – I'd swear it's a B29.'

'Not a chance.'

A siren sounded. The guards sprang into motion.

'Shewltah! Shewltah!'

'It's an air raid! A daylight raid!'

They had recently been forced to dig four large shelters in the camp for such an event. The Japanese knew that the chances of day raids were increasing rapidly.

A machine-gun crew rushed into the centre of the parade square and erected their weapon upon a tripod like a camera stand. Normally the Nambu Type 11 only appeared for special occasions – visits from area command or the *tenko* on the Emperor's birthday. With it mounted, they opened fire.

'What the hell do they think they're doing?' Norb joked. 'The gun's not accurate at over a mile and the B29's got to be at least twenty thousand feet up.'

Still, regardless of the hopelessness of the range, they emptied magazine after magazine at it until it disappeared.

The all-clear sounded.

Speculation was rife, especially as no bombs had fallen within earshot, either in the vicinity of the camp or further afield. A raid in the city to the west would have been audible.

'No doubt about it,' Frank Gough said with an air of authority. He had been an observer with the RAF. 'That was no bomber. That was a photographic reconnaissance. And we'd best protect ourselves.'

Within a week, the Japanese had provided the materials and the letters 'P.O.W.' were painted on the roof of the kitchen and on the Americans' barrack hut.

The late summer hung lazily in the sky over the timber works. They had tidied up the yard and were stood down from duty because there was no electricity to power the machines. A raid somewhere had felled the power lines or hit a transformer sub-station. That was not what they had been told, but it was what Mr Mishima had surreptitiously relayed to them.

The water was short in the yard, too. The lack of power had caused the pumping station to halt and, by three o'clock, the barrels were nearly empty and the men were getting thirsty. The lorry was not due to call for them until five-twenty. The shade was hot and the sunlight hotter, sultry and humid.

Sandingham was restless, as were the others. The guards, conscious of this, allowed them to pace about or shift from spot to spot in the shadows. They were certain no one would attempt an escape.

Behind the tall pyramid of felled tree trunks, awaiting the saw and the shaver, the barbed wire that surrounded the timber yard premises was loose and low. It was also close to the trunks that had rolled or slipped against it. From time to time Sandingham had had to go behind the mountain of logs in order to shift the stack for selection and removal. From the rear of the pile, throughout the summer, he had seen a papaya tree growing. That it was a rare plant in Japan and much prized by its owner were facts of which Sandingham was ignorant. He was similarly ignorant of the fact that the guards had their eyes on the tree in anticipation of the day when the fruit might grow to maturity.

At first, it had been a leafless pillar but, as spring came, so did large, palmate-like leaves. Under these, which grew only on the top, appeared exotic flowers that swifty died and changed into small, deep green rugby balls two inches long. As the summer developed, so did the fruit, watched almost daily by Sandingham. The fruit swelled, filled and grew longer. Towards the end of the summer the deep green altered to emerald and then to a faint greenish-white. This became, by degrees, a washed pink and then a peachy, soft canary-yellow colour. The fruit were ripe at last.

Under the guise of going to relieve himself, Sandingham made his way behind the timber sheds and then, when the guards were looking away, he hunched low and dashed behind the uncut supplies. There was a space here between the tree trunks and the wire that was several feet wide but narrowed to a point where the stock-pile leaned upon the posts supporting the wire.

Carefully, Sandingham surveyed the outside world. He had hardly ever looked through the encompassing fence.

The papaya tree was standing against the fence on a strip of land a little higher than the surrounding countryside, which consisted mostly of lotus and rice fields interspersed with patches of cabbage or daikon. A quarter of a mile away was a hamlet of typical Japanese houses and a small shrine beside a farm. He could hear ducks quacking. A good way off, a figure was slowly ploughing or fertilising with a bullock towing an implement of some sort. It was too far away to spot him.

Climbing the wood pile and peering over the top, he could see the road passing the timber yard. There was nothing moving on it in either direction for as far as he could see.

Gradually, he eased himself on to the top log, lying flat upon it and hoping that his brown skin and scrawny frame would camouflage him. When he was sure he was not being seen by the guards or the prisoners, he put his left leg over the top wire and flipped himself into the cover of the trunks. There was no shouting or fusillade of fire smacking into the logs.

He cautiously descended the wire, using the logs resting against it as footholds and stood on the earth. He was trembling with fear and excitement. He was so agitated, he had to piss so he stood against the wire and urinated through it on to the timber. He chuckled inwardly at the thought that he was doing this against the Japanese wood, a one-day suicide plane and the fence, and all from the free side.

Relieved, he started to work his way up the vertical papaya trunk. It was smooth and he was not strong enough to get to the top of it. Sliding down again, he measured the distance from the top of the wire to the ripe fruit. Too far. There was only one way to get the fruit down: shake the tree. He estimated that one good vibration should do it. He tested it tentatively. It was not an old tree and it would shake. He embraced the trunk, wriggled his feet into a good grip on the ground and, mustering all his strength, he gave the trunk a hefty heave. The foliage shimmered and hustled. The fruit swung against each other. One dropped. He tried to catch it but could not. It fell to the ground and split open. Within, he could see the sweet, juicy meat of the fruit around the black pips.

He picked up the fruit and shinned up the wood pile, slithered over the top of the wire and dropped into the space behind it. Here he pulled the fruit into halves and jammed one in a cranny in the wood pile. The other he hugged in close to his body. This he would smuggle into the timber shed and share with Mishima and Garry. The other half he'd eat himself later.

'Dorobo o tsukamaero!'

There was a man standing at the end of the trunks.

'Yoko ni nare!'

This other voice was over his head. He heard the rattling home of a bolt in a breach. He could envisage the brass case inserting itself into the barrel.

'Koko ni ki!' ordered the first voice.

Sandingham was unsure of what to do – lie down or go forwards. He decided on the former.

'Hayakushiro! Isoge!'

He stumbled out of the shadow of the trunks into the sunlight. The guard on the top of the stack jumped down to the ground. He grabbed Sandingham by the nape of his neck, pincering his thumb and fingers into his flesh until Sandingham felt his head hum, the blood fighting to get to his brain. He was pushed to the ground where the first guard turned him over and discovered the papaya.

The *hancho* came running from the yard office.

'Miro!'

He saw the papaya.

'No goot!' the *hancho* screamed and booted Sandingham in the side, just above his kidneys. He grunted and rolled over, spewing the little water he had drunk earlier. The *hancho* picked up the half-papaya and, as it was covered with sweat and grit, he threw it over the wire. Sandingham lifted his arm up to protect his face. The guard nearest him swung his rifle barrel at his head and cracked the steel against his ear; the foresight dug into his skull and he felt the blood begin to flow.

Going down the alleyway behind the felled trees, the *hancho* found the other half of the fruit. It was already covered with ants. He chose to toss it beside the first half where it thumped on the earth, spilling the seeds on to the dust.

With a length of hawser, they securely bound Sandingham to one of the pine trunks in full sunlight and left him there. The remaining prisoners and the Japanese workforce were herded into the nearest shed and instructed to sit or squat on the ground. The Japanese placed themselves apart from the PoWs. A shouted interrogation followed in which it was eventually divined that no one had assisted Sandingham in his climbing of the wire and thieving of the fruit. That understood, the prisoners were ordered to keep absolutely quiet until the lorry arrived.

After a little while, Sandingham felt the hawser stretching his

skin and his left arm grew numb. A close warmth ran down to his
wrist, though whether blood or sweat he could not tell. He
started to think about what would happen to him or to the others.
Fantastic and horrifying possible courses of action began to mill
in his head. He closed his eyes to obliterate them but they
continued to play inside his mind, private reels of ghastly con-
sequences running across a screen in his brain. When he opened
his eyes he could see the guards gazing at him with cold, dis-
interested stares.

What Sandingham could not see was the figure of Garry who
had been butted and prodded into the shed with the others. He
was taking action.

Very slowly, so as to attract no attention from either the guards
or the other workers, Garry edged himself towards a side door. If
he could get close to it, he could hide by it where there were a lot
of off-cuts propped against the wall. The others were talking in
whispers amongst themselves. It became apparent that Sandingham had been caught not because he had been seen but because
the guards had noticed the top of the papaya tree whipping to and
fro at his attempt to dislodge the ripe fruit.

He gained the cover of the discarded strips of pine and reached
up to open the door. The handle was round and smooth and his
perspiring palms made grasping it awkward, especially as he
dared not stand or even crouch up to get a better purchase on it.
He turned it and the door stuck. He looked down and saw he had
ignored the bolt at the base, which he now pulled. It cracked
open, but with a sound that seemed like a chasm opening in the
air. He listened for footsteps, ready to pull his penis out should a
guard come to find the cause of the noise and, subsequently, him:
he could pretend to be urinating. He had been a prisoner long
enough to know he'd get a thorough slapping for this, but that
would be all.

He looked upward. There was a bolt at the top of the door. By
great good fortune, it was drawn back.

The door did not creak as he moved it a half inch at a time.
When it was open by a foot he began creeping through into the
timber yard behind. He had never seen the door used but knew he
would come out by the buckets they used as latrines. Once
through, he closed the door as carefully as he had opened it. With

it shut on the latch, he stood and tiptoed to the corner of the building. He could see Sandingham across the yard, slouched in his ropes in the burning sun. In the shed the guards were talking loudly to each other.

By the corner he halted and listened once more. Nothing: all clear. Sandingham's head was lolling from side to side. His eyes were shut and blood had trickled from his mouth and ear, to congeal as a dark brown stain on his chest. Garry choked back the rage he felt as, impotently, he watched his lover just thirty feet away.

Going down like a sprinter on his blocks, Garry readied himself for the run. In four seconds he would be behind the wood pile to Sandingham's right. That was in deep shadow now. He could hide there and figure out what to do next. Quite what it was he was aiming to achieve did not occur to him: he would play it as it came. All he knew was that he felt he had to do something to help Sandingham.

Sandingham raised his head. He opened his eyes once more and saw Garry behind the angle of the shed. It was plain to him that his friend had in mind some sort of escape; perhaps he planned to cut him loose or maybe he was just bringing him water. His throat was parched. Yet he knew that to do anything at all was asking for a terrible retribution. Sandingham had to stop him, but he couldn't call out for that would attract the guards. Besides, his mouth was too dry to make more than a croak. He looked hard at him and shook his head. To do so caused rivers of pain to rush through his chest and his neck. His damaged ear rattled and bubbled as if it were full of liquid.

He made every effort to force a word out of his mouth, but he could not. It was dry and his throat was scorched with the bile he had puked up with the water.

Garry rose from his bunched position and broke cover.

'Miro! Dassoda!'

The bullets caught him in the side and, at such short range, he was hoisted off the ground and sailed fully six feet into the wire. His neck was split open below his Adam's Apple and the windpipe hung through the gash. His arm was shattered. His legs tore open at the thighs. He hung on the wire for a moment and then dropped, as if at his leisure, on to his knees. Then he pitched forward and lay still, twitching slightly.

Sandingham wanted to die.

The two guards advanced upon Garry's body with unease. They prodded it with their rifles, as they might a wild animal, before taking it by one arm and dragging it into the shade of the office. There, to stop his quivering, they bayonetted him several times through the spine.

With the heat building on to his grief and dazed state of pain, Sandingham passed out. When he came to the sun was much lower and the prisoners had departed in the lorry. There was no movement in the timber yard and no sound except for a lone bird. He turned his head in the direction of the wire and saw, through the fence upon which tiny shrivelled bits of Garry still adhered, a brown bird the size of an English thrush. It was whistling a plain song. Its breast and throat filled with air then deflated as it gave its call. After five minutes it stopped its singing and hopped, two legs together with each jump, to the papaya at which it started to peck, devouring the seeds from the dirt and then extracting them from the fruit itself. It was oblivious of the ants.

There was the steadily increasing din of a vehicle approaching. The *hancho* rushed from the door of the office into the yard and swung the gates open. A lorry drove in which Sandingham had not previously seen. From it issued five guards and an NCO, a *socho* or sergeant-major. He was heavily built and it was plain to Sandingham that he was not of Japanese stock. He spoke his orders with a gutteral accent. The soldiers obeyed him with considerable alacrity. They untied Sandingham from the log, retied him more tightly with his hands behind his back, a length of cord running from his hands to his ankles which were placed in a rope manacle. He was pulled to the lorry and bodily thrown into it. The guards positioned themselves around him.

In the meantime the Korean *socho* had been giving the *hancho* what Sandingham, in different circumstances, would have termed a 'right bollocking'. This culminated with the *hancho* bowing and the *socho* giving his face a resounding slap.

The lorry drove off in the direction of the camp.

At the gate, the commandant stood in front of Sandingham and punched and slapped him about a bit in front of a small gathering of PoWs. It was an object lesson for them to see the harvest of

criminal activity. He was then taken to an office in the commandant's building and given a third degree interview in Japanese,
much of which he did not understand, the translator being
absent. He was able to grasp that he was accused of stealing food
from the Japanese people which, under Rule Four on the board,
meant 'big punish and death may be': the Imperial Japanese
Army, he was told, was made up of the entire people of Japan, all
of whom were fighting for the glory of their land and Emperor:
so, to steal from a farmer was to steal from the armed forces.

He cowered at the sight of the guards. He pleaded and begged
forgiveness. He swore innocence. He screamed for mercy. He
screamed in agony. He accepted his guilt. He denied it. He
submitted to everything, for there was no alternative.

By midnight, Sandingham was semi-conscious. He had been
beaten in the ordinary sense of the word, had had one of his
thumb-nails wrenched off and the soles of his feet scorched with
matches and cigarette butts. Most of his interrogation took place
with his questioners seated and he himself standing with his arms
tied behind his back and just above his waist. This did not quite
dislocate his shoulders. He had been forced to drink over a gallon
of water after asking feebly at ten o'clock for a drink. The water
in his stomach now made him bloated and heavy. He had tried
hard not to urinate but had been unable to stop himself. At
eleven-fifteen he became aware, as if it was happening to another,
of the warm liquid running down his leg. It gave him the strange
sensation of childhood guilt, so out of place in such a bizarre,
wicked situation. The guards and the *socho* laughed at him for
this then punished his act by singeing his testacles with a match,
burning the hairs off as one might prepare a plucked chicken.

He was left standing until morning when he was cut down and
placed in *eiso*.

Solitary confinement in the camp was served in a cell with no
light. Sandingham stayed there for the winter months of 1944,
living on the most frugal diet necessary to keep him alive. He
heard little and saw nothing but the arrival and removal of his
food and his lavatory bucket.

At first, he tried pacing his tiny cell for exercise, attempting to
walk three miles a day, the distance from his father's house to the
Five Feathers public house. He worked it out in his head: one step

was 32 inches and he could take two steps across the cell. There
were 1760 yards in a mile, 5280 feet, 63,360 inches. Divide this
by 64 inches: here he found his mind at first fuddled but later
clearer when he worked it out in the dirt on the floor. That went
in 990 times so there were 1980 steps to the mile, 5940 steps to
the saloon bar of the Five Feathers. As he walked, he tried to
visualise landmarks on the way – the gate leading on to the
common, the Methodist chapel outside the village, the farm duck
pond, the derelict barn by the copse. But he found this an onerous
pastime and it made him sick with longing and nostalgia. He tried
doing press-ups and bunny-hops but they rapidly sapped his
strength. He thought to count the time off but was soon lost.

After a few weeks, he existed in a dream world of nostalgia,
hatred, fear, love, self-pity and loss. He relived his life and
worries. He grappled with his unwarranted guilt at being a homo-
sexual, a man who rejected God, a man who sought peace. He
was in turn an avowed heterosexual, a devout Christian and a
warrior. He was a king, a pauper, a demon, a god, a creature of
darkness. What he was not, in those months, was a man. All he
remembered constantly in his befuddled mind was Garry's
courageous stupidity and Mr Mishima's undercover friendship.

For hours in some of the ceaseless days, Sandingham tried to
reason why Garry had acted in such a way. Was it because he
planned to escape, and that was the easiest way? he wondered.
Possibly it hadn't been planned at all, was just some spur-of-the-
moment decision – or not even that, just an involuntary action, a
reflex spurred by some drive deeper than he or Garry would
know. At other times, he wondered if it was out of love. But the
more he tried to puzzle it out, the more he remembered and the
more it hurt until, finally, he actively pressed such thoughts out
of his mind.

And, spinning head upon heel through these waking and sleeping nightmares revolved the same tormenting thought, unanswered and unanswerable: Bob was dead. Garry was dead. He
was alive. What was it that was saving him?

In the cell, he passed his third Christmas in captivity, excluding
the one upon which he had been caught, and saw in 1945.

PART NINE

Hong Kong: Autumn, 1952

THE BRISK WIND was coarse with heat. The dust eddied in the dirt track by the Chinese middle school along the road from the hotel. Sandingham walked down the track, tripping and stumbling in the dry runnels made by the torrents of rain from the three tropical storms that had driven across the South China Sea in the first half of September. He had been up to Ho Man Tin 'village' to see if there were any chance of his obtaining by stealth, thievery or purchase a small amount of opium. He had remaining only his hidden emergency supply in his room.

Ho Man Tin was a squatter area in the heart of the Kowloon peninsula. Situated on a barren hill of gravelly earth interspersed with boulders, it was densely crowded and inhabited largely by refugees from Red China who had managed, against the will of the Hong Kong authorities and probably of God himself, to get into the colony.

The population of Ho Man Tin lived in a shanty town as ingenious as it was over-populated. The shacks were constructed out of whatever could be found at hand: metal sheeting, tea chests, scrap timber, cardboard and tar-paper, hessian sacking – the detritus of the city. This cramped town within a town was almost a state in itself, with its own map of lanes and alleys known by heart to every being who lived there. It had its own sewerage system of meandering, circuitous ditches a foot wide and six inches deep that slugged along through the shacks and lean-tos and flowed, especially when it rained, to either a *nullah* of the city planners' design or a low-lying sump of valley with a natural soak-away. The lack of laid-on water supplies – water was obtained from stand-pipes in the nearest streets, up to five hundred yards away – gave rise to a thriving business in the carriage of buckets and tins on bamboo yokes or the backs of bicycles. As in the big city outside, wherever a service was required there was an eager band of opportunists to fill the demand.

The closeness of the shacks made them a health hazard in the summer and a fire hazard in the winter. The inhabitants made a living by conducting any employment they could obtain or industry which required no capital investment – or as little as possible. Many were general coolies, labourers on building sites and in the streets. There were rickshaw drivers and petty smugglers, tricycle-pedallers and cricket-fighting gamblers and beggars. And there were those who fashioned hand-beaten pots, mugs and cheap vases, made soap and glue from bones and animal fat, joss-sticks from sandalwood powder and the bone glue, hair oil (from the same source as the soap), baskets from split bamboo, cotton from waste cloth, string, shoelaces . . . Some, more enterprising than the others, manufactured illegal matches, clay 'cherry' bombs and even fireworks. These, in the right season, could maim one man and make forty thousand homeless in an hour of holocaust, the flames fanned by a stiff, cool, winter breeze. Inevitably, some of the people of Ho Man Tin lived by crime.

The criminals were not in the same league as Francis Leung. They were pickpockets, burglars of the poor, stealers of food and the raw materials required by the area's little industries, whores and pimps for whores for the coolies, swindlers of tourists, illegal hawkers, bag-snatchers and minor drug-dealers.

The latter did not supply to even the small opium dens hidden in the back streets of Kowloon, such as the one Sandingham frequented. They did not provide the premises for chasing the dragon, only the opium with which to do it in the privacy of one's own shanty. Their supplies invariably reached them through the same channels, directed their way by the Leungs and other such big-time operators, but were often of inferior quality or cut with other substances not so likely to induce the dreams of content-ment and the bliss of heavens. Most of Hong Kong's opium came from the Golden Triangle, an area of inaccessible mountains and valleys on the Thai-Burmese border. It reached Hong Kong by way of Singapore and Manila, Saigon and Macau, Hanoi and China. Some came from China herself, but this was a comparatively sub-standard concentrate and usually ended up feeding the habit of the poorer addict. Sandingham had known, as he had walked up the track, that he would need more of the lesser variety to keep him going: it was not as powerful as that to which he had grown accustomed.

He need not have concerned himself. He was unable to purchase any at all. The sight of a European in a squatter area, unless he were wearing a police uniform or carrying a clipboard in the company of other civic officials, was about an unusual as a bacon sandwich at a bar mitzvah, as Norb once used to say. And whatever is unusual is generally unwelcome. His scuffed shoes and shabby jacket and trousers, his cheap wristwatch and frayed collar, the usual signs of the down-and-out, up here showed him to be a man of some substance and position, and men of position do not ask for an ounce of opium without having an ulterior motive beyond actually needing the stuff.

He was despondent as he reached the end of the track on Waterloo Road. He was more than reluctant to dip into his last-chance cache. He knew that he had to get some from another source. Where was the problem. He was certain that Leung would have put it about that he was not to be supplied.

The only alternative was drink: that would dull the craving for a while. But there again, booze cost money.

There were times when he cursed opium. Yet there were times when he blessed it, too. He had first taken it to dull the physical pain of his wracked body, in the immediate post-war years. Later, he realised to his relief that it also reduced his mental agony, the memories he could not exorcise even by the deepest gin- or scotch-induced sleep. Opium was a good servant and a fair master – except when he was without it, when it became a cruel god.

Fortunately, only two days previously, he had succeeded in stealing a wallet and a Leica thirty-five mm camera from a tourist in Hanoi Road. The money was not plentiful – the man carried mostly traveller's cheques – but the camera had fetched thirty-two dollars in a pawnshop off the northern end of Shanghai

Street. That his hotel rent was due again soon appeared of little
consequence; his nerves took precedent over his roof.

He looked right then left down Waterloo Road. The mid-
afternoon traffic was light. To his left, in a haze of heat rising off
the metalling of the road, he could see the bridge of the Kowloon-
Canton railway. Leung and his band of merry saboteurs had
blown that during the war.

On an impulse, Sandingham turned that way, crossing the road
by Victory Avenue and walking slowly up Peace Avenue. To his
left was the embankment of the railway line protected by a wire
fence and a sloping, narrow expanse of dry grass, stunted trees
and wind-lifted litter.

Peace Avenue: looking about him as he stepped along the
pavement, he wondered if the peace it celebrated was worthwhile. Urchins played in the gutter. A mangy dog rooted through
some garbage left by an alley. At the tiny square that terminated
the adjoining Liberty Avenue an old woman was sitting on a
wooden box with her grandchild, eating boiled rice and cabbage
from a bowl she held in her hands. Around her on the road lay the
bones of a small fish she had spat out. As he passed her, she
emptied a cup of tea leaves into the gutter. Above and all around
the square, washing hung out on poles from metal-framed windows. The newly laundered garments dripped into the street and
on to unwary passers-by. Chinese opera blared out from a third
floor balcony.

'Peace' was this semi-squalor. After the war there had been a
hope that a new world would rise phoenix-like from the damage.
The phoenix was a Chinese mythical bird related to the dragon,
born of fire and breathing the fire of redemption and renewal.
After every war, throughout history, there has been hope: and,
after every war, the selfishness and power hunger of politicians
and the greed of businessmen has quickly commandeered and
sequestered whatever was bright in that hope and used its means
for their own ends. What remained was an old lady eating a plain
meal in the street.

The Leungs of the world, thought Sandingham. The inevitable
bloody Leungs.

Like a long-distance runner, he paced himself with an amalgam
of those words – theleungs, theleungs, theleungs . . .

At the end of Luen Wan Street he climbed the steps to the small station. A notice informed him that a train would be along soon.

Within five minutes he was comfortably seated, looking out of the carriage window at the expensive suburb of Kowloon Tong. Here there were houses – not blocks of flats or tenements – each with its small, neat garden. The train stopped at a signal, and Sandingham watched a gardener watering plants with a red rubber hose while, behind, an amah hung out lace underwear on a line strung between two posts. This was where, in suburban comfort, the greedy adventurers and selfish profiteers lived with their families.

From the far end of the railway tunnel to Sha Tin station was only a short distance of two or three miles, the track surveyed from on high by the Amah Rock, a boulder pillar on a peak behind Beacon Hill, shaped like a Chinese woman with a child in a sling upon her back. The legend had it that she had been turned to stone for stealing the child. As a punishment, she was petrified while trying to escape over the hills.

At the station, Sandingham alighted and pondered which way to go. He had not planned to come to Sha Tin; he had simply gone there. Nothing had forced him except the confusion in his mind. If he crossed the road and followed a pathway up the hill, through a hamlet, he would come to the Temple of the One Thousand Buddhas. Taking that route, dogs would snap at him and the Chinese would stare in their hidden manner. He chose instead to take the road to his right, following the shore, walking by the small wooden houses and shops that formed Sha Tin fishing village, and then on to the open road. Beside him the sea lapped at the stone wall.

He walked on towards Tai Po, eight miles away. He passed a roadhouse which was open, but he did not enter. After a mile he came upon a two-storey stone building constructed on the very brim of the shore. It was derelict, and he was glad. During the war it had been one of White Pig's homes, his rural or weekend headquarters where, doubtless, plentiful supplies of Red Cross parcels had been stored and devoured by him, his Chink whores and his subalterns. Sandingham stood before the padlocked, rusty gate and hurled a stone through one of the glassless windows. It clumped noisily inside, the thud echoing.

His head began to echo with the falling stone and he realised he was both thirsty and hungry. He was taken with a vague curiosity as to why he had caught the train out to Sha Tin. Just to toss a stone into an empty house?

He retraced his steps to the roadhouse. On the parking space before it a number of cars were drawn up in the shade of several tall trees. One was a new Ford Consul, the bodywork painted in two-tone light and dark grey. Upon the front seat lay a leather case which he recognised as being from a superior pair of naval binoculars, the sort that would fetch a tidy sum from a pawn-broker. He tried the car door but it was locked.

He pushed open the glass door to the café and, finding a table that overlooked the cove, sat down and surveyed the menu. When a waiter came he ordered a twelve-ounce bottle of im-ported Carlsberg lager for one dollar fifty.

Across the bay the shore was in shadow, for the sun was lowering. Smoke drifted up from a distant village and flattened out into a streak of gossamer-like strands. The Amah Rock was clear-cut in black against the sky, sharp as a velvet Victorian silhouette. The tide was running and a fishing junk in half sail was sailing down the cove, close in to the shore. On the poop deck, Sandingham could see a young girl priming and filling pressurised Tilley lamps in preparation for the night's fishing.

The menu lay before him. It showed a photograph of the café with the legend underneath reading, 'The magic Kiosk by the side of the magic Tide Cove'. Sha Tin Hoi, known in English as 'Tide Cove', was unique in having four tides a day. On the reverse side was a section printed in italics. Sandingham read it without reason, certain of the phrases catching his imagination.

'This is the only place you can watch and feel a roaring train while you eat.' A train pulling a row of goods trucks shunted along the tracks the other side of the road: it did not so much roar as chuff and hump and jangle. 'Occasionally', he continued read-ing, 'you'll be thrilled by the shooting Vampires smacking out of the blue.' He looked up and down the cove but no twin-tailed jet aircraft appeared on cue, as the train had. 'Your junior folks may enjoy fishing, fording, boating, ferrying, crabbing, clamming or simply playing around in the shallow mangroves. This is the place you'll enjoy most! Please come again and save a trip to Miami or

Geneva!' He looked at the mud showing where the tide was rapidly ebbing, and imagined children clamming in it, albeit absent of mangroves. No child would be allowed to wallow in such mud. That was the preserve of very sick prisoners. He wondered if gulls nested nearby.

'You tea an' toas', sir.'

The waiter, with a 'Dairy Farm' crest on his jacket, slid a tray on to the table and started to pour out the first cup of tea from a pot.

'I ordered a beer,' Sandingham complained gruffly.

'Oh!' The waiter looked shamefaced. 'Ve'y sorwy, sir!' He studied his order pad. 'I get you beer now.'

He removed the tray and took it off to its rightful table. Sandingham's eyes followed him so that his glare of annoyance could be felt for longer in the small of the receding back. In this way, he saw the boy who lived in the hotel.

He was sitting with his parents and watching the sailing junk. Sandingham studied the family group. The mother was in her early thirties, blonde and slim with a lightly tanned skin and blue eyes. She wore a flowery print skirt and a cotton blouse. The father was of roughly the same age, a well-built man with dark hair and sunglasses with green lenses. His trousers were light fawn and his short-sleeved shirt was white with shoulder tabs. His shoes were highly polished and he wore an expensive gold wristwatch on a gold-band bracelet. The shirt betrayed his job to Sandingham: he was a naval officer.

The boy took after his mother in looks and there was a faintly feminine delicateness about him, especially in his thin wrists and long eyelashes. They were only a few feet away and Sandingham was able to eavesdrop easily.

'Coke all right?' The father pointed to the green bottle in front of the boy, from which protruded a wax paper straw.

'Yes, thank you, Daddy.' Pause. 'I like it when it's cold. It has a different taste somehow.'

Sandingham's attention returned to the junk.

'When will you . . . ?'

'Thursday, Beth. Could be late afternoon. More probably early evening. We'll be stored up by then anyway, so you could come on board for lunch. Thursday's curry puffs.'

'Can I come?'

'You'll be at school.'

'Can't I? I'll be ever so good. Promise.'

'Can you be?'

The father tousled the boy's fair hair and pretended to punch him on the arm.

'Yes.' He was emphatic.

'What do you think?'

'What do you have on Thursdays?'

'Let me see . . . ' The mimickry of adults, then, 'Swimming, Maths and English in the morning. RI in the afternoon.'

'I thought you liked swimming. And English.'

'How was his report, Beth?'

'Good in most things. Above average in sport. He still can't swim all that well.'

'You'll want to swim if you want to go in the Navy.'

'Grampy couldn't.'

'He certainly could. He was a diver.'

'Divers don't swim,' the boy retorted with puerile logic. 'They sink with lead weights on their belts and have to get pulled up by a rope.'

'*Touché!*'

'I don't see why not. It's not as if it's often.'

'Thank you, Beth,' the boy said. The gratitude was evident in his voice. To his father he then asked, 'Can I go on the bridge?'

'We'll see what Captain Rodgers says. But don't you ask him. He'll be exceedingly busy.'

'Exceedingly busy,' reiterated the boy, nodding as if with knowledgeable agreement.

Beth: how unusual, Sandingham thought, that the boy should call his mother by her Christian name. He had done that himself as a lad – his mother was always 'Fanny' to him, her nickname with his father. It gave him a shared bond with the boy and he wished there were some way to communicate with him. Sandingham wanted that so very much. He plotted quickly how he might accomplish it. Then he dropped his planning. What he had in mind at that moment would have him run to a worse fate than the unfortunate stone amah on the hills above.

The beer came and the waiter poured it into a tumbler. Sandingham drank deeply and with the pleasure of relief. The cold lager assuaged both his thirsts. His hunger faded.

Before he had finished his second beer, the boy and his parents stood up to go. He watched them leave the café, enter the twin-coloured Ford and back out into the road before driving off. As the car swung round, Sandingham became conscious of the boy looking at him through the car window.

'Mr Sandingham!'

Damn, thought Sandingham. He had hoped to avoid him.

'Good evening, Mr Heng.'

'Good evening. May I have a word?'

The hotel manager led him across to the corner settee by the bar. There was no one about; the bar had yet to open.

'I'm sorry, Mr Sandingham, but I have to ask you for another payment of your rent. I must ask you to give it to me within a week.'

'How much?'

'At least two hundred and fifty dollars.'

'Can I give you some now, on account?'

Mr Heng was surprised, but did not show it. He decided a bird in the hand was, with Mr Sandingham, worth at least a flock in the bush.

'Certainly.'

Sandingham reached into his pocket and took out one hundred dollars rolled in a rubber band.

He had had the most astonishing luck. Coming down Soares Avenue he had found the roll of bills lying in the gutter. At the time he had marvelled at the way Lady Chance did sometimes smile on poor, benighted bastards like himself. Fortune was with him, he felt, if only very temporarily.

Mr Heng took the notes, counted them out and issued Sandingham with a receipt. This should keep him going, Sandingham calculated, in equal debt but no deeper, until nearly Christmas. He still had no dope, but he did have a roof for a while.

He went under the lime-green, neon-lit plastic arch into the hotel dining room and ordered the evening meal. The manager followed him in.

'I'm sorry to bother you again, Mr Sandingham.' He held out a white, sealed envelope. 'This came in the post for you.'

It had a ten-cent stamp stuck on it and was postmarked in Tsuen Wan, on the way to Castle Peak. Sandingham slit it open with his bread knife. If only there could be half an ounce in it. A quarter of an ounce. There was no possible way he was going to get any unless it was from his old source.

Inside there was only a typed noted. It read, 'One hundred dollars, please, Joe. By Saturday.'

It was a warm, South China autumn afternoon. Flies buzzed intermittently upon the windows and butterflies flicked lazily from one blossom to another in the rows of chrysanthemum pots in front of the hotel. Insects could foretell, as Sandingham understood, the coming doom of December just as birds had sensed the quicker advent of a stranger winter at another time in his life.

He spent the hours immediately after midday in his room, smoking a small amount of his last supply of opium. The withdrawal symptoms weren't affecting him badly as yet. That would come, though, as he knew only too well. And when that happened it would be the end. Once in the grips of the shakes and fears he would be useless. A clinic would take him in, he would lose his opportunity to earn and the downward spiral upon which he had existed for so very long now would sharply accelerate and he would speed faster and faster towards the bottom. They would release him cured, albeit temporarily, but washed out and without a future. The addict's eternal curse, he knew, was to be saved from his demons.

After smoking he left his room, with the window open and the small electric fan on full, and went to the first-floor lounge where he sat in one of the easy chairs and thumbed through that day's edition of the *South China Morning Post*. Nothing attracted his attention for more than a few seconds until he came to a small paragraph in the centre pages which announced that the Japanese consulate general's office in Hong Kong had been re-opened upon the arrival in the colony of the new representative of the Government of Japan, Mr Osamu Itagaki. He had presented his credentials at Government House and the office was now officially reinstated.

Sandingham let the paper drop to his lap and he looked blankly at the potted indoor palm that stood by the glass screen dividing the lounge from the landing.

Normality was returning. Eleven years after the fall of Hong Kong, the blowing up of the Bren-gun carrier and the death of thousands, the consulate was open again. It was all water under the bridge, spilt milk, the passage of years lapped up with unemotional thirst. The politicians were back in control. Visas would be issued, passports stamped, trade links strengthened. Those who had died had died for what? he pondered. Eleven years of undiplomatic ties. He felt the anger surge up within him and he fought against it. Partly, he struggled so that the softness of the opium would continue for as long as possible; partly, because he knew that to lose his temper was futile.

The lounge seemed stuffy now, as if an excrescence was seeping from the newsprint. He folded the paper into its wooden clip and opened the glass doors leading on to the balcony. The sun was as gently warm as an English summer's day. He leaned on the parapet and thought of the two Australian officers he had had his contretemps with in the self-same spot. They would know he was right by now. If they were still alive.

A faint brrrmming sound reached his ears.

Glancing over the wall, he saw the boy below. Once again, he was playing with military Dinky toys in the hedge along the top of the bank to the driveway. Unlike the last occasion on which Sandingham had watched the boy bomb his models, this time the child was erecting a camp hospital. A new toy ambulance was added to the fleet of vehicles. It was guarded by the tank. A white postcard tent was hidden in the grass, its top decorated with a childish red cross.

The boy was engrossed in his game. With the hospital set up and well defended against brutish attack, he skipped to the other end of the lawn where a small airstrip existed on a manhole cover. From there, he took off and flew, in his hands and in his daydreams, a Hawker Hunter jet fighter painted in camouflage colours. He banked around the hedges, landed to refuel on the wall between the flowerpots, took off again and started a long bomb run on the card hospital.

Sandingham steeled himself. He wanted to shut his eyes but he could not bring the lids to close. He wanted to be blind and to see,

both at the same time. The bombs, however, did not shake down
from the sky. There were no explosions. The Avon cannon shells
did not strafe the hospital or attack the tank. The ordnance was
left intact.

Now the boy was the pilot, talking to the control tower which
replied to him.

'Hospital, George. I see a hospital. Over.'

'Okay, Bert. Don't bomb the hospital. Over.'

'Righto, George. Banking to left. Over.'

The boy's mouth spittled some static on the imaginary radio
waves.

'They've got tanks, George. Shall I shoot them? Over.'

'No, Bert! Do not shoot tanks. Repeat, do not shoot tanks. You
might hit the hospital. Over.'

'Roger, George. Returning to base. Over and out!'

The soliloquy finished, the boy turned the jet for home at the
other end of the lawn.

Sandingham returned to the lounge, sat in the chair and sank
his head into his hands. If games were real, he thought, humans
would be infinitely kind and good and just. But they weren't.

After a minute or two he got up, left the hotel lobby and
mounted the four steps from the covered porch to the lawn.
Sandingham saw that the boy was occupied in excavating further
defensive trenches around his hospital with his hands, scooping
the earth out and piling it over a hidden bunker containing a jeep.
He knelt on the damp grass by the lad.

'Hello.'

The boy started, for he had not heard Sandingham approach.
A look of quick terror flashed across his face.

'Hello,' he answered tentatively, looking around to ensure that
no one was watching him talk to the mad man, the crazy guy, the
mok tau.

Sandingham pointed to the tank and guns.

'Don't you think that having guns there puts the sick men at
risk? After all, if there were no guns there would be no need for
the enemy to attack the hospital.'

'No. Red Chinese and North Koreans don't care about such
things. They bomb anything. Everything needs guarding.'

'But the last attack came to nothing. Not one bomb fell.'

The boy chose to ignore this observation. He had been a British pilot then, on a mission against the Communists. The politics were reversed now.

'This is Korea, is it?' Sandingham changed the subject and cast his eyes along the hedge.

'Yes,' the boy informed him, surprised an adult should take any notice of his playing. 'The hedge is a forest and the bank is a hill going down to a river.'

Sandingham saw through the hedge that a trace of water was running in the storm ditch. The skull-headed gardener had been on his rounds.

'This,' the boy continued, indicating a line in the grass left by the hose, 'is the border between north and south. This place where the hospital is is called "Ping Chong Sing". The hospital is a MASH.'

'What's a mash?'

'Mobile Army Surgical Hospital. It's where wounded men go. So you were wrong. You said the sick men, but they're not sick. They're hurt.'

'How many doctors are there in the tent?'

The boy gave him a guided tour of the hospital with its surgical ward, its operating tent, the ambulance (the back doors on it opened), the defences, the bomb shelters, the underground jeep hangar and the guards hiding in the 'trees' of the hedge, ready to snipe at the aircraft.

'David?'

It was the mother's voice.

'Here, Beth.'

She came out of the shade of the hotel porch and on to the lawn, catching Sandingham standing up as she approached. There was a look of annoyance on her face. He wondered if he smelt of drink or dope or both.

'Good afternoon,' he greeted her. 'Your son's having a good game here.'

'Yes,' she replied with unforthcoming deliberation. To the boy she said, 'Get your toys together, David. It's time we caught the hotel bus.'

The boy collected his toys into a wicker basket and followed his mother into the building. In the street, Sandingham could hear the hotel Ford shooting-brake start up.

In the hedge remained a toy soldier. It was made of plastic and was a man in khaki battle-dress with arms extended, about to hurl a grenade. Sandingham put the figure in his pocket.

'I've got your grenade thrower,' Sandingham told him when next he contrived to meet the boy: it was the following day, and he was having his tea in the dining room.

'Thank you,' replied the boy. He sat across the white-clothed table. 'Can I have him back?'

Sandingham took the toy from his pocket and returned it to its owner.

'I've some other toy soldiers you might like to see. They're in my room,' he said.

'Thank you,' repeated the boy, 'but I'm not allowed to talk too long.'

To avoid confusion or the scotching of his idea, Sandingham stood up.

'Another time, then.'

As he pushed the chair back under the table, the boy asked, 'What's your name?'

'Joseph. But you can call me Joe. And you're Davy.'

'David', he was corrected. 'Why do they call you "Hiroshima Joe"?'

Sandingham was caught off guard.

'Who's "they"?'

'Everyone. They call you that.'

'It's because I was there once. Long ago. In the war.'

'Oh . . .'

The boy was obviously disappointed not to have had the name explained or at least expanded upon. In this way, he might just as well be called 'Bombay David', because their P&O ship had stopped there on the way out and he had stood in the Gateway to The East on the waterfront and gone to the hanging gardens where the tower was that the dead people were put on so that the vultures could eat them.

In the garage below the hotel, the childen of the guests used to gather after school or in their spare time to chat or play. Mr Heng was annoyed by this, fearing the cars would be scratched or some child would be run over, but he had difficulty in catching them.

The main attraction of the place was not the cars but the fact that one end of the garage was sub-let to three young Chinese men who repaired cars there, serviced guests' vehicles, maintained the hotel bus and took in outside work. Their area was always littered with the used parts of cars, razor sharp and springy turnings of steel from their lathe, replacement bits, tools and multi-coloured cotton waste, and the air under the bare strip lights permanently carried the pungent scent of hot engine oil and hydraulic fluid. The children collected what scrap they could like magpies.

David's speciality was ball bearings. He was fascinated by their weight and shining steel coats. They rolled truer than glass marbles and, dropped from a height – say, his mother's first-floor balcony – on to concrete, they bounced like rubber, especially the small ones. His prize was one specimen nearly an inch in diameter.

Tucked away behind a Dodge, talking in broken English to the mechanic whose head and shoulders were under the sump of a jacked-up car, he saw Sandingham weaving his way through the parked vehicles.

'Hello, David. What are you up to?'

It was an innocent question and betrayed the fact that he knew the boy was in the garage without the company of his peers who were flying paper darts from the lounge balcony and getting into trouble for it.

'Ah Chow is going to give me a present because I'm helping him while Ah Foong is out.'

There was a clunk under the car, something dropped on to the concrete and a Chinese voice swore to itself.

'Davit! You han' me big ren-ch, pleas'.'

An open palm appeared by the front wheel. The boy placed a monkey wrench in it.

'T'an' you.'

The hand withdrew and re-appeared.

'You wan' dis one?'

In the fist was a ball race three inches across and dripping light oil.

'Yes, please!'

His reply was near ecstacy. He took it.

'Thank you very much. *M koi.*'

The boy sat on the bumper of the black Dodge and spun the race in his fingers. Oil flicked on to his bare knees and he wiped them clean with a tuft of cotton waste. Sandingham leaned against the next car. He didn't talk to David, but merely looked at him.

Bob must have been like this once. Poor Bob who was years dead yet not dead at all. As long as there is memory of something, then a part of that something must still exist.

For several nights, Sandingham had lain awake, half-drunk, and dreamed of Bob. In his thoughts, the boy and Bob had become synonymous. One was the other. Now, as he watched the boy entranced in his wheel bearing, he could see his lover once more, untainted by war or fear and unstained by blood or sweat. There was a similarity between the boy and the much-creased photo Sandingham kept under the chipped glass top in his room. It wasn't age or even physical appearance. It was the naivety of youth, the unmarked experience of undamaged innocence. It was this that made him love the boy, though he had never consciously felt that way for a child before. Not that he could recall.

As he left the garage, he saw that the Chinese mechanic had marked the calendar over the workbench up to date. It was Saturday.

When next he saw David, the boy was sitting on his own in the lounge. He was sobbing and his face was moist. A dribble of saliva hung on his lip and he sucked it in. He sniffed and blew his nose. Sandingham wanted to hug the boy, caress him, kiss his tears. Of course, he did not dare and instead sat next to him, his heart pounding with the shared ache.

'What's the matter, David?'

The boy looked at him then bent his head to stare at his shoes. He held out a manilla envelope.

Sandingham accepted this and saw that it was addressed to 'David' and the address. No surname. He opened it and took out a buff sheet of paper with a typed message upon it; the names and places and the date were filled in by indelible pencil.

Dear David, [he read]

I regret that I must write to inform you of the sad loss of your relation/friend [the former was deleted] DANIEL KERRINS who was killed in action on Thursday last. He died bravely and without pain, fighting with honour and glory in the service of his country and the British Commonwealth.

He requested of me that I send to you the enclosed with his affection.

Yours sincerely,

Unit chaplain.

There was no signature: Sandingham knew that the padre had had to write probably thirty such letters that day and in his anguish and exhaustion had forgotten to sign. He couldn't have known he was writing to a child.

Tipping up the envelope, he let slip into his palm a felt uniform shoulder tab. On it was one word: AUSTRALIA.

He folded the letter, replaced it in the envelope with the badge and gave it back to David.

'I'm sorry, David. Very sorry.'

Died without pain . . . with honour and glory: so much army bull with which Sandingham had been familiar too often and for too long. To have given the priest the message to send the badge meant that Daniel Kerrins knew he was going to die and that meant he was in hideous pain. There was nothing honourable or glorious about dying with your guts hanging free or retained only by your tunic buttons or your webbing belt and flies. There was nothing magnificent about meeting death with your hand projecting from a wall of rubble or your body hanging from the mudguard of a Humber.

Back in his room, he lay on his bed and closed his eyes. Bob's faded photo gazed emptily up through the glass to the ceiling.

He telephoned Francis Leung at nine o'clock on the Monday morning at the only contact number he had for him. Of course, the call was taken by one of his men and Sandingham, in a telephone kiosk at the Star Ferry pier, was instructed to wait there until he was answered. Five minutes went by, then ten. Sandingham knew that Leung had received his message within seconds of the henchman hanging up: he was being kept waiting as a matter of protocol. To reply too soon would suggest eagerness, friendship, consideration even – emotions Leung did not want to have associated with him as far as Sandingham was concerned. Far better to keep him at arm's length.

It dawned on Sandingham that he might be kept waiting half an hour, long enough for the gardener from the house at Eleven-and-a-half-Mile Beach to drive Leung's car in to Kowloon, approach the kiosk and stab Sandingham once, neatly under the sternum. This was the reason for his choosing a booth at the Star Ferry at the height of the rush hour: it was surrounded by a tumult of people commuting across the harbour to Central District. He could scream or shout. He could fight and attract attention. Chinese would gather round, as they always did, the spectator nation, keeping back from the action but appreciating the drama of it. The Europeans crossing on the ferry would be the ones to take the initiative. They would come forward and beat off the assailant while another would have called the HKP who would screech up in a grey police Landrover and arrest the would-be assassin. He, in turn, would be traced to Leung. What happened after that would be in the lap of the gods . . .

The telephone rang. He let it ring three times in revenge delay then lifted the receiver.

'Yes?'

'Mista Sandinarm?'

He was disappointed. The delay had been meant to inconvenience Leung, not his go-between.

'Yes?'

'You wait.'

This was the inevitable instruction from any of Leung's men, be they on the phone or at the end of an alley. Several more minutes passed during which Sandingham's anxiety increased, which was exactly what Francis Leung intended.

'Is that you, Joseph?'

'Yes.'

'I did not see you on Saturday.' His voice was dense with reprimand. 'What do you want?'

'I need more time,' Sandingham pleaded. 'I can't get enough by stealing and I have no other means. And I badly need a pipe.'

'No sweat!' Leung told him with deliberate sarcasm, as if he were the master of the world who could shrug off disasters and disabilities as easily as a cloak. 'Just get some of the money and you will be allowed back to Ah Moy's place. Say two hundred dollars? Hong Kong, not American.' He laughed shortly. 'And as for time, Joe: tonight. Nine forty-five. You needn't come to me. I'll come to you, to save you the cost of the bus to Castle Peak. Be at . . . '

It was in his interests to keep Sandingham in a short supply of opium. Without it at all, Sandingham was useless and the money would be unforthcoming. In itself it was a paltry sum: it was the principle that counted. If one man got away with a small debt – especially a *gweilo* – then anyone would try it on.

'Wait. I need to write it down.'

'Don't!' Leung's voice was hard. 'Just listen and remember. You will.'

He gave an address in Kadoorie Avenue.

'And Joe – one more thing,' Leung added. 'Do not try and get anything from the shacks of refugees in Ho Man Tin. They have been given their instructions.' He laughed again but there was no humour in his voice.

The line went dead.

Sandingham spent the remainder of the morning preying on tourists, but with little luck. Now that the winter was almost upon them visitors were fewer and those who were present still were not of the wealthy summer variety. He succeeded in stealing forty-eight dollars from a woman in an Indian tailor's store in Kimberley Road. Knocking her handbag on to the floor, he had then picked it up for her, apologising profusely and removing her billfold as he did so. He obtained another twelve dollars, all of it in small change, in the cloakroom of a busy restaurant in Nathan Road, rummaging through coats left hanging in the gents while the attendant was out for a moment. But he was a long way short of the two hundred.

As he alighted from the Number Seven bus at the stop fifty yards past the hotel on the junction with Argyle Street, Sandingham saw David walking back from school. It was the midday lunch recess.

He was wearing khaki shorts, a white shirt and, sewn to the pocket, a yellow- and brown-striped shield-shaped badge with the letters 'KJS' along the top. He carried a small, square wicker basket containing his books, his coloured pencils, a towel and a few of his Dinky toys. Sandingham knew the sort of thing the boy took to school for he'd seen him open the basket and check the contents in the foyer one morning when he had been waiting for the rain to cease.

David had reached the pavement opposite the hotel, and now stood at the kerb waiting. The traffic was busy and fast-moving. He looked to left and right but seemed to be making no effort to step off the kerb. Sandingham was about to cross to help the lad over when one of the hotel roomboys appeared and, swiftly dodging between the passing cars, gained David's side and guided him through to the far pavement.

The opportunity lost, Sandingham was not upset. He knew that the first-floor roomboy was called Ching and he always helped him over the road whenever David's mother was out.

Sandingham went back to his room, hid his morning's takings and went to the dining room where he knew David would be eating his lunch on his own. He was right.

In a corner reserved for children in the lunch-hour, the boy was sitting eating cold chicken salad. In the absence of his mother's discipline, he had served himself with an over-abundance of mayonnaise of which he was more than fond. When he had the opportunity, he would put it on fried eggs and bacon and tomatoes, too. Sandingham had seen him do this. It reminded him of a Belgian Hong Kong Volunteer officer from the transit camp who, upon liberation, had done the same thing. It had made him violently sick.

He sat at the next table and ordered a sandwich and a glass of San Miguel. When it arrived, the beer glass was cold and perspiring. 'Good morning at school? Would you like a Coca-Cola?'

'Not very. We had fractions and decimals and I can't do them very well. We had Geography, too. About India and tea planting in Assam. And I should very much like a Coke. Thank you.'

Sandingham placed the order and it came in a glass as cold as the beer.

'Cheers!' said Sandingham.

The boy raised his drink but said nothing. He had not had another adult say this to him, except his father who did it in fun, not for real, like Hiroshima Joe did.

'What have you done today, Joe?' he asked.

David's use of Sandingham's Christian name gave him a warmth far inside his chest. It was good to be called 'Joe' by someone who wasn't out for something. He accepted the friendship and it fuelled his desire.

'I've had to go to work,' Sandingham lied, though it occurred to him that that was just what he had done in a manner of speaking. 'When you've had your lunch, would you like to see my soldiers?'

The boy thought about this for three mouthfuls. He had been distinctly and positively told by his mother not to associate with, talk to, be seen with, accept a drink or present from, or – above all – go to the room of Hiroshima Joe. To do so was strictly against her express commands. On the other hand, Joe was an adult. He was not a stranger, for everyone knew him. He was a bit cuckoo, but then so were many grown-ups. And his mother could make mistakes. She'd lost his monocular when they'd been at the beach in the summer, she had sewn his school badge on upside down and had had to unpick it, which was why the edge of it was frayed, and she had gone out to a party when his father was last in port and left her watch in the ladies' next to the officers' mess on the ship. And he was naughty: that he knew. She said so enough, but often smiled as she spoke. And he had put too much salad cream on his food, and she would have got batey at that if she'd been there. Surely one more tiny wrong was neither here nor there.

'Yes.'

And that was that.

When he had finished his meal, David went to his room and picked up one of his Grenadier Guards. The soldier's busby was a bit scratched and his rifle was bent. He carefully straightened it and filled in the scratch on the bearskin with a crayon. It looked as good as new. If Hiroshima Joe would swap this one for one of his own, it would be good. Grenadier Guards in dress uniform weren't much good in a war. They stood out and got shot at: the Hawker Hunter pilot could easily pot them off in the trees.

The guardsman in his pocket, he left his room with its door ajar and walked along the balcony towards Sandingham's.

For his part, Sandingham tidied his belongings and furniture, set his straight-backed chair beside the bed and switched the fan on rotate so that it spread its breeze.

There was a knock on the door. He opened it.

'Come in, David.'

The boy entered but did not shut the door behind him. Sandingham could not get past him to give it a shove and so he left it. There would be time enough for that.

'Hello, Joe.' The boy was unsure of himself, committing his sin. 'I've brought one of my soldiers. I thought you might like to swap him for one of yours.'

He fumbled in his pocket but the soldier's rifle got caught in the material and he had to use both hands to free it. The more he tried to get it out, the more entangled it became.

'Let me do it,' said Sandingham, leaning forward from where he was sitting on the edge of the bed. He waved his hand beckoningly, as a friend might. 'Come a little nearer.'

With childish trust, David stepped to the bedside. Sandingham started to shift the soldier through the material, but allowed his hand to brush against the front of the boy's shorts. Within a quarter of an inch of his fingers, Sandingham knew David's little cock was resting like a tiny caterpillar in his underpants. He let his hand slip on to the boy's bare leg.

'Just a minute. I think I can get at the soldier's gun. What kind of soldier is he?'

'A Royal Grenadier.'

'They stand very upright. He must be at attention in your pocket. Slope arms! Stand easy, private! I don't think he has. Let me pull the material tight.'

His hand slid down and up under the hem of the shorts. The boy felt nervous at this and Sandingham could sense him shivering a little with unreasoning fear. It was not the fear of terror, but the fear of the unexpected. He, too, had known that.

One finger slid under the elastic edge to the boy's underpants. He wanted the boy so much.

David squirmed.

'Keep still, Bob, it's all right,' Sandingham whispered. 'It's all right.'

'No!' said David. 'I don't want you to do that.'

He stepped back but Sandingham had a firm grip on his shorts.

'You stay here. I've still got to show you my soldier.'

It required little imagination, even in the mind of a small boy, to have a guess as to what soldier it was Sandingham had in mind.

David shouted, 'No!'

'Shut up!' Sandingham muttered, his temper firing up. 'I'll tell your mother you were in here if you're not quiet. Then she'll spank you.'

With a sudden tug, David wrenched himself backwards and against the door. It slammed shut. He was out of Sandingham's range but the door opened inwards and prevented his escaping without going back into Sandingham's reach.

'Stand still, David. Look.'

He did not. Instead, his eyes flashed with fright.

'Look at me, Bob. Look at me, please.'

Sandingham's hands were at the front of his trousers, his fingers shakily unbuttoning his flies.

'I'm not Bob. I'm David,' stammered the boy.

His words were quavering, for he was on the verge of weeping with fright and confusion.

The door handle turned and smacked against David's back. It pushed him on to the foot of the bed.

Sandingham, with all the speed he could muster, sat on the chair and at the same time propelled it back towards the desk. The further he could be from David the less could be inferred.

In the door stood Ching, the roomboy.

'What you do-in'?'

'Mind your own business and get out of my room.' Bluff was his only defence.

'Davi'. You come wif me. It time for you to go back to schoo'.'

David stepped towards his rescuer. The Chinese roomboy walked forwards to Sandingham.

'I know what you do. You dirty man! *Lun jai*! You filt'y man! You no like girl. You like small boy who no can fight you.'

He lifted his arm back and fetched Sandingham a powerful clout on the side of his head. It knocked him off the chair.

'I didn't mean to steal it,' Sandingham whimpered. 'I won't . . . Bob! Make him stop! Bob!'

The second explosion of agony hit him in the groin. The roomboy had kicked him as hard as he could in the testacles. It wasn't as vicious as it might have been or as straight a delivery as the Chinese had intended.

'Hiroshima Joe! Better you no talk Davi' nex' time. I see you talk to him one more time, I tell Mista Heng. You get t'rown out of hotel.'

He laughed at the man doubled up on the bed.

'You shi'!' he said and slammed the door.

Sandingham saw, as the door swung shut, David standing on the balcony corridor. He was grinning. In his hand was the guardsman, his rifle barrel snapped clean off.

As the ache subsided so Sandingham's self-reproach increased. He knew that it had been a foolish move. The one friend upon whom it seemed he might be able to rely, albeit only a small boy, had been rejected by a stupid approach governed by his plain yearnings and not by common sense.

He thought perhaps it was the lack of drugs that had heightened his sexual awareness. Opium was said to repress bodily desires. He had not wanted a man so much for a long while. And he had now to go and choose a mere boy.

At no point before had he ever had paederastic feelings. The very word 'paederast' made him flinch within himself. It was not in his code to consort with children and now he had broken that and was riddled with a shame which grew until he could no longer bear the guilt that flooded his thoughts.

If the mother discovered what had happened he was well and truly for it. It wouldn't take the roomboy to have him flung out; David's mother would call the police, her husband would fly back from Korea on compassionate leave and the case would be splashed about the pages of the *South China Morning Post* as he faced a judge in the law courts before the Bank of China on Hong Kong-side. They'd put him away in a secure hospital, dry him out from the booze, kill his habit and then incarcerate him in Stanley Gaol where the other prisoners would make his life a living hell. Child molesters – again the words struck a chill chord in him – were regarded as ordure by other criminals, whether they were petty thieves or hardened murderers. Accustomed as he was to being gaoled, he was not keen to relive the experience, even as a ward of the as-yet-uncrowned Her Majesty. It would be, he had to admit, no small poetic justice if he were to end up in Stanley: the Japanese had used the prison as their civilian camp during the occupation. All his liberty could have been thrown away for the failed seduction of a child.

Sandingham searched his memory of the encounter for a sign that he would be shopped. The roomboy had not said that he would tell the mother. But the Chinese had definitely said that he would the next time . . . Next time: never!

He tried to move and found the pain greatly reduced. The kick had glanced off his inner leg, and although the skin was badly bruised there his private parts were not as painful as he had supposed.

He lay back and tested straightening his legs. There was no pain. His kidneys did not hurt either. He stood up and it was not sore to stand or walk.

He pulled a cigarette from a crushed packet of Lucky Strike on the table, and lit it. Seated in the chair, he looked out of the window at the blank wall opposite and fell into a reverie in which Bob appeared before him on the concrete outside as if in a magic-lantern show. He was highly critical of Sandingham's behaviour and castigated him for even thinking of shafting a child in such a squalid manner. His words, partly invented by Sandingham and partly a retention of memories long submerged in his brain, flung themselves into Sandingham's face like blasted sand. He rubbed his eyes, but the particles of grit simply ground into his eyeballs. His tears were irritant. He scoured them aside with a shirt sleeve.

The cigarette, hardly smoked, had burned down to his fingers and scorched them. He dropped the stub and, as he leant over to retrieve it from the parquet floor, he lost his balance and toppled sideways, his head glancing off the mattress on the bed which took on a hardness it did not possess.

He lay and immersed himself in an amalgam of remorse, disappointment, self-disgust, recrimination and the anxiety at being found out.

By three o'clock he felt more himself again and, despite the lesson learned at the expense of his budding friendship, he sensed sexual urges stirring in him. There was only one way remaining for him to gratify these, and that lay in Lucy and her company.

As he left the hotel, he saw David once more on the front lawn. He was setting up his soldiers in their familiar battlefield. He did not look at the boy, but stared ahead down the driveway.

'*Mok tau!*' the child said through the hedge. 'That means "blockhead" in Chinese. That's what you are. A crazy man! You haven't got your marbles.'

Sandingham stopped. The boy's inept use of the idiomatic would have been funny in another context. He slowly moved his head to face him through the mesh of the hedge.

'You shouldn't play with soldiers. Every time you play with soldiers, a war is born in your mind. And in war, men are killed.'

'*Mok tau!*' was the only answer he was given.

'You will learn. One day, somewhere, David, you will know I'm speaking the truth.'

'*Mok tau!*' the boy tauntingly repeated.

'Your father might be killed in a war. In Korea – like Daniel was.'

He spoke the words but could not quite think at that moment why he had taken such drastic and spiteful recourse against a small boy's gibes.

David fell silent. Through the foliage, Sandingham could see his face. He looked more grave than Sandingham could ever remember a child appearing. He was instantly sorry for what he had done but there was no way he could let David know. That one sentence had wreaked more havoc in the boy than the entire episode of crude, lustful advances could have done. The sexual fingerings he only partially understood. This he comprehended fully.

Once on the street, Sandingham peered back over his shoulder. The boy was hunched up on the stone balustrade of the hotel frontage watching his receding back with all the hatred he could muster.

'Lucy no wuk here now,' he was told by one of the other girls in the bar.

'Where is she?'

The girl hoisted her cheong-sam higher up her thigh and eased the zip in the slit up a few teeth. She pushed her small breasts forward and upward with her hands, her nipples ridging through the silk. Younger than Lucy, she was a good deal more experienced, having started on the game at fourteen. Her name was, improbably, Araminta.

'I no know.'

'You do,' Sandingham cajolled her. 'You'll tell me, won't you?'

He leant against the bar and touched her arm lightly. If he showed he fancied her, her pride might let her tell him. She shifted enticingly on the tall stool.

The barman appeared from the back quarters. He did not welcome Sandingham as he used to on his visits to Wan Chai.

'You go. You wan't ta'k girl, you pay an' screw.'

'Screw yourself,' Sandingham replied, putting his hand in his pocket. The barman thought better of it and disappeared the way he had come. People could hold all sorts of things in their pockets.

'How much you pay?' asked Araminta.

'Five dollars.'

'Ten dollar.'

Taking his hand from his pocket, he reluctantly gave her ten ones and she gave him the information.

'Lucy wuk in Happy Palladize Bar. It a ve'y good bar, ve'y classy joint.'

'Where is it?'

'Five dollar.'

'I can get the address from the phone book,' he said, 'but I'd rather have it from you to save me the effort. Give it to me and now and for nothing, or . . . ' He replaced his hand in his pocket.

'Okay. Tonnochy Road. Not ve'y far.'

He left the Vancouver Bar and headed eastwards along Lockhart Road. Each step took him nearer to Percival Street.

One of a group of urchins, playing on the arcaded pavement, flicked a scratcher under Sandingham's feet. Scratchers, as the children in the hotel called them, were pellets of red phosphorus and sulphur bound together with glue. When one trod on one or scratched it on a hard surface it ignited, and jumped about sparking and crackling loudly.

Concentrating on his memories, which were temporarily dis-
lodging even Lucy from his mind, Sandingham failed to notice the
scratcher and stepped straight on it. It fizzled and banged,
dancing from his feet across the paving stones. He leapt sideways
by instinct, bumping into one of the pillars supporting the building overhead. He ducked behind the upright and pressed himself
into it. The firework continued for a few seconds and spent itself.
The ragamuffins were most amused by Sandingham's antics of
avoidance and at once set two other scratchers going.

He looked down the expanse of Lockhart Road. Cars were
going to and fro. A rickshaw was being pulled along with a pile of
cardboard boxes in it. A dog sauntered across the street. Nowhere could Sandingham see the Indians with their .303s, or the
Japs: he could not hear a Bren gun rattling but believed he could
hear the sputter of small arms fire. He could hear, too, the crump
as the mortar shell hit above his head and the ceiling caved in. He
rushed over the road. A taxi screeched to a halt to avoid hitting
him.

'Dew lay lo mo!' swore the driver out of his window.

The children cantered about with glee.

Safely over the road, Sandingham composed himself. He
mopped his brow with a handkerchief and carried on walking, all
the while getting nearer and nearer to the place where Bob had
been killed.

The Happy Paradise Bar was indeed as up-market as Araminta
had suggested. As Sandingham entered he was not met by a
surfeit of bad, cheap taste composed of plastic curtains, plastic
seats and plastic bar tops. The lighting was typically subdued but
the lamps were of an expensive type and modern. The floor was
carpeted except where there was an oval area of planking left
bare to serve as a dance floor. The bar was made of mahogany
with a brass rail and leather trim and the cubicles were curtained
on the inside of filigree carved screens. There was a scent of
lavender and jasmine in the air. The girls were not chattering
loudly and coarsely to each other but sitting almost demurely
upon padded chairs at a table by the far end of the bar. Mr Wong,
Lucy's previous pimp, was nowhere to be seen.

She saw him before he spied her and, leaving the other whores,
she wove through the empty tables to his side.

'Hello, Joe.'

He turned and saw her, held her by her upper arm and kissed her fleetingly on the cheek.

'You free for a bit?' he questioned her, adding, 'I've missed you so much.'

'You go, quick,' she hissed. 'This place no good for you. You will come to much trouble if you stay here.'

He noticed immediately that her English had much improved.

'Rubbish!' he exclaimed. 'I'm just coming in to buy you a drink, take you out for half an hour.'

Whereas previously she might have replied, 'No can do, Joe,' now she said, 'It can't be done.'

'Why on earth not?'

He was getting impatient.

'I am not allowed, Joe. I am special girl here, booked for special customers.'

'The hell with that!'

'You not understand, Joe. This police bar.'

This took a moment to sink in. Then he understood. This was not a watering hole for US sailors on R&R to get loaded in; not a boozing spot for beery squaddies from Nathan Road and Murray Barracks. This was a bordello more or less reserved for the European officers of the Hong Kong Police.

'Lucy, can I see you later? Tomorrow, maybe. In the morning?'

'No. I am watched all day and all night. Now I no have rooms in other building. I live upstairs.' She looked at the ceiling. 'Nice room, but . . .'

She looked over Sandingham's shoulder. In one of the cubicles sat a man. He nodded to her, ever so slightly.

'I must go now. Sit with other girls. You do not stay here, Joe. You go.'

She walked quickly back to her seat, rejoining the girls who had watched their conversation in curious and awed silence. Sandingham took a step to follow her and halted.

From the cubicle came a sighing noise as the occupant stood up from the padded settle upon which he had been resting. He came out on to the carpet and stood facing Sandingham. He was a large and powerful man, half-Chinese and half-Filipino with more than a dash of Yank ex-marine stirred in, dressed in a smart three-piece suit with polished, two-tone shoes. His muscles moved under his tight-fitting clothes like the plates of skin on a reptile's back.

'You leave now, Joe,' he ordered, his mouth twisting on Sandingham's name.

'I'll have a drink first,' Sandingham replied brazenly. He had to call the play to save face. 'This is a bar and I'll have a San Mig.'

He moved away from the girls towards the counter. The Filipino did not move or try to stand in his way. He did not lift his hand but snapped his fingers by his side. The barman put down a bottle of spirits he was inverting into a chromium-plated holder and reached under the rack of mixers. He lifted out a three-foot-long riot truncheon.

'That's his bottle opener,' the Filipino explained. 'He'll open your bottle for you, if you want.'

Sandingham moved nearer. The truncheon was lifted ready and, without his expecting it, it was swung full at him. He dodged nimbly backwards to meet the blade of the Filipino's hand in the small of his back. He stumbled and fell over a table.

'Get the drift?'

He got the drift.

'Now get out.'

He raised himself to his feet and, glancing quickly in Lucy's direction, took in the full impact of the look of sorrow for him on her face.

'One thing more,' the Filipino threatened as Sandingham gained the entrance, his accent gaining a thick Hollywood pastiche. 'Don't try to get off with Lucy – or any of the other whores in this place.' As an afterthought, he added, 'Else Mr L gets to know. Y' hear?'

Sandingham heard.

'And if Mr L gets to know, sure as shit sticks you'll get your ass whipped by the law.'

So, in exchange for the provision of high-class tarts with no hint of the clap, Leung had police protection for his business. Against that, what could a drunk bum, hungry for a pipe, do? Not a lot.

It was dark when Sandingham reached the Star Ferry pier, walking there along the waterfront from Tonnochy Road. In the harbour, several British and American warships swung at anchor, each of them illuminated by strings of bulbs hanging from the masts. Out in Kowloon Bay there was the darkened bulk of an aircraft carrier. The Royal Hong Kong Yacht Club building at the end of the mole at Causeway Bay appeared like another, ungainly craft seeking refuge in the calmer water. The lights coruscated upon the surface, rippling in a stiff, cold breeze.

He paid to travel on the cheaper, lower deck and waited in a crowd of coolies and amahs for the next ferry to pull in to the jetty. The longer he waited, the more he contemplated his position and how he might shake away from it. All the way across the harbour and up to the hotel on the crammed evening bus, he was lost in considering his alternatives.

At twenty past nine Sandingham counted out his entire money supply again. He had seventy-one dollars. Once again, he put it in a hotel airmail envelope, folding it double in the hope that it increased its value by thickness if not by worth. At nine twenty-five he quit his room and worked his way down the rear stairs to the hotel tradesmen's entrance, pausing *en route* to feel behind a box of tinned tomatoes for his hidden weapon. He was careful, slipping out into Emma Avenue, that no one saw him. It was only a few minutes' walk to Kadoorie Avenue.

The avenue was a tree-lined road that wound serpent-like up a low hill. The buildings upon it, some of them houses and others low-storied, luxury apartment blocks, were the homes of the exceptionally rich. Few people in Hong Kong could afford a house at all, let alone a garden, but some of these properties had substantial gardens with shrubs and flower borders and trees that kept the buildings cool in the summer and protected them from the strong, cold winds of winter which blew straight down from northern China.

The lighting in the street was subdued and provided by old-fashioned lamps in glass lanterns on cast-iron poles. The branches of pines hung over the stone or brick walls of the gardens, and the pavements were crisp with fallen needles. For this Sandingham was grateful, for the debris silenced his footsteps somewhat.

The gates to the house were shut. Mounted on the wall beside them, covered by a lintel in the shape of a classical-style Chinese roof, was a bell-push. Sandingham pressed it and the light in the switch went out as he rang. Over his head, in an adjacent pine tree, a light snapped on. A Chinese guard came to the gate.

'Who you?'

'My name is Mr Sandingham.'

The guard scrutinised his wristwatch, holding it at an angle to catch the light from the tree.

'You early. Not you turn yet. Qwartah 'our. You come.'

He walked off through the shrubbery.

It was certainly not what Sandingham had expected. He had thought he would be taken in, given a talking to, have his pecunary offering accepted and then be ejected into the shadows of Kadoorie Avenue within a matter of minutes.

Thirty yards up the road Sandingham stopped by a China Light and Power junction box on the pavement. It was between street lamps and in semi-darkness. From it he could see the gateway. To make sure he was unobserved, he walked past it and into a cul-de-sac on his left, then doubled back to squat down on his haunches by the metal cube. Thus camouflaged, he began his watch on the entrance to the gardens.

He did not have to wait long. A Cadillac drove up the hill and the chauffeur stopped it by the gate, the sidelights off and the engine running. The gate opened and a European came smartly out from the grounds, crossed the road and got into the car. It drove off; the headlights were not switched on until it was halfway to Prince Edward Road. As it passed him, Sandingham hopped his way round the junction box.

He rang again and the guard reappeared.

'Who you?' he asked again, although he could clearly see Sandingham.

The name given, he unbolted the gate and allowed Sandingham to enter.

There was a short driveway curving round to a circular area before a porch. The house was modernistic and square, with deep-set balconies along the top, second storey. To the left of the porch was an American convertible with the roof up. It struck a tiny chord in Sandingham's mind.

The guard pressed a buzzer on the front door and it opened.

'You go in. Wai'.'

He did as he was told.

The hallway was marble-floored, the walls hung with ornately framed mirrors and pictures of Chinese scenes in a mountainous region. Upon a table was a white telephone and, above it, a white-fronded pampas-like plant dipping its ferny seeds over the telephone directory. Sandingham noticed that the disc of card in the centre of the dial had been reversed. No visitor could tell the number. A stairway rose to an upstairs landing.

A door at the far end of the hall opened and an elderly amah in servant's uniform, black trousers and a loose white shirt, shuffled towards him. Her feet were tiny, having been bound in her childhood. She had a slight stoop and her hands seemed older than the rest of her body. She kept her eyes on the floor before her.

'Come,' she instructed without even looking at him and he followed her off to the right down a passage carpeted with coarse, colourful Afghan rugs.

The amah stopped at a deep-stained wooden door and knocked quietly. She waited for a moment, then twisted the brass handle, stepping aside that Sandingham might enter.

The room was large. The marbled floor was strewn with deep-piled Tientsin carpets and on the beige-coloured walls hung a miscellany of pictures. Sandingham recognised some of them as Chinnery's. A wood fire was burning. On the mantelpiece above stood another gilt-framed mirror before which stood a huge ivory statue of the Goddess of Mercy, Kuan Yin. Her frail figure was erect and hanging in wraiths of carved ivory cloth, as if she were dressed in clouds. Sandingham appreciated, in a morbid way, the irony of such a deity in such a room.

Before the fire was ranged a lounge suite in white leather, with maroon, emerald and azure Thai silk cushions scattered upon it. Two of the four armchairs had tall backs. The tables were all under a foot high and made of camphorwood. An antique brass tea urn rested on a trellis by the curtains that, Sandingham realised from their size, must cover a large glass patio door leading on to the garden.

'Good evening, Joseph.'

Francis Leung was behind him, had been there as the door opened. He was holding a goblet of brandy which he had just poured from a cocktail cabinet. He was wearing a dinner suit.

'Good evening, Francis.'

'Mr Leung, please. Sit down.'

Leung pointed to an armchair in the centre of the room. As Sandingham went towards it he discovered that there was another person present, seated in one of the high armchairs.

She was a remarkably beautiful woman in her late teens or early twenties. Such beauty could only be the possession of a Eurasian – and of Francis Leung. Her cheeks were high and her eyes almond. Her skin was smooth and held the inner glow of health. Her fingers, where they rested on the white leather, were long and artistically thin. Her hair was auburn and gleamed in the firelight. She was wearing an ankle-length evening dress of black brocade with a sparsely embroidered decoration of tiny blossoms.

'Good evening,' Sandingham greeted her. He had not expected anyone else to be in the room save perhaps a guard. It was unfortunate.

She tilted her head to him and smiled, but there was no friendship in her movements. Leung made no attempt to introduce them.

'Will you have a drink, Joseph?'

'Yes, thank you. I'd like a scotch.'

While Leung poured this into a cut-glass tumbler, Sandingham studied the room. He wanted to say, 'What a nice place you've got here,' but thought the better of it. Instead, he looked at the girl and then it came to him. He had seen her, months before, driving the convertible parked outside, on the day he had gone to see Francis Leung when the old man and the youth had tried to get his money off him at the bus stop by Kowloon City.

'Here.'

Leung handed him a glass with a mere splash of good whiskey in it. The amount was intended as an insult but Sandingham tried to ignore this and sipped it, enjoying the aroma in his nose as much as the burn in his throat.

'Thank you.'

'Now. Have you the two hundred?'

Sandingham reached deep into his pocket and produced the envelope. It was slightly stained from rubbing against oily metal.

He could smell it as it left his hand. As he walked across the room and took it, Leung did not.

'This doesn't feel like two hundred,' Francis Leung observed, slitting the envelope open with his index finger. 'It feels,' and he flicked through the notes, 'like seventy-five.'

'Seventy-one,' Sandingham replied, surprised that Leung could be so accurate. He drained his glass.

'I see.' He put his hand out. 'Another scotch?'

Sandingham lifted the tumbler.

Leung put it down on one of the tables, turning away as he did so and counting through the money.

'Seventy-one bucks,' he mused. He placed the money in his pocket, picked up the empty glass and, quick as a cat, smashed it into Sandingham's ear. The glass did not break but Sandingham's ear began to bleed.

'Not even the interest,' Leung said as if nothing had happened.

'I'm sorry? . . . '

Sandingham couldn't hear. His ear was twitching with the fluid movement of his blood.

Leung leaned over.

'Not even the interest,' he repeated. 'I still want the whole amount. This is inconvenience money.'

'How can I?'

'I do not know. How do I care? It is your business.'

'It wasn't my fault.'

'No. It was the fault of the Chinese Government. But you are responsible for my investment in you.'

It was time to appeal. Bargaining was useless and reasoning less so. Sandingham put a hand to his head to staunch the blood. It was congealing inside his ear.

'Does nothing of the past affect you? We were once equals, once in the same hell and we helped each other. In the trenches of Kai Tak. Against the Japs. We fought side by side.'

'No. We were never equals. We did not fight together. You were a prisoner, a slave worker. I was the fighter. I took the risks. I killed the Japanese, not you. You never ambushed Japanese in the New Territories. I did. You surrendered. I would never surrender.'

'But the circumstances – '

'They don't count,' Leung interrupted him. 'You should have died – fighting. That's the trouble with you Europeans. You value life too highly. Life in the East is cheap.'

Sandingham knew only too well life's intrinsic value. But nearly four years in prisoner-of-war camps had taught him the lesson that it was not cheap at all, but cost dear. And it wasn't just Europeans' lives either. Mr Mishima's face flashed across his mind's eye.

'So don't pretend, Joseph, that you are a comrade of mine. You are just like my guards. Expendable in time. They know that. Why do you not accept it?'

It dawned on Sandingham then that all that Number 177 had done for them in the war was not done for them at all. It was a part of business. That made him furious, but he locked his anger in.

'So now what?' he questioned Leung sullenly.

'So now you have at least three hundred dollars by Saturday. Or else I may have to accept that you are a loss and write you off as one.'

There was a knock on the door. Leung spoke and the amah entered with a miniature package the size of a matchbox. It was placed on the drinks cabinet. She left as soft-footedly and as limpingly as she had come. In her was epitomised, that moment, all the cruelty for which Leung stood: an old woman who had had her feet bound and deformed as an infant in the dictates of good taste and the sexual fetish the Chinese had for small feet.

He did not have to be told what was in the package, wrapped as it was in brown greaseproof paper, but Leung could not resist telling him.

'Opium,' he said. 'But not for you. Not until I get the settlement. Three hundred this Saturday, three hundred the next and then we'll see.'

Picking up the drug, he tossed it to the girl who caught it daintily and put it in an evening bag.

'A gift for a friend,' she said mockingly, the first words she had spoken. Her accent was very feminine and yet icily cold.

'Now you leave, Joseph. We have a supper party to attend on the other side of the harbour. I will show you out.'

He spoke briefly in Cantonese to the girl who stood up and smoothed her hair in the mirror.

Sandingham raised himself from his armchair, his right hand in his pocket. Leung half-faced him as he put out an arm to open the door.

'I'm sorry about the money,' Sandingham muttered as he got nearer to Leung.

The steel spike was so much heavier than he had expected it to be. But it was so fast. He tore it up through the material of his jacket, through the white front of Leung's evening shirt and under his ribs. He slid it in so easily. He wondered if perhaps the oil on it helped.

Leung spluttered. His left hand dropped from the unturned door knob and his right grabbed for his heart. He dropped on to the marble and his blood puddled out from his chest. Falling, the spike that was jammed in a rib-space tore free from Sandingham's coat.

The girl heard the brief commotion and looked over her own shoulder in the mirror. She saw Leung drop and she also saw Sandingham halfway across the room towards her. She opened her mouth but not a sound issued from it. Sandingham spun her round, hit her on the side of her head with his fist and knocked her to the floor. He then kicked her in the side. She grunted. He grabbed hold of the ivory statue. It must have weighed ten pounds. He bludgeoned her head with it. Her blood smeared the yellowing ivory.

By the door, Leung was moving. His free hand was trying to get at the inside pocket of his jacket. Sandingham kicked him hard on the side of his neck.

Sandingham secured the lock on the door, then turned Leung over. In a shoulder holster under Leung's jacket was a pistol. It was a Webley .455 Mark VI: standard British Army issue in the war. The weapon was in prime condition.

Leung was still breathing. Sandingham pulled the spike free. He would have liked to have used the pistol but it would have made much too much of a noise in the confinement of the room.

Leung's eyes were glazed with encroaching death. He attempted to say something.

'Don't try to speak, you bastard,' Sandingham whispered.

It would have been good, Sandingham thought, to have left Leung to die slowly, but to do that might have risked him surviving. He had to finish it.

'The debt's settled now, you son of a bitch,' he said. 'For me, for Lucy, for the whole fuck-up you've made of my life.'

Leung's eyelids fluttered, which Sandingham took to be comprehension.

From Leung's pocket he retrieved the seventy-one dollars in the tell-tale envelope. He was disappointed to find nothing in his wallet. Rich men hadn't the need to carry cash, he reasoned.

He held the spike over Leung's forehead for a moment, then plunged it into the skull. It took three attempts to get it through the dome of bone. At each strike, Leung's limbs jerked, marion-nette-like.

Sandingham returned to the girl and opened her handbag. He took out the money it contained and the opium and tossed what was left on to the fire.

He checked that the patio doors were not locked, then put out the lights.

The drinks cabinet was very well stocked. Good cognac, ordinary brandy, scotch, bourbon, gin, vodka, rice spirit, rum . . . more than one bottle of most. He started with the white rum and finished with the brandy.

The final bottle he emptied in a stream towards the fire. It ignited and the flames spread in a leisurely flow across the spilt alcohol towards the leather suite and the tables and paintings and the two corpses which Sandingham had replaced in their chairs, close to the fire. For good measure, he had dowsed both bodies with spirits. Looking back, he saw them both aflame but could not bear to stand and watch: he had had enough of that.

He drew the curtains after him, but left the patio doors open by a foot or so. Fires need to breathe.

The garden wall was eight feet high and decorated along the top with broken glass. He climbed a pine tree, stepped gingerly on to the glass and jumped into the street. Still no one in sight. Keeping as much as he could to the shadows, he went down the hill to Argyle Street, crossed over and was in his hotel room, shaking with uncontrollable excitement, within five minutes. He opened the window, but did not hear the fire brigade racing along Argyle Street. By now, they would be too late anyway. It was then he sliced open the opium.

He was not sorry that he had killed Leung. It was his only viable option. However, the act of killing both him and the girl had filled him with disgust. He lamented that the situation had left him only this way out.

To kill was so sordid, so messy, so incredibly irreversible. To destroy life was to eradicate creation and the beauty of existence, totally and irrevocably. His grandfather had once said to him that when you shot a rabbit you weren't killing an animal but causing a complex machine to cease functioning: you were stopping for eternity a living unit.

The girl had not been in his plans, and he was sorry he had been forced to get rid of her too. In her case, it was real beauty he was removing from the world. It was as bad as setting fire to the Chinnery paintings and the ivory statue of Kuan Yin. They could not be reconstructed from the ashes. The thought of ashes made him shiver. Setting light to their bodies had been the worst thing, far worse than killing them, even. He knew what they must look like by now.

Yet the more he thought over his actions of the evening the more he grew distanced from them. Like killing the guard in the wheelhouse of the *Lisbon Maru* – it was necessary. It was a function that had to be fulfilled. One didn't question it. One did it as a matter of course. For the python to live, the hare must die. Some Chinese sage must have drawn that conclusion, and stated it so.

The magical fumes from the pipe began to seep into his nerves.

He reassessed his day. A new friend lost through selfish blundering. An old friend lost through hatred and the inner conceit of men always to do better than their peers, regardless of the price. A killing – two killings – that showed to him he was just the same as ever, just as capable of inhuman behaviour as ever.

Drifting into the blissful mist of the opium, Sandingham allowed his regrets to fade. For a moment, though, just before the drug owned him completely, he wondered if the same reasoning hadn't been logically structured in the mind of Fujihara as he had commanded Willy's firing squad, or in Mr Hoshigima's son's thoughts as the undercarriage dropped away from his aeroplane or in the brain of Captain Parsons, in the belly of the B29, as he gave the last screw its final tweak.

The police did not arrive to arrest him. For three days, Sandingham remained in the hotel fearing that every footstep along the corridor was an inspector and two constables with a warrant and a pair of handcuffs.

The story did not reach the newspapers, either. There was no report of the fire or the deaths. A week later, however, there were a few column inches on an inner page about the remains of two bodies – a man and a woman – being found in the sea off Lau Fau Shan. They had been badly burned and identification was impossible. It was also impossible to discern the date of death. It was assumed they were illegal immigrants who had met with a grizzly fate trying to negotiate the treacherous waters of Deep Bay.

So, in this manner, Francis Leung and the girl were ghosted away by their henchmen.

It did not take Sandingham long after reading the article to realise that his threat came not from the law but the outlaw. Revenge would be sought.

He considered going to the police himself, giving himself into protective custody. They would surely be glad to welcome the killer of a drug runner, major fence and Triad leader. Then he remembered the Happy Paradise Bar and that put an end to that.

His safest bet was to stay as close to the hotel as possible. In a crowd he would be all right. On his own he would be at no small risk.

With the money he had, he paid Mr Heng for another fortnight. Heng, for his part, soon grew concerned by the fact that Sandingham now resided in the hotel all the while. As long as the Englishman was ensconced in his room, or the lounge, or the hotel bar, he was not earning money, no matter how he might obtain it as a general rule.

The owners of the hotel were getting restless about his being a paying guest, never mind a free-loading one. The tale of his enviegling David up to his room had run through the hotel staff and the manager had felt duty-bound to relay it to his employers.

They were worried in case the guests got notice of it. Many were on friendly terms with the employees.

Additionally, the end of Sandingham's fortnight would fall just before Christmas. To turf Sandingham out into the street at such a time would seem uncharitable in the extreme, petty even, and mar the festivities the hotel staff intended to put on for their residents. After all, he was a European.

Mr Heng tried his best to persuade his employers to allow Sandingham to remain until a week into the new year, but they were adamant. He was not to be given any more credit, not so much as a day's worth.

Sandingham accepted Heng's information with a calmness that took the manager aback.

'It's all right, Mr Heng. I quite understand how things are. I shall seek some alternative accommodation.'

'If I can help you, Mr Sandingham? I have a friend who manages a cheaper hotel near Jordan Road. I'm sure . . . '

'I appreciate that: thank you. But I think I'll be okay.'

Quite how this move was to be achieved was beyond him.

Even with the opium to act as a kind of restorative to his system, Sandingham did not feel well. Every now and then, even in the middle of doing something like holding a cigarette or a knife and fork, his fingers went numb and prickly. The irritation was not unlike the electric feet from which he had suffered in the war years. His skin, after the summer months of clearing up, once more started to flake. He attributed this to the winter, but he also knew that even in the severe snows of Japan he had not had this trouble.

Worse than this were other symptoms. His urine began to burn again as he passed water and his stomach started playing up. He put this down to eating out of a can in his room. Perhaps he had stannic poisoning or something. However, even after being careful and consuming his stolen food on a plate, the indigestion and diarrhoea continued. He examined the tins in the boxes on the back stairs one night by the aid of a torch 'borrowed' from a roomboy. None of them showed signs of rust or deterioration.

It occurred to him that he might have contracted a venereal disease. He studied his penis closely. There were no signs of inflammation, pustules or broken blood vessels. It looked quite normal, yet it hurt like hell to piss.

In the mornings he woke unrested. His back, calves and biceps ached as if he had rheumatism. One of his teeth was loosening in its socket.

A week before Christmas, he awoke one morning to find the pillow under his head streaked with hairs. He touched his head. The hair was loose. He could pull little tufts of it free without feeling any jab of pain whatsoever. He sat up sharply with alarm. He was hit by a wave of giddiness. The light, which he had left on during the night, hurt his eyes as if he had just been freed from the *eiso* cell. He grappled for the chair back, but could not judge the distance to it and missed. His hand fell on to his stomach and his fingers hurt badly where they touched it. Looking through a wave of nausea, he saw that his fingernails were bruised dark mauve beneath the cuticle and one of them was weeping a straw-coloured, plasma-like fluid.

'Christ!' he uttered to his swaying figure in the mirror. 'I'm falling apart!'

It was like a nightmare. Maybe it was a nightmare, induced by going back on to the dope after being half-weaned off it. Or perhaps he had the DTs. He wasn't aware he was an alcoholic, but what else it could be he could not imagine.

He realised that he had to see a doctor, although he was not registered with one and had not been to visit one since returning to Hong Kong in late 1947. Only, to go to a doctor was to present his addiction to opium, and that would lead to complications both medical and legal. He could do without that.

An idea came to him. If he were to cross to Hong Kong Island, he could present himself to one of the military hospitals, either the Army establishment at Bowen Road or, on the other side of The Peak, the Royal Naval hospital at Mount Kellett. If he were to arrive in the out-patients' clinic as an ex-serviceman in transit through the colony they might just believe him and treat him. It wouldn't matter if they found out about his habit because he would not be a resident or one of their regular patients. They might ignore that aspect of his condition.

With familiar skill, he concocted a tale and left in the hotel bus with the guests who commuted daily to Central District.

The Star Ferry was packed and there was standing room only. This was handy, for it not only afforded Sandingham the safety of numbers that he required but also provided him with the opportunity to filch over one hundred dollars from an overcoat hung on one of the seat backs.

He was not as safe as he had anticipated. As he was queueing in the jostle to disembark at the Hong Kong-side jetty a well-dressed Chinese, whom he had noticed was one of the last passengers to board in Kowloon, running down to ramp to the gangway as it was about to be raised, leaned over and spoke to him.

'Mr Sandingham, good morning. Travelling across the harbour to the office?'

He made no reply. He did not recognise the man at all, but guessed his mission.

'Perhaps we might have a chat the next time you leave your hotel?' The man's voice was urbane, polite and carried a San Franciscan accent. 'My name is Choy. We have a mutual acquaintance in Francis Lee-Ung. Or, to be more accurate,' he said with exactitude, 'we had.'

'Fuck off!' Sandingham muttered.

The gangway hit the jetty with a thud.

'Good morning to you, too, Mr Sandingham. Until we meet again in more friendly surroundings.'

The Chinese got off the ferry ahead of Sandingham who was very watchful when he gained the waterfront.

Here he was at his most vulnerable. A car could pull up to the kerb, he could be bundled into it and it could be away down Connaught Road before anyone could take any action – if, indeed, something appropriate occurred to them. Ten or fifteen minutes' drive would have the car parked in a secluded sideroad near Pok Fu Lam Reservoir. After a lengthy session of excruciating pain, he would be left to die tied to a tree on the lower slopes of High West, well away from the road so that he was not discovered, his mouth jammed with his shirt and one or two of his fingers and, for good measure, a wadge of his own dung.

There was no sign of 'Choy' who had vanished into the rush-hour crowds.

Sandingham allowed three taxis to pull away from the rank before he hailed the fourth. None of the drivers had sought his custom so he assumed that there was no one cab planted there to kidnap him.

'Bowen Road Hospital,' he directed and lay back in the rear passenger seat.

A dizziness began to wave over him again and he strove against it like a man fighting nausea. He had to remain alert in case the taxi driver was one of those sent to get him. Being in the rear seat gave him an advantage. The dizziness passed.

The taxi drove round the Hong Kong Cricket Club ground and climbed Garden Road past the Peak Tram station. At the top, by the Botanical Gardens, the driver changed down into second gear and negotiated the left-hand hairpin bend into Magazine Gap Road. As the car went over the Peak Tram bridge Sandingham looked down the hillside to see the roof of the house he and Bob had made love in that day. It seemed a hundred years ago.

Bowen Road was narrow and twice the taxi had to pull in to the kerb to allow through a private car approaching from the opposite direction. Each time this happened, Sandingham half-expected a bullet to crack through the window.

The taxi finally passed the sentry at the gate, who nodded them through and halted by a row of parked staff cars and an ambulance. Sandingham paid the driver and added a tip he could ill afford. He was relieved, even surprised, to have arrived safely.

The powerful smell of carbolic and medication met him at the door to the out-patients' admissions office. He knocked and walked straight in.

'Can I help you?'

The orderly on duty, a corporal, did not get up from behind his desk. He saw no need to rise for a civilian and especially one that wasn't all that well dressed. It was important for Sandingham to gain the upper hand.

'Don't you stand up for a senior officer in the RAMC any more, corporal?'

The veiled, threatening tone of sarcasm in his voice, if not his appearance, suggested an officer's grip on command.

'I'm sorry, sir.'

In struggling to rise, the orderly banged his knee firmly on an open drawer. The pencils inside rattled.

'I want an appointment to see a doctor. It is quite urgent as I'm on my way through to Seoul and due to take off this afternoon. Two . . . ' A slip was about to be born and he corrected it. 'Fourteen hundred hours.'

'Can I see your movement orders, please, sir?'

'No. They're with my baggage at Kai Tak. Under guard. You know how it is.' He winked the wink of an officer to a subordinate.

'Yes, sir. If you'll just sit here for a moment, sir, I'll see what I can do for you. May I have your name, sir?'

Sandingham gave it and sat on a chair by the door. The orderly picked up a telephone. He talked on it for a few minutes, trying several extensions. Finally, he hung up.

'Dr Gresham will see you, sir. If you'll . . . '

There was a rap on the door and another orderly came in.

'Garner. Take . . . '

'Captain,' Sandingham interpolated.

'Take Captain Sandingham to Dr Gresham. Room – '

'Yes, corp.'

He turned jauntily on his heel and went out into the passage, his boots scuffing on the polished stone floor. For effect, Sandingham raised his eyebrows as the private went out.

'National Service,' explained the corporal. 'Can't do nothing with 'em, sir.'

Sandingham followed the private and was conducted along corridors painted in cream and green gloss until they reached a matching green door. The private knocked, waited and opened it for Sandingham. The doctor was seated at a general-issue desk signing sheets of foolscap.

'Do have a seat. Be with you in a moment, Captain.'

His rank had evidently been phoned through ahead of him.

The doctor screwed his fountain pen into its top and looked up.

'What can I do for you?'

'I'm not feeling at all well,' Sandingham informed him. 'I wondered if you could help me.'

He described the symptoms in some detail while Gresham left his chair and came round the corner of the desk to perch on the front of it, listening in a friendly manner.

When Sandingham was done, the doctor said, 'Right-o. Strip to your underpants, will you?'

As he was undressing, the doctor watched him. These were not the clothes of a staff officer in civvies on his way to Korea. The undergarments were shabby, the trousers creased and worn shiny at the seat. They smelt faintly of sweat and cheap soap.

'Sit on the couch. Now . . . '

He examined Sandingham in silence for at least five minutes, except for a curt 'Breathe in' or 'Cough' or 'Does that hurt?' until he removed his stethoscope and straightened up.

'I'll go on with my examination,' he said, 'after you tell me why you've lied through your teeth to get in here.'

Holding back as much as he felt he could, Sandingham admitted that he was a resident in Hong Kong, had little money, had been in the Army and been a Jap PoW, was down on his luck and needed help. He made sure that he did not exhibit any of the signs of pomposity upon which he had relied with the corporal to get him the appointment.

Gresham sighed. 'I can understand why you are reluctant to go to a local quack,' he said when Sandingham stopped. 'How long have you been addicted?'

'Three, maybe four years.'

'Drink much?'

'Beer, some scotch. Not a lot. Can't afford it.' Sandingham smiled self-deprecatingly.

'Now that we know you don't have a plane to catch, we've got a bit more time. I think we'll need it.' Gresham picked up the phone. 'Rollings? Dr Gresham here. Cancel my rounds for the morning. Ask Dr Tailling if he'll take them. Or Dr Frazer. And ask Dr Stoppart if he'll be so good as to pop along to my room.' Pause. 'No. Now, if he could.'

He caught Sandingham's concerned look.

'No need to worry. I'm not shopping you.' He hung up the telephone. 'I just want another doctor to see you. Second opinion. Two consultations are better than one – like heads,' he joked, to put his new patient at his ease.

Dr Stoppart joined them within a couple of minutes. He was in his fifties, dangled a pair of pince-nez spectacles on a black ribbon round his neck and wore a charcoal-grey suit. Gresham had on his uniform.

The two doctors examined Sandingham for over an hour. As

they were drawing their study of him to a close, a Chinese orderly
arrived with a tea trolley and they each took a cup of tea,
obtaining a third for Sandingham, ensuring that his was weaker
than their own.

The cross-examination then began. They asked about his
general health prior to the appearance of the symptoms, his
appetite and diet, his sex life, his hotel room, his contacts, his
opium usage, his tobacco and drinking habits (again) and his
family background.

'Let me recap now,' Stoppart summed up, replacing his spectacles on his nose and scanning a sheet of paper upon which he
had taken notes. 'You live alone in a hotel, don't mix socially,
haven't had a woman for some months. You smoke opium at the
rate of about three ounces a week, but this has been greatly
reduced of late. You don't seem to drink too much but you don't
eat well. Your parents . . .?'

'My parents are dead,' Sandingham said.

'Can you tell me what they died of?'

Sandingham, leaning his elbows on his knees, looked at his
feet. The cup in his hand shook and the ripples converged on the
centre of the tea.

'My father died during the war,' he said, adding with embarrassment, 'I don't know what killed him.' He looked up with
muted defiance to defend himself against the critical stares he
expected: there was none. 'My mother', he continued, looking
down once more, 'passed on in the autumn of 1937. She caught
flu – it was very cold that winter – which developed into pneu-
monia.'

Stoppard sensed the emotion in Sandingham's voice and exchanged a professional glance with Gresham.

'Finally,' he asked, 'you've lived here permanently since 1947?'

Sandingham nodded slowly, heavily.

'Have you had.. . .?' Stoppard reeled off a formidable list of
diseases. Sandingham had had quite a number of them.

'Tell me, one last clarification – I'm sorry to have had to shoot
so many queries at you like this – you were a PoW in Hong Kong
and Japan.'

'Yes,' replied Sandingham.

Scratching his head meditatively, Stoppard admitted after a

long pause that he was unsure and wanted blood and urine samples tested.

'To tell you the truth, Sandingham, I can't be certain what is wrong with you. You could have a number of deficiency ailments and some of your symptoms are most likely related to your opium-smoking. You could be suffering from a sort of jaundice even, though your liver seems not too distended. Your blood pressure is up, certainly, but . . . '

'You are also anaemic,' Gresham commented.

'What I'd like to do is take a drop of your blood and get you to leave us samples of your urine and faeces. We'll keep your presence here quiet – completely confidential. But we must make out records and admit you on to our lists as an out-patient. We are able to treat ex-servicemen. And you can rely on our dis-cretion – the secrecy of the surgery. But you must return to us to keep your bookings. Will you do that?' He glanced at Gresham and Sandingham tried to interpret his meaning: perhaps, he thought, the doctor was afraid he'd turn out to be one of those patients who, once equipped with a bottle of pills, disappeared never to return. 'We're not going to take you on if you put yourself off most of the while.'

'Thank you,' Sandingham replied humbly.

Gresham dabbed surgical spirit on the vein in the crook of Sandingham's elbow and drew off ten ccs of blood. It oozed like scarlet oil into the glass syringe. He was given a specimen bottle and told to urinate into it behind the screen. This he did.

'We also want another sample, as you know,' said Gresham.

'A thought,' Stoppart said. 'Can we have a specimen of your semen?'

Forty minutes later, all the samples were provided and Sand-ingham was told to rest in a waiting-room for the duration of the lunch-hour. He asked if he might have a meal and Gresham gave him a chit for the purpose. He ate steamed fish, mashed potatoes and runner beans, with rice pudding for dessert, in a cafeteria with the male nursing and orderly staff.

At a quarter to three he was summoned back to Gresham's office where he found the doctor on his own.

'We've carried out early tests,' Gresham told him. 'Nothing firm as yet. Can you return tomorrow?'

Sandingham said that he could, and was about to go when Stoppart entered without knocking.

'Excuse me, Jim.' He handed a report card to Gresham and turned to address Sandingham. 'Where were you a PoW?'

Gresham read the diagnosis on the card: the most interesting feature was the result of the slide of semen. It wasn't that the patient had VD. It was that he was sterile.

'Sham Shui Po camp and then Japan. I think I told you.'

'You did. What was the name of your camp in Japan?'

He gave it.

'What was it near?'

'What do you mean?' Sandingham rejoined. 'The sea? The hills?'

'Were you near a zinc works? Did you work in a metal factory? Tin or electro-plating? Galvanising? Did you work with sulphur?'

'No. I was slave labour, all the time I wasn't in solitary confinement, at a timber yard.'

'Where was this adjacent to? What was the nearest city?'

'Hiroshima,' he replied.

Gresham looked at Stoppart and they excused themselves from the room for a moment. Sandingham could hear them muttering together in the corridor.

It must be a mental disorder, Sandingham thought. It must have turned my mind and the illness now is psychosomatic.

The doctors returned.

'Sandingham,' said Stoppart. 'I'll pull no punches for I don't think I should. It is my opinion, and I'm ninety-nine-per-cent sure, you have severe radiation sickness.'

With an uncomprehending look on his face, Sandingham said, 'I'm sorry, but I don't understand what you mean.'

They told him.

PART TEN

PoW Camp near Hiroshima: 1945

As THE STEEL bolts were drawn the hoard of newly-hatched bluebottles and emerald-backed flies, alarmed by the echo the metal had caused in the tiny room, rose to circle and settle on the ceiling.

'You com ow' now!'

He was prodded with a five-foot-long bamboo stick.

'Moof! Moof!'

Sandingham bent to pick up his chipped enamel bowl and the shredding oblong of smelly coarse material which had had to suffice as a blanket throughout the winter. His clean-shaven head itched and, as he scoured his fingers over it, flakes of the scalp clogged up the crevices under his inch-long nails. When he had scratched his head, he scratched his bandy legs, the broken scabs joining the dessicated skin. Small dried particles of shit had gathered under his nails. The bucket in the corner opposite his blanket had not been emptied for over a week. The floor was slippery with excrement.

The daylight was so intense he stumbled as he entered it. The sun was not shining – it was too early in the day and the spring mist had not yet lifted. The brilliance of the hour, however, burned into his eyes and he shoved the blanket over his head for protection. He was guided by the bamboo stick, which struck him on his right side to turn him left and his left to go right.

In the barrack that served as the camp hospital he was laid on the *tatame* farthest from the door and examined by a US Navy sick bay attendant. The doctor was himself too ill to be of any assistance and it was all the more advisable as the war ground on never to send a prisoner to the Japanese PoW hospital.

'Lie still,' he whispered to Sandingham, one hand soothing the Englishman's brow while the other dabbed the muck from his legs with a damp rag. 'You're in a helluva state. Nothing I can't fix for yer, though.'

Screwing up his eyes against the glare from the door and raising himself on his arms, Sandingham attempted to see the young man's face, but it was against the light.

'Are you sure? I feel bloody.'

'You are, here 'n' there. No sweat, though. We'll get you cleaned up. Have you . . . ?'

Sandingham knew what was going to be asked of him. The routine questions of name, number, rank, place of birth, father's name, pet dog's name, unit, regiment, place of capture, rough time, rough date: he had seen this done before, had done it himself and wondered whether this was the point when they'd be put to him.

'It's April, sometime,' he informed the medic. 'About eight a.m., from the sun.' It had risen while he was being attended to. 'I was captured in Hong Kong. Don't worry. I've not lost my marbles.' He lay back again. 'Thank God for Yanks!'

'Thanks, Limey,' the American retorted. Then, 'Some do. You seen 'em. I seen 'em. Ass over elbow after a month in the *eiso*. Solitary does things to yer. Had a guy in my last camp – up north – stuck in the slammer for two months for spitting out his snot, as you English call it – real quaint, that! – within sight of a Nip. A mere *jotohei*, at that. By the time he came out he thought he was Hirohito's nephew.'

It was all lies. Sandingham knew that as well as the American. And the American knew he knew. But the idea was to get those released from the cells 'rehabilitated' to camp life as soon and yet as easily as possible.

'I'm Hirohito's mother,' he declared. 'The war is over.'

The attendant became serious.

'You might not be too far off the target. A good bit's happened while you were in the dark.'

'I heard about increased bombing raids,' Sandingham said. 'I heard some Blondin singing it outside the block before he was moved on.'

'He got a good beating fer that. No' – the American lowered his voice – 'it's bigger 'n that.'

He wrung out the rag and rinsed it in a bucket. A film of slime floated on the surface: he skimmed this off with a piece of wood much as a milkmaid might whisk off cream.

'Food's shorter 'n ever. We guess Japan's blockaded. On top o' that, we gotten word.'

He dabbed the wounds again, dropping into them salt that had been obtained by evaporating sea water. Each pinch brought a wincing sigh to Sandingham's lips and a tear to his eyes.

'What word?' he questioned.

'Midway fell. Over eighteen months ago. The IJN got real thrashed. Yamamoto, the Nip admiral, accepted defeat and got the hell out. We heard four big ships sank. Now we got a rumour there was a helluva battle at an island called Truk. Seems the Jap supply fleet got fucked.'

'Eighteen months?' Sandingham was amazed. 'Why haven't they surrendered?'

'Pride. They got too much goddam pride, I guess.'

'And Europe?'

'Allied landings in northern France last summer. The Krauts are on their last legs, we reckon.'

When Sandingham was clean, the attendant transferred him to another *tatame* that had been rubbed with salt as a precaution against lice and bedbugs. As such it was only partially effective, but any success was welcomed.

'I'll get yer soup. Back in five. Okay?'

'Okay,' Sandingham confirmed.

Eighteen months. If the Japanese were that badly off – the major part of their Navy on the bottom, plus the supply fleet – then the end could not be far off. An American landing would happen, and the war would be over.

It was more than a fortnight before Sandingham was returned to work in the timber yard. Even the *isha*, the Japanese camp medico, had excused him for that long. At the time he wondered if the man were softening or preparing for the end of the war as a loser in the hand of an occupying force, but the violence with which the medic later struck another patient with a backhand slap drove such considerations from his thoughts.

The first days back were physical and mental agony. The *hancho* and the other workers, prisoner and Japanese alike, made the tasks he had to do light ones. These required that he leave the sawing sheds (there were three now) from time to time and the sight of the papaya tree over the woodstack and the spot where Garry had died burned his eyes and caused a lump to rise in his throat until he thought it might choke him.

On his fourth day back Mr Mishima managed to have a long conversation with him.

It was made possible by a power cut. These had become increasingly frequent over the winter, and speculation was rife as to the cause. Some claimed partisan action, some Allied bombing raids and others fuel shortages. None knew, of course, if the cuts were of a local, regional or national nature.

Just before the midday rest period the lights dimmed, brightened, flickered, then faded completely. The circular saws slowed and the band saw jammed. The planers hovered into a low howl then screeched to a halt. The plywood laminator lost its hydraulic pressure. The *hancho* cursed volubly and the Japanese workers giggled at his impotent anger. He shared the joke before instructing all present to clear up the dust and shavings, pile the planks and switch off the machinery.

The light rain falling outside was spring-warm and the workforce was instructed to sit in the compound. To wait by the machinery was not in the *hancho*'s book of emergency procedures. Drinking water was distributed before the thin midday soup. Mr Mishima beckoned to Sandingham to join him under the wide eaves of the building, partially hidden by three barrels of tar that were used to waterproof some of the plywood.

'How have you been?' Mishima enquired.

As he came closer to his friend, Sandingham noticed how the lines on his face were more prominent, the colour of his skin more paled and his thin eyes somehow set more deeply. It was, he realised, how he must appear now, too.

'In solitary confinement. I came out three weeks ago but was listed as sick. There is no food or light in the cells.'

'You have been there since the . . . ?' He stopped just before adding 'shooting'. The incident had obviously greatly affected him.

'Yes.'

'That is very cruel.' He drank from his bowl. 'It is not typical of Japanese peoples to be so cruel.'

'Hasn't your history been full of such violence? Like China's? Life is not to be counted as important.'

'Yes. There has been violence. The samurai fought terrible wars with each other and tortured many people. But they did not treat defenceless peoples so.'

'People,' Sandingham said. 'A collective noun.'

Mishima smiled. 'I need you to keep me correct,' he admitted. 'Without my pupils, I go rusty.'

A sentry was passing and they stopped speaking.

'But,' Mishima continued after the guard had disappeared around the back of the shed to check on those urinating at the buckets, 'haven't you, too, had violence in your history? In the Middle Ages of English history, did you not have an Iron Lady, a box whose nails embraced you with death? And a king who had two of his wives beheaded? Did you not drown innocent women who were said to be magicians?'

'Witches. Yes,' Sandingham agreed.

'So. What difference?'

Sandingham made no reply.

'In Japan, as well as warlike people and cruel people, there are good people. As in all countries. We have Buddhists who do not kill. Our religion is to keep life safe. How it is said?' He rubbed his head in a sage-like manner, causing Sandingham to smile. 'Sacred. Safe for the gods.' Mishima knuckled his eyes before carrying on. He was tired, he explained; had not been sleeping well. 'But throughout history it has always been the cruel ones who are in command. Who act. The peacemakers are never strong and so are overrun by the violence-lovers. We forget them. We must not. To forget the peaceful people is to forget the true centre of humans.'

'Do you believe that?' Sandingham asked.

'Yes. We must not forget.'

'I mean that peace is at the true core of the human being, the human soul?'

Mishima stared at the hazy horizon outside the compound. Even with the rain it was more humid than was normal for the time of year. Sitting motionless in the drizzle, they were perspiring.

'I don't know.' His response was melancholic. 'Yet if we do not hope for that, pray for that from our gods, then what chance is there for men to live together in the world?'

They fell into a meditative silence.

The sun broke weakly through and cheered them somewhat. The *hancho* walked between their groups, talking to the Japanese and curtly grunting to the prisoners, his nearest approximation to the English language. He was no longer concerned that camp inmates were speaking to his countrymen.

After a while, Sandingham interrupted Mishima's thoughts.

'How is your wife?'

'She is well. She is working in the city hospital as a – an orderly?'

Sandingham nodded.

'And your son? How is he?'

Mishima made no immediate reply to this enquiry. Then he said, 'It is the duty of every Japanese to work for the success of his country in the war. It is right we should help others, but for the war effort? That is pig-wash. Japan cannot win the war. Nobody can.'

Sandingham did not correct his idiomatic error, nor did he find it in the least bit amusing. He knew Mishima was right.

'Go for a leak,' his friend ordered him out of the blue.

This slang phrase did make him chuckle.

'Why?'

'Go beyond the buckets to the old tool chests. Open the top one. Inside is a small paper box. In that is a dried fruit. It is a plum. Eat it. It will do you good.'

'But if I get caught . . . '

'If I see a guard coming I will distract him. And it will only take you a minute.'

'That's a risk to you.'

Mishima shrugged. 'Do it.'

That night, lying on his *tatame* with the rain dripping steadily on to the ground outside, Sandingham re-counted all the tiny gifts Mishima had given him over the months, from the medicinal tea that killed cockroaches right up to the dried and salted plum which, he noticed, had a Chinese wrapper on it. That caused him to wonder. How on earth had it come to be in Mishima's possession? He fell asleep at last puzzling over this pointless detail and using it as other men might count sheep jumping over a gate.

The summer gathered its skirts about itself. The days grew hot and the nights sticky. Food supplies dwindled and the prisoners became hungrier as the pangs of starvation began to wheedle into them. Most lost weight while several, whose metabolism could not stand the reduction in already meagre rations, simply died. Others, little more than skinned skeletons, hung tenaciously to life with a will that surprised even themselves.

'Every night, when I shut my eyes,' Townsend, a RAF officer taken captive at Kuala Lumpur, told Sandingham as they lay on their bunks in the twilight of a rest day, 'I wonder if I'll open them again. In the morning I open them again with sheer amazement,'

'You shouldn't think about it,' Sandingham replied. 'We've all surely learnt to accept whatever God throws at us.'

'God? I doubt even he throws this.'

The lights went out.

'You know something?' Townsend's quiet voice sounded in the semi-darkness: he was merely a shadowy piece of the blackness on his bunk shelf.

'What?'

'When I was in Singapore, just posted out in '39, I went on the razzle with some of the lads. Junior officers from a couple of destroyers. We went to a bar, had a few beers and then took a couple of taxis to a whorehouse. Chinese girls, mostly. Hardly a Malay in sight. I'd fancied a Malay – my lay Malay, we used to say. It was a private joke in the mess.' He made no effort to show humour at it now. 'Anyway, the lads got the tarts lined up and chose them one by one. I was left with a choice of two. One was an old biddy, fat as a sow and filled with rice, no doubt. The other was a fine-skinned girl. "Girl" wasn't far wrong. I took her by the hand, went up to the room. No messing about. Soon as the door was shut she was starkers. I looked at her. Little fuzzy crotch. Long black hair. Little tits with nipples like brown, unripe raspberries. Tired eyes. You know, I couldn't shag her. She reminded me so much of my kid sister and I thought, "Someplace, you've got an older brother and if I was him . . . " So I paid her, kissed her and buggered off. She shouted something foul at me down the stairs. Thought I thought she wasn't good enough. She threw the money after me, too.

'After that, the lads up whoring in the rooms, I walked down the street. Stroll about until they were done. Came upon this Chinese fortune teller. "You want fortune?" he says. I gave him two dollars and he juggles with these sticks in a bamboo pot. They jump out one at a time. He looked them up in his almanac and sprinkled some sand in a tray. You know the sort of thing?'

Sandingham nodded, realised Townsend couldn't see him and said, 'Yes.'

'He tells me I'll get married to a yellow-haired girl and have two sons. Says I'll have a hard time around my thirty-third birthday but I'll get over it and live to be sixty-four.

'You know something?' he repeated. 'I was thirty-three yesterday: that was right. I married Sylvia – strawberry blonde – in July '39: that was right. She went back to Blighty – sailed from Port Swettenham on a latex carrier – in November of that year and I don't know what since . . . ' He tried not to sound too worried. 'I think she'll wait. Then we'll have two sons, I reckon. Funny, isn't it? A Chinese fairground act right as rain.'

In the morning, Townsend was dead.

'Can I show you this?' Mishima asked him.

The *hancho* was assisting with the replacement of a band saw. Putting his hand out over the steel bed of the saw machine, Sandingham accepted a piece of crisp card slid over the shining surface. It was a photograph.

'Who is this? Your wife?'

'The lady on the left is my wife. Her name is Noriko. The other you know.'

'Katsuo, your son.'

The lad had not been in the timber factory for nearly a month and after Mishima's response to his earlier query Sandingham had not liked to ask where he was. Now he thought that perhaps the photograph, which was obviously a recent one, was meant to prompt him to enquire.

'Where is Katsuo? He's not been here for a while. I hope he's not ill?'

Mishima's eyes followed the next log that was being brought to them by the four prisoners on lumber roster. They were staggering under its weight, and having difficulty lifting it on to the saw bench.

'He is dead.'

There was no sign of emotion on his face except for one tear that glistened on his cheek. His eyes saw little that was near at hand.

Sandingham could say nothing.

'Like Mr Hoshigima's son. He went to fly an airplane. A bomb airplane. The kamikaze. Two days ago . . . '

'Christ! Mishima . . . '

'It is done, that is all. No use crying over spilt milk, as you would say.'

'No, I wouldn't,' answered Sandingham. 'I wouldn't say that. I'd say what the fucking hell was it for?'

He felt the anger rising in him like bile. He wanted to hit someone, something. He picked up a spanner and smashed it against the electric motor casing. The tool clanged loudly and dented it badly but the *hancho* did not hear over the din of the working machines.

'It was for Japan,' Mishima reminded him. 'For the Emperor.'

He did not appear at all bitter, just beaten down by the death of his son.

'Death is the greatest defeat,' he added. 'Life is the greatest victory.'

The next day, Sandingham showed his faded photo of Bob to Mishima.

'When the war is over, you must come to England, Mishima. Try out your English on the real article.'

The reptilian hiss of the hydraulic rams on the plywood machine punctuated their conversation.

'I should like that. And you must come back to Japan, even though your memories of it are not so good now. There are many wonderful parts of Japan. Nikko and the Shinto shrines at Ise, Todaiji temple that has the biggest bronze statue of the Lord

Buddha in the world: Lake Ashi and Mount Fuji are most beautiful in the spring.'

The inner look of distant thoughts must have reflected itself on
Sandingham's face, for Mishima stopped speaking. He, too, then
let his mind drift to more peaceful places.

'You're right,' said Sandingham at length. 'We shall both
forget the horrors of this life and relive only the good things. And
those we shall share.'

'Maybe, after the war is long ended, you could come to the
temple at Todaiji with me. Or to Kofukuji Temple. We can burn
incense together. It won't matter if the Buddha is your master or
not. All our heavenly masters are one.'

Sandingham watched the adhesive and sap oozing from the
wood.

'You'd make a good priest, Mishima,' he said. 'You'd do well
here – plenty of potential converts. A captive audience.'

For a moment, Mishima looked hurt but the smirk on Sandingham's face betrayed his teasing and he, too, smiled.

The sheet of plywood in the press was processed and Sandingham tugged at one corner, Mishima at the other, sliding it off the
platen on to the pile of finished squares.

'The island of Shikoku is one hundred miles away,' Mishima
informed him erroneously. It was only thirty miles away at
the nearest point. Sandingham had ascertained that fact in a
moment of rash, escapist dreaming. 'On the island, not far from
Takamatsu, is the Kotohira shrine. Japanese people call this
"Kompirasan". It is a place where sailors and travellers have
worshipped for many hundreds of years. We should go there
together, too.'

'How shall we stay in touch?'

Mishima considered this obstacle while they laminated the
next sheet. The odour of the glue stung their nostrils.

'Not too hard,' he said. 'But quite difficult. I will give you my
address in characters – you can copy them on to a letter if you
write. If you come to visit me . . . Japanese cities have no street
names. But you can discover my house easily. If you go into the
city on the main road from the east, from Kure or Saijo, you come
to a temple on the right-hand side of the road. At a junction.
Opposite is a shop that repairs bicycles. Turn left here and my

house is eighteen doors down on the left.'

The following day, in the midday break, Mishima slipped Sandingham on oblong sheet of paper. On one side was the address and on the other a crude map with characters upon it, showing signs to watch out for on the way to the house.

Sandingham woke with a start. He could not tell what it was that had shaken him from a deep and dreamless sleep born of exhaustion, but something had.

He lay still and listened to the buzz of insects outside the barracks. A cricket in the roof beams was grinding its rasping song in counterpoint to another in the yard. From the pond outside the camp wire he heard a bullfrog blorting.

The windows and shutters closed upon them, but these were ill-fitting and, as his eyes readied to the night, he could make out a pencil of bleak moonlight ovalled on the paper panes like a torch beam played upon a frosted screen.

With great care, for he appreciated only too well the value of sleep to his comrades, he slipped off his *tatame* and wove his way through the hut to the shutter with the crack in it. He opened the inner window – an act which was strictly against the rules issued by the guards – and pressed his eye to the chink of light.

The camp was oddly cold in the moonlight, which seemed to detach it from reality. Whatever was illuminated was grey and the shadows were not black, only greyer. Even where there were low wattage lights switched on around the perimeter, the moon seemed to nullify their effect. It reminded him of the pen-wash paintings with which Victorian ladies decorated their diaries and, like those illustrations, was somehow hard and soft at the same time. The absence of colour was unworldly.

Yet the peace and calm in the scene was captivating. He wedged his elbows on to the narrow wooden sills and rested his chin in his hands so that his eye remained at the thin shaft of light.

The moon was not far off full, brilliant and alive. Small cumulus clouds scudded across the night sky which was devoid of stars until near to the horizon, so bright was the moonlight. The air was clear and pure.

A jab of colour showed itself to Sandingham. From the shadows of one of the low-built watch-towers a red spot glowed, swelled and faded. Watching its place, he saw it return and then a faint wisp of greyness lofted out into the moonbeams cast by the lattice-work of the structure. A guard was having a crafty smoke. Sandingham smiled to himself: the universal soldier skiving when the officer was away.

From the very far distance a vague, barely discernable howl commenced. At first he thought it was a love-sick dog in a fishing village on the inlet, baying at the moon. Unlike a dog, it did not change pitch.

The guard stubbed out his cigarette and climbed the short ladder to his lookout.

Air raid, guessed Sandingham.

The lights on the perimeter poles dimmed further and were extinguished, proving his hunch correct. The officer of the watch marched into sight and spoke in low, incomprehensible tones to the guard in the tower.

There had been a number of air raids in recent weeks, most of them very distant and not one had occurred within earshot of the camp.

When it came, it sounded like thunder. Not the bass thunder of a storm close at hand or echoing in the hills, which could shake things and set the nerves on edge. It was more like the gentle thunder that is generated by heat lightning at sea or off a tropical coast. It was a summer thunder made from sheet lightning and not the terrible thunder formed by the anger of forked lightning.

The cumulus clouds to the south-east grew pink-tinged in the moonlight, and it was this new, gradual hue that convinced Sandingham that the summer thunder was a massive raid upon the naval yards at Kure.

He watched for over an hour, held by a morbid curiosity. Under the delicate clouds, the dockyards and wharves and houses and streets of Kure were being flattened. People were dying. Oil storage tanks were exploding and ships were blazing. High above, pilots in the cockpits of USAF B29s were listening to the gabble of their observers on the intercoms, pressing their buttons and heaving in on their joysticks, banking away and up as the loads of explosives fell free. Sandingham strained his eyes to try to see the aircraft, but they were hidden by the camouflage of the moonlight. He made efforts to hear the bombers, but all he could pick out in the night, above the weak thrill of the thunder, was the raucous zizzing of the crickets, the scuff of the guard's *tabi* on the dry soil – he was back under his tower now, and had lit up another cigarette – and the peculiar, strangled whistle of a night bird.

'There was a big bombing in Kure the night before last,' Mishima told him, confirming his own assumptions and verifying the rumours that had run rife in the camp the day before.

'How bad?'

'Very heavy. Much damage was done. To houses. To the dockyards. Some warships were sunk. I heard this from a friend of mine who works for the railway. He could not drive his train into Kure yesterday morning.'

They carried on working together without speaking. The *hancho* was in a foul mood and stomped about the timber yard shouting at all and sundry in Japanese. He made no concessions to the prisoners and bellowed at them with no attempt to make himself understood. They had to guess what he wanted or rely upon their shaky knowledge of Japanese commands. Those who were fluent quickly interpolated a translation where they could.

With the arrival of three trucks loaded with logs the *hancho* left the building to supervise the unloading, and this afforded Sandingham an opportunity to communicate with Mishima once more.

He was about to question him about the Kure raid when Mishima spoke first.

'What worries me,' he confided, 'is that, in Hiroshima, we have not been bombed. The city is untouched.'

Sandingham asked him why he thought this was so.

'I can't say. Some people tell me it is because many of the citizens have relatives in America – there are many Japanese in California. Others say it is good fortune. A teacher who used to be with me in my school, Mr Sasaki, told me he thinks it is because the Americans want to use it as a main base when they invade. Maybe they will even land in this area.'

He appeared reticent, though. It was as if he were not sure any of these motives was credible, and Sandingham could feel him holding back.

'Come on, Mishima. I know you well enough now. You have your own reason worked out.'

He shrugged.

'I think there is another reason. Perhaps it is . . . I cannot . . . Perhaps I should not mention this to you, Sandingham, because you are – but that is ridiculous: how can I call you "enemy"? – but Hiroshima is a military base and industrial centre. Your fellow prisoners who work in metal factories and places like that – they are making materials for Mitsubishi shipyard where they build warships, and there is another Mitsubishi factory that manufactures tools and machinery. And there is Yoshikima Army airfield. And the Army has a big ammunition and gun store there as well as several soldiers' stores for equipment. And there is the headquarters of the Japanese Army ship communications regiment and the central command of the Second General Army. This we all know.'

He glanced with puzzlement at Sandingham who returned his look with equal bewilderment. Hiroshima sounded like a prime target for air attack.

'So why is it not attacked? I think it is because of something I do not comprehend.'

He raised his eyebrows.

'Yes,' Sandingham assured him. ' "Comprehend" is right.'

'Some people in my street talk of *bukimi*. In English, that word means "grim" or "awesome" or "weird" or "unearthly" or "ghastly", I looked it up in my Japanese/English dictionary. They think Hiroshima is waiting for a terrible thing to happen.'

'But what could that be?' Sandingham answered.

'I do not know. No one knows. Maybe something bigger than an air raid. It is not in our knowledge to say. It is just a – think to see – premonition.'

'How long do you think the weather will hold like this?' he was asked as he washed himself in the ablutions. The water was cold and welcome as he rinsed the sweat and gluey covering off his skin in preparation for a new layer of the former that would start to sheen on him as soon as he stepped out into the late evening air.

'I've no idea. One can't tell. It's not like England where you can hazard a fairly safe guess. Red sky at night means nothing here.'

'It's getting as hot as Hades down in the docks. Smudger was near fainting in the godown and that was by mid-morning. This afternoon we were put to unloading a cargo of ore of some sort. The dust rose from the hatches and just hung in the air. What breeze there was only shifted it to and fro. One of the Nips gagged on it. Then the *hancho* gets uppity and starts bellyaching about something or other. Nip that threw up gets a slap for his efforts.'

The soldier wasn't actually talking to Sandingham, but simply addressing the wall before him, letting whoever was there accept his news and views. When he was finished with sluicing himself down he left, muttering to himself as he crossed the compound.

'It's getting pretty grim in the timber yard,' observed another voice from one of the doorless 'crappers'. There was no privacy in the latrines.

'It is,' Sandingham replied. 'But at least the sap from the wood is pleasant compared to dust.'

'Might be for you. As for me, I never want to smell a pine tree again, even if it's on the estate of Balmoral.'

'Better than the farts you're dropping at present,' a third voice butted in. 'You got lucky and ate beans?'

A half-hearty laugh rattled in the long hut.

A wizened man entered through the door halfway down the wall behind Sandingham. He was an Australian merchant seaman, not over five feet high and with scrubby ginger hair all over his head and chin; his blue eyes were watery and diluted in their orbits. His hands were stringy but strong.

'Hello, Stoker Blue, me old chum!' welcomed one of the men.

The wizened head nodded. The corded hands dipped a wooden bowl into the water tub and carefully poured several pints into a metal basin on a stand. No one wasted water: it had to be carried too far to make it other than precious.

'Tell you something,' the small seaman said as he rubbed his wet hands over his stubbly crown. 'The Japs have about had it.'

'How do you reckon that, SB?' questioned a Canadian accent from the latrines.

'Easy, Seattle. Our truck had a puncture today. Right in the city. Right by the side of the road. Guards get batey and we get herded on to the pavement and made to sit cross-legged while the driver and his mate jack up the rear axle and bolt the spare on.

'Chanced we were stopped by a small street-market. Couple of shops and stalls. Nothing special. 'Cept that there was bugger-all in them. The rice shop had no rice, only millet, and that looked none too sharp. The butcher's had only a few scraggy cuts and that looked like it was cat meat it was so small. The greengrocer's stalls had very little on them. Daikon, some greens, but nothing much else. No fruit in sight.'

'Hey, Ozzie! You were too late. Maybe you got there after the sale,' shouted one of the wits, facetiously mimicking him.

Stoker Blue from Adelaide ignored this wisecrack.

'Billy, who understands Nippo, travels in our truck to the plating works, told me he heard one of the shopkeepers say he was clean out of something he couldn't quite make out and he wasn't sure when or if he'd get a new supply.'

'Think they'll pack it in?'

'Who knows?'

'Anyway, who gives a brass farthing if the bastards are hungry or not? Let 'em bloody starve. Taste of their own sodding medicine. If they got any.'

This irony was greeted with hoots of derisory guffaws and slow hand-clapping. The friendly mockery quickly petered out as soon as a guard appeared approaching across the yard.

A week later the weather broke. Great clouds gathered on the horizon in the middle of the day and, by evening, the sky was covered with a dull blanket. The rain was a dismal drizzle at first but it gradually increased until it was a torrential downpour. Water spouted off the roofs and cascaded into the dirt. The guttering could not cope and the latrine sumps filled to overflowing. The honey-carters did not call and the prisoners were obliged to dig a pit at the edge of the compound in which to pour the effluent of their community.

Digging the pit in the pelting rain was back-breaking work. The wind had risen as well to make matters more difficult. Sandingham took his turn at the shovels, lifting the cloying mud out of the quagmire to be slapped and paddled into a wall around the rim. In this way, they hoped, the dug earth might act as a dam and deepen the volume of the cesspit. By the time it was completed it was twenty feet long by ten wide and ten deep. Before they commenced using it it was a foot deep in greyish-brown water. The remainder of the rest day was spent filling the pit from the latrine with a bucket chain.

When the rain abated and they returned to the timber yard the prisoners were faced with a panorama of semi-dereliction. The wind had lifted part of the corrugated-iron roof and twisted it back on itself. The wing of metal sheeting sticking up had acted as a funnel and guided two inches of rainwater into the sawing shed. The damage and chaos were considerable.

'Look at it,' remarked CPO Bairstowe. 'Like the deck after a mess night. Only no broken bottles or smashed pianos.'

The machines were damp, the electric motors shorted out with the water. The stock of planking was dripping wet and the plywood, soaked through, had warped and buckled to uselessness.

'No wuk!' bawled the *hancho*. His next sentence translated approximately into, 'Let's get this bloody shambles tidied up.'

It took more than that day, amidst squally showers, to get the roof battened down and the shed cleared and dried out. The wet timber and plywood was stacked in the farthest corner of the yard and ignited with a can of diesel fuel and used gearbox oil, for which act the *hancho* got a resounding telling-off from the touring foreman late in the afternoon. Vehicular fuel was scarce enough and the oil could have been better used for heating in the winter.

Twice in the week following the storms the timber yard was subjected to air-raid alerts. When the sirens were heard from the city ten miles away, or relayed by phone from a command centre of some sort, the *hancho* would rush into each of the buildings and blow three short blasts on a football referee's whistle. This was a signal to switch off all the machinery and lighting and line up at the door in Indian file. At a command from the *hancho* the file would jog out of the building and over towards the stockpile of untouched tree trunks. In the centre of this a bunker of sorts had been constructed. It was really just a low log cabin affair, over which the raw trunks had been piled higgledy-piggledy until they were ready for the saws and planers. Although makeshift it seemed likely to provide ample protection from anything but a direct hit.

Once in the bunker, which had only the one entrance, the guards would squat by the door while the prisoners and their Japanese co-workers would sit cross-legged in rows. They were forbidden to speak. When the all-clear sounded, or the *hancho* was called to the telephone by the ringing of the exterior yard bell, they struggled out in lines and paraded in the yard for ten minutes' physical jerks, conducted by the *hancho*, to shift the cramp of the air-raid shelter.

The first raid was a non-event. They could hear the high-altitude drone of bombers but not bombs dropping or any form of retaliatory ground-to-air fire. The second was not a raid as such but the timber yard was buzzed five or six times by a pair of fighters. They flew in low from the coast, the hum of their engines expanding to a crashing crescendo as they passed overhead at under five hundred feet. They banked towards the hills inland and returned. No gunfire occurred either from the cannons on the aircraft or the ground.

When they were gone, the prisoners chattered about the visitation.

'Recce. They'll invade near here. US Marine landing zone.'

'Wasn't a strafing run . . .'

'Maybe this area'll be a parachute-dropping zone. It's flat. Got some cover.'

'Chump! Got muddy fields as well. Fancy dropping into the clag?'

'Sussing out the lie of land for likely targets.'

'Looking for the camp, maybe. Liberation plans?'

Their ideas swerved from the possible military justifications of such a flight mission to the optimism of release.

'Today's 27 July.'

'So what, Smudger?'

'It's me wedding anniversary.'

No one replied. A year before, someone might have offered to send him flowers or beg a peek at his sexy letters – of which he had received none – or rib him for remembering. Now they threw each other glum looks which took on an even sadder air from the guttering peanut-oil lamps.

To change the subject and draw Smudger off his misery, someone said, 'What do you think that mission today was for? Not bombing again.'

'I know what it was all about,' commented one of the Americans. 'We saw it in the docks. Leaflet raid. A B29 flew over at about twelve thou' and dropped leaflets. I got one. Some drifted on to the quay. The Nips were fast as hell collecting them up so that we didn't get to see, but I found one later blown under a crate. It's in Nip.'

He rummaged between the cracks of his bunk, under the centre of his straw mat, and extracted a many-folded sheet of white paper.

Sandingham handed the leaflet to one of the Dutch officers who could read Japanese. The man studied it for a few minutes, holding it at an angle and close to the smokey flame.

'What's it say, Jan?'

'It is from the American High Command,' he explained. 'It is quite long but what it says, in short, is that if Japan does not surrender then the Allied forces will destroy Hiroshima.'

Mishima, thought Sandingham, and *bukimi*. The idea was there. All that was to follow was the act itself.

'What did the Japs in the docks think of this?'

'Not a lot, sir,' said one of the others who worked in the dockyards.

The senior British officer had entered the barrack in time to hear the translator's interpretation. Now the dock-worker was speaking.

'I only heard a few of the guards chattering and couldn't understand much of their jabber. But the Jap who works the crane hoist on my jetty, who's a decent sort of bloke – he let me know they were laughing at it. Scoffing at it. They don't think it's on, I suppose.'

On his bunk, Sandingham resolved to tell Mishima of the leaflets and, the next day, as soon as the opportunity arose, he did so.

'I, too, have seen one of them,' was the reply. 'It scares me very much. I think there will be a big air raid on Hiroshima.'

He confirmed that many people took the threat the leaflets promised lightly.

'There is one good thing,' Mishima said later in the day. 'My house is a long way from the centre of the city or the industrial sites where they will drop their bombs. My wife and I shall be safe or have time to run. The nearest place to bomb to my house is the railway station, and that is nearly a mile away.'

All day long at the timber yard Sandingham had had a sense of apprehension which he could not quite put into words.

The day had started cloudy but had cleared to become a warm and fine afternoon. By evening the rainy weather was a thing of the past but it left its legacy of air filtered clean of dust and summer heat. Driving back to the camp in the lorry, he had seen the countryside around bathed in a charm and beauty hitherto unseen or unacknowledged.

His uneasiness transferred itself to his friends.

'What's up, Joe? Feeling ill?'

'No. Just odd.'

'Gut-ache?'

'No. Not exactly. Sort of emptiness. Sort of butterflies or stage-fright mixed with a little nausea.'

He stared at his arms and legs in the pure rays of the evening sun and studied the shadows that lingered under his taut skin. His joints were boney and his muscles, though not badly shrunken, showed very obviously the fact that he was starving. He looked at his comrades as if for the first time and knew that they too, were slowly dying of malnutrition. He caught a glimpse of his reflection in the rear window of the driver's cab. His cheekbones were becoming prominent and his eyes sunken with the mascara of hunger tingeing the lids and spaces under his lower lashes. His skin was pallid and the paleness was accentuated by the bare sunlight. Yet he was still, to his own astonishment when he gave it thought in the sleepless night hours, unscarred by any of the terrible diseases that wracked some of his colleagues.

'Empty belly, empty mind,' advised a fellow officer.

That night there were two air-raid warnings but the prisoners were left undisturbed in their barracks. Only four times in the previous three months had they been taken to the shelter constructed beside the main guardhouse, between it and the *eiso*. Even then the aircraft had flown on. The guards were certain that the bombers were either not interested in their area or else knew of the lettering on the roof and therefore avoided the place. The hassle of getting all the prisoners up, out to the shelter, through the inevitable *tenko* that would be necessary, and back into their huts was just not worth the effort.

Sandingham could not doze off. Each time the alert came he slipped softly through the sleeping, grunting, fidgeting sleepers to the shutter crack and peered out. The starlight was prominent but he could not see or even hear aircraft.

Eventually he was able to let his mind slip into an uneasy doze from which he kept waking himself by moving and itching.

At morning *tenko*, just after six o'clock, the prisoners were informed that the truck taking those who were employed in the timber yard to work would be an hour late. The five lorries transporting those who went to the Mitsubishi shipyards and the docks left on time at a quarter to seven.

At half-past seven, after the commandant had been informed of the all-clear having being given, Sandingham and the others boarded their truck and settled themselves into the back. There had been a warning given just after seven, as the truck was arriving, and this had delayed their departure. The warning had apparently been a false alarm.

The tarpaulin cover had been removed from the framework several weeks before and, instead of the well-patched canvas awning, they now had a morning-blue summer sky over their heads.

The road to the timber yard was busier than usual, Sandingham thought. Cyclists and some motor vehicles came and went in both directions. Pedestrians were somehow more numerous, too. He wondered why, then realised that it was probably due to the fact that the air-raid warning had delayed some from leaving home and now they were seeking to catch up on their daily routines. What was more, he was usually in the timber yard by now and so was not familiar with the public activities of this time of the morning.

At a crossroads, the lorry stopped to allow a bullock cart to negotiate the junction. The animal was nervy and did not want to get too near to the vehicle. To allay its fear, the driver backed up the side lane and switched off the ignition.

There was a comparative silence punctuated only by the owner of the cart trying to cajole the bullock forward.

'Hear it?' Toni asked.

Toni Ardizzoni was from New York. Little Italy. Corner of Greene and Spring, where his father had a delicatessen, of which Toni was inordinately proud: he hoped to inherit it, or at least manage it, after the war. Toni had been responsible for making the shop's fresh tortellini. He had also flown B29s as a navigator.

'What?' Sandingham could hear nothing in the aftermath of the chuddering of the motor.

'Another aircraft.'

They all looked up. Even one of the guards gave a quick turn of his head towards the sky.

'Can't see anything.'

The bullock was padding the ground, its hooves kicking the dirt about with fear and frustration.

'I can. Left of the small cloud. It's a plane. No – it's two, I think.'

'Got it.'

'What is it, Toni?'

'That high, it's gotta be one o' my babies. Movin' slow, too.'

As he spoke, they saw the dot alter course. Another dot and possibly a third followed it on a parallel change of direction.

'They're veering off. Weather planes?'

'Mebbe.'

The bullock was smacked on its rump with a bamboo cane. It took some tentative steps forward. The cart lurched behind it and the driver waved his hand to urge the animal on. It jittered and tried to skip in its shafts. A wicker basket containing two emaciated cockerels fell off the rear of the cart and rolled in the dust, the occupants squawking with annoyance. Once over the crossroads, the carter waved his thanks to the driver who returned the gesture.

Reaching to the ignition key, he was about to twist it when it happened.

There was a sharp flash on the horizon. It was a blue colour, like an electric spark of magnificent proportions. A few seconds later there was a warmth in the air like a summer breeze but not blowing, not moving at all.

No one said anything.

It was followed by a cloud bellying outwards and upwards over the distant city. There was a silence lowered upon them. Sandingham became acutely aware that there were no birds singing or insects chirruping. The bullock, he saw, was standing as still and firm as a statue. It was as if someone had stopped the projector running the film of life on to the screen of the world – just for a few frames. There was then a rumble that quickly swelled to a thunderous bang.

The film recommenced. The bullock jerked into action. The birds sung again.

The driver started up the lorry and crashed the gears. The guards were shouting to him, gesticulating wildly through the rear window of the cab and through the doors. He did not reverse and drive back towards the camp but on towards the timber yard, the horn blaring to clear the way through the cyclists and walkers.

The gates to the yard were open, swinging wide on the hinges. The driver slewed the truck through them and skidded to a halt. The guards bullied and chivvied the prisoners off the rear bed of the truck and herded them into the woodpile bunker. With them all in there, they pulled the door to and wedged it firmly shut with a heavy log. The prisoners heard the truck drive off. Still nobody spoke. They could hear nothing from outside.

'They've gone. Buggered off,' someone said incredulously.

'Let's get the door down.'

They shoved and heaved but the log held firm in the earth.

'Roof. Have a go at the roof.'

The bunker was not well constructed, depending for its security upon the weight of timber on and around it. It was, furthermore, never intended to be a prison. Without too much difficulty they managed to ease aside some of the logs and Sandingham, being thinner than most, was hoisted up and started to weave his way through the mesh of trunks resting on the bunker. In ten minutes he was out.

Gathering his breath, he shouted down through the wood pile, 'I made it. I'll get the door.'

It was then that he looked up.

Over the city was a cloud, thousands of feet hight, as it seemed to him. It was shaped like an umbrella toadstool. It was black and

deep purple and grey all at once. At its base was a thick layer of
smoke, turning in and in and in upon itself like dough being
kneaded.

'Christ!' he muttered involuntarily.

The log was no problem. He tugged it aside and all the
prisoners crawled or crouched out into the sunlight.

'Look at that!'

They gathered in the yard and gazed up at the cloud. Even now
it was growing taller as they watched.

'That was some kinda raid!' exclaimed Toni.

He studied the face of his scratched and battered watch in a
perplexed manner.

'What's up, Yank?'

'I don' get it. It's only twenty to nine.'

'So?'

'You see a raid like that come together in under twenty minutes . . . ?'

They scattered about the timber yard, searching for the
workers or the guards. There was no one there, not even the
hancho. There were no weapons, either. In the office, they found
some clothes and shared them out.

Sandingham was excited and afraid and exhilarated. It was like
being a child let loose in an adult world from which all the adults
and their constraints had been miraculously, irrevocably removed. Yet he was simultaneously terribly afraid for Mishima.

The two dozen or so of them met in front of the office.

'What the hell do we do now?' puzzled 'Harris' Tweed,
confused by the possibility of freedom.

'Get back to camp or stay here. One or the other. What we
can't do is piss off as we like.'

'Why the hell not?' asked Mick Harwood in his Liverpudlian
accent.

'You heard His Majesty the Nip Emperor free you? You see US
Marines chargin' over th' hill? Ain't no cavalry in this man's war.
For Chrissake, think, you guys!'

'Toni's right. If we run loose, we'll be judged escapers and shot
by the Kempetai. If we get seen at large in the countryside we'll be
done for. If that is a flattening of Hiroshima by a raid, and the
Japs want scapegoats to punish, we'll be the best they could
have.'

They sat in hasty council and took a quick show of hands. The majority was for getting back to the camp where there would be guards to protect them against the local population. The calculated risk of making their way through the farmland was accepted as inevitable. It was deemed better than remaining in the timber yard for a lynch-mob.

'How far is it back?'

'I reckon it's five, six – mebbe seven miles.'

'If we go on the road . . . '

One person ran to the gate and cast his eyes up and down the road. There were few people in sight.

'Not many about now.'

'Where they all gone?'

'See here. I reckon we could cut across country. The camp is over there . . . ' The prisoner from the gate returned and pointed with a six-inch nail he had picked up as the only weapon he could find. '. . . And if we marched as fast as hell we could do it in less than two hours. There's no steep hills or anything.'

To assist with their journey, they put on all the Japanese clothing they could find in the office. As they dressed, Sandingham realised that the clothes were the property of the Japanese workers. It confirmed that they had been there that morning, but had left in a hurry before the prisoners' arrival.

He lifted Mishima's jacket off its hook. As he did so, through a window, he caught a glimpse of a bicycle haphazardly leaning on a wall.

In one pocket of Mishima's jacket, he found some currency notes, some coins and a small rice cake wrapped in a cotton napkin. In the other was a small wallet-like folder. Inside were identity papers of some sort, two letters and a photo – it was of the three of them: Mishima, Noriko and their son, Katsuo.

Pushing his arms through the sleeves, he pulled on the jacket. It was a good fit, although it would not have been had he not lost so much weight. The sleeves were much too short. To disguise his head, he put on one of the peaked caps that were regulation issue to workers and soldiers alike.

The others had assembled in the yard.

'Are we ready? We don't go as a column. That'd be too obvious. Split into two and threes. But walk in sight of another group. If you get stopped, keep going. If you see one group being done over, join forces. Okay? Let's go!'

In their worry, no one noticed Sandingham holding back.

When they had gone, he ran behind the office to where he had seen the bicycle. He mounted it and pedalled out of the gateway. In the distance, on his left, he could see the groups making their way along the road; the leading pair were striking off along the banks between the rice fields. To the right, ahead of him as he shifted his weight and turned the handlebars, was Hiroshima. Above it the cloud now looked less like a toadstool and more like a tall-bodied oak tree with a fearsome, awful canopy thousands of feet high.

The bicycle was old and heavy and his legs were not strong enough to propel it forward at any speed. At first he had wobbled: it was six years since he had last ridden a bike. This one was plainly a poor man's model, for it lacked gearing and there was a metal-framed shelf behind the saddle for the carriage of packages and boxes.

The road wound through paddyfields and vegetable farms, many of them partially harvested. The few hamlets he pedalled through contained knots of people talking excitedly to each other. Everyone was facing the city.

The nearer he came to the city limits the more people he found to be travelling with him. Some were on cycles, some on foot, a few in cars or on lorries. As he came alongside the railway line to Kure the road took a bend. Here he decided to stop, to regain his breath. He squeezed on the brake levers and halted by the kerb under the shade of a tree that grew over a stone wall.

From around the corner he could hear a mysterious sound. More accurately, it was a great number of disparate sounds melding together to make one orchestration, much as many notes join in unison to make a complex chord. He tried, leaning over the handlebars, to recognise any one of the noises but he was unable to do so, for whatever they were they registered in his brain as unlikely to unite. They did not fit into a pattern – much as a cawing crow would not be expected to join in harmony with a harpsichord.

His breath regained, Sandingham shifted the pedals and took

the pressure of the chain. He rode away from the kerb and around the corner.

Ahead of him on the road, half a mile away, there was what appeared to be a tide coming in his direction. As he pedalled on and approached it, he saw it was a multitude of people. Behind them was the smoke of what Sandingham took to be the burning city.

When he caught sight of them he assumed the crowd he was riding up to was made of refugees from the air raid. He had seen Chinese in droves leaving a district under fire in Hong Kong. As he got closer, he saw that he was only partly right.

Within easy sight of them, he stopped again. He could not quite believe what he witnessed in front of him.

The crowd was silent except for the shuffling of their feet and the creaking of the axles on their handcarts. A few moaned but none spoke. Many of them were injured. Cuts about the face and hands had bled into streaks upon their clothing. Some limped, while others were riding on the handcarts, sitting on an assortment of mundane household belongings. As they passed by, he saw that they were all stunned, bemused even. Refugees were usually more alert than this, eager in their escape. These people were strangely apathetic.

He was about to set off the way they had come when an elderly man in a dirtied *ukata* – a light indoor kimono used by Japanese much as Europeans might use a cotton dressing-gown – touched his arm. Sandingham looked down at the man's hand. It was badly grazed as if he had rubbed it along a rough surface. Straw-coloured plasma was weeping from the wound.

The man said nothing but looked Sandingham straight in the face, then shifted his eyes to the bicycle. He pleaded through the telepathy that pain brings to the injured. Without a thought Sandingham lifted his leg over the saddle and relinquished his machine. The old man said nothing at all; he did not even smile his thanks. He steered the bicycle through the crowd and, propping it by a pedal to the opposite kerb, helped a middle-aged woman on to the saddle, precariously balancing a child on the crossbar between her arms.

Sandingham watched them rejoin the crowd.

Walking was easier for him than cycling. His legs, after initially feeling weakened as he dismounted, set back into the stride to which they were accustomed.

It was not long before he reached the outer limits of the blast damage. House walls were askew, trees leafless: windows were blown out and fences down. Debris littered the road.

The more he walked, the worse the damage became.

All the while, from the city, there rose the vast pall of smoke and dust. It was so wide and huge now that it entirely cut off the sun. The head of the tree-cloud over-toppled him and was widening its branches.

Sounds increased. From the city came the noise of human turmoil, of burning, of disintegration and the musical tinkling of metal bending or breaking, glass shattering. In the firestorm were the popping detonations of houses igniting in an instant and exploding. It was the symphony of destruction.

He walked with his head lowered, his brain struggling to recall the instructions from Mishima on reaching his Japanese friend's home. If he looked up, what he spied wiped his thoughts clean with horror.

Around him, few buildings stood. They were heaps of wood and tiles, cloth and glass and metal. Some smouldered. Brick or stone edifices were cracked and leaning. Everything had collapsed. The narrower sidestreets between the houses were filled with rubble. Further on, the sides of buildings were burned as if scorched. Telegraph and power poles were charred down one side. Flimsy upright objects, like some of the street lamp-posts, were bent over. The air was filled with the acrid stink of the ruination of war.

Everywhere, there were the people. Or what was left of the people.

To one side of the street was a shambles of wooden planks, beams and plates. Shattered roof tiles underfoot hurt his soles through his *tabi*. Woven into the fabric of the wreck of the building were bicycle frames, wheels, chains, mudguards – a carton of saddles lay strewn on the pavement like an obscene dried fruit. Opposite was a stone building: most of it had collapsed but enough had survived to assure Sandingham that it was a temple. The smoke rising gently from the ruins was scented with incense.

'Eighteen doors down on the left,' Sandingham uttered.

He shut his mouth up promptly. To speak in English was to commit suicide. He tugged the peak of his cap down further and stepped over a tangle of power cables and began to clamber over the first hillock of rubble that had been the cycle-repair shop.

It was impossible counting off the houses: they were all so utterly destroyed that there was no way to discern one from the next. He tried to guess how wide each property might be and then assess how far down the street he had gone; but there was little to guide him.

He kept his face lowered, studying where next to step or balance. Often he stumbled or slipped over splintered wood, torn cloth and more tiles. Pieces of furniture stuck out from the wreckage like decorations in a macabre sculpture.

When he had gone what he estimated to be one hundred yards, he sat on the protruding end of a cupboard and shouted.

'Mishima? Mishima? Mishima-san?'

He scanned the destruction around him, oblivious to everything but a sign of his friend.

'Mishima-san . . . wa doko desu ka?'

Nothing moved except a hot wind. The only sound was the wind in the crannies and around the tangled wires of the ruins, and the murmur of the fire raging in the centre of the city.

Smoke drifted towards him. It choked and confused him, cut into his lungs and made his eyes and nose run. It was pungent and foul.

He clambered further over the ruins, keeping to the street. Another fifty yards and again he halted, precariously standing upon the ridge of a roof that had slid sideways into the street.

'Mishima-san!'

He was quiet, listening for a reply.

It came from a place below and to his right, out of his line of vision. It was not a voice so much as a grunt. Someone was tugging at debris under a nearby roof, partly fallen in and smouldering.

Sandingham skidded and slithered down his roof and up the next until he could see into the roof space. At first he could make

out little: the smoke from the depths of the building was digging
into his eyes and he had to keep rubbing them and screwing them
up to keep them from being blinded.

When he saw the person, he knew it was not Mishima. This
was a younger man. His hair was matted with blood and one of
his eyes was shut. The lid was closed and sunken in over an absent
eyeball. He was buried to the chest in a cross-hatchery of wooden
planks and earth. One of his hands was pinned under him. The
other was free and, in this hand, he held a single chopstick. With
this, he was uselessly trying to prise up one of the planks pinning
him down. He was mumbling unintelligibly.

There was little Sandingham could do for him. He lowered
himself to the man's level and lifted the obstruction against which
the man himself was fighting. As it came away, a shower of dust
and rubble caved in along the man's side and clattered into an
empty space below him that had been the main room of his home.
The tumbling debris intermingled with his intestines that were
hanging half out of his stomach.

Retching, Sandingham turned his head away.

As he did so, the ceiling upon which the man was standing gave
way and he fell into the room below. He dropped like a doll
discarded by a wanton child. He hit the wooden floor with a
drumming thud and lay, grotesquely twisted, upon a low table.
Smoke wraithed over him.

'Sandingham?'

He jumped. Above him, on the roof ridge, was Mishima. He
was covered from head to foot in what looked like flour. He was
bare to the waist and his ill-fitting trousers were torn. His feet
were also bare and badly lacerated. His hands were red.

'Mishima!'

It was with relief as well as love that Sandingham spoke his
name. He reached his friend's side and touched his elbow.

'What on earth has happened?'

'Look about you.'

For the first time, Sandingham extended his horizon. Now that
he had found Mishima somehow everything would be all right.

As far as he could see in any direction, there was utter desola-
tion. Not a building remained that was less than three-quarters
demolished. Streets and lanes were mere dips in the landscape of

rubble. Some were catching alight. In the distance, the city was a blazing inferno.

'Can you help me?'

It was a rhetorical question and Sandingham followed Mishima over the remnants of two houses that had been set back from the street, one behind the other.

The first had simply dropped upon itself but the second had folded sideways before accepting a third on top.

To assist him down a drop of ten feet into what had evidently been a small, neat garden, Mishima gave Sandingham his hand. As he lowered him down, Sandingham gazed up at the Japanese's face. It was then he saw that the dust and grime was besmirched with tears. And he knew what it was he was going to help him to do.

Mishima had dug a tunnel into the house from beside a willow tree that was stripped of its foliage. The tunnel was angled upwards and bent through fifty degrees at the same time. Sandingham crawled into it and hoisted himself up with his knees and elbows. At the end of the tunnel was a bulbous cave and in the side of that was a woman's face. It was bloodied but had obviously been wiped, for the blood was smeared with sweat that had stiffened with the powdered plaster that had dusted everything. The rest of the body was hidden completely.

Sandingham thought the woman was dead. He started to edge backwards when the eyes in the face opened wide and the mouth moved.

'Ak-arm-ast-ute-di,' it said.

Then the eyes closed but the mouth stayed open, avidly and awkwardly sucking in the stale air of the tunnel.

Once out, Sandingham gripped Mishima by his shoulder. He knew who the face belonged to, though it was unrecognisable from the photograph he had in his pocket.

'Your jacket,' he explained needlessly. 'It was hanging in the office.'

He felt for the wallet, closed his fingers on it and gave it to Mishima. He opened it and quickly glanced at the photograph of the three of them before flicking it shut and tucking it into his clothes.

'What is best?' Sandingham asked. 'You know the house better than I do.'

What a stupid thing to say, he realised. Of course he did. Sandingham had never been there before. He had hardly been invited to dine in their home. It was, he knew then, a miracle that he'd located the house in any case.

'Nothing,' Mishima replied. 'There is nothing to do.'

'Bollocks!' Sandingham's barrack-room slang seemed oddly in place in such a situation.

Mishima stoically shook his head.

'What about a room underneath? Isn't there the possibility of a cavity underneath her?'

The woman at the end of the tunnel was no longer a person, a human in trouble, but an objective, a goal towards which to strive. Sandingham had missed having something to aim at in his years of imprisonment. All he had had to keep him going was the will to see it through, to survive. Now that he was out of the camp, he wanted to transfer that to Mishima's wife. He was desperate that she should also pull through.

Mishima shrugged, saying, 'There is a room, but it will be flat now or filled with . . . '

'Show me! Quickly!' Sandingham saw the smoke that was wafting through from beneath the wreckage. 'We have not much time.'

Pointing to an indentation in the cliff of shattered wood, he jumped down on to a section of black roof tiling that had somehow toppled in one piece, and now leaned over the indentation. Instead of digging horizontally, he began tearing the tiles free until he was through to the ceiling beneath. This he kicked inwards and discovered a large space beneath it big enough for him to stand doubled up in and certainly to move.

'Here!'

Carefully, Mishima stepped on to the roof and gave his hand to Sandingham who let himself down into the hollow. It was filled with an aroma of foodstuffs and pinewood. Looking up to Mishima's face framed by the entry he had booted through, he saw the man's features marbled through dusty smoke. He coughed to rid his lungs of the clinging fumes he had disturbed with his arrival.

'What direction?' he asked his friend. Mishima seemed blankly uncomprehending. 'Which way?' This time Mishima tipped his head and vanished from sight.

A solid bank of plaster, glass, wood and tiles dissected what had been a kitchen. Some of the split wood had buckled and, behind him, Sandingham saw the cause of the smoke. Cloth and wood had fallen into the *hibachi* on which Mishima's wife had cooked their breakfast. The charcoal had not yet died and was now a dangerous fire hazard. As he regarded it with fear, a small flame licked free and smoothed its tongue around a thin beam. Having nothing to extinguish the fire with but his own resources, Sandingham pulled himself free of his *fandushi* and urinated over it. The steam was foul but it put out the fire.

He estimated that Noriko Mishima was above him and to the left, about six feet into the rubble. He began yanking and scrabbling away at the debris, piling up to his rear whatever he pulled free, but making quite certain that he did not cut off his exit.

For twenty minutes, he worked solidly and with speed, thinking of nothing. His brain kept reissuing to his mind's eye the panorama of the city interspersed with a vision of the old man who had silently begged his bicycle of him, but his consciousness wiped it away as soon as it appeared.

He was making some progress when Mishima shouted down to him from the hole in the roof.

'You stop, Sandingham. No need.'

He ceased digging and hauled himself out of the ruins. Mishima's face was expressionless. The anguish and pain were gone. In its place was an emptiness that stretched down to the very foundation of his soul.

Sandingham reached out for his hand and took it in both of his own, stroking it in a futile attempt to comfort him. He knew he was crying but through his tears he saw Mishima merely stand and show no reaction whatsoever, gently pulling his hand free.

'I'm sorry . . . Mishima.' He wiped his eyes on the sleeve of the other's borrowed jacket. 'Maybe it's for the best. This city is . . . '

He lifted his head. The vortex of the firestorm that was roaring in the city was edging nearer. It was already up to a low hill less than a mile away.

'It will not burn this far,' Mishima whispered, divining what Sandingham was considering. His voice was hoarse and dulled by sorrow. 'It cannot cross Hijiyama Park or the river.' He sat on the roof, bringing his hands to his brow, forcing the furrows into a frown. 'My first name is Tadashi,' he said after some moments. 'Please do not forget that.'

'I won't.'

'And your name?' His softened voice choked as he spoke.

He knows my name, Sandingham thought. Why does he want it again? Yet he answered.

'Joseph,' he confirmed. 'But they call me Joe. My friends call me Joe.'

'Wait here, Joe.'

Mishima made his way down the roof and went into the remains of what had been his home. Sandingham could hear him shifting things about as if he were searching for something: then he was quiet. Finally, he reappeared with a white cotton kerchief tied round his forehead. In his hand was a square of white paper with black characters upon it. He bent and knelt on the roof tiles beside Sandingham.

'Joe,' he said, 'I am sorry for what my people did to you and your people; just as you will one day be sorry for what your allies, the Americans, did to the Japanese people. Never forget that it is men who are mad, not nations. Men make wars. Nations do not. Leaders do – who need never fight but send others to die. Politicians are the corrupt ones. They decide but it is we, the common men – the innocent people of the race – who act for them. And suffer in their place.'

He unfolded the paper.

'This is my *jisei*,' he explained. 'Do not take it away from me.'

Sandingham was nonplussed. Why he should take away a sheet of notepaper did not occur to him. Perhaps it was a prayer sheet, he thought.

'I won't,' he said again.

Mishima moved on his knees to the far end of the roof, near to the entrance to his tunnel.

Half-turning away from Sandingham, he said over his shoulder, 'Sayonara, Joe. Tengoku de aimasho.'

With his elementary knowledge of camp Japanese the words meant nothing to Sandingham.

Mishima held the paper at arm's length and read it in a murmur to himself. He then slipped something out of his clothing and wrapped it in the white square.

Sandingham, who thought Mishima was about to pray for his wife, respectfully averted his eyes and stared up instead at the thick clouds of smoke that canopied over him several thousands of feet high.

A spluttering snapped his thoughts.

Mishima was still kneeling but leaning a little to one side. The white scarf round his head was awry.

'Tadashi? Is there anything wrong? Can I . . . ?'

He received a gurgled and garbled response.

Mishima tipped sideways and rolled down the roof. As he twisted over, Sandingham saw the knife pressed in under his sternum, the polished sharkskin hilt flush with Mishima's stomach.

He fell down the roof after Mishima, vainly trying to stop his descent. Yet it was to no avail. Mishima was dead.

It was raining. Overhead there was a dense black cloud and he could vaguely hear thunder.

Sandingham stood up, his spine aching from the exertion of gathering the rubble with which he covered Mishima's body. He knew it was not a grave: a bulldozer would come one day and level the area. But in the meantime at least no birds or scavenging dogs would feast off his friend's corpse.

The rain fell in big spots, not heavily but consistently. He did not know for how long it came, nor indeed for how long it had been falling. He just became gradually aware that it was settling upon him in its own sad way.

The drops hit the skin on his bare forearms where he had rolled up the sleeves of the jacket. As each one touched him, it left a charcoal-grey stain, as if someone with a cruel sense of humour was bespattering him with diluted classroom ink, the Stephens' black ink of his schooldays.

The fall of rain terrified him, though he could not appreciate why. His flesh unaccountably crept, and he scuttled over the roof and into the safe shelter of the area beneath.

The tram was gutted. Only a steel skeleton remained. The side-panelling had warped, fractured and prised loose. The glass that had been the windows had melted and run down the sides, cooling like a coating of speckled sugar on the wheels and road surface. The paint was seered off.

Sandingham walked up to the tram, not knowing why he did so. Nothing was making sense to him. Inside, the seats had disappeared and only the frameworks remained in their original rows, twisted crookedly. On the floor of the tram cabin was a partly congealed liquid slush of greyish-brown matter in which lay some broken branches, stripped bare of their bark.

It was more than a minute before he realised that the floor-covering had been people, the branches nude bones.

He did not vomit at this realisation. His stomach did not even lurch towards his throat. There was nothing left to throw up – not food nor bile nor rage. He was growing devoid of new emotion, his inner store insufficient for what he was experiencing.

He simply cried. It was not a loud venting of tears but a gradual, miserable sobbing, such as a child might make when its toy was irretrievably lost.

Their hair, eyebrows and eyelashes had been scorched off and, when they closed their eyes, the upper lids snagged under the lower. Few had skin left on the fronts of their bodies. Some were smeared with vomit that had stuck to their chests and breasts. Some walked with their arms held out before them, as if in supplication to a greater power for a hint of mercy. Many were naked and, of those, some had even their pubic hairs singed short.

They all moved with their heads hung, not speaking, not complaining. Their submission chilled Sandingham even more than their hideous wounds.

As he studied them shuffling past him, he saw upon the backs of a few the patterns of straps or elastics, of flowers or birds or delicate designs printed indelibly upon their skin.

A boat was being punted across a river by a Japanese man. Helping him was a priest. He was European. His soutane was besmirched and stiff with sweat and grime.

Sandingham watched them guiding wounded over the water.

They worked with little conversation, passing instructions to each other but saying little else. He thought at once that he should give them assistance, to help them as any man might another in a crisis, and began gingerly to step over the debris to where a flight of stairs was cut into the bank.

As he neared them the punter spoke to the priest in German. 'Da ist nichts zu machen.'

Joe thought better of offering his assistance and turned aside, keeping his face to the rubble-strewn ground.

'Wakarimasen,' the old man uttered.

The teenage boy lifted his index finger to the smoke as if instructing his elder on one of the finer points of warfare.

'Molotoffano hanakago.'

He overheard this as he shuffled by the pair. They were sitting on an inverted and much-dented trader's tricycle. No other words passed between them.

Hanakago, Sandingham knew, meant flower-basket. He wondered how a bomb could bear blossoms.

In the middle channel of the river there sailed a gunboat of the Imperial Japanese Navy. It made slow headway. In the bows stood an officer. He was holding a megaphone through which he shouted unintelligibly.

The marvel to Sandingham was not that the gunboat had appeared but that it was so trim and tidy, so unadulterated, its shape clean and purposeful, deliberate and ordered. And the officer was so neat in his uniform, so dispassionate. He was almost serene.

It was nearly evening and the fires were dying in the city centre. Against a wall that had withstood the blast because it had been end-on the epicentre, Sandingham paused. He was utterly tired but unable to consider sleep quite yet. He slid down to a sitting position against the wall and hunched his knees to his chin, hugging his calves with his arms. So far, no one had recognised him as a foreigner. Few people were in a position to care.

Wherever he went there were bodies. He had never seen such carnage. In Hong Kong at the fall, when someone died, they just –

died. The bullet that did for them might make a small hole going in and a large hole coming out, but that was all. Someone freshly shot in the head was not mutilated but simply broken. Those caught in the ambush at Wong Nai Chung Gap had lain on the road looking like humans that were now ceased. Even those caught in a crossfire of mortars were still recognisably human until the flies and the ants started their forays.

The dead he now saw littering the wreckage of the city were not like that at all. Many were as unlike to human form as was conceivably possible. They were not necessarily dismembered, but hideously disfigured. Sandingham was used to seeing the dead lying in grotesquely contorted positions, but not like these.

He had found a man bent backwards over a post, his head touching the backs of his knees, his stomach unsplit but stretched so tight it had contouring under it the coiled map of gut. The man's skin was maroon and his arms hung back against the shoulder sockets.

At one point in the afternoon, he had paused by a water butt to drink. His throat was parched from retching and swallowing smoke. He also wanted to try to wash off the blotches the rain had given him.

He reached into the water. It was cool, indescribably cool. It was luxurious. He slopped water on his arms and rubbed at them. The rain spots did not even smudge let alone show signs of washing clean.

Resigned to leaving himself dirty, Sandingham leaned over the edge of the barrel to press his face into the surface and suck up the water. His reflection stared back at him. Beside his face was another. It was floating a foot under the surface. The eyes were holes. The mouth was a slit cavern of darkness. The hair willowed around the scalp. He did not drink but watched. The face folded up in the water. He was dreaming. It was the effects of exhaustion. He thrust his fingers into the clear jet-black of the water and felt for the face. There was nothing hard there. No skull. No corpse. Yet something soft brushed against the back of his hand and his forearm. As he brought his arm clear, something clung to it. It was light and wrapped itself on to his arm like algae. He straightened his arm. Clinging to it was the face: no features, just a flat mask of skin, peeled from its owner and cast into the water.

Sandingham screamed. He flicked and threshed his arm trying to dislodge it, but it would not move. It was glued to him by the water and its own grossness. He could not bear to touch it: instead, grabbing a piece of wood, he scraped it off, all the time hollering. The face fragmented and came away like curds off milk.

In a temper of panic, he toppled the butt over, the water soaking invisibly into the dry ground.

By the time he reached the river again it had become a tide of dead. The once-living wallowed to and fro in the wash, rising and falling with the slow motion of obscene lovers. Old men, young women, children. For fifteen minutes, Sandingham had blankly watched a baby floating next to its mother, her hand entangled forever in the infant's clothing. Between the bodies, where they were not log-jammed together against the shore or a collapsed waterfront building, hundreds of tiny fish floated belly-up. An occasional seabird filled in the occasional space. In death, they were all equal.

He found himself talking quite loudly to himself in English and instantly jammed his mouth with his fingers. This slip of concentration brought him out in a cold sweat of fear, for leaning against the wall a few feet away was a young Japanese man.

Sandingham glanced sideways to see if he had been overheard.

The man was bruised all over his side and was nursing a broken left arm. The shattered bone was protruding not just through the skin but also through the shreds of clothing he was wearing. He was moaning.

Sandingham edged along the ground to the man's side.

'Doshita no desuka?' he asked.

The man raised his face to Sandingham but made no reply. His open eyes saw nothing. It was quite obvious that he was blind.

Finally he mumbled a reply. Sandingham, not understanding it, said, 'Doshite agema shoka? Nanio motte kimashoka?'

'Mizu,' answered the man, his fingers pressing to his arm. Then, again, 'Mizu. Mizu.'

Sandingham could do nothing. There was no water.

After a while the young man got to his feet, rubbing his back up the wall. He staggered off in the direction of the river but, after going about a hundred yards, he fell on to his side, gave a yodelling howl and lay still.

All through the late afternoon, wounded figures had been continuously going by him, walking aimlessly, stumbling, tottering, lurching, feeling their way, crawling even. For the last half-hour, however, this traffic of pain and despair had eased.

The evening sun was trying to sever the clouds and smoke. It was weak and lifeless.

Leaning now against the wall, Sandingham sensed he was not on his own. He looked around him. No one alive was in sight. The dead youth lay in the road. The dead girl opposite was still there, partially covered by ash that had drifted against her like snow. The little group of dead by the remains of the food shop was unchanged. The dead cat beside the burnt-out car had not moved. Yet he felt he was with someone.

His eyes focused on a section of the wall to his right. There was someone there. They were standing in the centre of the street. Their shadow was plainly outlined on the plaster of the wall. Sandingham gazed at it. Yet in the street there was no one.

He stood up hurriedly and ran to the point where the person should be. Still no living person in sight; yet the shadow was still there, imprinted on the wall.

He took two quick strides and his own shadow merged with the other. He was where the person had been, should still be. If that person had had a soul and that soul had had a shadow it would be inhabiting his body now. They would be in him, safe in the deep recesses of his marrow. He heard himself shout – a shriek, his dry throat ripping apart as the sound rose to a whistling falsetto.

He ran, his own shadow flitting over the rubble of the houses and the bodies of the dead; his voice he left behind in the air, hanging there like the shadow that had lost its owner.

He was worn out, totally enervated. All he wanted to do was sleep, lose consciousness forever, just as Mishima had chosen to do.

After leaving the shadow he had fled along a maze of streets and, as darkness fell, found himself on the edge of what appeared to be a public park. There was a mass of people on the ground within it, lying or squatting upon the grass. Their silence shocked him deeply. Some were moaning or wheezing, some keening in undertones of anguish, but no one was speaking.

From a gate pillar there hung a gate. It was still, miraculously, on its hinges. Pointlessly, for the second half of the twin gate had disappeared, he pushed it open and stepped on to a pathway.

As soon as he passed a group of people on the ground, and they noticed that he was unhurt and standing upright, they begged water of him, or help, or comfort. They did not clamour or shout or demand. Nor did they really ask. They merely said it in soft, lovers-like voices.

' . . . awaremi tamai,' they pleaded. ' . . . awaremi tamai.'

He had no pity left to offer.

An old woman was going from one corpse to another, skilful in her ability to distinguish between the living and the non-living: there was often little apparent difference. From any corpse that wore spectacles she helped herself to them, trying on pair after pair before discarding them. Sandingham followed her movements until she discovered some that suited her vision and disappeared behind a clump of trees.

One man lying beside a split tree trunk captured Sandingham's attention. He sat cross-legged on the ground, stark-naked like a grotesque holy man. His body was covered with dancing stars. He was muttering something to himself, over and over. Curious, Sandingham went up to him and listened to his liturgy.

'Tenno heika, banzai, banzai, banzai, banzai.'

The stars around his body were made by the brittle evening light splitting apart in the hundreds of glass splinters that were embedded in his skin.

Towards the centre of the park the people thinned out and the shrubbery that had survived the blast rustled in the hot night breezes. Behind him, the pitiful congregation were illuminated by the dying fires in the city.

The bushes offered Sandingham the shelter and protection he needed to sleep. His eyes were leaden and his brain numbed by all he had seen. He pressed the branches aside and entered the cavern of the undergrowth.

The men were sitting in a row, their legs stretched out before them.

Sandingham eased himself on to the earth, not noticing them. Gradually, he felt their presence. He looked up at them.

They were all alike. Their faces were entirely burned and the frail skin hung from their cheeks and foreheads like the flaking surfaces of the hoods of ripe mushrooms. Their sockets were red voids and the mucous of their melted eyes shone glutinously on the raw, hanging flesh of their faces, like the glass from the tram windows. Their lips were gross, swollen slits surrounded by creamy pus and plasma.

He jerked back. They heard his movement and whispered through the cracks of their mouths. They hissed like creatures of the underworld. They spoke as insects might.

One of them tried to get up, rocking himself from side to side on his buttocks. Another raised his arms very slowly towards Sandingham. As he did so, Sandingham could hear the tissues in the man's armpits tearing.

He grunted with fear, with ultimate horror. He wanted to scream but could not.

The dead were coming to life.

He picked up a clod of dried earth and hurled it at the man with the crackling arms. The ball of soil hit him on the chest and disintegrated like a tiny grenade. The earth made a radiant pattern on the man's flayed skin which darkened as the blood soaked into the dirt, absorbing it into the meat.

Sandingham ran pell-mell through the park, standing on people's hands, tripping over their prostrate bodies, oblivious of everything. He ran until there was nothing in his life but the next step following the last step and the cartoon strip of all he had witnessed that day flickering in an endless loop through his brain.

He was lying in a ditch. Over his head, thin leaves were shifting in a breeze. A bird was cheeping somewhere, readying itself for dawn. Far off, a dog was howling and barking.

Opening his eyes, he stared upwards at the pattern of the tree against the vaguely lightening sky. Mud was caking on his chest and his left cheek. His right cheek was cushioned by wet clay. As he lifted his left arm to pull himself upright, the dried mud cracked. He shuddered and checked that it was just mud and not his flesh.

He took a deep breath and slapped his hand on the mud to reassure himself. The grimy splash spattered his soiled skin.

'I'm alive,' he said to the tufts of grass by his face. 'Filthy, agreed. But alive. Definitely!' He raised his eyes. 'But why? Why on earth me?'

His *tatame* stank of sweat. He lay on his side, hunched up like a foetus, trying to exorcise his memories. The other prisoners avoided him, for they had listened to his description of the city and what he had seen and they knew what he must be thinking. For some of them his concern was unexpected. The Japs had given the prisoners a time in hell and the dropping of what they all assumed to be a vast cluster bomb had come as a just retribution.

The guards kept well away from the prisoners. They still mounted watch over them but they seldom interfered with what they did and there were no more work parties sent out to factories, the shipyards or the timber works. No punishments were meted out and no fatigues ordered. Two prisoners in the *eiso* were released without explanation.

Five days after Sandingham had returned to the camp, walking in through the gates which the sentries held open for him, a turmoil was caused by an American aircraft flying low overhead. He heard the first pass.

'Joe! Joe! For Chrissake, get on out here! We've been spotted! It's the USAF!'

He walked listlessly to the door of the barrack and squinted against the bright morning sky. Out to sea, he could hear the whine of the aero engine. It gathered in volume.

The Grumman Avenger flew over so low that Sandingham could even make out the features of the pilot's face as he gazed down from the cockpit. Every rivet and exhaust-oil stain was pin-sharp. On the third run over, the aircraft climbed to a thousand feet and littered leaflets across the camp and the surrounding fields.

One of the leaflets fluttered down to the ground by Sandingham, who picked it up.

'What's it say?'

He turned to find that Mick Harwood had joined him in the sunlight. His sightless eyes stared flatly at Sandingham but the remainder of his face betrayed his eager inquisitiveness.

Sandingham up-ended the leaflet. It was a single sheet of paper printed on both sides, the front in English and the reverso in Japanese. Others gathered to hear him read it.

"To all Allied Prisoners-of-War," ' he started. ' "The Japanese forces have surrendered unconditionally and the war is over." '

'Well, I'll be damned! exclaimed Pete Krasky, known as 'Rancho', for he hailed from San Antonio. 'It's finally finished.'

No one else said a word.

' "We will get supplies to you as soon as is humanly possible," ' Sandingham continued, ' "and will make arrangements to get you out but, owing to the distances involved, it may be some time before we can achieve this.

' "You will help us and yourselves if you act as follows . . . " '

The senior officer now stood by Sandingham's side. In deference to him, Sandingham stopped reading and offered him the leaflet.

'Carry on, Joe,' the officer commanded, adding, 'and the rest of you pay particular attention.'

' "One: stay in your camp until you get further orders from us. Two: start preparing nominal rolls of personnel, giving fullest particulars. Three: list your most urgent necessities. Four: if you have been starved or underfed for long periods do not eat large quantities of solid food, fruit or vegetables at first. It is dangerous for you to do so. Small quantities at frequent intervals are much safer and will strengthen you far more quickly. For those who are really ill or very weak, fluids such as broth and soup, making use of the water in which rice and other foods have been boiled, are much the best. Gifts of food from the local population should be cooked. We want to get you back home quickly, safe and sound, and we do not want to risk your chances from diarrhoea, dysentery and cholera in this last stage. Five: local authorities and/or Allied officers will take charge of your affairs in a very short time. Be guided by their advice." '

'Not much trouble obeying that,' 'Harris' Tweed stated. 'We all stay on watery soup, eat as much as we have been and avoid fruit and veg. No problem.'

There was a general chuckle. Sandingham, raising his eyes, noticed another bunch of men over the far side of the parade-ground huddled around another reader.

'It has a translation of the Japanese on the back,' he went on. 'It reads, "In accordance with the terms of the surrender of all Japanese forces signed by His Majesty the Emperor the war has now come to an end. These leaflets contain our instructions to Allied prisoners-of-war and internees whom we have told to remain quiet where they are. Japanese guards are to ensure that the prisoners get these leaflets and that they are treated with every care and attention. Guards should then withdraw to their own quarters." '

'Remain where I am, I will,' CPO Rye said. 'But quiet?'

He coughed and started singing 'Rule Brittania' and even the Americans joined in. The senior officer, in the meantime, with the barrack leaders and the *hanchos*, marched off to confront the commandant with the leaflet.

Sandingham folded his copy and put it in the pocket of Mishima's jacket. It was then he saw Mick Harwood, tears streaming from his emotionless, unseeing eyes: Sandingham realised that he, too, was crying, but was not quite sure why.

The long table was laid with bowls, chopsticks and, by every fourth place setting, a tiny china pot of matchwood toothpicks. By every bowl was a sake cup and a flat dish. At intervals down the centre of the table were nests of condiments.

'Attention!'

The sergeant-major by the door squawked rather than barked his words. He had suffered from diphtheria and it had affected his voice box.

They stood in their places, their folding chairs scraping on the wooden planks of the floor that had been scrubbed by some of them over and over in the past years. A few, Sandingham amongst them, felt mildly guilty stepping on to the floor with their *tabis* or boots on.

The commandant entered. He was wearing his formal officer's uniform. His collars bore red patches and on his sleeves were gold stripes and five-pointed stars. Across his chest and around his waist were the regulation cross-strap and belt. By his side was his sword. His deputy accompanied him.

He went to the seat at the head of the table and stood erect

behind it; then, to the consternation of the silent prisoners, he
bowed low to them, undid the leather hanging strap of his sword
scabbard and handed the weapon horizontally to the prisoners'
senior officer.

'Senso wa owatta,' he said, his shrill voice now muted but
strident at the same time.

Half a dozen of their former warders then served a meal
consisting of a thin fish soup, a raw fish dish, tough steak – each
prisoner being served the equivalent of at least a previous month's
meat ration for the whole camp, if not more – and sake rice wine.
Several toasts were made but Sandingham, as he took to his feet
for them, did not hear the toasts and offered his thoughts not to
'King and Country' or 'The President' but to Bob, to Garry and to
Mishima.

When the dinner was over, they returned to their barracks and
fell asleep pondering on their futures.

'Dog-shit,' said Daphne, a brawny merchant seaman stoker.
'Definitely Dog-shit.'

'What about Snuffles? He was the . . . '

'Ssshhh!'

They were silent.

Sandingham cleared his throat to announce his arrival from the
ablutions.

'Okay. 's Joe.'

'What about Mickey Mouse?'

'I say Dog-shit.'

'I have to agree with that.'

He lay back on his *tatame* and sniffed at his hand: the soap had
been soft and its perfume was almost as tangible. He could not
remember when he'd last used scented soap. Perhaps it had been
his mother's, he thought, or Bob's. He had been issued with it
from the supply of Red Cross parcels the commandant had been
holding 'in reserve', as he meekly put it.

'Dog-shit it is then.'

'When?'

There was a pause.

'Well, I must say there's no time like the present.'

'What are you talking about?' Sandingham asked.

'Dog-shit,' replied Daphne from the dark. 'We're going to even an old score.'

'Don't you think there's been enough of that?' he answered.

'On a national scale, maybe, but we're thinking a bit more personally.'

'Want to join in, Joe?'

'No. I don't think so.'

'Suit yourself. But don't think for a sec that all Nippos are nice like that mate of yours in the timber shed. He was a rare un' – most of them are just little yellow pigs. Human runts.'

'And we're going to get the bacon.'

They left the barrack on tiptoes, letting themselves out into the warm night that would be the last in which Heicho Dog-shit would puff on his cigarette under the guard tower.

Holding his breath down low, Sandingham listened to the blackness, trying to pick out the sounds of death in the insect hubbub. He heard it, that rapid scuffling of feet and the thud of the length of waterpipe followed by the hurried plugs of kicking feet meeting flesh. By morning, Dog-shit's weighted body was being nibbled by fish under the reeds in the stream half a mile to the west.

'Nothing like a job well done,' commented Daphne as he wriggled under his thin bed quilt. 'Nothing like a bit of the old one-two.'

Soon he was snoring.

Over the next ten days three air drops were made to the camp. The first consisted of twenty canisters of supplies that swung to earth under cream silk parachutes. The prisoners were inundated with simple luxuries the like of which they had not seen since well before their capture. Tins of beef stew, fruit cocktail, butter and jam, sardines, fresh apples, magazines, cigarettes and even cigars fell like manna. The second drop, the following day, was made up of clothing, an assortment of civilian clothing and military articles, mostly of American origin. The last delivery was medical.

The prisoners were kept occupied making lists. Armies love lists and at first the prisoners duly pandered to this weakness, eagerly writing a host of lists but soon tiring of the exercise. When they grew bored they started to retreat into their private thoughts

and memories. For some, the cessation of war removed their
reason to fight for a hold on life and, in those last weeks, they
wilted and died. In contrast, many of those who were terribly ill
fought on. The arrival of saline drips, quinnine, iron and vitamin
pills, iodine, sulphur, procaine, mercurochrome, gentian violet,
swabs, surgical instruments and sterilised bandages were
weapons in their solitary battles, and they recovered slowly but
surely.

The sadness of the deaths of some of the inmates was compounded by the crash and killing of the aircrew of the plane that
dropped the medical supplies. The pilot had misjudged his
approach, and although he dropped his chutes on target in the
paddyfields east of the camp he failed to pull out of his run
in time. The aircraft hit the hill a mile inland from the perimeter fence, exploding on impact. A search-and-rescue party of
prisoners, with four guards, set off for the crash site immediately,
but when they arrived there was nothing they could do except
offer prayers and rummage through the smouldering wreckage
for dog-tags and identity bracelets.

That evening, as they left after their evening meal of mushroom
soup, Irish stew and tinned cheese, the prisoners were greeted by
a querulous wailing from one of the barracks.

'Who in God's name is that?'

'You mean "what". Sounds like a badger mating.'

Joking about the shindig, Sandingham and several others went
to investigate.

In the barrack hut, at the end by the *hibachi*, was a naval rating
called Giles Gilly. His nickname was 'Wrong Hole', derived from
a dirty tale about a Bombay tart who shouted 'Gilly, gilly' to any
cherry boy who missed his mark.

'What's up, WH? Got the trots?'

He was alternately hugging and punching his belly.

'Have a good fart and shut up.'

'But have it outside. You'll upset the bordello pong of Joe's
soap.'

Wrong Hole made no retort to this crudery. Instead, he
stopped wailing and started chattering like an ape, shivering until
his teeth clicked hard enough to chip.

'Pack it in. You'll have the Old Man in here.'

'Jesus Christ!' shouted Sandingham. He had gone past Wrong
Hole to the sailor's bunk. 'Get the MO!'

'What?' Disbelief and confusion hung in the question.

'Get the fucking MO. Fast as you can.'

From under the slats of the bunk Sandingham tugged the
gyroscopic flight compass from the crashed plane. The pressure
glass cover over the dial was unscrewed, the brass ring shining on
the floor.

Wrong Hole set off his banshee wailing again. He rubbed his
eyes hard until his fists were slick with tears and blood.

The camp doctor rushed in.

'What's up?'

'Wrong Hole, sir,' Sandingham reported. 'He's drunk the
methyl alcohol in this.' He held up the compass.

Wrong Hole went into a spasm like an epileptic. He thrashed
his limbs about and bit the leg of the table, clamping his jaws on it
like a rabid dog. He died blind and mad, strapped tight like a
lunatic, at dawn.

It was more a rural halt than a station, with a single shack of a
building at a point where the track divided into two: there was no
formal platform, just a smooth patch of dusty gravel by the rails.
A fence held at bay a marauding bank of late summer weeds and
the single signal gantry stuck up from the centre of the bank like
an alien tree. The wires that controlled the signal arm passed in
runners along the side of the track: alighting passengers had to
beware of stepping upon them.

Sandingham leaned against the fence. The wood was hot and
he turned his back on the other prisoners who formed the first
draft to be expatriated. In the weeds, crickets sawed. A yellow
butterfly jerked its wings up and down in a lazy flight as it dipped
from one small blossom to the next. It did not perch long at any of
them: the nectarial harvest had been robbed by the bees.

His mind was empty, but his emotions were in conflict. For
three and a half years he had had but one aim in life – to be free.
Not only of the camp, but of the Japanese military, the sickness
and the continual presence of the dark angel, the incubus of death
that waited to suck at any one of them at any time. He looked
down at the well-polished boots which pinched, at the khaki

trousers that rubbed at his crotch, at the white, laundered shirt that was crisp with starch and chafed his neck, and wondered if he would ever get used to wearing real clothes again.

Now he was free, liberated by an American lieutenant and his three sidekick GIs who had arrived in a jeep and distributed cigarettes, news and packets of Wrigley's spearmint chewing gum. The night before their liberation he had slept uneasily. His dreams were crammed with images of the years: of the beatings and Mishima's photo, of Garry's mad run and the *hibachi* glowing in the barrack, of the lousy food and the lousy clothes and the lousy *tatami*. Over all of these hung the mushroom-shaped cloud and the row of men in the bushes. He had twitched in his sleep and bruised his ankle against the wall.

It was only as they had formed ranks to march to the station that Sandingham had realised at last that he was leaving. A great sadness had come over him which he could neither control nor explain. He had looked back at the foul latrines, the kitchen block, the parade ground; had stared lastly at his own barrack; and his mouth had seized up and gone dry, and the lump in his throat had hardened into a stone of pity and sorrow for all those who had not made it. And he thought of those graves which were, even as he marched out of the gate, being exhumed for shipment home to the UK, or the USA, or Holland or some other benighted corner of the world where relatives would weep for an hour at a fresh graveside before continuing with their peace.

The barrack: his own corner of it had been home. He had lived there for – he tried to count the months, but his misery wiped time out. He steered the tears off his cheeks with a forefinger.

The train steamed in to the halt. It had five passenger carriages behind a coal tender. They lined up at the doors and heaved themselves into the compartments, eager as schoolboys to get a window seat. Once aboard, Sandingham stood by the door and closed it. The window was open and he leaned on the metal sill, looking down the way the train had come, from Hiroshima. He could not see their camp.

A toot on the train steam whistle heralded the judder of the couplings taking up the strain; then, with the locomotive pouting smoke, they slowly set off.

Beyond the signal, where the railway was crossed by a lane, a small group of local peasants had collected. Upon their shoulders they carried mattocks or hand scythes and their cart was piled with straw. They watched the train approach and Sandingham, in turn, watched them come nearer. As the train drew alongside the crossing some of the peasants bowed. Others just stood, silent and immovable spectators watching the procession of history pass them on a single-line railway track. A dog gambolled along the shingle, snapping at the wheels.

The docks were packed and bustling. Sandingham, having been 'processed', joined a contingent of other British prisoners from camps all over Japan. He befriended, in the transient manner that one strikes an acquaintance with fellow travellers, a soldier with a trim, pointed beard who was known to his comrades as 'Yagi'. It was a nickname Sandingham laughed at: *yagi* was Japanese for a goat.

Once aboard the ship they were shown to their berths and left to organise themselves until the vessel sailed. There was little to organise. Sandingham's worldly possessions were contained in a newly-issued cardboard box tied round with stout twine. He had nothing of real value, even to him, except the photo of Bob and the jacket that had been Mishima's. Other knick-knacks they all saved or hoarded were the stuff of souvenirs: gift material for sons or nephews.

He pushed the box under the shelf in the closet and lay on his top bunk. Beside his head was the cabin porthole. He spun the retaining clasps and opened the heavy glass disc, clipping it back against the storm plate. He thrust his head out, to discover that he was near the stern.

Amidships, the prisoners were still coming up the gangway: those too sick to make it were being helped in through a door level with the quay. The activity in the dock buildings hummed and resonated against the galvanised metal walls.

On the dock below him, between his ship and the one lying alongside aft of her, was a corral in which was massed a throng of silent Japanese. Not one of them was under thirty-five; women predominated.

'What are you watching?' asked Yagi in his musical Welsh accent.

Sandingham had forgotten how beautiful a South Wales voice could be.

'I'm sorry?'

'What are you looking at?'

'Nothing much. The warehouses, the docks, a crowd of Japs.'

'Poor blighters!'

'Why?'

'They're waiting there for the remains of their dead. Shipped back from all over the Pacific.'

Duty rotas were established as soon as the ship was at sea. They were light, for many of the prisoners were too weak to undertake heavy work. Sandingham was assigned to the galley to make buttered toast every breakfast. He also accepted the task of brewing up mid-morning coffee and heating the doughnuts that were issued with the mugs.

He spent his afternoons lying in his bunk reading or lounging about on the deck with a detective novel: another luxury he had forgotten. The sun tanned him and he dozed off from time to time, only to wake ten minutes later with a guilty conscience, feeling that he wasn't doing his chores and would consequently be beaten for his idleness. Then he would see the sky and the smoke pluming from the funnel and a warm contentment would seep into him again.

One morning, the chief cook asked him to fetch more ham. The toast was made and he was about to leave.

'Where do I get it?'

'C'mpanyon way fo-er,' the Texan told him. 'Fridges 'e'en.'

Sandingham found companionway four and descended the steep incline of the steps. At the bottom, in the bowels of the ship, he found himself in a corridor into the walls of which were set heavy steel-plate doors. The nearest was labelled 'TWO/2', the next 'THREE/3' – both numbers and letters made it simple for the military uneducated. He walked down the dimly-lit passage until he reached 'SEVEN/7' and wrenched the retaining levers down. The bulk of the door swung open. He twisted the switch and low wattage bulbs came on in the refrigeration compartment.

He lifted his leg over the door sill and looked about him for the sides of ham.

The metal shelves, six high, reaching as far as he could see ahead and to left and right, were loaded with corpses sewn into canvas sacks, each one stencilled in black – the one by his elbow was marked 'PEARLMAN: KEVIN/342688'.

They steamed past Corregidor Island, into the Bay of Manila, the sun set astern of the ship with a vast godly blaze of yellow, orange and red. The sea was a smooth, dark green and the tropical undergrowth on the island was already so lush as to cover over the scars of the intense fighting that had taken place there. The bay itself was strewn with sunk or scuttled ships and minefields, indicated by brightly painted buoys, were scattered either side of the shipping lane.

On the quayside, US Red Cross girls were dispensing Coca-Cola and coffee, doughnuts, packets of peanuts and chewing gum, cigarettes and copies of *Life* magazine.

Peering down on them from the deck, Sandingham realised that they were the first European women he'd seen since the week before Christmas, 1941.

PART ELEVEN

Hong Kong: Christmas, 1952

THE HOTEL LOUNGE was bedecked with paper-chains, tissue Chinese lanterns, silver and gold tinsel and fairy lights. After the guests had retired for the night the first-floor roomboys had taken the decorations out of storage and hung them. When they had completed the lounge they moved down to the main lobby. The square wooden pillar by the reception desk was spiralled with red, white and blue crêpe, the bar was surrounded by blinking lights, each bulb the shape of a distinctly oriental Santa Claus, the ceiling was criss-crossed with more paper-chains and, on the main glass doors, there was a matching pair of wax-paper and plastic holly wreaths. The younger children, coming down for breakfast the following morning, were entranced by the translation of the business-like lobby into a psuedo-grotto of magical proportions.

Up in his parents' room, David studied his diary. It was nearly full. His grandmother had sent it to him from England the Christmas before and he knew that she would send him another this year. She had said she would in the letter that had accompanied her birthday card to him in September.

Thumbing through the entries, he relived bits of his and the world's year. After a few pages, he read sections out loud, pretending he was the BBC World Service announcer recapitulating upon 1952:

'February: King George VI of England dies; the nation and the Empire mourn. 22 June: I have a cholera jab; very painful. 7 September: my birthday; I have a party and Andrew gives me a BRM Dinky, godfather gives me a fountain pen with a solid gold nib . . .'

He stopped reading. His finger was in the page on which he had written of his encounter with barmy Hiroshima Joe in his room. The meeting had scared him, though at the time he was not so scared as puzzled and apprehensive. It had taught him that adults were certainly not all to be trusted to behave rationally, and Hiroshima Joe in particular seemed to have a code apart from his parents, from Jonty and Margaret, Biddy and Major Binniss, Sally and Mike Prentice and others of his parents' friends.

Adults, he concluded, were utterly unpredictable and not to be relied upon. The one exception was in areas in which experience or tradition governed them – such as at Christmas: then they were safely predictable. In the run-up to Christmas Eve they would secrete parcels in cupboards (heavily taping or tying them against tampering); they would become jovial – sometimes falsely so – and free with praise; or alternatively they would become threateningly strict at odd moments when they knew they held the whip-hands of present-withdrawal or Father-Christmas-absence.

On Christmas Eve itself they were particularly jolly. The anticipation of giving, which David himself appreciated as a momentary warm and pleasing glow, affected them as much as receiving did the children. They invariably spent the morning shopping or going to work where little work was done. At lunchtime they went to office parties and in the evening they drank with friends, went out to other friends', had friends visit them or a mixture of all these. Their children either accompanied them, which was uncommon, or stayed at home in the charge of the amah, which was commonplace. During the night, as David now knew, one of them stole into their children's bedrooms and filled their stockings; later they would giggle as they arrayed presents under the tree. The following morning Father, a majesterial head-waiter-cum-master of ceremonies, handed out the spoils to Mother, children and, in David's case, the roomboys who serviced their hotel rooms.

This year, he mused, Christmas would be different for him, at least. His father was not going to be there. He was in Korea, and would not be back from his tour of duty until the second week in January.

David's mother told him that his father would telephone on

Christmas Day, but she was not sure when, for the lines were always busy at Christmas with people ringing their loved ones. He pointed out that they *were* loved ones, which his mother indeed assured him was so, but he also understood that there were lots of men in the war who wanted to talk to their wives and children, too. And parents.

Recalling this conversation as he looked at his diary reminded him of his letter. He pulled it out of the flap at the back of the book, next to an old map of the London Underground and Southern Region commuter lines. Somewhere, surrounded by pastures of grazing kangaroos and wallabies and dingoes, Mr and Mrs Kerrins would not be getting a phone call. This no longer gave him the sad ache that it had, but it did still hurt him a little to think that the call would not be connected.

The door opened and his mother came in, carrying in her arms two large brown-paper bags.

'What's in them?' He looked from one of them to the other.

'Specialities,' she said mysteriously.

He knew better than to ask, for at Christmas 'specialities' could cover a multitude of items, many coded 'Top Secret' until the day itself.

'Don't you want to know what they are?' she asked. This went further to prove David's theory of adult unpredictability. 'It's not like you to be uncurious.'

He had done suffixes and prefixes at school in the last week of term. With Christmas drawing nigh, however, he considered it would be unwise to correct his mother's grammatical error which, he reasoned, was in any case probably made to check his knowledge. Whenever David caught his father out over such mistakes he would first scowl, just for a split second, then cheer up, saying, 'Just testing you, David. Well done!'

'What is there, then?' he replied, causing his mother to smile indulgently.

She lifted the articles free of the bags one at a time and laid them on the coffee table.

'Walnuts,' she began, 'hazlenuts and almonds; crystallised fruit; dried figs; dates; a bottle of gin, a bottle of whiskey, a bottle of rum' – she winked at him – 'a bottle of vodka; some maraschino cherries – green and red – not,' she emphasised, 'to be eaten by others beforehand – and stuffed olives; crisps and prawn crackers, cashew nuts and peanuts . . . ' She opened the second bag. 'And decorations. We're going to decorate this room.'

'We haven't a tree,' David pointed out with the unmoving logic of his age.

There was a knock on the door. With perfect timing the duty roomboy entered carrying an artificial tree. It was not very large, and when he stood it on the suitcase shelf by the bathroom door it did not reach to the ceiling. But it was a tree, and it delighted David.

'On Christmas Eve we're going to have a party. And on Christmas Day we're going over to Commander Fisher's for lunch. You'll like that, won't you?'

'Yes,' David answered truthfully. The Fisher boys were friends of his and they lived on Hong Kong Island with a wooded hillside right behind their bungalow. They had found a dead cobra there in the summer. 'But what about Daddy's phone call? He won't know where we are.'

'That won't matter,' his mother said. 'We're going to ring him on the way. We're going to stop off at the Cable and Wireless office in Central District and call him ourselves. I've got the call booked for Christmas morning. We've got three whole minutes.'

She busied herself putting away the Christmas fare and, together, they spent the rest of the afternoon decorating the room.

Sandingham had been staying more and more in his room, raiding the cardboard cartons of canned food on the back stairs and going down to the hotel dining room for a meal every other day, so as not to arouse suspicion. Much of the stolen food was wasted and he flushed it down the toilet: he was seldom hungry, and losing weight. A week before Christmas he had risked venturing out after dark to obtain as much opium as he could; he managed to purchase enough to keep him going for a few days, but no more. The word was out that he was a marked man.

Living almost entirely in his room was rather like existing in a more luxurious *eiso*. There was no one to talk to, no one to confide in, no one with whom to share his troubles. On the Friday before Christmas, when the telephone rang, it made him jump and shake. He had not used it for more than two months. He let it jangle for a full minute before lifting the receiver. It was the hospital: an orderly had been instructed to ask after his health and to invite him to attend the doctors' surgery that afternoon.

'I'm afraid I can't make it until after Christmas at the earliest,' he lied.

'Dr Gresham is most anxious to see you, sir. He asked me to say that if you were too ill to cross the harbour then he would be willing to visit you.'

Sandingham looked about his room. He was ashamed of it and would not want to display it to another European. But there was no escaping the fact that, one way or the other, the doctor would get to see him.

'I think I can possibly make it. This afternoon? What time?'

'Two-thirty, sir. And could you please bring a urine sample, sir?'

The festive atmosphere around the hotel bar did not impress or exhilarate Sandingham very much. He was struck initially by a sense of revulsion at its hearty seasonal *bonhomie*, then by a feeling of deep nostalgia. He shrugged this off as he pushed through the glass doors to the waiting hotel shooting-brake.

As the vehicle swung right along Waterloo Road a black Ford Prefect slipped out of a parking place and followed it at a discreet distance. This did not fool Sandingham. He had known it had been standing guard over him for three days.

'Nat'han Low?' enquired the driver.

'Star Ferry,' answered the American who was sitting with his wife next to Sandingham in the seat by the window. 'And you, sir?'

Sandingham could trace no irony implicit in the 'sir' and guessed that its utterance was the result of a good mid-western upbringing rather than a hint of New York smart-assedness.

'Star Ferry as well, please.'

'Clayton Sellers, Junior.' The American offered his hand and Sandingham shook it once. 'My wife Blanche. We come from Omaha, Nebraska.' Sandingham tipped his head to her. 'You residin' in the hotel?'

'Yes.'

'Been here lawng? I mean, you live here in Hawng Kawng?'

The rhyme caused Sandingham to smile. Few things did these

days, but this ludicrous man struck him as funny and, for that reason, Sandingham liked him.

'Since the war, more or less.'

'That's a helluva time, sir.'

His wife chipped in, 'Can you recommend any sights for us to see? We are just passing through, you understand. My husband is on business. He works for . . . '

She named a big corporation, but Sandingham missed it. The black Ford had come alongside the hotel bus at the traffic lights on Nathan Road. A man in the passenger seat was speaking rapidly to the hotel driver in the Shanghai dialect of which Sandingham was ignorant. The driver made a reply and the lights changed. He shuffled the steering wheel through his hands and the bus shooting-brake turned left. The Ford continued across the junction. Sandingham could tell the driver was worried.

'What's the matter, Ah Cheong?' he asked in Cantonese so that the American couple could not understand.

'That is a bad man. He speaks bad things.'

'What sort of bad things?'

Ah Cheong cast a quick glance over his shoulder.

'He says you a wicked man. He says I should not take you in the hotel bus again. I told him that I had to because you are a hotel guest. He said if I do that, he will make trouble for me and my family.'

'Don't worry about it, Ah Cheong. I'll not use the bus after today. Not for a while.'

The driver looked relieved and thanked him. Sandingham put the problem to the rear of his mind.

'Sorry about that,' he said. 'Places to visit? How much time have you?'

'Until January two. We fly out Pan American on January two.'

'Ample time. You must visit Hollywood Road – they call it "Cat Street" – and the temple there. Then you must go out to Repulse Bay and to the floating restaurants in Aberdeen. You should do a tour of the New Territories, too. Don't miss Kam Tin: it's a walled village, centuries old. Have you been up The Peak?'

'Not yet. We're on our way there now. Going up the mountain railroad.'

'It's often best to travel up by taxi and down in the Peak Tram, as they call the mountain railway.'

In that way, Sandingham obtained his escort across the ferry and up to the hospital.

'How have you been, Joe?'

'Not so well. The shakes are worse and I'm off my food a bit. My throat's a bit worse. It still hurts to pass water.' He handed Gresham a beer bottle with an inch of urine in it. 'Best soak the label off before leaving it around. Especially near Christmas,' he joked.

Gresham chuckled and said, 'What are you doing over the holiday?'

'The usual, I suppose. Stay in my room, have a drink or two. Listen to the radio. Be a Queen's speech this year.'

'It's a lousy time, Christmas, when you're single. I remember it from when I was a medical student. My parents were killed in the war so I had no family.'

Sandingham made no reply.

Shuffling through the medical papers on his clipboard, Gresham added, 'And chase a dragon?'

'Probably. Yes – chase a dragon.'

Lying on the couch, the white sheet under him, seemed to accentuate Sandingham's illness. His legs, with their rough sore patches, appeared more starkly diseased against the blue-white of the hospital linen. His hand shook more visibly and his thinning hair was somehow thinner with the overhead spotlight shining through it. Gresham picked up Sandingham's right hand and pressed the fingernails. The quick was white and remained so after the pressure was released.

'That hurt?'

'A bit. Not a stabbing pain. More a throb.'

The doctor held an ophthalmoscope to Sandingham's eye, the thin pin-beam of light making Sandingham dizzy. He tightened his fist on the rim of the couch.

'The light bother you?'

'Yes. Strong light has been affecting me for some months.'

'Let me see . . . sit up, will you?'

Sandingham sat up and dropped his legs over the edge of the

couch: they did not reach to the ground and he felt like a child in too high a chair. Gresham felt under his jaw, under his arms and around his sides. He prodded his liver. He pulled Sandingham's eyelids down and studied the faintly pink mucosa. He took his pulse. He depressed Sandingham's tongue with a wooden spatula and peered into his pharynx with a pen torch.

'Glands bothering you?'

'I don't think so. I have noticed blood passing out with my faeces.'

Gresham weighed him, wrapped a sphygmometer around his arm and pumped up the rubber bulb. The mercury column rose and bobbed in its tube. Gresham made notes.

'Your diverticulosis – the blood in your faeces – how long has this been happening?'

'A while. I can't be sure.'

'As long as your easy bruising?'

Sandingham's arms and shins were mottled with bruises in various stages of discolouration. Around them his skin had a shiny white pallor to it which was flaking.

'I suppose so, yes.'

He scratched at his thigh, a dust of himself gathering under his nails. He sucked them clean.

'I seem to have dandruff all over,' he remarked.

The doctor made no comment but pressed into his back and listened to Sandingham's lungs through a stethoscope. When he pulled the black nipples of the instrument from his ears his face was grim.

'I'll not beat about the bush, Joe. I don't think it is fair for me to do so. I'm going to lay it on the line, as the Yanks say. I could try to fool you, but you know and I know that is wrong and I think I should spell it out to you. Frankly, I've bad news and Dr Stoppart will confirm it.

'Your samples have been tested here but we've also had some of them flown back to the UK for analysis and a second opinion. They have better testing facilities there than we have here.

'It's not dandruff you have but a kind of skin cancer. There is no cure for it, but we can slow it down with a new ointment from the USA. We've got some of that . . . ' He picked up a tube from his desk. It had yellow and black printing on the label. ' . . . And want you to use it. It's still experimental in that it's going through clinical trials. You're one of them, a guinea pig, so I need you to be on hand for testing in the future. Will that be okay?'

Avoiding Gresham's eyes, Sandingham said that it would. Leung's private army permitting – but that he did not add. A murder charge on top of all this was not something to relish.

'That's not all, I'm afraid. You know you are anaemic: you also have, we are fairly sure, acute lymphoblastic leukaemia. This is because the marrow in your bones is malfunctioning, to put it crudely. This may be the cause in part of your passing blood: you may have thrombocytopenia – internal bleeding. We need to test further to know this for sure.'

'What does this mean?' questioned Sandingham, though he was aware of the implications from the earlier briefing he had had from Gresham and Dr Stoppart.

'You'll likely fall prey to common illnesses and some not-so-common ones, too. Your resistance is lowered, and what resistance there is will be further reduced by your drug habit. Before you ask, I must say we are pretty sure. And there is no really useful treatment. There are some drugs we can offer you, but they are new and largely untried in the field, so to speak.' He tugged the stethoscope from his neck and folded it into its black wooden box. 'I'm really very sorry. It's a sod of a thing to tell you at Christmas.'

'You mean, at my last Christmas.'

It wasn't a question but a statement of fact that Sandingham had absorbed and which he had, without proof, been expecting for several months.

'Yes.'

'How long?'

'It depends. I can't calendar it. Next month, possibly – that would be the earliest. Two years at the most, if you were lucky. You have a lot going against you.' He looked straight at Sandingham. 'Why don't you chuck in your habit? It would help you.'

Yet Sandingham knew that it wouldn't. It would make things worse. He made no reply.

As Sandingham dressed to leave, Gresham said, 'You must keep in touch. We'd like to see you at least weekly. Today's

Friday. Boxing Day next Friday. Can I see you the Monday after Christmas?'

Sandingham nodded. 'Why not?'

He went on foot to the Bowen Road station of the Peak Tram. There was little point in maintaining a low profile from what he now thought of as 'Choy's Boys': if they didn't kill him, the radiation would do the task for them. The only difference would be the pain: perhaps it would be best to let nature take her foul course than let some Chinese hood have his pleasure with sharpened bamboo strips and a razor.

He boarded the up-bound tram, giving his fare to the be-spectacled Chinese ticket collector who stood at an angle of forty-five degrees to the tram cabin floor. As it passed the down-bound above May Road he saw Mr and Mrs Clayton Sellers, Jnr, sitting close to each other in the front seat. Blanche Sellers – was she 'Junior' too? he wondered – chanced a quick wave to him before grabbing on to the window frame again out of repressed panic. May Road was the steepest part of the track.

At the top station, below Mount Austin, Sandingham crossed the junction by the taxi rank and set off down Harlech Road. He walked as briskly as he could, but was soon out of breath and had to lean against a railing to rest. It dented his palm painfully, and he heard himself say, 'For Chrissake, driver!' in an exasperated voice.

His strength regained, Sandingham started off again at a more leisurely pace. As he strolled under the winter trees he let his past gather about him. Vague voices returned that he had not heard for years.

'Iron railings on either side. Try not to decorate them with khaki . . . the British Army doesn't survive on tea, tinned jam and powdered eggs . . . Very good, Bellerby . . . If your pecker stays aloft, your men's will . . . Jay! We've got two hours . . . '

He halted at the fork in the road where the left took him either down to the old gun implacement or along the north slope of High West and the rifle range. He looked down the mountainside to the Hill above Belcher's.

'Fancy a little snort for the road? Sit down, dear boy!' chortled a voice in the wind.

The butts of the range were made of concrete and Sandingham

took shelter in them from the drizzle that was seeping out of the fog a hundred feet higher up. On the ground, by the target frames, there was a small pile of spent copper bullets dug out of the rear bank of the range by children. He picked the bullets up, one by one, and tossed them to and fro in his hands.

Choy had been waiting for him at the entrance to the Star Ferry pier. As the crowd surged forwards down the steeply tipping gangway he took Sandingham's elbow.

'Allow me to help you down, Mr Sandingham,' he said amiably. 'A man in your state of health needs a helping hand.'

'Fuck off!' Sandingham muttered. He shook his elbow free and promptly stumbled. The gangway was at such a clumsy angle he had difficulty finding his step on the slats. He felt momentarily dizzy as he sat heavily on a bench.

Once on the ferry, Choy sat down next to him.

'You are very sick. You need to see a doctor.'

After his earlier statement on the gangway Sandingham had wondered if Choy had managed to bribe or threaten his way into the Bowen Road hospital records, but his speech now suggested that he wasn't in full control of the facts.

'I may have something that might cure your illness,' Choy continued. 'Look.'

In his hand he was carrying that morning's edition of the *Hong Kong Standard*; wrapped in it was a thick-handled bowie knife, the steel blade of which glinted along its cutting edge. Sandingham felt an involuntary shudder course through his body.

'Consider this, Joe.' Choy's voice was low yet crystalline with menace as he bent slightly to Sandingham's ear. 'If I were sitting where you are, and you were here, even with all these people about us, I would need only to strike the palm of my hand against this to push it through your clothing and into your stomach. Then I could toss it away into the harbour. Do you know the bottom of Hong Kong harbour is thick with mud? It would sink from sight forever. Then I would shout for help. I would get away as soon as the ferry arrived on Kowloon-side. But you, Joe? In your health, you would not live long with your stomach torn.'

'Then do it,' Sandingham offered. 'Go ahead. I shall scream you did it. But so what? Go on then, Mr Choy. Kill me.'

He spoke loudly and a few Europeans sitting nearby, laden with bow-tied Christmas packages, stole a glance in his direction. He heard one person exclaim, 'Oh, really! These white Russians. Pickled at four.'

'You see, you are a cast-off of your kind. And now you are not to be touched by Chinese people. Soon you will die. In my time, not in yours. You'll have poison in your food; maybe some heroin mixed into your opium – I know where you bought your last supply: that man is dead now – or a knife will stab you in the street. Even in your hotel room. See?'

Choy slid an expensive calfskin wallet out of his well-tailored jacket and flipped it open. From the stamp pocket protruded a brass key. It bore the same trademark as the hotel door locks.

'The skeleton,' Choy explained, though he need not have bothered. Sandingham was well aware what it was.

The ferry bumped against the piles of the Tsim Sha Tsui pier and the passengers rose to leave. The deck tilted under the weight of the people standing around the gangway.

'Bus or taxi, Joe? Take the bus. Maybe the conductor will let you fall from the step. Take a taxi. A Kowloon taxi? One of the orange and red ones? Maybe the driver will not go to Waterloo Road but to a hillside behind Kai Tak. Near to Sai Kung. It is very lonely over there. Little traffic. Or you can walk. But it is a long way, and it will be dark before you enter your hotel.'

At the taxi rank, Choy vanished into the crowd. Sandingham queued as if to catch a cab. A rickshaw coming along to the ferry concourse conveniently collided with a private car. A crowd quickly gathered to watch the slanging match and Sandingham escaped into the columned portico of the railway station. He purchased a ticket to the station near the hotel and, in this way, got home safely. It was, as Choy had reckoned, now dark.

He sneaked into the hotel through the rear tradesman's entrance and was about to climb the back stairs to his floor when he heard music issuing from the front lobby. Curious, he went along one of the ground floor corridors, through the tiny garden courtyard where the trees were now bare.

The decorations were lit. The oriental Father Christmases blinked on and off, the paper lanterns were illuminated and the tinsel shimmied like a shoal of landed fish. The lobby was packed with children. In the centre, by the bar, was a juggler dressed in classical Chinese costume. Upon his head was a pork-pie hat of black silk with a pom-pom on it. His jacket was embroidered with dragons and clouds in azures and turquoises and jade greens. He was tossing, as high as the ceiling, five cups and a orange. Behind him was a Chinese band with a wailing flute, a zither and a small drum.

The juggler passed the cups to an assistant and bowed, then gave the orange to a boy in the front row. Sandingham noticed that this was David.

His act over, the juggler waved on a man with a rosewood xylophone. The musician started to plink out his melodies, parodies of European jazz band tunes and current popular songs from the radio. He was accompanied by a small grey monkey with eyes like bloodshot berries, that pranced and tumbled in time to its master's music. To complete the show, the little primate was dressed in a tricorn hat, elasticated pants of canary-yellow silk and a tiny brocade jacket. It carried a classical Chinese sword constructed of wood and papier mâché which it smacked on the floor and bit. Around the monkey's waist was a collar, to which was secured a length of thin chain. The children laughed uproariously until tears of merriment ran down their cheeks.

Standing by the dining room entrance, Sandingham saw nothing amusing in the monkey's cavorting and tomfoolery. It was trapped by its japes, despite its fine clothes, in a spiral of living and dying that was as sordid as his own.

As he turned to go up the main staircase Sandingham saw Heng studying him and he eased his way towards the manager, pressing through the standing parents behind the children.

'A party for the guests' children,' the manager said. 'The owners thought it a good idea.'

'Very good indeed,' Sandingham agreed. It was, after all, Christmas.

'But you don't like it?'

Heng knew what he was thinking, Sandingham realised. The worldly old codger had him summed up in one.

'The juggler – what I saw of him – was excellent. But I can't avoid feeling sorry for the monkey.'

'You know what it is to be tied up, Mr Sandingham. Maybe not by a chain or by rope, but . . . '

Looking into the manager's eyes for a moment, Sandingham thought he recognised a flash of sympathy, a spark of friendship that was not suggested or forced by the season.

'Yes, Mr Heng. During the war . . . ' His sentence too tailed off.

'And now also, perhaps.'

'Perhaps.'

Sandingham knew that, by the end of the week – by Christmas Day – he would be in debt again for the rent. It was already overdue.

The step had been slick with a sudsy water that the floor amah had failed to mop up. Running to his room late on the Wednesday morning, David had slipped and fallen awkwardly on his left arm. The roomboy on duty, Ching, who was the one to see him safely over the road to school, heard his fall and the short yelp that went with it. He comforted David, sat him up on the rubber mat that ran down the length of the corridor and called for his mother. She thought his arm was broken, called the doctor and half an hour later, David – much to his joy – was rushed to Kowloon Hospital in a Daimler ambulance. The X-rays showed no fracture. A severe sprain was diagnosed and David was released with his arm in a white cotton sling.

'Will it mean I have to stay in bed for Christmas?' he asked the casualty doctor fearfully. He did not want to ruin his mother's Christmas nor lose out on the festivities and the trip to the Fishers', not to mention the telephone call to his father in Korea.

'No, young man. I don't think so. Just you stop in bed for the remainder of today, get some rest and get up tomorrow. But keep your arm in the sling and don't use it. Can you unwrap your presents single-handed? I expect so.'

He was taken the short distance back to the hotel in a taxi. His mother helped him into his pyjamas and put him to bed at four o'clock. The day was fading and he did not feel so out of place. To cheer him up, his mother gave him one of his presents early.

'It's just a little one,' she informed him, 'to take away the pain.'

He duly succeeded in removing the wrapping with one hand. Inside was a cardboard box with a battle scene printed on it. He lifted the lid to discover one of the presents he'd hoped for and had included on his list: a machine-gun crew. There were three soldiers and what David assumed was a Vickers machine-gun. One of the soldiers was sitting with his legs bent up: he was the firer. A second knelt by his side: he was feeding the belt into the gun. The third was opening an ammunition box. They were dressed in khaki and mounted on a square of stiff card on to which was outlined a hill, trees and a shell-burst in the sky.

'I like them,' he thanked his mother. 'I like them very much.'

He lay on his side and positioned the gun crew in a foxhole punched in his pillow, inches from his face. That close up, they looked real, almost alive.

'It won't hurt so much in the morning, David. Now you get some sleep. I'll come in during the evening with some supper for you. Would you like a warm milk? Ching can get you some.'

'Yes, please. And some digestive biscuits. And some salted cashews.' After all, he thought, it was worth trying it on.

'Biscuits yes, nuts no. A sprain is one thing. You being sick is another.'

She closed the door and he heard the lock snap home.

It was dark on the stairs. The light-bulb must have blown on the landing above. Sandingham gave no thought to the coincidence that the bulb below had also seemed to have burnt out.

He felt his way downwards and reached the first of the food boxes. It contained cans of peaches. If he took more of these the missing quantity would be noticed, so he passed his hand over this to the next box which held tins of Carnation milk. He took two of the smaller size and wedged them into his pocket. Omitting the next two cartons, he slid his thumb under the flap of the third and lifted out a tin of clear vegetable soup. From lower still, he removed three flat tins of sardines and, by mistake, a tin of potatoes. He shoved the tins into his shirt.

There was a sound above him on the stairs: someone had opened the landing door. He held his breath and did not move, knowing he was secure from discovery if he did not give himself away. It was too dark for him to be seen. He heard the door close with a swish of its hydraulic hinge. He waited. No other noise happened.

Carefully, to be on the safe side, he edged up the stairwell. There was no light to guide him apart from an exceptionally faint glow through one of the small, grimy, frosted-glass windows facing the back street.

He halted, and listened. He could hear something. It was a far ticking, which he decided was emanating from somewhere towards the front of the building.

The flurry of a soft garment and the zizz of something being thrown came to his ears as two quite separate entities. He dropped his head. A light metallic object clattered down the stairs behind him. A second later a powerful torch shone momentarily in his face. The bright burn of the reflector hung in his retina and made him giddy. Aim restored, the torch was clicked off and another light object was hurled at Sandingham. However, as soon as the torch had gone out, he had flattened himself into the wall. When he did not tumble on to the cartons and boxes, and the torch was switched on again, he was ready.

His attacker, he estimated, was about fifteen steps above him, next to the door to the landing above. He shut his eyes and hurled himself upwards, his feet slapping on the concrete. He grabbed the man around his knees and twisted him sideways. The tins next to his chest gouged dents in his skinny ribs. The other, not to be overbalanced, got a firm hold of the doorknob with one hand and as best he could lashed out at Sandingham with torch and feet.

Letting go of his assailant's knees with one arm, Sandingham flailed with his free hand at the torch, felt it slap into his palm, closed his fingers on it and wrenched it free. He heard it roll against the wall in the darkness.

A fist as bony as if it were devoid of flesh began pummelling his skull, forcing him to loosen his tackle-like hold. He thrust his hand into his pocket and wrenched out one of the tins. He swung his arm back, hoisted himself up on his feet and brought the tin down on the point of darkness he assumed hid the man's head. The tin connected.

The man let go of the door handle and slumped to the floor. He was not unconscious as Sandingham hoped and his feverish scrabbling suggested he was searching for the torch.

The next moment Sandingham was booted on the thigh and

went down. He struggled rapidly to his feet and kicked back at the darkness but his foot only hit the wall. As he was knocked down once more with a vicious punch, he found the torch. Spinning it in his hand until the rubber stud was under his thumb, he pressed and the light scorched out to show the skull-like face of the hotel gardener: the first of Choy's inside men. He had evidently known of Sandingham's thieving excursions down the back stairs, learning of them when lying in his sleeping corner at the roof door, and had used one of these to lay his ambush.

Keeping the man confused with the beam, Sandingham struck out with his foot at the man's groin. The gardener grunted as the air was pushed from his lungs and he doubled over. Sandingham brought his knee viciously into the lowering face. There was a mouse-like squeak as the gardener's nose broke. The gardener flailed his arms, clutching at his face: he lost his balance and fell on to the steps in a groaning heap.

In his room, Sandingham locked the door and levered the bedside table against it. Nowhere, he now knew, was safe.

David sat in the armchair by the french windows of the lounge, gazing out at the balcony. It was bare of the potted chrysan-themums and kumquat bushes of the summer. The grey sky did not even hint at it being Christmas Eve. On the parquet tiles by his chair was the machine-gun crew guarding a Bedford army lorry.

Sandingham pulled the glass door open and entered the lounge. He was careful to leave the door ajar so that the roomboy on duty could see that he meant no mischief.

'Happy Christmas,' he said. 'What have you asked Santa Claus for?'

David did not turn round. He had seen Sandingham enter through his reflection in the glass before him.

'There's no such person as Santa Claus. Your father and mother – and grandpa and grandma and people – buy you presents and your parents give them to you. And,' David added, a little scornfully, 'you can't say "Happy Christmas" yet because Christmas's not until tomorrow.'

Sitting himself in the chair across the room, Sandingham leaned forward and rested his elbows on his knees. The pressure of his arms hurt his legs, which had pained him continuously since the fight with the gardener the night before.

'I have a present for you.'

He offered a small package to the boy.

David's first inclination was to refuse it. He was very wary of Sandingham now and had taken to heart the warnings he had received from his mother, Ching and the other hotel staff. The more he considered the outstretched gift, though, the more he realised that it would be churlish to refuse. Besides, he was inquisitive and eager to discover what was in it. If he told his mother he had received it, it would be all right. Then it occurred to him that he could not reciprocate.

'I've nothing to give you,' he apologised. 'So I shouldn't accept anything.'

'That doesn't matter,' Sandingham replied. 'I think I've got all I want.'

David took the package.

'What have you done to your arm?' Sandingham inquired.

'Sprained it. Can you please start the paper off?'

He handed the gift back and Sandingham tore the string away and peeled back the paper from one end.

Inside was a small box. It was dented, and had obviously been used for other things before. David removed the top and looked inside.

There was an envelope there, one of the PAA airmail ones from the desk rack in the lobby. He slit the flap. Inside was a faded photo of a young soldier.

'Who's this?'

'It was a friend of mine,' Sandingham explained. 'In the war. A very dear friend. He is long since dead.'

'Is this my present?'

'Part of it,' Sandingham said mysteriously. 'There's more if you feel in the box.'

David took out a figure cocooned in crisp tissue: it was a soldier, not a private or sergeant but a major-general. The toy soldiers in his set boxes never had officers in with them: they were always other ranks. And, unlike David's soldiers that were cast in a cheap alloy and clumsily painted on a production line, this staff officer was cast in solid lead and had been carefully and painstakingly painted by hand. Even his medals were accurately coloured, and the brown paint hadn't gone over the edge of his Sam Browne belt once. This impressed David, for even the loader of his machine-gun crew had the paint from his helmet run on to his neck.

With the major-general was a shining half-crown. David had not seen a half-crown since he was on the ship coming out. His grandfather had given two to him on the dock at Southampton as a parting gift. The coin was heavy with a shield design on one side and King George VI's head on the other.

At the bottom of the box was a third envelope.

From it, David slid a postcard. It was an ordinary black-and-white photograph and on the back of it a space for a message. Next to that were a few ruled lines for the address and a square where one should stick the stamp. There was printing on it in characters, but not Chinese ones. Chinese ones were all angles, and these were more rounded off at the corners.

'Are these all for me?'

'Yes. If you should like them.'

'I would. Thank you very much. Thank you very much indeed.'

A moment of childish cynicism suggested to him that he might have to do something in exchange for the presents and he wondered what this might be. He was still puzzled by the photograph.

'But why,' he asked, 'have you given me your friend's picture?'

'So that someone will remember him. His name was Bob. He was killed in Hong Kong. He is buried on Hong Kong-side.'

'Do you visit him?' David probed. His grandmother – the other one, his mother's mother – went every first Sunday of the month to visit his grandfather who had 'passed away', as she put it, when David was three.

'No. I never have.'

Sandingham peered out on to the low slope of the hillside opposite the hotel. He sniffed once and David thought he had a bit of a cold.

'You'll remember Bob, won't you?' he continued. 'Like you remember your Australian friend who . . .'

'Well, I have a photo.'

'Keep it safe.'

David rotated the postcard. It was a funny picture. There was a river in it. On its bank was a building on top of which was a dome made of rafters but no tiles. There was a cube-shaped building to the right with a dent in the roof. All the land around was brashy and bitty-looking, as if it were coated with cake crumbs. The two buildings had no windows.

Watching the boy trying to figure the picture out, Sandingham said, 'You asked me once why they called me Hiroshima Joe.'

'Yes,' David said. 'I'm sorry.'

'You don't need to apologise. And I'll tell you. In the war I saw something very horrid and I can't forget it.'

'Everyone sees something nasty in wars,' David interrupted. His father had told him that one evening when he'd asked what an 'offensive' was, which he'd heard on the radio.

'This was something worse than nasty, David. It was very, very ghastly. I'm not going to tell you about it because I don't want you to have a nightmare.' Sandingham smiled. 'Especially on Christmas Eve. But I have nightmares. The only time I don't get them is when I chase a dragon or have a lot to drink in the bar.'

'Chase a dragon' meant nothing to the boy. Sandingham did not pause to explain it. He was talking now without paying any attention to David, his concentration far removed from the lounge, the hotel or Hong Kong.

If David daydreamed like that in school, he knew only too well, the teacher would flick his ear with her nail to wake him. He was loathe to wake Hiroshima Joe.

'And what I saw makes me very cross sometimes. Mad with anger. And I don't like loud noises or bright lights. What I saw made me ill.'

He tapped his head signifying he was crazy and David smirked, not understanding that Hiroshima Joe meant it. He thought it was just a joke. Lots of people tapped their heads if they thought you were off your rocker.

'I hope you won't ever see anything like that yourself.'

Sandingham had returned to the present.

'So do I,' David assured him innocently.

'That postcard is a place in Japan called Hiroshima. That's where I saw what was horrid, more horrid than anything before. That's where I went – bonkers. And that's why they call me Hiroshima Joe.'

He got uneasily to his feet.

'Keep my presents. I hope you like your general. When you play with him and your other soldiers, try to remember me and keep my friend Bob safe and sound. And remember, too, that war is all right if you play it with your toys, but it's bad for real people to do. More than anything else, war is the worst thing people do.' He took one pace towards the door. 'Happy Christmas for tomorrow.'

'Happy Christmas, Joe,' said David.

Sandingham looked down at the little boy with his arm in a sling and the general lying on his back in the boy's palm.

'Thank you, David.' His voice was quiet and strained.

'What for? I've not given you anything.'

David resolved in that second to buy Hiroshima Joe a bottle of beer from the bar for Christmas. He'd spend the half-crown on it and have it sent up by room service as a surprise, with a note, just like they did in films.

'For calling me Joe,' Sandingham said.

David bent down. The general now commanded his machine-gun crew. The glass door brushed on the floor. When he raised his head, Sandingham was gone.

His mother was not at all pleased.

'I told you, David,' she remonstrated, 'quite distinctly, not to talk to that man.'

'I didn't say much,' David defended himself. 'And, anyway, he talked to me.'

'What did he talk about?' his mother quizzed him.

'He gave me the presents and told me he got his name because he was at a place in Japan — and that's how he got his name.'

'Well, I think you ought to spend the half-crown on his present as you suggest. Then you'll be equal. I don't want you to be in debt to him; one shouldn't owe people like him something. If you give it to me, I'll change it into dollars for you.'

He handed the coin to his mother, placing it reluctantly into her outstretched palm.

'I'd rather pay for it out of my pocket money,' he said, hoping to wheedle the half-crown back.

'Very well,' she answered curtly, returning the money to him.

For his part, he hastily secreted it into a pocket in case she altered her mind. 'But that'll be your weekly dollar for next Saturday. And I don't see why he wants you to have the photo of his friend.'

She picked this up from her dressing-table and studied it: the young man in it was a junior officer – that much she could see between the cracks and creases – dressed in drill shorts and a battle-dress blouse. He was standing in ankle-high grass and smiling wryly. She read the faded blue ink. 'Bob: Penang, 1939.'

Evening was coming. David enjoyed watching the street lamps switch on. They popped as the power charged into them and hissed until the filaments were fully alight. In the summer, as soon as they even began to hiss, insects congregated round them.

He folded his good arm round his bad one, inside the sling, and rested them cautiously on the lounge balcony wall. Inside the cave of his sling the luminous numbers on the watch he'd got for his birthday glowed spirit-green. He was pleased, for he had ordered the beer to be sent up to Joe's room on Christmas morning, just before the hotel Christmas lunch. If he was in the bar at that time, then the boy had requested that it be served to him there, 'with the compliments of a small friend.' He'd thought of that himself.

The street lamp clicked on. He watched it gather in intensity.

There was a rasping sound above his head. He glanced at the hotel roof two storeys up, squinting to drive the street lights from his pupils. A stout rope had been thrown over the parapet, forming a U.

Against the evening sky, in which the last fragments of day shone, was silhouetted Joe Sandingham. He was standing stiffly to attention, his face rigid and his eyes fixed on the darkening eastern sky.

He jumped.

David held his breath.

Sandingham fell twelve feet, stopped abruptly in mid-air, made a noise like a man snapping his fingers, coughed and started to spin round slowly, like an acrobat.

PART TWELVE

Hong Kong: Summer, 1985

'WHAT CAN YOU see?' Annabelle asked, her hand resting upon his own. 'Anything?'

'Nothing yet,' David replied, but he was lying – not spitefully but deliberately, so that he could savour the moment for himself.

'It must be very strange for you,' his wife commented. Her hand left his and he heard the ice rattle in her glass as she drained the last of her gin and tonic and handed it to the stewardess.

'What is?' he said, without turning his head.

'Coming back. Returning to the place of your childhood. It must be weird.'

'Not really,' he lied again.

Through the puffballs of moonlit clouds below them, that looked like spent shell-bursts and into which they were descending, he could see the ocean sparkling minutely. An island hove into view directly under his face. He pressed his cheek nearer to the perspex, forcing his spectacles askew, and saw the waisted centre of the fragment of land. On the thin causeway, lights prickled in the summer night.

There was a chiming ping over his head. He sat back and raised his eyes to the rack above. Between the cooling vents, the call button and the reading spots, the no-smoking and seat-belt notices were still illuminated.

Cheung Chau, he thought. We're making our approach from the west.

He marvelled at how clear the world always looks from the air, especially on a tropical night. It was uncomplicated, two-dimensional and yet emotionally charged. The romantic sense of foreignness lifted itself up and seemed to embrace him in its mysticism and oddness. A voice from the air around him interrupted his thoughts.

'Ladies and gentleman, we are now making our final descent to Hong Kong-Kai Tak. On behalf of Captain Lee and the crew may I thank you for flying with Cathay Pacific. We hope you have had a pleasant flight and look forward to welcoming you again aboard one of our aircraft in the near future. After we have landed, please do not leave your seats until the aircraft has come to a standstill at the terminus buildings.'

The 747 entered a cloud bank. Wraiths of mist swept by the window and, across the wing, taut bands of vacuumed moisture trailed back from the leading edge.

He was at the window once more, eager as a child to catch his first glimpse. There was a hum and bump under his feet as the undercarriage lowered and locked.

The rim of the cloud disappeared at two hundred miles an hour and there, arcing out below him, was the whole of the waterfront of Hong Kong Island, from Kennedy Town to North Point. The scene and its suddenness took his breath away.

The skyscrapers were a mass of lights. The whole city looked like another world, an exquisite waterfall of electric sparks splashing down the sides of The Peak, around which roads were hung like shining necklaces. Traffic shimmered and scintillated. Every single dot of light seemed replicated in the waters of the harbour, upon which ferries glittered like the living bugs David knew one could buy in expensive jewellers' which had had semiprecious stones glued to their carapaces.

Annabelle leaned across him and said, 'It's beautiful beyond words.' She was amazed at the panorama.

'Yes,' he agreed. 'It is.'

It had always been beautiful. After they had left the hotel and gone to live on Plantation Road at the top of The Peak, David had realised just what beauty was: it shocked him as a child, took his breath away.

There were nights when his parents were out at a dockyard function, or to dinner with friends, when he tricked his amah into believing that he would be good and was left undisturbed in his bedroom. He used to slip from between the cool starch of the sheets, drag a chair to the window and sit staring out on the whole of Hong Kong and Kowloon laid before him. The ferries had glistened on the black carpet of the harbour and he imagined them to be slow-falling meteorites in a heaven laid at his feet. If he looked up, the stars in the sky were as sharp and as magical.

The broad peninsula of Kowloon projected from under the belly of the jet. Down the centre, through the plain of the sparkling tinsel of neon and halogen, of red and green and yellow and white, ran the spinal column of Nathan Road.

By now the aircraft was at only a few hundred feet. It banked sharply to the right and dropped on to the runway that fingered out into the black sea of Kowloon Bay for nearly two miles. The strobe in the underneath of the Boeing hit and dragged grass blades and air traffic control number-plates into garish, instantaneous sight. He could remember seeing seaplanes landing in that same bay when he was a boy.

They were met by an Englishman in his late twenties who had been sent by the Far Eastern office to welcome them and smooth their passage through immigration and customs controls.

'Mr Merriton? I'm Frederick Sawyer, sir.'

'Good evening, Sawyer. Thank you for coming to the airport. Most kind of you.'

David extended his hand and introduced his wife to the junior executive.

'I have a car waiting to take you to the Mandarin, sir. Your bags are already taken care of. Do follow me. I trust you've had a comfortable flight?'

The company Mercedes was parked by the kerb and the Chinese chauffeur was holding the door open as they stepped out into the humid night from the air-conditioned atmosphere of the airport buildings. The smells of the Orient, the sounds of the baggage coolies and the gutteral Cantonese voices washed over them and David wondered what had happened to the thirty-odd years in between.

'Sawyer, would you ask the chauffeur to drive down Argyle Street and Waterloo Road *en route*, please?'

The representative gave his orders to the chauffeur in fluent Cantonese before joining him in the front of the car.

The junction of Waterloo Road and Argyle Street was tra-
versed by a flyover. The hill opposite the hotel had disappeared
and, in its place, there were apartment buildings. The hotel, too,
had gone. Just after the railway bridge, the only landmark he
could remember and one that reassured him that not everything
had altered unequivocally, they took a left turn and were soon on
to the link road to the cross-harbour road tunnel.

The hotel was sumptuous. Once in their suite on the twelfth
floor, they showered and dressed for dinner. As the warm water
flowed over him, David shed the discomfort of the long flight
from London and then sat at the window in his bathrobe as his
wife bathed.

The vista before him was much the same as the one he had seen
from the plane, only now he was nearer and lower to it, feeling it
becoming an intrinsic part of him once more. Even though it was
so changed, he knew that under its veneer Hong Kong was still as
it had always been, with its tiny crowded streets and food stalls,
its temples and alleys, its throngs of people and never-ending
state of motion.

The Mercedes was waiting in front of the hotel, as David had
ordered it should be. Peter Gordon, their local manager, had kept
it free for him. All through the working breakfast he had had with
the Chinese representatives and the man from the Los Angeles
office he had been thinking ahead to this moment and now, as the
car door was opened for him by the commissionaire, David felt
the cold air swing outwards at him and it caused him to shiver
involuntarily. He settled into the back seat.

'Is your wife joining you, sir?' the driver enquired politely. He
was not allowed to park for too long before the hotel lobby.

'No. She's gone shopping and sight-seeing with Mr Gordon's
wife. Over on Kowloon-side.'

'Where do you wish to go, sir?'

'Drive out towards Big Wave Bay. Go through Wong Nai
Chung Gap and down Repulse Bay Road, not the other way
round through North Point. Through Tai Tam.'

'Yes, sir.'

When they reached the T-junction of Tai Tam Road with Shek
O Road he knocked on the sliding screen separating driver from
passenger.